PRAISE FOR THE NOVELS OF AMY BELDING BROWN

FLIGHT OF THE SPARROW

"Brown's voice transforms a remote period into a fresh and immediate world and, in Mary, gives us a heroine who is broken by sorrow but determined to survive. This is a novel about the true meaning of faith and freedom."

—Kelly O'Connor McNees, author of *The Island of Doves* and *The Lost Summer of Louisa May Alcott*

"The story of Mary Rowlandson is the story of one of the darkest episodes in our nation's history, and yet Amy Belding Brown manages to turn it into a soaring tale of light and hope. In telling her story of a courageous woman's search for freedom, independence, identity, and love, Amy Belding Brown never strikes a false note, never lets us down by snatching us out of time and place. While keeping faith with existing historical fact, she fills in the gaps with the delicate strokes of her art, transforming historical figures into living beings, vividly resurrecting long-lost ways of native and Colonial life. *The Flight of the Sparrow* reminds us of the promise of America and that the fulfillment of that promise relies on every human heart."

—Sally Cabot Gunning, author of *Benjamin Franklin's Bastard*, *The Widow's War*, *Bound*, and *The Rebellion of Jane Clarke*

"A fresh, engaging chronicle of the human heart that breathes life into a vital but oft-neglected chapter of our history. Amy Belding Brown has turned an authentic drama of Indian captivity into a compelling, emotionally gripping tale that is at once wrenching and soulful."

—Eliot Pattison, author of the Mystery of Colonial America series

continued . . .

"A mesmerizing tale of survival and awakening. *Flight of the Sparrow* breathes life into Mary Rowlandson's captivity narrative. The deftly depicted cross-cultural friendship reminded me of *Caleb's Crossing* and the fast-paced story kept me up turning pages. Belding Brown has crafted a fine-limned portrait of a remarkable and resourceful woman."

—Donna Thorland, author of *The Turncoat*
and *The Rebel Pirate*

MR. EMERSON'S WIFE

"This is the book I longed to read. It is the story of Lidian, the fascinating woman who was loved insufficiently by Emerson and perhaps too much by Thoreau. Amy Belding Brown has brought her back to life in a novel that glitters with intelligence and authenticity."   —Geraldine Brooks, author of *March*

"In this extraordinary book, Amy Belding Brown has brought the nineteenth century to life. We may think of Ralph Waldo Emerson and his family and friends as static daguerreotypes, but in this story they lightly spring off the page with all the inconvenient desires and ambitions that are the texture of our own lives. A soaring imaginative leap, this book combines detailed history with a page-turning illicit love story. It's a look at a rich moment in American history and a great read, a rare combination."

—Susan Cheever, author of *My Name Is Bill*
and *Note Found in a Bottle*

"Amy Belding Brown's novel is a beautiful work that renders effortlessly the sentiments and sensuousness of a woman who is, to use Ms. Brown's own terms, 'at war with herself,' a woman of opposites who yearns to reconcile her mental acuity with her emotional sensitivity.' The spiritual, emotional, and intellectual lives she is after illuminating for us are wonderfully ambitious, and it is quite refreshing to see that ambition backed up with a quality of writing that bears up to the weight of its subject matter."
—Bret Lott, author of *Jewel* and *A Song I Knew by Heart*

"*Mr. Emerson's Wife* explores the complex relationship of the famous philosopher and his less well-known partner in a novel that has a sturdy fabric of fact, embroidered with imagined events and emotions. . . . Brown's writing is graceful, at times giving Lidian a poetic voice. . . . In an age when scholarly biographers meticulously document every detail in the actions and settings of their subjects, Brown has escaped to the freedom of fiction to suppose 'what might have been.'"
—Ruth Johnstone Wales, *The Christian Science Monitor*

"In *Mr. Emerson's Wife*, Amy Belding Brown creates a fascinating view of one of America's greatest minds, the brilliant Transcendentalist Ralph Waldo Emerson, and, more specifically, his wife, Lidian. This is a story of just how restrained women were only two centuries ago and how choices can affect one's life."
—The Copperfield Review

Other Novels by Amy Belding Brown

Mr. Emerson's Wife

flight of the sparrow

A Novel of Early America

AMY BELDING BROWN

 New American Library

New American Library
Published by the Penguin Group
Penguin Group (USA) LLC, 375 Hudson Street,
New York, New York 10014

USA | Canada | UK | Ireland | Australia | New Zealand | India | South Africa | China
penguin.com
A Penguin Random House Company

First published by New American Library,
a division of Penguin Group (USA) LLC

First Printing, July 2014

REGISTERED TRADEMARK—MARCA REGISTRADA

LIBRARY OF CONGRESS CATALOGING-IN-PUBLICATION DATA:
Brown, Amy Belding.
Flight of the sparrow: a novel of early America/Amy Belding Brown.
p. cm.
ISBN 978-0-451-46669-3
1. Rowlandson, Mary White, approximately 1635–1711—Fiction.
2. Indian captivities—Massachusetts—Fiction.
3. Indians of North America—Massachusetts—History—Colonial period,
ca. 1600–1775.
4. Massachusetts—History—Colonial period, ca. 1600–1775—Fiction.   I. Title.
PS3552.R6839F58 2014
813'.54—dc23   2013035277

Printed in the United States of America
10   9   8   7   6   5

Set in Adobe Garamond
Designed by Spring Hoteling

Dedicated to the memory of my mother,

Eleanor Kellogg Belding,
1922–2012

In the face of adversity
she chose hope, curiosity, and grit:
the thirsty leaf reaching for the rain,
the night moth questing at the window,
the bloom that does not fold at twilight.

GRATEFUL APPRECIATION TO

my dear friend and first reader, Margarite Landry, for her insightful comments, her companionship over countless lunches, and her encouragement through many revisions and other hard times;

my aunt, Patricia W. Belding, for her meticulous reading of my manuscript, her contagious passion for reading and poetry, and her unflagging intellectual curiosity;

my friend and fellow contrarian, Wallace Kaufman, for his critical eye and straightforward advice on the early versions of this novel;

my agent, Susan Ramer, for her assistance, reassurance, support, and patience over the many years of our association;

my editor, Ellen Edwards, for her warm enthusiasm, generous guidance, and good humor;

my children, Daryl, Nathan, Samara, and Matthew, for their affectionate toleration of my eccentricities, and their compassion in providing me with so few reasons to worry about them;

and especially my husband, Duane, for his steadfast devotion, which has been a daily miracle for more than forty years.

Our soul, as bird, escapéd is
out of the fowler's snare:
the snare asunder broken is;
and we delivered are.

—Psalm 124, Verse 7
The Bay Psalm Book,* 1640

. . . .

*The Bay Psalm Book, the first book printed in British North America, is a translation of all the Psalms rendered in rhymed, four-four meter for singing. First printed in 1640, it remained in use for more than one hundred years.

flight of the
sparrow

CHAPTER ONE

Later, Mary will trace the first signs of the Lord's displeasure back to a hot July morning in 1672 when she pauses on her way to the barn to watch the sun rise burnt orange over the meetinghouse. She feels a momentary sinking in her bowels as it flashes like fire through a damp haze, putting her in mind of the terrors of hell. She has never been adept at reading omens. That is the gift and duty of her husband, Joseph, and other Bay Colony ministers. Mary sees the world matter-of-factly, as a practical, intelligible creation fashioned by God for the convenience of His people. As she plucks a paltry three eggs from under her anxious hens and slips them into her pocket, her chief thought is that by noon the heat will be suffocating. Yet, when she comes out of the barn, the ginger-colored hairs on the nape of her neck rise and she thinks she hears the Devil's footsteps rounding the corner of the lane.

A moment later, she sees it is not the Devil, but Edmund Parker, in nightshirt and breeches, pounding toward her in his bare feet, hair flying about his head like tufts of white flame. His eyes bulge and the mottled birthmark on his left cheek burns dark red. Mary hurries to steady him when she sees his legs sway. They look as rickety as a babe's.

"Mistress Rowlandson!" His fingers dig cruelly into her arm, yet she does not shrink from his distress. "I beg you, help me!" he cries. "'Tis my Bess. Her time has come."

Bess. The daughter who has shamed him by conceiving a child during her indenture to Deacon Park in Roxbury. Bess, who has refused to name the man who got the child on her and so was cast out with no place to go except back to her father's failing farm. The girl of whom the goodwives speak only in whispers, for fear the Lord will punish all of Lancaster for her sin.

"Where is Goody Turner?" Mary asks, wondering why he has come to her instead of the midwife.

His beard winks amber in the ominous light as he shakes his head. "Her daughter says she lies abed with the summer flux. But I think she refuses out of malice."

"Malice? I cannot credit that." Mary frowns, though she suspects what he says may be true. Every pious, God-fearing woman in this frontier town has kept her distance from Bess. They all believe that evil is contagious, that proximity to sin provides a foothold for the Devil, who can easily pass from one person to the next. "I'm sure she must be ill, if her daughter says so. The sweating fever has been abroad for a fortnight."

"Fever or no, she will not help. Nor will any other." His fingers dig yet deeper. "I've knocked on every door. There is no one else. I beg you, as a Christian, help us!"

Mary sees plainly enough where her duty lies. Indeed, how can she refuse? Did not Jesus command his disciples to help the poor and lowly? Did he not mingle with sinners? Edmund is beside himself with worry and she is the wife of the town's minister. She has no choice but to assent.

Mary has been present at a dozen births, though never in place of a midwife, and never alone. The prospect frightens her, not only because of the risk to her soul, but because the girl is young and may not be well formed enough to safely deliver a child. Mary has no birthing stool or linens with which to practice a proper midwife's art. Yet Edmund is in such a state that she cannot delay any longer with talk of flux and fevers.

She hurries into the house, empties the eggs from her pocket and stuffs it with scissors and thread and what rags she can quickly find. She briefly considers taking her eldest daughter with her. Marie is dutiful and steadfast and could provide an extra pair of hands. Yet she is so young—only a few months past her sixth birthday—Mary does not want her badly affected if things do not go well. Even in the best circumstance, childbirth is a perilous business, and if Bess should die—or the child be born a monster—it could set Marie's mind against childbearing for life. She instructs Rebekah, the servant girl, to keep a close eye on Marie and little Sarah, who is still so young she could easily toddle into the fire or drown in a puddle. She knows her son, Joss, will be tending the flax field with Joseph this morning. Her glance falls on the eggs she placed on the shelf and, at the last moment, she ties them up in a napkin to carry with her.

She and Edmund say little as they hasten over the hill to his farm. Neither has much breath to speak. Though it is just past dawn, the sun already pours down so fiercely that Mary has to wipe her face with her apron many times. There is no breeze; the heavy air reeks with the stink of pig offal and swamp water. The branches of the great chestnut tree by the meetinghouse droop while its leaves curl and wilt. They look gray in the light. Even the birds are still, as if they, too, sense the evils of the day.

As they approach, Mary can hear Bess moaning. It is not a house, but a hovel, so rudely built that few men in Lancaster would see fit to house their oxen there. She sees rot along the sill and cracks between the clapboards. There is only one room, for Edmund's farm never prospered. Who can tell why some fields flourish and others do not? Some people question Edmund's skills as a yeoman. Others insist he once committed a dark and unspeakable act that now prevents his success.

The door stands open, sagging on its hinges. Mary steps inside. There is no fire in the hearth, no bedstead, no boards under her feet, only hard-packed earth for a floor. The single window is covered with a torn flap of parchment, heavily oiled with hog fat. Bess is hunched on a pallet of blankets, her skirts hiked up and her fists jammed into her thighs. With every moan she tosses her head and rocks back on her heels.

Mary hesitates, shocked at how young the girl looks. Her bones have only recently knit into the shape of a woman. Beneath the grime-streaked face, her features are soft—almost delicate. How old is she? Fourteen? Fifteen?

Her brother, John, sits beside her on a low stool but he offers her no comfort, merely sits with his hands dangling between his legs. He deliberately avoids looking at her, but gazes up at the smoke-blackened rafters. Mary takes in the slump of his thin shoulders, the restless tapping of his feet, and is reminded of her favorite brother. Josiah had the same awkwardness and coltish looks at that age. Mary was six when he was born, old enough to be responsible for watching over him, yet still young enough to enjoy his company. They had fashioned their own secret language as she showed him how to do the children's chores: feeding the chickens, gathering eggs, weeding the kitchen garden. It saddens her that she cannot remember a word of it now. She wipes her face with her apron. The morning's heat has already penetrated the hut's thin walls. Buzzing flies crisscross the room and swarm over the parchment window.

Bess makes a sudden sound—a combination of grunt and groan. Mary collects her wits and puts her hand on the boy's shoulder.

"John, you must lay a fire and fetch water. We will need a tub of it before we're done." He scrambles to do her bidding, clearly glad that he has been asked to do something that will free him from the stool.

Edmund comes in and stands just inside the open door. He looks stricken, and is plainly waiting for a sign from Mary as to what he should do; men are usually banned from witnessing a birth. She asks him to close the door, and then thinks better of it, for she will need all the light and air available. Unlike Goody Turner, she cannot gauge the progress of a labor by her hands alone.

"Nay, leave it open," she says, and begins giving orders. "Bring in as much straw as you can. We must cover the floor to soak up"— she hesitates—"the fluids. Find something clean to wrap the child in when it comes. And collect whatever strengthening food you have."

He shakes his head. "We have naught but scraps of bread."

"Then you must beg some from a neighbor. Broth. Stew. A pottage. Go to Goody Kerley's house; she is my sister. Tell her I have sent you and she will provide. Your daughter must have food and drink or she will faint with her pangs." Mary turns from him and kneels beside the girl.

"Bess!" She puts her mouth near the girl's ear. "Bess, I've come to your aid." To her own surprise, she adds, "All will be well." She's not sure what possesses her to say this, since she has no assurance at all that it is true.

Bess turns her head and Mary sees the childbed fear in her eyes—a fear she knows well. She has seen it on the faces of her sisters as they labored. She has felt it on her own. Everyone knows that bearing a child can carry a woman to her grave.

She also knows that Bess has another reason to be afraid—a reason Mary dreads—for it is required of all women, wed and unwed, that they confess the name of their child's father. They must do this during the most difficult moments of labor when the pain strips all self-control from them. Though she knows this is for the good of Bess's soul, and will assure her a chance of salvation if she dies, Mary has no taste for the custom. She has endured the pangs of labor herself and knows that in the darkest hours of travail, a woman can be persuaded to reveal her most shameful secrets, to confess the vilest sin. A woman is not herself at that time, but only a vessel for the terrible power of her womb. Mary has no desire to press Bess for a revelation. The girl is without a husband—isn't that shame enough?

Gossip has it—and all Lancaster believes—that the child's father is her master, Deacon William Park, that he likely forced himself on her and then threatened her with the lash to procure her silence.

As the only woman present, it is Mary's duty to extract a confession from the girl, yet she wishes with all her heart that it was not required. What good can come of it? Deacon Park is wealthy and proud, with a reputation as a righteous man. All the shame will fall on Bess's thin shoulders. She will be branded a liar and temptress, and worse. She will be doubly condemned for trying to bring down a God-fearing and pious man.

Soon a fire is leaping on the hearth and John has hung a kettle of water over it to boil. Edmund brings in armfuls of straw and he and John spread it over the floor. Edmund leaves and returns with a wedge of cheese and a pot of broth. He warms the broth while Mary rubs Bess's back to ease her pain. She persuades the girl to walk with her, up and down across the room.

"It will hurry the babe along," Mary assures her, supporting Bess with an arm around her waist.

They walk only a short time before Bess's pains are too strong to continue. Mary eases her down onto the pallet and asks Edmund to leave. "There are duties I must perform," she says. "Things that must be kept from the eyes of men." He nearly runs out the door in his haste to escape these women's mysteries. Mary quickly closes and bars it behind him.

She whispers a prayer, begging God for strength, then kneels beside Bess. "The time has come, as you knew it would," Mary says. "You must confess the name of your babe's father."

Bess shakes her head and sets her teeth in a desperate grimace.

"There is no protecting him, Bess. The truth will be revealed. You cannot save him, but you can save yourself from the flames of hell."

"I cannot," she whispers, then moans and clutches her belly as another pang overwhelms her.

"Just speak his name," Mary says, "and you will have all the aid you need." She leans over the girl and places her hands at the base of the swollen belly, pressing firmly. "I beg you, Bess, say it. All Lancaster knows this was your master's doing, but *you* must declare it true." When she does not answer, Mary presses harder. Bess's eyes snap open and she screams.

Edmund beats on the door with his fists. "Stop!" he cries. "For God's sake, you must not torture her! Let me in!"

Mary ignores him. "You must speak the name. Else I cannot help you."

Bess screams again. "'Tis no Christian thing you do, Mistress Rowlandson!" Edmund shouts. "This is a Devil's game!"

"The name of your master," Mary says, the words scraping raw in her throat. "Just say it and be done with this."

Bess shakes her head violently, setting her teeth and closing her eyes, her whole body thrashing beneath Mary's hands. Mary begins to lose her purchase, yet she knows she should not relent. Suddenly, Bess goes limp; her face grows dark red and seems to fold in on itself. She sobs; tears run from the corners of her eyes and Mary's own eyes blur. Beyond the door, Edmund is silent.

The girl's mouth opens and an unholy wail escapes her. It has in it the sound of bones scraping across broken rocks, the sound wind makes as it rages through desolate winter forests; it makes Mary think of ice crusting on the doorsteps of burned houses. It makes her think of death.

"Say it," Mary whispers, but her resolve has turned to water. "Just speak his name. I beg you." Her voice catches on a sob. Duty or not, she cannot continue.

She takes her hands away and stands up. Silently, she berates herself as a poor, weak woman who does not have the resolve to do what is required. Yet she cannot make herself do more. She wants only to comfort Bess and ease her pain. Mary kneels again, puts her arm around her, and tells the girl she will not hurt her anymore.

"Have no fear," Mary says. "Your travail will soon be done." Bess moans again. Mary opens the door and motions Edmund in. She helps Bess move higher on the pallet and asks Edmund to sit behind her, to support her head and torso while Mary helps to ease the child out. "Hold her well," Mary says as she parts the girl's knees and bends to her task.

M ary stares down at the wet infant wailing in her arms. A healthy, strong boy, with a sheath of wavy black hair slicked to his scalp. His skin is the color of well-steeped tea. It takes her a moment before she believes what she is seeing—the child's father is clearly not Deacon Park.

She looks up and meets Edmund's eyes. He, too, has seen the boy's dark skin and black hair. He smiles.

"A boy," Mary announces. "You have a son, Bess."

"Is he well?" The girl's hands reach for the infant.

"Aye," Mary says. "'Tis a fine, lusty boy. Hear how he cries!"

"I have named him already," Bess whispers. "Silvanus."

It is unwise to name a child so soon; there are too many dangers to be faced in the first weeks after birth. But Mary has no heart to warn her. Let her enjoy what little peace she can.

The girl lies back against her father, and closes her eyes. A long sigh escapes her; a faint smile turns up the corners of her mouth. Edmund gazes down at her and strokes her forehead in a gesture so tender Mary's heart wrenches to see it.

She turns her attention back to the babe, who squirms vigorously in her arms. There is still much to do: The afterbirth must be delivered; the birth cord must be cut and at just the right length. It must not touch the floor, or the boy will not be able to hold his water. Two eggs must be broken and stirred over hot embers and applied to a plaster for Bess to assure her future fertility. She must eat a poached egg and suckle the babe.

Mary cuts the cord, cleans the child, swaddles him tightly, presents him to Bess and shows her how to help him latch onto her nipple. She makes the egg plaster and prepares the food Bess must eat. She washes the girl's legs and private parts and collects the soiled rags to take home. When her tasks are finished and both Bess and the child have drifted off to sleep, she steps outside, where Edmund is sitting on the doorstep.

"I thank you for your kindness to Bess," he says. He offers her a pipe of tobacco and she realizes suddenly that she is exhausted. She takes the pipe and sits beside him, enjoying the tobacco's bitterness on the back of her throat, the sweetness of the smoke as it threads into her lungs.

"Did you know about the babe?" Mary does not look at him. "Did she tell you of his father?"

He grunts softly. "She named no names, but spoke of an African slave who had been hired out to Deacon Park. Kind, she said. The kindest man who ever lived."

"Kind?" Mary asks. "What sort of kindness is it to get a child on her?"

He is silent a moment. "I believe she loves him."

"Aye, love," Mary says, nodding. So Bess consented to the union; she was not defiled after all. No wonder she hasn't revealed the man's name. Mary takes a long draw on the pipe. She knows about love, felt it running through her own veins when she was but a few years older than Bess. It seems so long ago now.

"The townsfolk will not be charitable to her," she says. "Or him. The child is not only a bastard but the son of a slave."

"He is my grandson," Edmund says in a hard voice.

"Aye," Mary says. She thinks of the tender way he soothed Bess, how he tried to protect her from interrogation. He is a kind man, Mary thinks, and for a moment she wants to tell him so. She has not known men to be kind. Her father was strong, courageous, often reckless, sometimes ruthless, but never kind. Her husband is a forceful man, righteous, insistent, and steadfast in his faith. He strives to be just and charitable, but kindness is not in his nature; his gentleness is confined to their marriage bed.

Yet Edmund Parker, poor though he may be, appears to be deeply kind. Mary remembers his wife, Ruth, who died five years ago of a wasting disease. She was a hardworking, silent woman who had not joined the church. Mary had pitied her for being yoked to a man who could not make his farm prosper. But perhaps Ruth knew deeper satisfactions.

On the far side of the field, John comes out of the woods. His hair is the color of straw in the sun. Mary thinks of the black-haired child inside the house, sleeping in his mother's arms.

She takes a final draw on the pipe and hands it back to Edmund. "I must go," she says, rising. "I have many duties to attend." She thinks of what she will likely find at home—her children ill-tended, the fire burned down to embers, a pot full of slick, gray porridge, her husband inconvenienced by her absence. She will have to tell him what she has witnessed—that Bess Parker has borne a black babe. It will shock him; it will shock all the good people of Lancaster.

At Sabbath meeting, he will pray for the Lord's mercy. He will beg God not to rain down His righteous anger upon the whole town. "Spare us from the wages of this woman's sin!" he will cry. The congregation will murmur and tremble and whisper, "Amen."

Mary hurries down the lane to her house. In the west, the sun is sliding behind George Hill. The sky is the color of blood.

CHAPTER TWO

"*Bess* must repent and make her confession before the whole congregation," Joseph says. He is sitting by the hearth in the heavy oaken chair Mary's father gave them when they married. His open Bible rests on his knees. "If she is to be restored, she must submit without complaint to her punishment."

Mary pictures Bess trembling as she is led out of the meeting-house, bound to the whipping post, and stripped naked to the waist. *How many lashes will the magistrates require?* "She is but a child," Mary protests. "Surely she has suffered enough."

Joseph gives her a disapproving look. "She is woman enough to bear a son," he says. "And she has caused more suffering than she has endured. I do not understand you, wife. What confusion has disordered your mind since you attended this birth?"

She wants to tell him she is perfectly sane, that any transformation she underwent was clarity, not confusion. But she knows he will regard such words as defiance. She keeps her head down and studies the bread dough as she kneads. It is brown and elastic, slightly warm under her palms.

"And, Mary"—he closes the Bible and rises—"you must not visit the girl until she is restored." When she does not answer, he crosses the room to stand behind her. "You have risked much in attending the birth. Further contact will taint you. Will taint all of us."

The skin between her shoulder blades stings suddenly as if pricked with quills. She wonders how he knew her intention. She forms the dough into a ball, covers it with a cloth and wipes her hands on her apron, focusing on her fingers as the coarse fabric scrapes away bits of dough, until she has control of herself. Finally she turns and looks at him.

"Is there no place for Christian charity, then?" she asks, her voice quiet, measured. She must not threaten his authority. "Is not kindness a fruit of the Spirit, after all?"

His eyes go hard and his jaw stiffens; she realizes she has gone too far. "It is not for a woman to decide such things," he says. "You raise yourself too high. Your pride will be your undoing."

She knows that it is entirely proper for her husband to correct her, yet she resents it. Has always resented it. "I must see to my spinning," she says, glancing at the small flax wheel in the dark northwest corner of the room.

He wraps his hand around her wrist. "Hear me, Mary. I forbid you to visit the girl."

She assents without meeting his eyes, a submissive bob of her head, so that he will release her. But as she seats herself at the wheel and moves her fingers over the distaff, her face is bright with anger.

For sixteen years, Mary has striven to be a steadfast and godly wife to Joseph Rowlandson. She has submitted her will to his, accepted his corrections, and regularly joined her body to his in conjugal union. She was twenty when they wed, seventeen when she first met him. She will always remember opening the front door of her father's new-built house and finding Joseph standing on the stoop: a sturdy, well-built man with wide shoulders, a long nose and dark hair that curled cunningly over his ears. He told her he was the town's minister, come to call on her father.

This was not surprising; it would serve any minister to make himself friend to John White, the wealthiest proprietor in Lancaster. He had spent years moving his family restlessly from one place to another, always seeking a new, more profitable opportunity. Mary was two when the family fled England in 1639, part of the Great Migration of Puritans to New England, seeking relief from the apostasy of King Charles. She remembers the crossing dimly: a haze of sunshine and black water, dirty white sails pasted to the sky, and the creaking, rocking hull.

Her father settled the family in Salem; six years later he moved them to Wenham, where the number of children grew to nine. When, in 1653, he announced that he had purchased land in Lancaster, a frontier town deep in the wilderness, his eyes had flashed with excitement. But Mary had had to look away as she felt a great sinking in her chest and saw her mother's face sag with fear. Only Mary's married older sister and brothers had been able to stay in Wenham.

Since coming to Lancaster, Mary had tried unsuccessfully to conquer her misery but, as she looked up at the minister that afternoon, something in his sharp blue gaze suggested that she might have prospects in Lancaster after all.

Now, for the first time in her married life, Mary defies her husband. On a warm, gray day when Joseph is called to the neighboring town of Groton to investigate a case of witchcraft, she packs a basket of food and carries it to the Parker farm. She finds Bess sitting in the yard, suckling Silvanus.

The girl smiles when she sees her. Mary lowers the basket and admires the babe, brushing his cheek with the tip of her finger and tucking her thumb into his tiny fist. She is touched when Bess asks if she'd like to hold him.

Mary cradles the small, warm body against her breasts, inhaling the milky perfume of his breath that rises from between his parted lips. She rocks him back and forth and closes her eyes. She remembers her own newborns so vividly that tears rise.

"He's a sweet babe," she says, handing him back to Bess. "And you. How do you fare? Have you ample sustenance?"

The girl's face reddens and she briefly looks away, then back again. "You are the first to visit," she whispers.

"I have brought some food," Mary says, removing the square of homespun covering the basket. "Cheese and bread. A slice of salted ham. Peas. Three good onions."

"Thank you." Bess's voice is ragged. Mary sits down and puts her arm around the girl's shoulder.

"What will become of me?" Bess whispers. "The goodwives scorn and shun me. They walk the other way when they see me in the lane."

Mary swallows against something sticky and hot in her throat. "They will receive you again if you confess and repent."

"I cannot." Bess's head drops lower; she will not look at Mary.

"'Tis not so hard a thing," Mary says gently.

"But I *cannot* repent." Bess looks up at her, her eyes dark with sorrow. "I would lie with him again tomorrow, if I could."

Mary can think of no satisfactory response to the girl's sinful declaration. She is plainly demented with love. Mary recognizes the condition, for she was once demented herself with love for Joseph. She remembers how kind and attentive he was the spring after they moved to Lancaster, when her mother took to her bed, complaining of pains in her bowels and chest. Throughout her long dying, he came daily to offer prayers and Christian comfort. He often ate at

their table. Mary became acutely aware of each time Joseph's gaze
fell on her. His glances caused something at the base of her spine to
shiver with pleasure. When he departed, she felt strangely exhausted
and yet she wanted to run all the way up the hill behind the house
and spin in circles under the trees.

Mary recalls lying next to her sister Elizabeth on their pallet in
the chamber over the kitchen, telling her everything. She was in
love, she said. She would not rest content until she became Joseph
Rowlandson's wife. She thought Elizabeth would sympathize because she had recently become engaged to Henry Kerley. Instead,
her sister clucked her tongue and told Mary what a foolish girl she
was. Love was not something that fell on a person out of a clear sky,
but a warm affection that slowly grew from years of sharing life's
toils.

Mary removes her arm from Bess's shoulder and presses her
hands together with sudden resolve. "You must not despair," she
says. "All will be well." The guilt from disobeying her husband suddenly falls away and she feels a resolute determination to shower the
girl with kindness and hope. "Fear not," she says. "I will see to it
myself."

A week later, Mary spends the morning heckling flax, pulling
the broken fibers through the series of combs to ready them
for the distaff. Early in the afternoon, she steps out on the front
stoop to catch what breeze there is, when the mastiff, sleeping in the
shade of the house eaves, heaves himself to his feet, barking. Mary
wipes her brow with the tail of her apron and turns to look, shading
her eyes from the sun's glare.

A man carrying a basket is walking on the road. For an instant
her heart lifts; the figure is the image of her father. She has to squeeze
her eyes shut to erase the illusion, for she knows what she sees cannot
be real. Her father is too frail these days to be out walking.

She opens her eyes and sees truly. "Goodman Parker," she calls. "How fares Bess this day?"

"Well enough." As Edmund comes closer, Mary sees that what he holds is not a basket but a crudely constructed cage. Perched on a stick inside is a bird.

Marie crosses the yard from the barn, hauling Sarah on her hip. Sarah points. "Bird!" she cries.

"I made you a thanking gift." Edmund holds the cage out to her. "For your charity to Bess. Your visits lift her spirits."

"How kindly thought," Mary says, though she is reluctant to take it. The only birds she knows how to care for are ducks and chickens. And she is certain that Joseph will object, for he will see the gift as frivolous, of no practical use.

"'Tis a singing sparrow," Edmund says. "To gladden your heart." His smile is so wide and Mary is so touched by his generosity that she cannot refuse. She holds out her hands and takes the cage.

The bird is russet and gray with a white breast; there is a dark triangle under its bill. It cocks its head at her, hops off the stick, and flutters briefly upward before returning to its perch.

"Bird!" cries Sarah again, clapping her tiny hands.

"May we keep it, Mother?" Marie puts Sarah down and brushes her skirts into place. "Will not Father complain?"

Mary smiles down at her daughters. "How can he complain?" she says. "Did not our Lord Himself promise that no bird is outside the Father's care?"

Mary hangs the cage on a peg by the window. She studies the cleverly made door, which latches with a hook and swings back on tiny pegged hinges. She sprinkles flax seeds and bits of bread in the bottom of the cage, and sets a saucer of water there, too. Throughout the afternoon she finds herself crossing the room to reassure herself that the sparrow is well. By the time Joseph comes in from the field with Joss that evening, the sun has gone down and the cage is in shadow. Her husband is weary and out of temper; even his prayer is short and bitter. They eat in silence, and when the meal is over, they retire to their bedstead and draw the curtains.

They are wakened at first light by birdsong.

As Mary expected, Joseph condemns Edmund's gift as foolish and worldly. When she reminds him of the many passages in Scripture relating God's concern for the birds of the air, he is not persuaded. He insists she must return it.

She looks at the cage, where the sparrow is now making chipping sounds. She is sure it is hungry. "But surely it is unwise to give rumormongers reason to think your wife has been ungracious toward a parishioner," she says, knowing his weak point is his reputation. When he doesn't reply, she presses her advantage. "Even though Goodman Parker is of lowly estate, a minister must still be mindful of the good name of his family. Have you not said so yourself many times?"

When Joseph acknowledges her point with a grunt, she knows that she has won. He will let her keep the sparrow and cage. But he warns her again that she must not visit Bess. "Goodman Parker's gift is recompense for your mercy, not a license to contaminate yourself."

Mary nods, though she has no intention of curtailing her visits to Bess.

Mary's sisters Hannah and Elizabeth are charmed by the sparrow. Whenever they visit, they bring a biscuit and break it into crumbs to sprinkle in the bottom of the cage. They like to sit near it, hoping to hear the sparrow sing.

"I have heard of birds caged in great houses in England, but not here," Hannah says one late summer afternoon as the women sit spinning flax onto their distaffs. "I am surprised your husband sanctions it." Her son, Josiah, who was born only twelve days after Sarah, sits at her feet rocking his infant brother, William, in Sarah's old cradle. Mary smiles, remembering the summer of 1669 when Hannah, Elizabeth, and she were all with child.

"Joseph complains it sometimes disturbs his studies," she says. "Yet I think the truth of it is that he has grown to delight in the song."

Joss, who is eight and solemn like his father, warns Mary that the sparrow will die. "'Tis a wild creature," he says. "Not meant to be clapped in a cage."

"It seems happy enough," Mary says. "Look how it sings."

"What choice has it?" he asks. "A captive may sing but still perish."

But the sparrow does not die. It seems to thrive on the food and attention Mary shows it. Marie tries to imitate the song, trilling high, sweet notes as she does her chores. Sarah finds worms and beetles in the kitchen garden, and pokes them one after another into the cage with fierce earnestness. Because she cannot yet say the word "sparrow," she calls it Row, which quickly becomes the bird's name.

Mary visits Bess when she is able, bringing food and the comforts of prayer and Scripture. On her fifth visit, as they sit in the dooryard sewing while the babe sleeps, Bess talks about her child's father, who languishes in the Boston jail. His name is Silvanus Warro. He was born on a plantation in the colony of Maryland, and brought north to the Bay Colony by his master, Daniel Gookin. He lived in Cambridge for many years and was treated well. Then Mr. Gookin hired him out to Deacon Park.

Mary listens, frowning as the sun warms her hair and scalp through her bonnet. She has heard of this Daniel Gookin somewhere before. Has her husband mentioned him? Has she met him somewhere? She remembers suddenly—he is the superintendent of the Praying Indians. A tall man with a narrow face and pale blue eyes, she thinks.

Bess's voice draws her back to the present. "Silvanus was exceeding kind to me when I first came to Deacon Park's. He helped me when my chores were burdensome. He comforted me when I longed for home." Bess's voice thickens. "How could I not have loved him?"

Mary thinks of Bess in the arms of a black man, imagines their limbs entwined in an embrace. She finds it difficult to believe that a woman can love a man so different in appearance and background from herself—but it is plain that Bess and Silvanus have tasted the fullness of love.

"When I discovered I carried his child, he said we must wed," Bess tells Mary. "I asked how that could be. I was under an indenture and he was a slave. But he kissed me and told me that he would find a way." She hunches low over her stitching. "One night he told me to collect my belongings and tie them up in a napkin. He stole a horse from the stable and some money from the deacon's strongbox. We fled but they caught us before we reached Plymouth." She falls silent for a moment. "They arrested him and sent me back to my father. Silvanus was tried and sentenced to twenty lashes. He's in jail until he can pay restitution."

Mary looks up and sees the girl's eyes glisten with tears. Instinctively she places her hand on Bess's knee to comfort her. These visits have brought Mary an unexpected solace—a respite from the burdens of mutual watch, the relentless scrutiny of each other's conduct required of all church members. Despite her youth, Bess has become a friend.

"'Tis said our true freedom is in Christ," Bess says after a while. "But I warrant a person ought to be free from human bondage, as well." She looks at Mary. "Would not Christ agree?"

Mary cannot think how to answer, for she has never considered this question before. Like all Puritans, she has been taught that the world is ordered according to God's will. Bondage is part of the human condition, recognized and authorized in Scripture. She thinks of her servants. Rebekah, just fifteen, who has been indentured for four years, and Peter, bound out from Duxbury, to help Joseph with the farmwork. She remembers Timothy, the son of a Nashaway sachem, whom they took in as a slave when he was orphaned. He stayed three years before running away. Mary never understood why he left a civilized English household with all its goods and godliness to return to the wilderness. At the time, she blamed herself for not properly schooling him in the Christian faith. Now, she wonders if there is another reason, a deeper need for freedom she did not recognize.

"We cannot know the mind of Christ," Mary says, though her voice lacks a forceful conviction.

"Nay, I think we can!" Bess says.

"'Tis a dangerous thought, Bess. I'm sure you know what befell Mistress Anne Hutchinson for such heresy."

Mary is shocked when Bess shakes her head. Is not every young girl raised on these tales whispered in the corners of dark rooms as warning to stay humble and mind the authorities? It occurs to her that the death of Bess's mother put her at grave risk, for it seems the girl has been raised in ignorance. "Mistress Hutchinson believed she had visions from the Lord," Mary explains. "People flocked to hear her revelations, though they were heresies. She was reprimanded by her betters, but she would not listen and persisted in her rebellious ways. She was tried and banished from the Bay Colony. Yet the Lord Himself continued to chasten her."

"How?" Bess whispers, plainly frightened.

"She suffered a monstrous birth after a long and torturous labor," Mary says. "The child in her womb was rank and misshapen. No one could even determine its sex. It died quickly. A mercy," she adds. "Later she and all but one of her living children were slain by

Indians. 'Tis a warning to all of us not to venture into realms which properly belong to men." Even as she speaks, Mary remembers her mother reciting the terrible curse Mistress Hutchinson spoke at her trial: *God will ruin you and your posterity and this whole state.* She does not repeat the words to Bess, but she is suddenly struck by how similar the words are to her husband's pronouncements. Was Anne Hutchinson a prophet after all?

Bess is silent, bending to her stitching. Mary hopes the girl grasped her admonition. She has told the story so many times to Marie and Sarah, they both know it by heart.

After a time, Bess speaks again. "It may not be a revelation from the Lord, yet still I believe it is evil to hold another person enslaved."

"'Tis the order of things," Mary says. "Ordained by God. Does not Paul in his first letter to the Corinthians enjoin the slave to stay in his position and serve the Lord?"

"He says that we are bought with a price, and that we ought not to be servants of men," Bess says quietly.

Mary turns to stare, surprised that the girl knows her Bible so well. She says nothing, knowing she should consult her husband for his greater knowledge of such matters. Knowing, too, that she will likely never trouble him with it.

On an afternoon in early September, Goody Cooper spies Mary carrying a loaf of bread to Bess and soon word spreads that the minister's wife is associating with a harlot. Joseph is furious. He reminds her that she could be beaten for wifely disobedience. He tells her it is only God's mercy that stays his hand. He forbids her to visit Bess again.

Mary protests, pointing out that Christ himself mingled with sinners, but Joseph will have none of it. "You are tainting my ministry!" he shouts. "You contaminate not only yourself but *my* children!" He reminds her that a woman must be subject to her husband in all things. He warns that if she disobeys him again he will have her pilloried in front of the meetinghouse.

Mary's visits end. But the gossip does not. Elizabeth tries to stanch it in public. But in private, she berates Mary for her foolishness.

"Bess Parker is no better than a strumpet," Elizabeth says one afternoon the next spring, as they work side by side in Mary's stillroom, making cheese. They are straining the whey from the curds and their arms are wet to the elbows. "Worse. She's a jezebel who minds not who she lies with. Think on it—a Negro slave!" She shakes her head. "'Tis vile. She imperils us all."

"How?" Mary asks. "What harm does she do *us* because she loves a slave?"

Elizabeth wipes her dripping hands on her apron. Bits of curd fall to the floor. "Mary, you cannot mean that!"

"But I do!" She feels a rush of blood to her cheeks and bends over the pan of curds. "Is it not for God to judge?"

Elizabeth is silent—but only for a moment. "God's people may judge in His name. *Must* judge. Else His wrath will destroy us all." She frowns. "Do you not listen to your husband's sermons?"

"I listen," she says. "But I also pray for God to guide my actions. And I believe He does."

Elizabeth sighs. "You have always had a rebellious nature, Mary." She pushes her hands back into the curds. "I fear for your safety." She slides a look at her. "For your well-being."

Mary is tempted to tell her to see to her own well-being, but holds her tongue. Of all her sisters, she is most closely bound to Elizabeth, who is four years older. Elizabeth has always been her chief protector, has acted as a mother when their own mother was in her sickbed or overwrought in the fevers of conversion. She patiently taught Mary how to sew hems, spin flax, and gather roots and herbs for medicine. She taught her to read and helped her memorize Scripture. She allowed Mary to sleep curled in the nest of her arms when she had been punished with the birch whip or wakened by terrifying dreams. Even now she looks to Elizabeth for counsel, though Mary's status as minister's wife is higher, for Elizabeth is only the wife of a yeoman soldier.

"Promise me you will strive to curb your inclinations," Elizabeth pleads.

Is not compassion an inclination that should be followed? Mary wants to ask, but instead she nods submissively and concentrates all her attention on her work.

In the winter of 1673 Mary's father takes to his bed and dies the next May, just as the earth is greening. Joseph reminds her that she ought not to feel any sorrow, for surely her father was one of the elect. His wealth and influence in the community prove this, for God blesses the righteous with his favor. He instructs her to pray for God's peace to fall upon her and she does. But she also seeks the counsel of her sisters, who share Mary's feeling that the world has become a strange and alien land, now that both parents are gone.

A year later, when Bess Parker's son is nearly two, news comes that the Court has determined the child rightfully belongs to Deacon Park. Mary can barely contain her outrage.

Joseph tries to reason with her, explaining that the Court's decision is just and final. That Silvanus is the son of a slave, and thus a slave himself. He assures Mary this is for the best, pointing out that Edmund can barely support his own two children. How can he be expected to provide for the babe and raise him to adulthood?

Mary knows Edmund will fight the edict, for he dotes on his grandson. "It is *evil* to take a child from his mother!" she cries. All she can think of is losing her first child to a sweating fever on a cold January morning when the babe was the same age as Silvanus. Mari had been a sweetly gentle child; even her death was gentle. Yet when she breathed her last, Mary did not want to hold her body, nor even touch it. She refused to look at the trundle bed where Hannah and Elizabeth had laid her out. She felt as a ship in the midst of a tempest, helpless before towering waves of grief. The wound to her heart has never healed.

"Calm yourself," Joseph says, stroking her cheek. "Do not let sentiment master you. Is not self-control a fruit of the Holy Spirit?"

Mary cannot refute him, but her outrage does not subside. When she learns Joseph has been selected to lead the delegation of six men who will separate Bess from her son, she begs to accompany him.

"Bess will need some Christian comfort from another woman," Mary insists.

But Joseph refuses, and will not be moved, no matter how much Mary prays and pleads. She waits at home while the monstrous deed is done. She cannot sit still, or concentrate on any task. She flits from one chore to another like a distracted girl. Row, agitated by her distress, flutters in the cage and emits loud, rasping *cheep*s. When Joseph returns, he reports that Edmund barred the door, requiring the men to force their way in. "I tried to calm him," Joseph says. "I assured him that I brought with me the peace of Christ and reminded him that he must do as the Court has ordered."

Mary pictures the scene as he describes it—Edmund roaring that he will not allow them to take his grandson. The men breaking down the door, subduing Edmund and Bess. Seizing Silvanus. She imagines the boy, John, bravely trying to beat them off as Silvanus throws his head back and wails with terror. Bess, frantic and weeping as her babe is carried away to his new owner.

Mary can think of nothing to say to her husband, though she wants to ask why he agreed to participate in such a wicked enterprise. She believes he ought to fall to his knees and beg the Lord's forgiveness. She prepares a basket of food—a beef pottage, a loaf of bread, turnips, and potatoes—and makes her way in secret to the Parker farm.

There is no calming Bess. She clings to Mary, sobbing and moaning, wetting her cloak all the way through. Mary wishes she could assure her that Silvanus will thrive, that he will be well cared for. Yet she does not know what will become of him. There can be no assurance that his owner will be kind—or even regard the boy as a child of God.

When Mary leaves, it is near twilight. She walks away with a stone in her heart. It seems that she can hear Bess all the way home, continuously moaning in the most broken voice Mary has ever heard: *"Silvanus! Silvanus! Silvanus!"*

CHAPTER THREE

That summer, the land parches to dun under a sun that sears everything—crops, earth, even livestock. Wells dry up, obliging the men to dig new ones, but the water tastes brackish and bitter and dusty, as if God has dipped in a dirty finger. For the second year in a row the wheat harvest fails. Strange lights blaze in the night sky. Witches are found in pious congregations. Barns burst into flame and children drown. Entire families are struck down by the pox.

Even Mary can discern these signs. Clearly, sin and darkness have ensnared New England in a deadly net. When she learns that Deacon Park has sold both Bess's lover and her son, and that Bess herself has been bound out again—this time to a judge's family in Salem—she is certain the day of God's wrath is at hand.

Thus she is not surprised when, in late June of 1675, word comes from Boston that Indians have attacked the village of Swansea, in Plymouth Colony. Pagan tribes have joined to form an army and are marching north into Massachusetts Bay. In mid-August Indians lay siege to Quabaug, a frontier town west of Lancaster. A

fortnight later, on a hot Sabbath morning, they attack farms in the
north sector of Lancaster itself, butchering George Benet and all his
animals outside his barn and leaving Lidia widowed with five babes
and no relation to come to her aid. Joseph Farrar meets the same
fate. His poor wife is in a stupor for weeks, abandoning her children
to fend for themselves. The MacLoud family is slain in their dooryard as their house burns before their eyes. The Indians do not even
spare four-year-old Hannah. Two days later, a violent storm rips
trees from the ground and ruins the fields of wheat and maize.

Weekly, Joseph's brow glistens with the exertions of his preaching. He cries out and smacks the air with his fists. God, he reminds
the congregation, does not hesitate to rebuke those He loves. Has
He not visited earthquake, fire, and plague upon the Bay Colony? Is
not Lancaster's disobedience as great as any of the Bay towns?

By November, the Indian situation has grown so desperate that
the selectmen consider enclosing the entire town. Someone calculates that it will require a fence eight feet tall and twelve miles long
and they abandon the plan. Instead, the largest homes are designated garrison houses. Two men are appointed to build a stockade
around the Rowlandson house, providing a measure of safety but
spoiling Mary's view from the dooryard. Where she was once able
to see trees blanketing the hills beyond neat fields of wheat and flax,
now she faces only stout posts set close together like the brown teeth
of a great beast.

Winter comes, and an icy wind sweeps the hills and cracks the
branches of trees. Rain falls and freezes on the doorstep. One night
the full moon darkens and turns red as if drenched in blood. Cakes
refuse to rise and bake into dense dry bricks. The sparrow no longer
sings in its cage. Jonas Fairbanks reports that he heard the blaring
of unholy trumpets early one Saturday morning when he walked on
George Hill. Thomas Hosmer tells of the birth of a calf in nearby
Groton whose head was so monstrously deformed the animal could

not stand. Witches' stones crash against the Sawyer house three nights in a row and it is said that the dung of a passing crow struck a man dead on the Concord Turnpike.

In January, everyone in Lancaster is ordered to take shelter nightly in their designated garrisons. Mary's sisters and their families are assigned to the Rowlandson garrison, as are their closest neighbors, the Joslins and the Kettles. By day everyone goes about their duties warily, the way a farmer harvests his ripened grain with one eye cast toward a fretful sky. At night, more than forty people crowd into the house, bringing their blankets and food stores and little else, for there is no room to accommodate furniture. Mary's household, which she strives to order daily, becomes a place of noise and disarray.

In early February, Joseph tells Mary that he has decided to travel to Boston and beg the governor to send troops for their protection. Mary tries to dissuade him. The night before his departure, as they lie in bed, she pleads with him. "Can you not wait till spring?" She tries to keep her voice low, mindful that the bed curtains do little to muffle sound. She can hear the snores and sighs of her relatives and neighbors who sleep on pallets only a few feet away. "'Tis the dead of winter and travel to Boston is arduous."

"Mary, hush." He rolls to face her. Even in the dark she can see that his forehead has knit into a frown. He strokes her cheek, trying to gentle her as she does the children when they are fretful. "You will infect others with your fears. You must be strong in the Lord."

"Send Lieutenant Kerley in your stead! Surely he is more suited to the task." She whispers the words, hoping that her sister Elizabeth is not awake to hear Mary offer her husband in place of her own.

"Henry *will* go. Did I not tell you? He has already agreed to accompany me. But in Boston they will be more persuaded by a minister than a yeoman soldier."

Mary struggles to still her tongue, to submit her will to his. Yet fear assaults her again, sliding up her back like a cold snake. "And what are we to do if the Indians attack while you are gone?"

He clicks his tongue irritably. "Do you think I would leave if I thought that likely? The very reason I go is to insure that we will *not* be attacked."

"But if we are—"

He cuts her off, and tells her what she already knows. "I do not leave you without protection. The house is well garrisoned. John Divoll and John Kettle are here. Abraham Joslin, John MacLoud. My own nephew—"

"Thomas is but a boy," Mary protests.

"Hush you, now! He is nineteen and more skilled with a musket than I am."

Again Mary strives for silence. Again she fails. "Can you not wait until the house is fully secured?" She thinks of the flankers the men have begun building at the corners of the house, spaces a man with a musket can squeeze into and sight the enemy through long vertical slits.

She hears him sigh and realizes their conversation is over. "The Lord will be your safekeeping, Mary," Joseph whispers. She feels his warm breath against her ear. "Sleep now. You must trust always in Him."

She nods *yes*, her forehead lightly brushing his chest. She breathes in his warmth, his familiar scent. Joseph is her husband, the head of her house, as Christ is head of the church, and she owes him loving obedience. She must trust him. Though she sleeps little, she says no more that night.

The sun is rising as Mary follows her husband into the yard the next morning. Joss has brought the bay mare from the barn and is stroking her neck. Elizabeth's husband, Henry, is already mounted on his black gelding. A sudden gust of wind sweeps down from the ridge behind the house, and Mary shivers, for it is plainly an ill omen. She sees Joseph glance at her, and forces a smile of encouragement. She does not want him to discern that her bodily humors have turned to vinegar.

Elizabeth comes out of the house and goes at once to Henry, who is shivering in his thin uniform. Mary sees that Joseph, too, is shivering—though with cold or excitement, she cannot tell. She takes his hand, but fleetingly, for the journey to Boston is long and grueling, and he and Henry must ride in daylight because of the Indian menace. He mounts the mare.

"Godspeed you," Mary manages to say, shielding her eyes against the brightening sky so that she can make out his features.

"We will return before the week is out," he promises, leaning down. "The Lord will keep you. Trust in His mercy."

She nods, accepting his instruction, knowing he means to comfort her. Yet, as the men guide their horses up the bank and into the lane, Mary has the evil thought that she will never again see her husband alive. She feels a wave of self-pity that she fears will dribble out of her all day in small, bitter drops.

CHAPTER FOUR

For four days Lancaster waits for Joseph and Henry to return with soldiers, but no word comes from Boston. The women and children keep to the house. Mary goes about her duties with the other women, tending the fire, scrubbing floors, washing clothes, watching over the children, preparing food. They make porridges of dried peas and beans, stews of boiled parsnips and ham, loaves of bannock bread and pans and pans of biscuits. There are so many in the garrison that they have to set two boards at midday. Everyone eats quickly from common trenchers; even the children are subdued.

Mary minds her own children vigilantly, keeping a singular eye on six-year-old Sarah. Marie is now ten, sturdy and obedient, stalwart as her father. Joss is two years older, rangy and impulsive, desperately needing to be put to work. There is never enough for him to do in this confined space. Mary often sets him to cutting firewood at the back door, yet his liveliness is never sated.

Each night, after their day's labors are done and the children asleep, the women sit together while the fire burns down. They mend and knit and talk of their fears. On the third night, Priscilla Roper says something that turns Mary's blood to ice.

"Do you not suspicion," Priscilla says, "that Bess Parker's sin has brought this menace upon our town?"

Elizabeth speaks before Mary is able to collect her tumbling thoughts. "Has not Bess gone to Salem these many months now? We cannot fault her for our present trials."

"But her father still lives among us," Priscilla says. "It is said he has turned to witchcraft."

"It has not been proven against him," Mary says sharply. "He has simply done what anyone would do—seek to protect his child and grandchild."

Priscilla casts a skeptical glance. "When was he last at worship? When did he last sit at the Lord's table?"

"I know not," Mary says. "But his absence does not make him a witch."

"Perhaps not, but we dare not ignore the signs."

Mary wants to say that they have long ignored signs of injustice and intolerance, but she holds her tongue. Such talk will only set her against her neighbors and sisters, and no woman in a frontier town can afford such disaffection. They depend on one another for their very lives—especially in these perilous times.

"The girl's sin was severe," Ann Joslin says. "Surely we have not forgotten the child was a Negro?"

"Aye," says Elizabeth Kettle, nodding.

"Does that make him less her child?" Mary asks. "Does it make her heart less desolate when he is lost to her? Think on it. What would we feel were one of ours sold into slavery?" And then Mary says what she has not spoken before outside Joseph's presence. "If the Indian menace is indeed the chastening hand of God upon Lancaster, I warrant it is not brought down by Bess's sin, but by our own insufficiency of compassion toward her."

The women instantly fall silent and none of them—not even Elizabeth or Hannah—will look at her. Finally Elizabeth coughs and, to relieve the awkwardness in the room, begins to speak of Indians. She declares they are without mercy. She says that her husband heard some ghastly particulars when he was in Concord the past week. "'Tis said in Swansea they slew seven men and cut off their heads and set them on poles in the wilderness. And I have heard it whispered that in another place they bound all the men together and made them watch as they butchered their cattle and swine before their eyes."

"They kill our animals to provoke us," Priscilla says. "To unhinge our minds. They know how we prize them."

Mary nods, for she too has heard of this cruel Indian practice.

"That is not the worst of it." Elizabeth lets the linen napkin she is hemming fall into her lap and strokes it, as if it were a purring cat from which she seeks comfort. "They delight in torture. It be both sport and pleasure to them."

Ann Joslin moans and Mary feels her hair rise, though it is safely tucked beneath her cap.

"Some they cut off their hands and feet," Elizabeth continues. "Some they take their scalps and flaunt them as trophies. Once they have exhausted their cruelties, they dispatch the men with a blow to the head. And before they kill the women, they defile them."

Mary is frightened, yet something perverse in her makes her want to hear more, to probe each horror. She bites the inside of her lip hard, to still her querying tongue. "If the Indians come to Lancaster," she says firmly, "I will never let them take me alive. I would rather die than subject myself to their depravities."

"Pray God that we all be spared," Ann Joslin whispers and folds her hands over the unborn child that has already grown large within her.

"I doubt they will come," Hannah says. "Why would they come

in winter, when they must wallow in snow? If they attack Lancaster, I am sure they will wait until spring, when they can strike quickly. And, in any case, soon we shall be well defended."

"Let us hope so," Mary says. "For I have not heard that Indians govern themselves by reason, let alone good sense."

The women fall silent. For months, they have worried their memories with the August terrors as one dabs at a sore that will not heal. They have repeated the details over and over: the bloated, mutilated bodies, the charred timbers of the MacLoud house, the poor fatherless Benet children. Their horror is like a blaze that singes the hairs on a woman's arm when she stirs the pottage.

When the fire dies down, Mary banks it and the women retire—Mary to the bedstead where her daughters are already curled together in sleep, her sisters and neighbors to their pallets. Though it is late and she is exhausted, Mary does not sleep but lies staring at the shadows that move across the curtains. She hears children's gurgles and sighs as they sleep, the drowsy murmurs of adults. She wonders how Bess Parker fares. She thinks about Indians and their fierce pagan ways, their disquieting stealth. Even now they might be skulking through the woods nearby. Or laying a trap to butcher Joseph and Henry on their way home from Boston.

It begins to snow and with the snow comes sleet, small hard flakes that tick against the windows and clot on the doorstep. Mary whispers a prayer of protection as her mind finally empties into sleep.

The wind comes up before dawn, whining against the roof and clapboards, waking Mary from a troubling dream in which Joseph has lost his way in the wilderness. She sees him caught fast in a tangle of undergrowth beneath great trees while savage beasts and Indians circle him in ever-tightening rings. She can do nothing to save him, but stands watching while he cries out for mercy.

She sits up, praying that God has not sent the dream as a prophecy. Marie lies sprawled on the far side of the bed. Sarah whimpers in her sleep. Mary pushes the curtains aside, ignoring the familiar catch in her back and knees as she stands. She relieves herself in the chamber pot and quickly puts on her bodice and skirts over her shift. She takes her apron and pocket from the hook by the bed and straps them on before making her way to the hearth, where the dogs reluctantly rise and make room for her. The fire has burned down to embers and it takes a long time to coax it back to life, time spent kneeling on frozen stone and carefully rearranging the coals, blowing and feeding strips of bark to the embers to rekindle the flame.

She is still crouched on the hearth when she hears the first shriek. She tells herself it is but the wind against the flankers and adds another handful of sticks to the small fire. Then she hears it again and knows it is not the wind, for the shriek is followed by musket fire.

The dogs lift their heads, ears pricked. Mary gets to her feet, praying it is merely a hunter from another garrison, tracking deer in the fresh snow. But there comes another shot, and another, like the sound of dry twigs snapping under a heavy foot. She moves to the window, stepping carefully over her sleeping neighbors, and uses her fingernail to scrape frost from one of the small diamond panes. Her view is distorted by a ripple in the glass, but the black smoke rising beyond the snow-topped stockade is clear enough. It comes from the Kettles' house. Mary takes a step back, pressing her hand over her mouth, looking around the dark room. Everyone is still asleep.

The sound of muskets grows louder and closer. She tries to remember what Joseph said must be done if the Indians attack, but her mind is as blank as the snow in the yard. At her feet, a pile of blankets stirs and Hannah's husband, John Divoll, emerges. She can make out his features only dimly in the half-light, but she sees him rub his forehead and cock his head toward the sound.

"They have come," she says, whispering because she cannot seem to make her voice work properly. "The Indians are upon us."

He scrambles to his feet. "Awake!" he bellows, already pulling on his breeches and coat. "The enemy has come!" He heads for the cabinet where the guns are stacked.

People tumble out of their blankets and rise from their pallets. Row sets up an alarmed chirping. Mary sees Ann Joslin on her feet, clutching a struggling Beatrice in her arms. From the parlor come the sounds of an infant's wail and a man barking orders.

Hannah appears at her side, sweeping a tangle of dark hair from her face, pulling a blanket around her. "Mary?" she says, her voice catching at the back of her throat. Mary can think of nothing to say, no sisterly word of comfort or solace.

Joseph should be here, she thinks, and a dart of anger jabs her throat. She scans the room for Joss as she hurries to the bedstead, finds Sarah still asleep, Marie awake and huddled in a nest of blankets.

"Come," Mary says, throwing back the covers. "Put on your clothes, girls. Hurry."

"Are we going out?" Sarah frowns up at her.

"Nay, not yet," Mary says. "But we must be ready in case we are required to make an escape."

"Escape to where?" Marie asks. "Why?"

"The Lord will guide and protect us," Mary says, knowing it does not answer her questions, yet it is all she has to offer. "Hurry now. Make ready."

Musket balls rattle like hail against the house and men are shouting and slamming closed the shutters. What little light was inside is gone now, the rooms plunged into blackness. She searches her heart for hope, snatches at the fact that the Indians have not yet broken into the house. Perhaps Joseph, at this very moment, is close to Lancaster with the troops that will drive off the enemy.

Elizabeth is suddenly at her elbow. "We must pray!" she whispers. Mary nods but she cannot bend her heart toward God before locating Joss.

She pushes through the crowded room to the narrow stairs and climbs to the chamber where her son sleeps. She stares at his empty pallet and tossed blanket, and her heart thumps hard. She glances at the ladder that leads to the attic, and sees a shadow drifting between the rafters.

For an instant she frowns, puzzled; then she smells smoke and hears the hiss of flame on wood.

She nearly tumbles down the stairs. "The Indians have fired the house!" she shouts. "The roof is burning!" She runs to the bedstead and yanks Sarah to her feet, ignoring the girl's bewildered protests. Marie is suddenly next to her, moving like a shadow. Mary drops her free arm over her daughter's shoulder and hugs her tightly, briefly. Then—finally—she sees Joss carrying a water bucket, weaving purposefully between people. He disappears up the stairs and for one instant she admires his valor. In the next, she fears for his life.

Ann Joslin, crouched now on the floor against the wall, begins a wild weeping. Mary kneels to calm her. "Fear not," she says. "I am assured my husband will soon come with the soldiers. Even now, I warrant he's but a few miles from Lancaster." She wants to believe this—*must* believe it—for she sees how plainly her own fear is reflected in the other woman's face. Ann lapses into whimpers, and then there is only the clout of close-fired Indian muskets and the thud of balls tunneling into the front door. It sounds to Mary like the Devil's own knuckles, endlessly rapping. She knows she is doomed. They are all doomed.

Joss runs down the stairs, trailing smoke. Water drips through the ceiling boards. He stands in front of Mary, coughing, eyes bright with excitement even as he confesses that he could not stanch the flames.

"We must go out!" she cries. "The house has been fired!" In front of her, John Divoll staggers backward with his hand on his neck. Blood runs between his fingers and drips onto the floor. He sinks down on one knee.

"John!" Hannah's scream makes the infants wail louder. The dogs moan from the corner but, strangely, they do not bark.

Mary turns to the knot of children huddled, coughing and weeping, in the middle of the room. She grabs Sarah's arm and the hand of Elizabeth's four-year-old daughter, Martha. "Hurry! If we stay here, we will burn alive." She wonders if they can hear her over the cries inside and the pagan howls outside. Smoke pours into the room, threatening to smother everyone. She doubles over, coughing and coughing into her apron.

As she straightens, the fire suddenly surges forward from the back of the house. Flames roar overhead. "Joss! Marie!" she screams, dragging Sarah and Martha toward the door. "Everyone! Make haste!" Elizabeth moans and falls back against the chimney wall.

Sarah begins crying and jabbing her free hand in the direction of the east window. Mary looks to where she is pointing and sees the birdcage hanging on its peg. She cannot make out the bird. Likely it is already dead, killed by the smoke.

"Mother!" screams Sarah. "Save Row!"

Mary shouts to be heard over the din. "Nay, Sarah. Come now. We must save ourselves."

"No!" Sarah yanks her arm from Mary's grasp and scuttles back through the huddled people behind them. Martha starts to make the gulping sounds that herald a wail, and Mary picks her up. "Hush, child. I have you now." She looks for Elizabeth but cannot find her.

Sarah suddenly appears at her side, carrying the birdcage, which is nearly as big as she is. To Mary's surprise the sparrow is still alive, fluttering and flapping against the bars. Mary puts Martha down, plucks the cage from Sarah and orders both girls to hold tightly to her skirts. "Do not let go," she warns, in a menacing voice that does not sound like her own. She moves again to the front of the house.

The youngest Kettle boy is crouched by the door. "Open it," Mary cries. "Hurry!" He scrambles to do her bidding. She glances back to assure herself that Joss and Marie are following and then takes a deep breath, pulls the two little girls close, and steps resolutely over the sill.

She fully expects this to be her last moment. The only thing left to feel is a war club crushing her skull, or a musket ball shredding her lungs before she crumples into a slick of her own blood.

Yet she stands stock-still on the wide granite door stoop, holding a birdcage, miraculously unscathed. All her senses have exploded wide open. Terror has rendered the world fiercely, acutely luminous, as if even the smallest thing in it is vibrating with meaning.

CHAPTER FIVE

The sky is an unholy blue. Wind has blasted away the snow clouds, and the rising sun flares above the meetinghouse. The tang of gunpowder fills the air. Scalloped in fresh snow, the shattered stockade wall gapes open. Oddly, the whitewashed fence at the bottom of the yard is still standing, its gate latched.

Smoke pours from the roof, unfurling a black curtain over the open door. Heat flashes into Mary's lungs. John Divoll, carrying his son Josiah, bumps her hip as he lurches past into the yard, knocking the cage from her hand. It rolls across the stoop and into the snow. Mary stumbles after John, unable to draw her gaze from the blood still running down his neck, streaking his linen shirt. She feels Sarah take her hand, and then she thinks to grasp Martha's. She moves forward, pulling the girls along. Her shoes sink into the snow.

The Indians are everywhere, like a plague of vermin, flowing up the slope from the swamp and down the long hill behind the house, assailing the garrison like crazed rats. They have infested the barn and stand on its roof and peer from its windows; they crouch behind each tree and stone; they turn themselves into stumps in the dooryard, into hummocks of land, into saplings, into the earth itself.

At the bottom of the slope, the northeast corner of the barn is swallowed in flames. Great red and yellow coils lash the sky. Ropes of smoke trail up from the eaves and thrash across the roof, as if binding it with gray cords. The cow staggers through the snow, bawling; pigs run squealing in all directions. Mary sees Brindle, one of the oxen, swaying beyond the gate. Her great belly has been split open. As she lurches forward, her intestines unravel across the ground.

Mary's stomach twists; she bends and retches into the snow, dimly aware that Martha's hand has slipped from hers. When she straightens, she glimpses the child running back toward the house. She shrieks and starts to follow but immediately loses sight of her in the smoke and confusion. She tightens her grip on Sarah, who is straining toward the cage.

Mary feels a wedge of dull anger slide between her ribs. She reminds herself that the child is too young to understand their peril. Mary lurches back, grasps the cage in her free hand and carries it away from the house. Sarah, finally cooperating, tries to hurry along beside her, but the snow is deep; their progress is difficult and slow. Mary stops behind a barrel, crouches and draws Sarah down beside her. "We must let Row go," she says, setting the cage in the snow and unhooking the little door.

As she reaches inside for the sparrow, she is aware of the absurdity of what she is doing. Why is she taking time to release a bird when the world is being sundered before her eyes? When her life and the lives of her children are in terrible danger? She grasps the sparrow firmly, feels the tiny heart quivering against her palm. She glances down to see if Sarah will protest, but the child has buried her face in the heavy folds of Mary's skirts.

Mary opens her hand. The sparrow does not move. She hears

women screaming and the fire snarling behind her like a great beast. She throws the bird up into the air, but it drops to the snow, flaps its wings twice and flutters toward the cage.

Mary stares down at it. She realizes dully that she should have anticipated this. The cage is the only home Row has known for more than three years. Impulsively, she rises and with all the strength she can muster kicks the cage away. It rolls toward the burning house while the startled sparrow flutters over her head. The bird rises, turns west, then north, darts over the roof of the house, and is instantly gone.

Mary hears a groan and turns to see Ann Joslin staggering toward her. She is carrying Beatrice, balancing her oddly on her swollen belly. Suddenly an Indian leaps in front of Ann, flourishing his war club. She shrieks and cowers. Mary instinctively moves to turn Sarah away, to prevent her witnessing what will happen next. Yet the Indian does not kill Ann, but grabs her arm and shoves her through a break in the stockade.

Mary peers over the top of the barrel, looking for Joss and Marie. Everything appears dim and distant in the smoke. Shapes have become shadows. With a roar and the sound of splintering wood, the barn collapses and a dark cloud rises in its place. Mary twists away. She sees that Sarah's cap has come off and her flaxen curls are flying around her head. Mary lifts her hand to tame them—a simple, foolish gesture in the maelstrom of terror. But it strangely calms her—the feel of her daughter's small skull beneath her palm, the feathery mass of silken hair, her smooth, sleep-warmed skin. She gathers Sarah closer and looks west, where the forest begins beyond the field.

She wonders how many more Indians are concealed in the trees. She prays that Joss and Marie have made their way to safety. Perhaps they fled up the hill to the meetinghouse. Surely even Indians would not set fire to a place of worship. She starts in that direction, but again Sarah holds her back, shaking her head, refusing to move.

"Come!" Mary can hear the fear in her own voice and tries to banish it. "Do not disobey me now, child!" Still Sarah refuses to move. Finally, Mary picks her up and half drags, half carries her as fast as she can toward the gap in the stockade. Her arms shake with the unfamiliar weight and her skirts drag in the snow. Each step seems agonizingly slow.

She hears a man scream and turns. Hannah's husband, John, is at the bottom of the yard, halfway between the burning house and barn. He is no longer carrying Josiah but staggering toward the lane, a dark figure against the snow. Even as she watches, he falls.

The Indians swarm over him, chanting and shouting. They pull off his breeches and shirt and wave them like banners. They yank him naked to his feet and throw him down again. One raises a knife. John shrieks as his entrails pour out onto the snow. The Indians howl.

Mary cries out, the sound rising the way a blackbird startles from a tree—there suddenly, and as quickly gone. In the next instant, she feels a blow in her left side and staggers back. For a second her whole body is numb, and then pain stabs her.

It takes her a moment to realize that she has been hit by a musket ball; her skirt waist has been shredded, exposing bloodied flesh. In the next instant Sarah begins to scream, and Mary looks down to see her daughter's hand, spangled in blood.

A wave of nausea overcomes Mary and she sinks, pulling Sarah down with her. Her legs fold crookedly under her. She tears off Sarah's apron and uses it to bandage the girl's hand. Sarah struggles and cries out.

"Hush!" Mary whispers, her mouth close to the girl's ear. "Help me, Sarah. I must stanch the bleeding."

Sarah sags and the iron smell of blood fills Mary's nostrils. It is then that she sees that it is not only Sarah's hand that is wounded; her entire midsection has been torn open. Mary bites down on a moan, rips off what remains of the girl's apron and presses it hard against the shredded flesh. At once, blood soaks through the fabric and begins pooling in her lap. Mary feels a great darkness suck her downward. If the ball has entered Sarah's bowels, she will die. A cold numbness comes over Mary, as if the snow has invaded her heart. She tears a long strip of cloth from her underskirt and wraps it tightly around Sarah's stomach, then gathers her daughter to her bosom.

Three of Elizabeth's sons pass Mary, only yards from where she sits on the frozen ground. Henry and William carry muskets. William is bent forward in a low crouch, dragging his leg, which he injured a few weeks ago in a fall from the barn. Joseph, who is but six months older than Sarah, runs by, his feet throwing up clots of snow. An Indian springs from behind a cart and knocks him to the ground with a single blow to his head. The child does not move but lies on his back in the snow. His eyes are wide, staring at the sky as if surprised, but Mary knows that he sees nothing.

William turns and wildly swings his musket at the Indian, who howls and dodges away. Another warrior appears and leaps on William's back. The boy's good leg buckles and he goes down. Both Indians fall on him at once, instantly crushing his head and neck with their war clubs.

Stunned and sickened, Mary watches it all. William thrashes briefly and then lies still. The tallest Indian squats over him, draws a knife from his leggings, and cuts away the boy's scalp. He begins leaping around, waving his hideous prize. Pinwheels of blood stream from his hand onto the snow.

Mary cannot see Henry. Has he escaped? She hears violent coughing and whirls to watch Elizabeth reel out the door and onto the stoop, smoke roiling around her. Her dark hair has spilled from her cap and she clasps an infant to her bosom. Mary wonders briefly whose child it is.

Elizabeth sways and takes one step forward, then sinks to her knees. For a moment Mary thinks she has been killed, but then she struggles valiantly to her feet. Nearby an Indian rises from behind a barrel. He wears nothing but a short cape and breeches. He raises his musket and fires straight at Elizabeth. Her arms open, as if reaching for some unseen rescuer and the infant falls into the snow. Mary sees the white horror on her sister's face before her expression goes flat and she slumps forward. She almost seems to be arranging herself as she collapses next to the infant.

The Indian scoops up the child in one hand and, holding it by the feet, dashes it against the side of the house. The skull splits open and the snow blossoms suddenly with blood. The warrior contemptuously kicks away the tiny body, as if it is a rotten gourd, then turns to his friends with a triumphant cry.

Something unlocks inside Mary and, covering Sarah's face with her sleeve, she lifts the girl into her arms and struggles to her feet. She heads for Elizabeth, who has not moved. Her face is pressed down deep into the snow and it is Mary's thought that she must turn her sister's head so she can breathe. When she is only a few feet from Elizabeth, Mary glimpses an Indian rounding the house and coming toward them.

Her mind is slow and murky, as if the smoke has invaded her head. She stops, sways, starts to turn. Suddenly a war club is thrust in her face and Mary finds herself staring at strange pagan designs etched into the wood.

The warrior is breathing heavily, so close she can smell the wild, rank odor of his breath mixing with the stink of charring wood. His head is shaved on one side, his remaining hair caught into a long braid decorated with feathers that falls over his chest. He studies her, his eyes moving slowly up and down her body, then fixing on

Sarah. Her mind clears and she realizes he's weighing their lives, deciding whether to kill them.

"Please," she says. Her tongue burns and tastes like smoke. "I beg you, do not slay her."

Their eyes meet and he lowers his club. Mary steps back, away from him, but before she can take a second step, he stops her with his free hand and plucks off her cap. He flips it into the wind, where it swirls on an updraft toward the ruined barn. Her hair falls down her back and shoulders. He stares at it, perhaps startled by the color, then grasps a handful and brings it to his mouth. Like a snake, his long tongue comes out of his mouth and he licks one strand. Mary shivers in revulsion, but when he tilts back his head and laughs, it occurs to her that her hair may have saved Sarah.

He catches Mary's wrist and pulls her quickly across the yard. When she stumbles under Sarah's weight, he jerks her impatiently. They go down through the yard of blood and churned-up snow, moving past the mangled bodies of her nephews William and Joseph, and past the naked, bloodied corpse of John Divoll. They pass a dead boy's body sprawled facedown on a rock, his arms twisted in impossible positions. Mary recognizes the tousled hair; it is Josiah, Hannah's son. She looks away but cannot stop the heaving of her stomach. They go past the barn and out to the lane, where many Indians are milling around. Someone hands her captor a length of braided rope. He fashions a loop and knots it around her neck, tying the other end to his waist. Mary is grateful that he does not try to pull Sarah from her arms. The child is still moaning. Blood runs from her stomach, dripping thickly onto the snow in multiplying spots. Mary's own wound repeatedly stabs her, but she forces herself to stand tall, sensing that drawing any attention could mean the instant death of her daughter.

Her eyes burn, her mind swirls, and she cannot hold a thought. Her throat hurts, as if the tears clotted there are barbed. She tries to concentrate on what is happening, but everything is fragmented, confused. Did she not swear she would rather die than fall captive to Indians? Yet now that the hour has come upon her, where is her courage to resist these heathens? Why can she not gather the strength to flee?

The chanting and cries die away, and for a moment there is no sound except the fire crackling and soughing up the house walls. The air reeks with burning wool and hair. Mary looks back over her shoulder at the house, where flames are busily licking at the three laundry barrels that stand by the door. One of the barrels erupts in flame and breaks open. Its staves fall across the stoop onto Elizabeth's legs. Mary can watch no longer. She turns away from the sight of her sister's body, even as Elizabeth's skirts burst into flame.

She hears a crow call from the tree by the meetinghouse, and the sound of women weeping. She spots Hannah standing a few yards away. She, too, has a rope around her neck, and is carrying her four-year-old son, William. Mary wants to signal her, but Hannah is not looking in her direction.

The Indians begin to push the captives into a long line. There are warriors everywhere, hundreds of them. Finally Mary sees— sorrow mixing with relief—that both Joss and Marie are far ahead of her in the line with other children. Two of Hannah's children are there, and Elizabeth's three daughters, including Martha. All their necks are bound by ropes. A few yards away, young Henry Kerley sags between two warriors. His arms are pulled behind him and bound to a pole laid across his upper back. Mary feels a great plunging hopelessness fall through her. Her nephew did not escape as she had hoped. Likely no one escaped.

She begins to shake. The tremors are so strong she has to struggle for breath. She wonders how much blood she has lost. She sees Elizabeth Kettle weeping, her hands covering her face. She, too, is tied to her captor. Nearby, Ann Joslin stands with her head bowed, clutching Beatrice, whose small arms are clasped tightly around her mother's bound neck.

Mary hears a woman scream behind her. She turns to see Priscilla Roper stagger and fall as an Indian strikes her on the side of her head with his club. Priscilla keeps her arms around her young daughter as she falls. But the girl is trapped beneath her and starts to scream. The Indian yanks her out from under Priscilla's body. For a moment Mary thinks he will hand her to another woman, and she even extends her own free arm to accept the girl. Instead, he tosses her high into the air, swings his club and smashes her skull. The girl drops at his feet, dead.

Her captor tugs on her rope and Mary lurches forward. She is shaking so hard she is afraid her legs cannot hold her. Sarah moans and she hushes her urgently. The whole line is moving. Mary loses sight of Joss and Marie as they are swallowed in a great shifting chain of people. The Indians are hurrying the captives away, leading them south along the lane like cattle at a market. Abruptly, they turn west into the field, pulling and jerking the captives toward the forest. It is strangely silent; the only sound Mary hears besides feet shuffling through the snow is the warning shriek of a jay.

Mary sways under Sarah's weight; her daughter slows her as surely as shackles. She feels blood from her own wound flowing down her left side. Waves of vertigo sweep through her. Where the snow has drifted and lies deep in a small hollow, she stumbles and nearly falls. The air is foul with smoke. They march in a long ragged column across the field, in snow up to their calves.

Only once does Mary look back. Their blood has made a jagged pink trail in the snow. The walls and roof of her home have fallen. A smoking pyre rises over the place where her sister's body lies.

Then they go into the trees, and Mary feels as if she has come to the end of the world.

CHAPTER SIX

The snow is not as deep under the trees. It has been packed down by the feet of the Indians and captives in front of Mary, so she no longer has to wallow through drifts. Yet they move slowly, on a trail that only the Indians know. The tree trunks, black against the snow, remind her of a stockade wall.

They begin to climb a steep path disordered with roots and rocks. She hears children moan and cry out for their mothers, but they do not stop walking. They are strung out in a long line—Indians and captives tied together—a line that twists like a snake into the forest. Mary sees a group of warriors herding pigs and an ox. Some carry dead chickens and tools—kettles and rakes and shovels. A young warrior holds a leather flail in his left hand, idly flipping it back and forth as he walks. It is clear the Indians have plundered many houses.

She hears Indians talking in their garbled language. Several times she trips, but manages to recover before she falls. In her fear and fatigue, she begins to imagine that the warriors will drive them on and on until they all fall dead, never reaching any destination. The wound in her side burns and her chest and arms ache from

carrying Sarah. The rope chafes her neck. She knows they must be
climbing George Hill, though it feels as if she's walked much farther than a mile. The light is muted under the trees, which makes it
difficult to see the path, especially with Sarah in her arms. When
Mary stumbles, the rope nearly chokes her.

Finally the land begins to level off and she sees the roof of a building poking over the brow of the hill. It is the old trucking house, or
what is left of it, for it has been long abandoned. But it is shelter, and
at this moment of exhaustion the sight of an English house gives Mary
hope, especially when she sees the Indians preparing to stop for the
night. Apparently even devils have to sleep.

Mary is still tied to her captor. He has stopped to talk to a warrior wrapped in a red blanket. She wishes she knew their language.
She thinks of Timothy, the young Nashaway servant who ran away.
She regrets reprimanding him for using Indian speech. If she had
learned those words, they might prove useful now.

She looks around for Joss and Marie, but cannot find them in
the semi-gloom. She gently lowers Sarah to the ground and cups
some snow into her palm. She holds it until it melts, then dribbles
the few drops of water into her daughter's mouth. Sarah moans
constantly and seems half asleep, though from time to time she
rouses to ask where she is. Blood still oozes from the wound in her
stomach; the stain now covers not only her waist but her bodice and
skirt front. And it's smeared all over Mary's apron.

Mary lifts Sarah again and shifts her higher in a vain attempt
to relieve the ache in her shoulders. Her own wound pulses and
burns as she steps toward her captor. "Please," she says. "Let us use
the house." She points to the sagging roof, hoping that he understands some English. "To sleep. For the women and children."

He frowns, spits on the ground, and then wipes his mouth with
the back of his hand. "What, you love English still?" He forms the
words slowly behind his teeth. They come out as throaty sounds
that remind Mary of a dog's bark. But the meaning is clear enough.

"Aye, I love them," Mary says. "Am I not English? What has that to do with taking shelter?"

His eyebrows rise and he erupts in a burst of grunts that she slowly perceives is his peculiar mode of laughter. The man he has been talking with joins in. Her captor says something in his own tongue and laughs again. The other Indian begins hopping around, clucking and screeching like a crazed hen.

A third Indian approaches. He is tall, with even features and a steady gaze. He wears leggings of deer hide and a dark blue blanket over his right shoulder. But his face has not been painted, and when he gestures, Mary glimpses an English waistcoat beneath the blanket. He speaks to the warriors in their tongue and then looks at her.

"Do you understand your situation?" He speaks English clearly, without a strong accent.

"My situation?" The pain in her side is coming in sharp waves, wringing sweat from her despite the cold. "Tell them that I am the wife of Lancaster's minister. My daughter is sorely wounded."

"They know who you are," he says. "It was ordered that you be taken."

She frowns. "Someone planned my capture? How would they know me?"

He looks at her hair. "You are easily marked. They looked for a woman whose hair is the color of the fox." He smiles.

Her captor looks at her and speaks, a torrent of incomprehensible words. She looks questioningly at the tall Indian. "Kehteiyomp says you are of no importance now," he tells her. "You must remember that you are a slave."

Slave. The word lashes her. She thinks at once of Bess and her lover, who is a slave, of the child who was torn from her. She recalls Bess saying that slavery was a great evil in God's eyes. She recalls her own assumption that it is God's will. Now the Lord's judgment has come upon her with an exquisitely crafted punishment. She herself is enslaved and will soon become intimate with its rigors.

"He wants to know where your husband is," the tall man says. "He wants to know why he did not defend you."

Mary studies her captor's face, wondering if she should tell the truth. "He has gone to Boston," she says. "He will rescue me when he returns."

Her captor laughs and makes a cutting motion across his neck. "He not save you," he says. "Men slay him when he come." He gives the rope a sudden, sharp tug, and Mary lurches forward. Sarah cries out. Her captor turns and moves quickly along the ridge, forcing Mary to clutch Sarah more tightly and hurry after him.

In front of the empty house, several men have dug a pit and are building a huge fire. Mary is shaking with cold and hunger. But instead of leading her to shelter the warrior pulls her to a large stone two rods away from the fire, and sweeps it clean of snow.

"Here," he says, pointing. "You sleep here."

Mary cannot imagine sleeping ever again, let alone on a frozen rock with no blanket. She shakes her head. "Please," she says. "Let me sleep in the shelter with my children."

He strikes her so hard she loses her footing and tumbles back onto the rock. Sarah falls, thrashing, on top of her. Mary sprawls there, wondering at her own foolishness. She had reacted impulsively, without thinking of the consequences—as if she and Sarah were not in the gravest danger.

Her captor gestures that she must sleep where she fell. Mary pulls Sarah to her and spreads the cloak over both of them, though it is a poor barrier against the bitterly cold night. Her head swims and her side feels as if a hot iron is pressing against it, pressing deeper with every breath. She closes her eyes and prays—for her husband's safety and for God's mercy upon her and her poor captive children.

Mary starts awake. Unearthly, piercing cries swirl through the darkness, lifting the small hairs on her neck. She raises her head. The Indians have gathered in a wide circle around the fire.

Some are making the rhythmic yelps and shrieks that awakened her, while others writhe before them in grotesque postures. Like creatures from hell, she thinks. They hop and twist around the fire, their bodies black against the bright flames. It takes her a moment to understand what she is seeing. But she finally realizes—their cries are an unholy music, and their convoluted movements are a barbaric form of dancing. She is witnessing a celebration, a pagan thanksgiving.

The men have butchered livestock. The leg of a cow—perhaps her own milk cow—roasts on a spit over the fire. A sow's head lies near a pile of unplucked hens. Mary does not move, yet as she watches, she grows angry. It is *English* food they are eating, the fruit of *her* labor feeding the enemy, while she has not even a morsel to nourish herself or her child.

She sits all the way up and pulls Sarah into her lap. The girl's eyes blink open and shut and she whimpers, "Mother." Her skirt and bodice are torn at the waist, the fabric soaked in blood. Mary tries to examine her wound without hurting her, but every time she starts to open the bodice, Sarah moans and flails her arms. After several attempts, Mary admits defeat. Even if she could clearly see the wound, she has no salve to treat it. She resettles Sarah against her bosom and rocks her back to sleep.

The chanting and dancing go on and on. Mary feels herself slide into a sort of trance, brooding on what she witnessed that day and wondering what lies ahead. She reminds herself that it is God's providence that Sarah still lives, and that she herself has been preserved to care for her daughter. Perhaps He wants Mary to prevail against the heathens. Didn't He show the people of Israel again and again that their strength was in Him? Didn't He lead them out of Egypt?

In the flickering light, Mary notes that the rope that binds her neck has been thrown over a branch above her head, with the other end tied to a tree some distance away. As she studies the arrangement, she sees its cleverness—it permits her some limited movement, but if she tries to go too far, she will quickly strangle herself.

She peers into the trees that rise beyond the firelight. The Indians are occupied with their celebration and pay no attention to her. If she moves slowly and quietly, she might be able to untie the knot, carry Sarah into the concealing trees, and find her way home.

Home. She has no home. Her house is gone, no more than charred beams on the frozen earth. Yet she reasons that there must be some building or shed in Lancaster left standing, a place where she and Sarah could shelter until the troops that her husband promised come to their rescue. She wishes she knew where Joss and Marie are. She has not seen them since they were marched across the field out of Lancaster.

She lies down again and works her fingers into the thick knot at the back of her neck. Slowly, she begins to loosen it. When an Indian looks in her direction, she closes her eyes and opens her fingers, feigning sleep. She works at the knot for a long time, but cannot free herself. Her captor has tied it with such cunning that her only escape is death.

The dancing and chanting last through the night. Mary lies on the rock next to Sarah, covering them both with her cloak, trying not to move. She remembers the biblical account of Joseph and his captivity in Egypt. How God protected him and raised him up. After some time she sinks into a fitful sleep.

When she wakes, the sky has lightened, shining like a gray pearl. Her legs and shoulders ache and the wound in her side throbs. She lifts the cloak and looks at Sarah. Her eyes are closed and she makes no sound, but her cheeks are flushed, and when Mary kisses her forehead, she feels the dry heat of her fever. She sits up but Sarah does not wake. She is as limp as a doll on the cold granite. Mary says her name, praying for strength. But there is no one to give her any comfort, except the Lord. And He seems very far away.

She thinks of the English-speaking Indian, wonders where he has gone. Perhaps she could prevail on him to help. He is so well-spoken he must have lived among Englishmen for some time. Perhaps he is a Praying Indian, one of John Eliot's converts. Mary knows that the minister in Roxbury has converted many heathen natives, organizing them into small villages in the wilderness where only Christian Indians live.

Embers glow in the fire pit. The dark forms of sleeping Indians lie scattered nearby. Some have begun to move around. A stocky Indian approaches her, a wide-shouldered man with dark eyes. He gestures to Sarah. "Is very sick?"

Mary has heard it rumored that some tribes eat English children in lewd ceremonies, even murder their own offspring if they show signs of weakness. "She is strong," Mary says. "She will soon be well." The Indian reaches down and flips the edge of the cloak off Sarah's head and shoulders. He touches her neck with two fingers. His fingers are black with grime. Mary feels a shiver of revulsion when she sees them set against Sarah's fair skin. Is he going to choke her? After a moment he withdraws his hand. He frowns but says nothing. When he leaves, Mary expels a breath she did not know she was holding.

She gets to her feet and pulls the cloak over Sarah again. The sun is rising. She walks as far as her rope allows and relieves herself behind a bush. As she stands up, she turns east and, through a gap in the trees, glimpses far below the hillside what remains of Lancaster: a scattering of burned houses, dark smudges strewn in the dooryards. Smudges that she knows are the bodies of people she loves.

When Mary returns to the rock, her cloak lies in a heap on the ground and Sarah is gone.

• • •

She runs back and forth, as far as the rope will allow, crying her daughter's name over and over. She knows Sarah is not strong enough to crawl away on her own. Someone has taken her. Mary falls to her knees and begins to scrub the stone with her hands, as if she could pry Sarah from its icy interior.

She senses someone behind her, and then feels a hard hand on her shoulder. She looks up at the tall, English-speaking Indian.

Mary stares at him as his hand moves to the deerskin pouch that hangs from his belt. He takes out a knife.

She cannot help herself—she cries out a pitiful mewling bleat, like a lamb.

"Do not fear," he says.

But she is afraid. She is terrified. He points the knife at her throat and Mary is certain she is about to die. The sorrow that covers her like a shroud is not for her alone, but for her lost children. For Sarah especially.

"Please," she whispers, even as she bows her head to take the knife. "Please, I beg you. Have mercy." She closes her eyes.

She feels the blade against her throat, feels it move back and forth across her skin. She is certain now that he is going to torture her with a slow death. The force of the blade finally becomes so great it cuts off her breath.

The pressure is suddenly released and the rope falls to the ground. It takes her a moment to realize the Indian has not hurt her. He has set her free.

She takes three deep breaths. "Thank you." Her voice scratches the air and then she is suddenly, brutally cold. Her jaw shakes and her teeth clatter in her head. The Indian picks up her cloak and hands it to her. Mary wraps it around her body, though she realizes, as the cold settles into her marrow, that it is not cold alone, but the chill of death.

"Do you know where my daughter is?" She can barely form the words. "Do you know where they have taken her?"

He returns his knife to its pouch. "Monoco's son carries her on a horse."

The name *Monoco* is familiar. He is the one-eyed sachem of the Nashaway tribe that sold land to her father and the other Lancaster proprietors. Mary has seen him swaggering along the town roads as if he built them himself. "Where? Where can I find her?"

He points, and without a backward glance, she runs in that direction, though the path is crowded with Indians. She races past them, thrashing through the snow. On the far side of a ridge she sees a horse and rider. Her legs sag under her and she grabs a sapling to keep from falling, briefly leaning against it before pressing on. An Indian calls out, mocking her flight, and another grabs her arm, but she wrenches away. When she finally draws near, she finds an Indian boy about Joss's age riding the Kettles' mare, clasping Sarah around the waist. Her daughter is moaning. Mary runs her hand over the mare's flank and reaches for Sarah. The boy stares down at her without expression.

"Thank you," Mary gasps. "Thank you for carrying her."

He does not respond. She doesn't know if he's proud, stupid, or simply doesn't understand English. She does not care. Walking beside the horse with her hand on Sarah's leg, Mary is flooded with gratitude. For the Lord, who has preserved Sarah's life and given Mary reason to hope. For the Indian boy who carries her daughter. And for the tall Indian who cut her free.

CHAPTER SEVEN

They walk west through frozen wilderness, stopping only to sleep when it grows dark. Mary trudges along, trying to keep up with the Kettles' mare, to stay as close as she can to Sarah. On the third day, the boy riding the mare offers her his place. His kindness surprises her and she briefly wonders if it is a trick, if riding the horse will cost her more than she is willing to pay. Yet she quickly accepts, unable to resist the opportunity to hold and comfort her daughter, though the awkward heft and twist of her torso as she climbs on reopens the wound in her side.

Every motion causes Sarah pain. She groans and grinds her teeth and rolls her head back and forth on Mary's chest. She cries out, "I shall die!" over and over, while Mary alternately tries to hush her and murmur encouragement.

From the mare's back, Mary sees the line stretching out in front of her. She watches warriors hurry the captives along, prodding them with their war clubs when they stumble. She looks in vain for Joss and Marie, but spots Ann Joslin, sees her reel and nearly drop Beatrice. Elizabeth Kettle has her head bowed and weeps as she walks, continually rubbing her face with her sleeves.

It begins to snow. The flakes fall fast and the wind catches them. Snow stings Mary's cheeks and clots on her eyelashes. It is difficult to see more than a few rods ahead. As they start down a long hill, the mare stumbles. Sarah and Mary fly over her head and crash to the frozen ground. For a moment, Mary cannot see and gropes wildly for Sarah. She hears a scream and wonders if it comes from her own throat. Then Sarah groans and Mary's eyesight clears. She runs her hands over her daughter, seeking broken bones, new wounds. The mare has disappeared. The snow has stopped and three warriors stand nearby, pointing and laughing, plainly mocking Mary's plight. Shaking with pain and humiliation, she picks up Sarah and moves back into the column of walkers. She feels as if her brain is banging against the wall of her skull. She has had nothing to eat or drink except melted snow since the attack. She wonders how long it will be before her strength gives out. And what will happen then?

The warrior who captured Mary, whom she has not seen for two days, appears and signals that she must walk behind him. They come to a place where the trail widens and climb a low ridge. In front of her several warriors have stopped at a wide gap in the trees and are pointing at something in the distance. When she reaches the spot, she sees a great Indian village spread out below her, hundreds of clustered domed shelters of varying sizes stretching along a river like knots on a rope. The word *wetu* comes into Mary's head. She has heard of these Indian hovels but she never imagined there would be so many in one place. Threads of smoke rise from the dwellings into the frigid air. Huge trees line the river, which is silver with ice under the gray sky.

The column's pace picks up; some of the warriors run down the hill; others hurry the captives along. Mary hears women's voices chanting high, hawklike notes. As they enter the village, Mary is able to take only a few steps before the women are upon her, crowding around and peering, jabbering in their strange tongues, plucking at her clothes. They prod Sarah's cheek to see if she will respond, but she lolls senseless in Mary's arms.

Some of the women carry infants on their backs, strapped so tightly to boards they cannot move their heads. They gaze out at the world like tiny statues. Older children, dressed in shirts and furs, chase one another, laughing and weaving among the groups of women. Mary is shocked that no one scolds them, or even seems to notice them at all.

Her captor pushes his way through the crowd of women, gesturing angrily. Mary plods after him, carrying Sarah in her weary arms even as she searches the crowd for a glimpse of Joss or Marie. They come to an open place where hundreds of Indians are milling around. A few rods away Mary sees a warrior who seems to be selling Ann Joslin's son to an Indian woman. The woman waves her arms, shakes her head, and repeatedly pokes the boy's chest with her fingers. Fear is written plainly on the boy's face. Mary wants to comfort him, assure him that all will be well, though, in truth, she has no such assurance. The Indians are as fickle as the weather, changing their demeanor on a whim, fierce one minute, charitable the next.

She has little time to ponder, for in the next instant her captor sells her. *Like an ox at a market fair,* she thinks. Her buyer is a straight-backed warrior whose long hair is drawn back and caught at the nape of his neck with a band of beads and feathers. He has broad shoulders and well-muscled arms. His features are regular except for his large nose, which looks as if it has been broken several times. His eyes, nearly as black as his hair, make Mary think of demons.

He hardly looks at her, but grabs her sleeve and pulls her along twisting paths to a large wetu covered in bark, where he throws open a flap of grease-stained skins and signals her to enter. When she does not move, he gives her a shove and she stumbles through the opening. The skins fall back across the doorway behind them with a dull thump. Sarah moans. The smell of dirt and smoke and grease nearly overwhelms Mary. All she can see at first is a fire, sunk in a stone-lined pit. Smoke rises straight up and disappears through a square opening in the roof.

Her owner says something in a rush of words that sounds like the grunting of pigs. Mary stands, weak with fear, as a woman comes forward from the shadows. She has a long face and a straight nose, wide-spaced eyes and a strong chin. She stares with a gaze so hard that Mary looks away.

The woman takes Mary's chin in her hand and turns her face from side to side, studying her closely, as a man might study a cow or an ox in the marketplace. She pokes Mary's cheek, pries open Mary's mouth and runs her fingers over her teeth, curls her hand about Mary's upper arm and presses the muscles there. She lifts Mary's skirts and rubs her legs, touches her breasts, examines her wound. At last, she seems satisfied.

"Mattapsh," she says, gesturing. *"Yo cowish."* Mary does not move. When the woman speaks again, the warrior puts his hand on Mary's shoulder and presses her down hard onto a mat of skins. She kneels there, uncomprehending, as he lectures her in his tongue.

The woman steps forward. *"Quinnapin,"* she says, dropping her shoulders toward Mary, as if a closer proximity will help her understand. *"Quinnapin."* She touches the man's chest and nods vigorously. *"Quinnapin."*

"Quinnapin," Mary repeats, slowly understanding that she is speaking the man's name.

"Nux," the woman says, nodding. *"Sachem."*

Mary recognizes the second word as a title of authority. She dips her head, indicating that she will cooperate. She will not resist or try to run away. Not while Sarah lies dying.

The woman places her hand on her own chest. *"Weetamoo,"* she says, firmly. *"Sachem."* She taps her chest again. *"Weetamoo."* She turns back to Quinnapin and rattles off a long string of Indian words. Dizzy and weak, Mary resettles Sarah on her lap, doubting that either she or her daughter will live.

Quinnapin abruptly leaves the wetu. Weetamoo sits down next to the fire and takes up a wide strip of deer hide onto which she begins sewing small black and white beads. Mary has seen wampum before, strung onto necklaces and belts; she knows it is made of shells and the Indians place a high value on it, treat it like money. It has always seemed to her an amusing form of currency, but she finds herself fascinated as she watches Weetamoo. So much time and care are required to string the tiny beads, let alone to craft the elaborate black and white patterns, that she wonders if the Indians value wampum not for its intrinsic worth, but for the patience required to prepare it.

Mary kisses and strokes Sarah's feverish face and examines her wounds. The torn red flesh of the girl's abdomen is no longer seeping blood, yet the smell that rises from it tells Mary it is going putrid. She tears a new strip of cloth from her underskirt and ties it over the ragged flesh. She says a prayer, begging God for mercy. She can think of nothing else to do. She peers at the great mats of woven reeds hanging on the sides of the wetu. Rude wooden platforms draped with animal skins stand along the walls. The stink of dirt and furs fills her nostrils. She lies back on her mat and falls away from the pain, sliding into a blessed darkness.

Mary wakes to the realization that she is warm. For the first time since the attack. Some time has passed, though she cannot tell if it is minutes or hours. The door flap opens and a young woman enters, carrying an infant strapped to a cradleboard. She sits beside Weetamoo, who puts down her beadwork, gently unwraps the child from the board, folds him into her arms and begins to suckle. Weetamoo and the girl talk in low voices. The sound, combined with the soft suckling of the baby, makes Mary think of music.

When Weetamoo is done suckling, she places the baby in her lap and plays with him for a long time. Mary cannot stop watching. She has never seen a woman treat a child so tenderly. She was taught when she was still a child herself that showing such affection spoils children and endangers their souls, so she has always been careful not to treat her children too gently in public. Yet she recalls the many times she cosseted them in secret, when no one was watching. She knew she was sinning, yet the sweetness of her infants so overwhelmed her that she could not help herself. As she watches Weetamoo, Mary longs to rock a new babe against her breasts once more.

Weetamoo stops playing with the infant and straps him back onto the board. She says something to the girl, who rises, dips a bowl into a small kettle over the fire and hands it to Mary.

It seems to be a stew of some kind—chunks of meat swimming in a thick broth that smells slightly rancid. Mary would not have touched her lips to it only a few days ago, but her hunger is so urgent that she doesn't even sniff it before she begins scooping it into her mouth with her fingers.

She tries to feed some to Sarah, but the child refuses to swallow. The gruel runs down her chin and stains her shirt and neck a silty brown. "Where is Row?" Sarah whines. "I want to hear Row sing."

Mary hushes her. "Row is well and safe. I am certain of it." She thinks suddenly of Joseph. Why has he not rescued them? She feels anger thread into her chest, then rebukes herself. Warriors are waiting to kill him. She must pray, not for her deliverance but for his safety. Nearly swooning from pain and fatigue, Mary bends her heart toward God and dutifully begs Him to keep Joseph from all harm, to spare him such a trial as hers.

CHAPTER EIGHT

For a week, Sarah lies insensible in Mary's lap, burning with fever. Mary watches, terrified, as the wound festers. She knows how quickly such fevers can take a child, and she has no poultices or balms to soothe her. In desperation, she scrapes dirt from the floor, mixes it with her own spittle, and smears it over Sarah's wound, hoping that it will at least cool her skin. But Sarah only moans and tosses more fretfully. With hand gestures, Mary begs Weetamoo for salves, but the woman ignores her. Mary sits hunched over her daughter, certain that Sarah is dying, and wild with guilt that she can do nothing to save her.

Preoccupied by Sarah's condition, Mary scarcely notices that the Indians are feeding her. Several times each day, the girl—whom she learns is Weetamoo's maid, Alawa—sets slabs of flat bread, cups of water, and bowls of gruel into Mary's hands. When she is too distracted to eat, Alawa tears pieces from the bread, dips them into the stew and presses them to Mary's lips. She chews, unthinking, like a child. Alawa encourages her with gestures to feed Sarah in the same manner, and Mary does. It seems as if she spends hours working Sarah's mouth open with one hand and sliding tiny bits of broth-soaked bread onto her tongue. She spits out at least half of it, but she does manage to swallow some. So Sarah feebly clings to life, while Mary clutches the hope that the Lord will save them both.

She is vaguely aware of the comings and goings of Weetamoo and Quinnapin. She knows they sleep naked at night, curled together under heavy animal skins, Weetamoo's babe tucked up between them. She sometimes hears him suckling. One night she hears Weetamoo and Quinnapin join together as husband and wife. The sound of their lovemaking sends such a bolt of longing through Mary that it is all she can do not to cry out for Joseph. She burrows deeper under the skins they gave her, hoping to shut out the sounds. She weeps for all she has lost. She wonders if Joseph has fallen into Indian hands and been slain.

As Sarah grows more feeble, Mary can do little but hold her. She sits for hours, rocking her, watching Weetamoo decorate belts and skirts with wampum beads. The woman carries herself like a queen. Mary feels oddly diminished in her presence and prays that the Lord will grant Weetamoo a merciful heart.

Instead, Weetamoo rises up like a demon in the middle of the night, pulls Mary from sleep and casts her out of the wetu. Mary pleads with her, begs for mercy, and tells her over and over that Sarah is dying. But Weetamoo's only gesture of compassion is to throw a blanket over Mary's shoulders, fold Sarah's legs and arms inside it, and secure her to Mary's bosom like a swaddled babe.

It is snowing, a hard stinging snow mixed with sleet that blinds Mary and scrapes her face. Her skirts and cloak swirl around her. Tendrils of smoke curl above the wetus. Everything is gray and white. Mary begins to move along the path. She has no destination, no home. She leaves it to God to guide her. Snow flies into her eyes. When Sarah thrashes against her, Mary shifts her daughter higher

to ease her burden, but Sarah is so heavy she staggers. Mary wonders how far she will be able to walk before she collapses and they
both freeze to death.

Dimly, through the streaming snow, she sees a figure. A storm
wraith, dark wings flapping and spinning, wild hair etched in
white fire.

The figure speaks and Mary sees it is a woman. What she perceived as wings is a blanket. There is no fire but only snow. The
woman pats her chin and leans toward Mary so she can be heard
over the roar of the wind. *"Quenêke,"* she says.

"Quenêke," Mary repeats.

She points to a nearby wetu. When Mary doesn't move, the
woman grips her arm and pulls her inside.

The wetu is filled with sleeping Indians. They stretch out on
their platforms and lie clustered on mats around the fire. The air is
tangy and hot. Quenêke points to a space near a platform. Mary's
joints feel frozen into their sockets. It is difficult to move even the
few feet to the side of the shelter, and even more difficult to push
Sarah under the platform and slide down beside her. Quenêke
squats, urging haste with small motions of her hands and low grunting sounds. When Mary has settled, Quenêke pulls a heavy bear
hide over her and creeps away.

Mary wonders why this stranger has taken her in. Does this
mean she is now Quenêke's slave? Is this strange mixture of cruelty
and kindness an Indian custom? The hide smells of smoke and rancid grease, but it warms her. She lies with Sarah in her arms, her face
raw, her mind empty. She tries to pray, but no words form in her
mind and her tongue lies still in her mouth.

After a while, Sarah stops moaning, and her breathing becomes
ragged. Mary sits up and pulls Sarah into her lap. Her body has
become oddly dense, almost too heavy to move. Even as Mary holds
her, she feels a dark cold filling the child.

Mary does not release her, even though she knows Sarah is dead. She presses her face into her daughter's hair and inhales the fragrance of her scalp through the bitter smoke that clings there. She begins to comb the hair with her fingers, pulling the twigs and burrs from the fine yellow strands, smoothing it, braiding it. Only when she finishes does she see that her fingers have trailed streaks of blood into the hair.

Tears come and images float through Mary's mind: She remembers the terrible cries of Bess Parker after her son was taken from her. She remembers the death of her own firstborn daughter. Remembers the fever, the seizures, the slick hot sheen that covered the tiny body, the thrashing, the shrieks, her own desperation. Nothing at all would soothe the child, not even her breast, which had always calmed her. How angry—how furious—she had been at Joseph and his stern counsel to submit her will to God in Christian resignation. She had wanted none of it. She had wanted to scream and rail at God. She had wanted to curse Him, and to curse Joseph for imparting His cruel requirements.

Now, as she tries to remember little Mari's face, she cannot, though she can still feel the round head under her palm, the pink skin stretched over the skull, the heat coming up through the fine hair, soft as milkweed. After Mari died in her arms, Mary handed the body to her sister, and could not bring herself to touch the child again.

But Sarah is different. Holding her body brings Mary comfort and solace. She is her last connection to English life. Her hands and arms are fastened to Sarah's cooling flesh, as if bound there by sailor's knots. She prays that none of the Indians will wake and discover she is dead. She prays again for strength. Even as she prays, she feels herself drowsing, falling toward sleep, and this time she does not try to prevent it. For there is no longer any reason to stay awake.

She dreams it is spring. She is standing on the doorstep of her house, looking across the muddy yard to the barn. The sky overhead is clear but there are low gray clouds in the west. She is troubled by the sensation that there is something she must do, but she cannot think what it is. She becomes slowly aware that she is all alone. There is no one else about the farm, or walking on the road. There are no birds in the trees, no sound of animals coming from the barn. She looks down at her hands and sees that they are bleeding. The skin has torn away in long strips and hangs from the ends of her fingers.

M ary wakes, blinking. A thread of light slides through the smoke hole overhead. Her hands hurt and after a moment she sees why: Her fingers are locked around Sarah, who lies on her lap, rigid and cold.

A few feet away a man is snoring. Mary can see the top of his head—a ribbon of coarse black hair—poking up from beneath a deerskin. She sees Quenêke squatting by the fire, fanning the flames with a turkey wing.

Quenêke looks up at Mary. She speaks, but Mary shakes her head—she does not understand. Quenêke's voice crackles like fire. She points the wing at Sarah.

Mary looks down and sees that her daughter's eyes are wideopen. She covers them with her hand and draws them gently closed. Sarah's skin is icy and dry. It is strange to see her so still. The girl was so quick about everything, so eager to learn about the world. And so quickly gone from it. Suddenly Mary is weeping again, surprised that she has any tears left in her.

"She is dead," Mary cries. "I must bury her."

Quenêke touches Mary's shoulders. "Haste," she says in English. "Go. Weetamoo."

Mary focuses on the whites of her eyes, her flashing teeth. Fear rises in her, like a hot ember scalding her bowels. She stands and starts to lift Sarah's body, but Quenêke stops her, braids snapping back and forth as she shakes her head. "Go Weetamoo," she says.

"Weetamoo?" Mary frowns. "She banished me."

"It is bad to die in wetu of sachem," Quenêke says slowly. "It calls bad spirits. You go now. Not give Weetamoo anger."

"No." Mary shakes her head. "No. Please, let me stay here."

It takes several minutes before Mary understands that she has no choice, that when Weetamoo turned her out of her shelter, it was a temporary exile. "Go haste," Quenêke says, taking Sarah's body from Mary's arms and pushing her outside.

Weetamoo does not seem surprised when Mary steps into the wetu alone. She begins giving her orders, assigning her chores with impatient gestures: She must scrape strings of meat from a smoked deer hide. She must keep the fire burning. She must stir the fibrous stew that fills the iron kettle. Mary's face burns from the heat though her mind is frozen. She can think of nothing but Sarah. Sarah writhing in her death throes. Sarah's last breath. Sarah's body lying in her lap as she sat on the dirt floor of Quenêke's wetu. An icy despair fills her. Life itself no longer matters. She has lost her soul.

Mary knows that grief is a sin. Joseph often preached against it, admonishing the congregation for their attachments. *Do not attach yourself to the things of this earth, but to Heaven alone. 'Tis a sin to place your affection in the flesh, for you belong to the Lord. Forsake your sins, for in sinning you forsake God.* He had lectured her in private, warning her that a mother must not cherish any of her children, for it is too easy to slip into the Devil's snare of serving them instead of the Lord.

Mary prays as she works. Or tries to, forcing her heart toward God, pleading with Him for mercy. After several hours, mercy comes. Weetamoo sends her to the river for water. On her way, Mary passes Quenêke's wetu. She cannot keep herself from entering.

Quenêke is cutting a deerskin into laces. Sarah's body is not in the wetu. Mary cannot hide her panic. "Where is my daughter? What have you done with her body?"

Quenêke looks up at her and puts down her knife. *"Monchuk,"* she says. "Girl gone."

Mary begins to shake. "Where have you put her?" She asks her again and again—falls to her knees and begs—but Quenêke gives no answer and goes back to her work. Finally out of patience, Quenêke pushes her from the wetu. Mary stumbles along the path, her sight blinded by tears, and almost bumps into the English-speaking Indian who cut her rope. He is squatting on the path, studying the ground. He leaps to his full height and looks down at her. She cannot read his expression.

"'Tis you," she says. Then, realizing how foolish she must look and sound, she steps back and tries to recover some composure by wiping her face with her sleeve.

It does no good, for her tears seem to have a will of their own and will not be stanched.

"You seek your daughter," he says. It is a statement, not a question.

She stares at him, stupefied, wondering how he knows. "Yes." Her voice is little more than a croak. She feels as if she's been screaming for hours. She swallows. "Sarah died in the night."

She sees him nod through the haze of her tears. "They buried her this morning."

She does not realize until that moment that she has been imagining some pagan desecration of Sarah's body, not a simple burial. "Do you know where?" she whispers.

"I do." She detects a kindness in his expression that she had not imagined possible in an Indian face. She has always perceived the natives as a stern, humorless people. But here is this man, looking down at her with eyes filled with compassion. "I will show you the place," he says, and gently takes her arm, turning her on the trail.

He leads her out of the village along a narrow path that winds through a stand of hemlocks, to a small hill that has been cleared of snow. He points to a mound of broken earth. "There," he says. "She lies asleep in the Lord."

Startled, Mary looks up at him. "You are Christian?" she asks.

"I was," he says slowly. "I was baptized by Mr. Eliot as a boy."

Mary's mind fills with questions, but they flutter away, like dark moths in the night. All she can think of is her poor dead child lying without coffin or shroud in a shallow grave deep in the wilderness.

She cannot help herself. She flings her body down, full length, on the frozen clumps of dirt, weeping. An icy cold rises from the earth, penetrates her skirts and bodice and shift, then slides under her skin. As the chill enters her bones, Mary feels a strange comfort. A peculiar thought enters her mind. If she stays here long enough, she will be reunited with Sarah. And with Mari. She senses hazily that she has finally found something real, something true, in the midst of the chaos.

She feels a hand on her shoulder. The Indian lifts her under her arms, pulling her to her feet. With great reluctance, she stands. He murmurs something and brushes her cheek with his hand. It is the most tender of gestures—and it is like a knife to her heart. Mary is undone; her legs wobble beneath her and she is about to collapse when he catches her.

She clings to him like a child. Tears pour down her face and her body is wracked by great, wretched sobs. He holds her, and she feels his compassion covering her like a cloak. When her sobs finally subside, she looks up and sees her own sorrow mirrored in his eyes.

Gently, he leads her back to Weetamoo.

CHAPTER NINE

For days, Mary's thoughts are a jumble of sorrow and confusion. She cannot wipe Sarah's wilderness grave from her mind. Nor can she stop thinking about her encounter with the English-speaking Indian, the troubling memory of clinging to him as she wept. The comfort she felt as he held her. The way she completely surrendered to the consolation of his presence. Not of his presence only, but of his *body*. Even at the thought, her face burns with shame. She is as miserable a sinner as Bess Parker.

She feels crazed and savage. She cannot concentrate on the tasks Weetamoo assigns. She is too restless to sit still. Her feet twitch and she cannot control her hands. She rises up and paces around the wetu until Weetamoo threatens her with a stick.

She walks through the village, wringing her hands, without destination, without reason. She stops people on the path to ask, with gestures and signs, where she might find Joss and Marie but receives only averted glances and frowns. It occurs to her that the English Indian might know, but she does not see him. Her pocket knocks against her thigh like a child's hand tapping for attention. She considers what it holds—a spool of thread and a needle, her short knitting needles, a scrap of sweet cake that crumbles to dust in her fingers. Her mother's silver embroidery scissors, their points sharper than a pup's teeth. She imagines taking them out and drawing the short blades across her wrists. She wonders how long it will take for all the blood to run from her body. How simple to walk a short way into the forest and sit down with her back to a tree and take her life. No one would notice her absence. No one would care when they found her dead.

There is no greater sin. It is as if God Himself speaks in her ear. She stops and stands still. She remembers Joseph's sermon the Sabbath after Martha Bard drowned herself. His voice had been filled with fury as he reminded the congregation of their duty to God and to the community. "Who amongst us is so foolish to conceive that we belong to ourselves, that we have the right to choose the day of our death? Who would so *tempt* the Lord to forsake us? Remember, we live on the frontier by His mercy alone!" Joseph had set everyone in the meetinghouse trembling. Even Mary was shaken.

She is so absorbed in her thoughts that she hears her son's voice before she sees him.

"Mother?"

She looks up and claps her hand over her mouth. Joss looks taller than she remembers, though it is less than a fortnight since the attack. He is too thin. His breeches and coat are ripped to rags, and his face is filthy with soot and grime, but he is smiling. She nearly falls to her knees.

Shaking, she takes his shoulders and presses her fingers deep into the fabric of his coat, to assure herself it is truly her son's flesh beneath the wool, and not some specter of her fevered mind.

"Sarah?" he asks, escaping her grasp. "Is she well?"

Mary chokes on a wave of despair. All she can do is shake her head. Her hands, still trembling, fall to her sides. She manages a whisper. "She has perished."

"Dead?" His eyes grow wide.

"Aye," Mary whispers. "She was sorely wounded, but she went like a lamb. My sweet babe." Words are like charms, she realizes. If said often enough, they will make it so. "They buried her, but I fear I cannot show you her grave. I know not how to find it on my own."

He puts his hand on her arm. "The grave is no matter, Mother." How like his father he is! She feels a wave of pride. "I have seen Marie," he tells her. "We prayed together and I promised to watch over her fate as I am able."

"Oh, my son!" She embraces him shamelessly. "Tell me—where is she? Can you take me to her?"

He shakes his head. "It was mere accident that we met. She is closely watched by her mistress."

"How did she seem?" Mary thinks of her daughter's slight frame and quiet demeanor. She has always been a sweet, compliant child. Too compliant sometimes. She hates the thought that she is now a captive. "Is she well? Have they harmed her?" The words rush out of her. What she wants to know, but cannot ask her son, is if Marie has been violated.

"She weeps a lot," Joss says. "But she says 'tis out of homesickness, not harm. I know she would like to see you."

Mary's eyes blur with tears, which she tries to quell. Joss takes her hand and strokes it, and his gesture undoes her. The tears run down her face and drip off her chin. He pats her shoulder, murmurs words she does not try to untangle. When she is finally able to control herself, she thanks him and begs him to tell her where he dwells.

He says he is living with a family in another village a few miles north. They have come to Menameset so his master may join the other warriors in a raid on Medfield. Mary is disturbed by the glint of excitement in his eye. "Pray to the Lord they are defeated," she says. "Are you treated well?"

He nods. "Aye. Like a son."

A great upwelling of dismay begins in her stomach and rises through her chest. "A son?" She struggles to collect her thoughts, to divert her mind from this new peril. "You must not forget whose son you are," she says. "Do you pray, Joss? Do you wait daily on the Lord?"

She catches a twitch of deceit on his face, but it is instantly gone—if it was even there in the first place—and he nods earnestly. "Every day, Mother," he says. "All my hope is in the Lord."

It is the answer she wants—the answer she *needs*—and despite her doubt, Mary feels a flooding reassurance that her prayers will soon be answered. If her children—all but Sarah—are delivered from torture and death, then there is hope for her. Surely God will spare her husband, and with His help, Joseph will soon rescue them.

"You must be strong." She squeezes Joss's shoulder. "Do not submit to the Devil's temptations. The heathen life can be seductive for a boy. Remain firm in the Lord."

"I will, Mother." He is again solemn, earnest.

"I pray for you always." As Mary embraces him again, she feels his resistance in the slight rigidity of his shoulders and the brevity of his response. When she releases him, she turns and quickly walks away, for she can no longer bear the awareness that she cannot care for him. Knowing that another family has embraced him. Knowing that the only balm to her sorrow is prayer.

When Mary returns to the wetu, Quinnapin is standing outside. When he sees Mary, he passes his hand in front of his nose and flips his fingers at her. "When you wash?" he asks.

Startled by his use of English, Mary gapes up at him, but when he wrinkles his nose in disgust, she looks down at her skirts. They are streaked with mud and blood and the hem is in shreds. Her stockings are caked in filth.

"'Tis some months now," she says slowly. "'Tis unwise to wash in this season. It opens the body to toxic humors and weakens the constitution."

He snorts derisively. "You wash," he says firmly. "Now. And every day." He grabs her shoulder, his fingers pressing painfully through her heavy wool cape, and shoves her into the wetu. Mary sees at once that whatever is about to happen has been arranged, for Weetamoo and Alawa are waiting for her. They advance—one on either side—and begin pulling off her clothes. Mary resists, thrashing and grappling with the women, but Alawa yanks at her skirt, and Weetamoo rips the sleeve from her jacket. When Mary cries out in protest, Weetamoo slaps her face hard, a blow so powerful that Mary staggers backward and falls to her knees. Weetamoo stands over her, spraying a torrent of Indian words that Mary cannot understand, but their meaning is plain enough—Mary must remove the rest of her clothes. Shaking, Mary obeys, loosening the laces and peeling the grime-encrusted layers away one after another. She takes off her latchet shoes and unrolls her stockings. When she is finally naked, Alawa gathers the clothes into a bundle and throws them outside. Weetamoo shoves a clod of sphagnum moss into Mary's hand, points to a pot of water, and signals that she must wash. Mary crouches near the fire, and obediently begins to scrub.

When Mary is clean, Alawa hands her a deerskin dress and a pair of moccasins and signals her to put them on. The deerskin is old and worn, thin as linen in some places. Mary holds the dress against her breasts and looks up at Alawa in alarm. "What of my shift?" She cannot abide the thought of wearing the deerskin against her naked body. Like all Englishmen and -women, she has worn a layer of linen under her garments since she was born. Alawa shakes her head. "No shift," she says slowly in English. Weetamoo frowns impatiently and makes a hurrying gesture with her fingers. Mary pulls the garment over her head and rises. The deerskin's folds fall over her like a caress. She is surprised at how easily she wears it, at how comfortable it feels against her skin.

Quinnapin steps into the wetu. He stands with his arms crossed over his chest, staring at her. He inhales a big sniff and smiles. "You clean now," he says. He draws a small English looking glass from his pouch and holds it up in front of Mary.

She sees a woman she barely recognizes. Her face is drawn; her eyes lie like gray river stones deep in their sockets. Her wet hair shines in the firelight. And she is wearing Indian dress. A sinking sensation overwhelms her. Will Joseph recognize her when he comes to rescue her? Will he assume that she has given herself to a warrior?

She starts to pull at the deerskin. "I cannot wear this," she says, shaking her head. "I must have English clothes."

Suddenly Weetamoo is in front of her, brandishing a stick. *"Maninnapish!"* she shouts and jabs her free hand at the doorway. *"Monchish!"*

"Go," Quinnapin says. "Weetamoo want you work."

What work? Mary wonders, but does not ask, for Weetamoo has raised the stick again. As Mary stumbles toward the door, Alawa throws a heavy blanket over her shoulders.

Mary's clothes lie in the snow in front of the wetu. She stares down at them, considering whether it will be safe to take them. She examines her skirt and jacket. The filth-encrusted skirt has been badly torn along the seam and the jacket shorn of buttons. Her hard English shoes are unharmed, but she has no desire to put them on again; the moccasins are soft and make her feet feel as if they are cupped in a huge, warm hand. She bends and roots through the pile until she finds her pocket. She ties it around her waist and starts along the path. After a few steps she goes back and retrieves her apron, stockings and shift, tying them into a corner of the blanket, unable to leave behind all the bloodstained tatters of her former self.

She wanders through the village, surprised to find she is not uncomfortable without her jacket and skirt. The dress is surprisingly warm and the blanket is an efficient barrier against the bitter cold. She ventures down the path to the river and stands on the bank for a long time, staring out at the shadows of the trees on the surface of the snow-covered ice. There are several star-shaped cracks in the ice and a black circle of open water pushed up against the shore—a place where she has fetched water for Weetamoo. She feels as if time has slowed down since she was taken captive; she has more occasion to observe the world around her.

She makes her way down the bank and squats beside the water. Even before she lowers her hands into the river, she knows the icy cold will make her fingers ache. She unties the corner of her blanket and lets the stockings, shift and apron roll into the water. She takes a deep breath, plunges both hands in after them and begins washing the garments, scrubbing them vigorously between her numb hands. She pulls them out and twists them hard to wring the water from them and then slaps them against a nearby boulder. She works with a fierce intensity, determined to draw every drop of blood from the cloth. When she is finished, she ties the dripping garments back into the blanket and resolves to dry them by the fire in the wetu when chance allows.

It is dark when Mary returns to the wetu. Quinnapin is gone and Weetamoo is playing with her baby by the fire. Alawa greets her as a friend, as if she had not savagely ripped her clothes off a short time before. Mary wonders if her status among the Indians has changed along with her clothes. She feels confused and weary—and grateful when Alawa scoops a bowl of stew from the pot and hands it to her. They eat in silence, side by side, listening to the babe's happy chortling as Weetamoo dandles him. Later Alawa makes a poultice of oak leaves and helps Mary apply it to the wound in her side.

Mary washes herself every day, first at Alawa's urging, and later because it makes her feel refreshed and calm. Slowly her wound heals. It no longer pains her to strap the pocket around her waist.

One day she puts on the apron. Alawa plucks at it and frowns, but no one tells her to take it off. The next day she rolls on her stockings and wears her shift under the deerskin dress. When Weetamoo sees her, she smiles and something in her face reminds Mary of her sister Elizabeth. She feels a brief wave of pleasure, followed by a sinking sensation. She looks down at her feet and sees that the hem of her shift is visible below the deerskin. Her cheeks burn and she tugs at the dress as if she might lengthen it. She knows she looks foolish but finds unexpected comfort in the strange assemblage of clothes.

Mary and Alawa spend much of their time working side by side. Gradually, they begin to communicate more easily. Alawa teaches Mary some Indian words. She asks Mary about her life before she was captured and Mary describes her children and sisters. She tells her about her childhood in Salem and Wenham and explains that she was born on the far side of a great sea.

When Mary asks about her childhood, Alawa tells her that she was born Mohawk and captured by Nipmuc warriors when she was very young. They sold her to a Narragansett, who sold her to a cruel English family in Plymouth Colony. They beat her and made her labor all day and late into the night, so one summer afternoon, when she was sent to fetch water, she ran away. One of Weetamoo's warriors found her sitting under a tree. She recounts this all matter-of-factly, as if it is not surprising or out of the ordinary. But Mary is stunned; it had not occurred to her that Indians might capture and sell one another.

"So you are a slave as I am?" Mary asks.

"I was slave with English," Alawa says. "But I not run from Weetamoo."

Mary thinks of Timothy and her face flushes in private shame.

Weetamoo's wetu is daily filled with talking women, and sometimes Mary slips outside and sits with her back against the sturdy bark wall, shivering beneath her blanket. Everyone is waiting for news of the Medfield attack. They are anxious for their men, worried they might not return. Their anxiety reminds Mary of the mood in Lancaster after the Indian raid in August, of the winter evenings she and her sisters sat sewing and talking. Yet it unnerves her to consider that Indian women might be so very much like Englishwomen.

She is surprised at how often Weetamoo leaves her to her own devices. She must realize Mary knows she cannot survive alone in the wilderness long enough to make her way home. Her disinterest grants Mary an uncommon freedom, and often little to do. All her life, Mary has been closely watched, and required to toil from waking to sleeping. She has been taught that idleness is a sin, and has long resisted its temptations. Yet, in her new position as a slave, she is often forced to it.

Slowly, Mary discovers in idleness a strange expansion of time and a growing awareness of the natural world. She begins to watch the flight of sparrows through the winter air and the dance of red squirrels in the trees. She notes the changes in clouds, the slant of sunlight as it falls on snow, the tight red buds of winter trees. All these things she has seen before, but only as background to her life's duties. Now she begins to understand that trees and birds and clouds and animals have a significance of their own that is independent of human activity.

It is an astonishing thought. She has never heard anyone express such an idea before.

One afternoon, squatting in a small pool of sunlight that is all the warmth the season has to offer, listening to the calls of birds, she hears a shout in the distance. It is echoed by another, and then a third, and soon by an entire chorus of whooping shrieks. Alarmed, she gets to her feet.

All around her, women rush out of the wetus and hurry along the path through the village. Mary follows at a distance. She does not wish to be observed, but is determined to discover the source and significance of the cries.

In the center of the village a circle of women is singing and shouting. The women laugh and sway as they sing. They raise their arms joyfully. Their song is wild and disharmonious, but Mary feels strangely moved. She finds herself swaying at the edge of the circle in time to their music.

Slowly she begins to understand what she sees and hears. The women are echoing the shouts of returning warriors. The attack on Medfield has been successful. The Indians have killed many English. They have brought the scalps to prove it.

Mary stops moving. The truth lies like a stone in her heart. She pictures the bloodied snow of her yard, Elizabeth's body lying broken before the door, her skirt in flames. Again she hears William's screams as war clubs crush his skull.

In shame, she leaves the circle and the singing to return to Weetamoo's wetu and its solace of shadows. She cannot stop trembling.

CHAPTER TEN

At dusk, Weetamoo orders Mary and Alawa to attend the celebration in the center of the village, where a great fire pit has been dug, filled with logs and surrounded by stones. The fire is roaring, wood snapping and flinging embers high past flames that rise to the full height of a man. The scent fills Mary's nostrils, reminding her of her burning house.

Men and women mill about and cluster in small groups, talking. Children chase one another, laughing, as they dart in and out among the adults. Four men sit around a drum of tanned deerskin stretched over a huge wooden hoop. They beat it with sticks, striking together so the drum makes a deep rolling *boom* each time, one that rings in her ears and thrums in the soles of her feet. Warriors bob and writhe in a circle around the fire, striking the grotesque poses she witnessed the night after her capture. Many are shirtless, despite the cold. They have painted their faces and chests in strange patterns of red and black. A group of women stands near the circling, singing; their strange undulating chants make Mary's skin prickle.

Alawa clears away snow near a tree and invites Mary to sit

beside her. Mary cannot draw her gaze from the dancers. Their wild joy bewitches her. She sees the man who first captured her and the one they call Monoco. Then Quinnapin steps into the circle. He seems almost regal to Mary, his movements at once graceful and commanding. The longer she watches, the more enchanted she is by the dancing. The drums beat on into the night and she feels her own heart echo their rhythm.

Some men dance for so long they stagger and collapse when they leave the circle. One falls as he dances. His friends quickly carry him away. After a time Mary finds her own shoulders swaying to the drumbeat. Dismayed, she closes her eyes and beseeches God to rescue her from this captivity before her soul is unalterably corrupted.

She hears Alawa say something and opens her eyes. The English Indian is standing in front of her. He is naked, except for a breach clout and a pair of leggings. A black feather is stuck in his hair. His face and chest are painted in jagged red designs. He kneels, and reaches into a pouch hanging from a cord around his waist. He draws forth a book and holds it out to Mary.

"Take it," he says, dropping the book into her lap. "It may bring you some comfort."

She looks down, but does not touch it.

"'Tis a Bible," he says. "The spoils of battle. I bargained hard for it."

She feels a terrible confusion—gratitude and longing mixed with caution. Did he fight in the battle? Did he slay English soldiers? She wants the Bible but fears what taking it might cost her. "What do you want for it?" Her voice is hoarse.

She detects a flicker of irritation under the paint. "I want nothing. It is a gift."

She picks it up and opens it. It is, indeed, a Bible, cunningly made, covered in leather, the pages nearly as white as the snow that lies around them. "I thank you," she says, glancing up to meet his eyes. "It will be a great solace." She looks away, for her face is suddenly warm.

Alawa jumps up, takes her arm and tugs her to her feet. The Indian says something to Alawa in a language Mary cannot understand.

"Be diligent and wise and they will not harm you," he says to Mary as Alawa releases her.

Mary nods. She feels Alawa standing behind her, watching.

"I am most grateful," Mary says. "But tell me, please—may I know your name?"

He hesitates for only an instant, and she senses he is studying her, looking for some sign of sincerity in her face. "Wowaus," he says. "But you will find it easier to call me James. 'Tis my English name."

"James," she says. "'Tis a good name. The brother of our Lord was James. You are a Praying Indian."

He nods. "I am also called the Printer."

"Printer?"

He nods again, smiling this time. "I was a printer's apprentice."

She knows that Praying Indians are farmers—and poor ones at that. From what Mary has seen, most are little more than beggars. "I have not heard of any Indian taking up a trade."

"You do not believe me," he says. She realizes—too late—that she has insulted him. A poor payment for his kindness.

"I meant no offense," she says. "I was merely surprised."

"There is much about Indians that will surprise you—if you but open your eyes."

She is stung. She looks down at the Bible in her hand. "Will I be punished if they see me reading it?"

He shrugs. "I think it is of little importance to them."

"Thank you, James," she says, reaching toward him this time, and then quickly withdrawing her hand, for she is afraid that if she touches him, she will not want to let go. "Thank you for everything."

He nods once more and turns away. She watches him leave, watches the muscles in his shoulders and calves as he moves into the shadows, until all she can see is his silhouette against the fire.

The Bible is a comfort. Mary keeps it in her pocket, thankful that it is small enough to be stowed there. When chance allows and Weetamoo's attention is elsewhere, she takes it out to read. It is her hope and consolation—a raft she can cling to as she tumbles in a pagan sea. She thanks God for James; she tells herself that the Lord sent this kind man to watch over her, like a guardian angel. These thoughts help her to forget the troubling feelings that invade her in his presence.

She does not see him for some time after he gives her the Bible. The more days that pass, the more she finds herself longing for another encounter. She knows such feelings are wicked, yet it is a comfort to know he is somewhere in the camp.

Mary becomes gradually aware that a man is following her around the village. When Weetamoo sends her to fetch water or gather wood, Mary sees him skulking behind her. Finally she identifies him as Monoco. He has a strong nose and wide brow, smooth skin and a long neck. He might be handsome except for his ruined left eye, which is sunken deep in its socket. He does not speak to Mary. Yet when she glances in his direction, he gives her a leering grin. His face reminds her of a picture of the Devil she once saw in a book of Joseph's. She makes a point of avoiding the lonely places at the edge of camp, places where the forest rises up to block the sun, where she cannot be seen.

One afternoon, as she gets water from the river, Mary sees Monoco sitting with Quinnapin under a tree. The two men are laughing and talking, smoking long pipes of tobacco, the spicy scent drifting on the wind. As she approaches, they stop talking and study her. The hairs on her neck rise. She feels as a hunted deer must feel—wary and doomed. She quickens her pace and ducks inside the shelter, where Weetamoo sits playing with her babe. Mary has learned that he is nearly four months old, a solemn black-haired boy whose dark gaze has often fallen on her. Weetamoo has unwrapped him from his cradleboard and is caressing his arms and legs, moving them in some rhythm Mary cannot follow. He looks too thin, yet he chortles heartily. She thinks immediately of Sarah and feels a terrible grief. She turns away and bumps into Monoco, who has followed her into the wetu. Quinnapin stands behind him, grinning.

Monoco grasps her shoulders and takes a strand of her hair between his fingers. Weetamoo looks up from her child and says something to him. He responds with a string of Indian words. His tone is eager but deferential.

"Matta!" Weetamoo says sharply. *"Monchish!"*

Quinnapin laughs. Monoco drops Mary's hair and backs away. His expression reminds Mary of a small boy whose knuckles have been rapped. She is shocked at what she has just seen—a man publicly chastised by a woman. It would never happen in Lancaster.

Mary looks at Weetamoo, who is once again absorbed with her babe. She is puzzled that she can treat a man with such insolence and suffer no public rebuke. Yet Mary senses that she has in some way saved her from a disagreeable fate. She feels a welling, if reluctant, gratitude, which she has no idea how to express.

For a week, the village lies under a spell of quietude. Then a great restiveness begins. The women go about their tasks with quickened pace. The men gather at dawn in small groups and disappear into the forest, returning with freshly killed animals. The new vitality is infectious—Mary feels her own slothfulness fall away and performs her assigned tasks with new liveliness and vigor. She begins to understand Weetamoo's words and grows alert to her moods. The woman has the capricious temper of a tyrant—content one minute and vexed the next. Mary forages for wood, fetches water, scrapes hides, and grinds corn on a stone. She tends the fire, searches for groundnuts and berries. She repairs the great mats that line the interior of the wetu, weaving bulrushes and hemp with a double-pointed needle made from the split rib of a deer. She smokes squirrel meat and sweeps the wetu's earthen floor with a pine branch many times each day. Her mind quickens and she casts aside her grief.

It is the Bible, she tells herself. God's word has come down upon her like rain on a parched desert. The knowledge that it lies in her pocket calms her as she works.

When Weetamoo gives her permission, Mary goes in search of her children, but the only person from Lancaster she finds is Ann Joslin, who is hugely swollen with her unborn child. Mary feels a rush of pity when she sees her sitting by the path between two elderly Indian women, picking nits out of her daughter Beatrice's hair. Mary thinks of the difficult final days before she brought forth her own children. She was clumsy and uncomfortable all the time.

"Good day, Goody Joslin," Mary says, hoping the familiar greeting will cheer her. "You look well." Though, in fact, she does not. Her cheeks are sunken, her eyes furtive; her arms beneath the dirty sleeves of her linsey-woolsey dress are little more than bones. Mary draws a scrap of dried corn cake from the bottom of her pocket and holds it out. Ann takes it, glancing warily at the two Indian women.

"Have they worked you very hard?" Mary asks.

Ann shakes her head. "They have given me little to do. Yet they do not allow me out of their sight." She touches her belly. "I believe they wait for the child." The whites of her eyes are yellow, like scraps of old parchment. "I fear they will take him from me once he is born. They have a special fondness for the flesh of—"

"Come," Mary says quickly. "Let us talk." She picks up Beatrice, who does not protest, and walks a short way up the path. Ann follows. The girl's weight is a sweet burden in Mary's arms, reminding her of Sarah.

"How long before you deliver your babe?" Mary knows Ann must be terrified of the ordeal ahead. A woman's travail is dangerous enough in a civilized English home.

"A week, I think. Not more than two."

Mary tries to reassure her. She tells her that she will seek Weetamoo's permission to attend her labor. That she will pray for a safe delivery, for the health of the babe. Ann nods respectfully, but her attention is scattered and fitful. Finally, she confides in a whisper that she plans to escape and make her way home.

Mary stares at her. "You cannot mean that. We are at least thirty miles from an English town." She takes her arm, as if to hold her. "There are hills to climb and rivers to cross. You cannot hope to survive by yourself."

"I have begged them to let me go." Ann's voice is clogged with tears, though Mary sees none on her face. "All they do is mock me. I can bear it no longer."

Mary wonders if Ann has gone mad. This is more than a woman's ordinary fretfulness as she nears her time. "You must not flee. For the child's sake, if not your own. It would be a terrible sin."

Ann looks at her as if her words are nonsense. "What matter is sin? God has abandoned us."

The words fall like a blow. Mary feels suddenly afraid. "Ann, you are not well. Your spirit and your body are feeble. You must listen." She sets Beatrice on the ground, draws the Bible from her pocket and begins to read Psalm Twenty-seven aloud. Ann stands with her head bowed, Beatrice slumped against her skirts. When

Mary is done, she looks up and sees immediately that Ann has not absorbed the words, for she is shaking her head. "I shall not see you again," she whispers.

"No! You must not speak so." Mary cups Ann's face between her hands. Her fingers make jagged streaks in the grime. "You must wait upon the Lord."

Ann sags away.

"Promise me," Mary says. "Say you will wait upon the Lord's deliverance."

Still, Ann says nothing, but stands gazing at the wetus and the frozen river beyond.

Weetamoo kicks Mary awake early the next morning and orders her to fetch water. As Mary hurries through the village, she sees women packing blankets and pots and kettles and loading them into baskets and onto small sleds. When she returns, Weetamoo orders her to help Alawa roll up the sleeping skins and remove the wall coverings inside the wetu. Mary works diligently to quickly untie the great woven reed mats. Her heart is beating too fast. She senses the sluice of excitement and worry swirling around her, feels part of it. Soon only empty shelters remain.

Alawa tells her that everyone is leaving Menameset. Mary feels a rush of panic. The longer she stays in one place, the greater the opportunity to find her children. And the greater likelihood they will be rescued.

"No," she says. "I cannot go." She shakes her head and waves her hands in the air to demonstrate her urgency. She goes to Weetamoo and begs to be allowed to stay. "Leave me here under guard," she says. "I will only hamper your travels." She hunches over and takes a few shuffling steps to demonstrate how weak and slow she will be on the trail.

Without warning, Weetamoo slaps her across the face. The

blow is so hard, Mary staggers back and nearly falls. When she claps her hand over her stinging cheek, Weetamoo yanks it away and strikes her again, shouting words Mary cannot understand. But she doesn't need words to know her life depends on Weetamoo, that she must do her bidding to keep it.

Her heart fills with rage as she fills the large carrying baskets under Weetamoo's direction—some with corn, some with skins, some with small pots and pouches of herbs and tobacco. She has never been treated so cruelly, certainly not by another woman. It is unnatural, a perversion of God's order, she thinks. She works with a cold fury, yet it occurs to her late that morning that this indignity is what Bess suffers in her indenture. What slaves everywhere suffer. Her positions as minister's wife and the daughter of Lancaster's richest landowner have protected her from perceiving this. Now she is no longer a woman but a slave. She has become a beast of burden, an object to be used and discarded at the whim of her mistress.

CHAPTER ELEVEN

They set out at midday. The sky is gray with low clouds. Mary is given a tall basket filled with corn. Alawa shows her how to carry it on her back and secure it with a strap across her forehead. Mary walks behind her on the trail, the last in Weetamoo's group and burdened with the heaviest basket. Her feet hurt and pain runs up and down her arms and legs. Her head aches from the pressure of the strap and soon she is so dizzy she has to stop and lean against a tree so the world will stop whirling. When Weetamoo happens to turn and see her, she shouts and brandishes her club. Mary forces herself to continue walking.

Trees rise like black pikes against the sky. It seems to Mary that the heavens are always gray in this bleak season, always threatening snow. She tries to pray. She thinks about the Israelites who wandered forty years in the wilderness, remembers how they struggled to be faithful to the Lord. How wickedly they strayed. She reminds herself that her chief task is to stay vigilant every moment so that evil will not overtake her while she busies herself with living.

At sunset they come to a clearing. It is a barren place—a ridge of snow-covered rocks with no trees or hills to break the wind. The Indians mill around, trampling resting places into the snow, and Mary realizes that they've stopped for the night. The women pile up pine boughs to lean against and then build fires and take out mats and skins from their packs.

Weetamoo directs Alawa and Mary to build a small shelter of mats, barely big enough for Quinnapin and herself and their infant son. Then she shoos them away. Alawa builds a fire and scoops out a hollow in the snow nearby, and she and Mary huddle together under blankets. Snow clings in clumps to Mary's back and thighs. Her dress is wet from hem to waist, and she is so cold she cannot stop shaking. She edges close to Alawa for warmth, curling up next to her, trying to sleep. Alawa's breathing slows and deepens, yet Mary cannot relax. After a while, she takes out her Bible and tries to read a few lines by the fire but the light is not sufficient. She finally dozes with her head on her knees. When she wakes in the morning, her arms and legs have stiffened so that she can barely move.

Weetamoo seems to have forgotten her. She does not give her orders or access to the stew pot. Mary must fend for herself or starve, so she walks through the camp, lighting on scraps of food—a few crumbs of corn cake here, some dried berries there, a chestnut begged from an old woman.

She searches for Ann Joslin to see how she fares, but she is not in camp. Later, Alawa tells Mary that when the Indians left Menameset, they divided into several groups and went in different directions, taking their captives with them. Mary wonders which direction her children have gone and when she will see Ann again. It distresses her that she may not be able to keep her promise to attend her labor.

The men come and go. She assumes they are hunting, but their luck must be very poor, for there is no sweet smoke of roasting game, no cries of pleasure that would accompany a successful hunting party's return. In fact, the quiet is profoundly unsettling.

Near sunset, a warrior comes into the camp. Mary is cheered to see that her sister Hannah's son, John, is among the party. She sees him from a distance—his face is smeared with dirt, but his eyes are bright and he does not have the lean look of the hungry about him yet. She follows him and finds him playing a game with pebbles on a patch of earth cleared of snow. When she inquires, he tells her that his master's sons taught it to him.

"You must be wary of taking their customs," Mary chides. "Be firm in the Lord lest you turn heathen. The Devil is very cunning."

He nods but does not look at her. He seems completely absorbed in his game.

"Have you seen your mother?" The thought of Hannah makes her ache, for she has not laid eyes on her since the day of the attack.

John shakes his head and then, suddenly, drops his pebbles and breaks into tears. Mary touches his shoulder, wishing she had taken more care in speaking. "What troubles you?" she asks gently.

"I have seen what they do." He swipes fiercely at his eyes. "My mother—I do not think she is strong enough to bear it."

"To bear what?" Mary feels alarm on Hannah's behalf. She puts her arm around his shoulder. "Be strong," she says. "We must trust in the Lord that all will be well."

He looks at the ground. Slowly, he begins to explain. He tells her that Goody Joslin was one of the captives in his group when they left Menameset. She trailed after the others because of her condition, and also because she had to carry Beatrice. She complained constantly that she was miserable, claiming that her time was near, begging the Indians to let her go home.

"She *wailed*. It was terrible to hear," John says. "We begged her to be quiet, but she would not. She appealed for mercy to one Indian after another. None would heed her. After a time they grew vexed." He picks up one of the pebbles and lets it fall again. "We stopped to rest. They ordered all the captives to stand in a circle. Everyone, even the children. Then they put Goody Joslin in the center. Two women stripped off her clothes. They made us all dance and sing around her."

Mary is scarcely able to breathe.

"I danced," John whispers. "I had to. If I had not, they would have slain me."

She does not want to hear his story any longer. Yet she understands he needs to tell it, and that she must know the truth. "You did no wrong," she assures him. "'Tis no sin to do what you must to live." She thinks—even as she speaks—that she might be wrong in this. Joseph would surely think so. Yet it seems important to her now to console the boy.

"She was shaking and weeping. It was so cold her skin was turning blue. I could not bear to look at her." He takes a loud breath. "After the dancing, the warriors beat her head with their clubs until she fell dead. Beatrice cried and so they killed her too. Then they built a fire and threw both bodies in it. All the Indians danced and cheered." He sniffs. "They made us watch until they were burned to ashes. Then they told us that if we tried to run away home, the same would happen to us."

Mary feels sick. She can summon no words of assurance or comfort. She knows now that she counseled Ann in vain; the poor woman was unable to endure the trial God set before her. *Because it was too hard,* she thinks. *Some trials are monstrous. Sometimes God asks too much.*

At daybreak the next morning, they begin to march again. They walk all day without stopping to eat. They are to gather what food they can as they walk. But Mary finds nothing. That night they make camp and this time they build a wetu. Mary is nearly euphoric with gratitude when Weetamoo invites her inside to share the thin gruel that simmers over her fire.

They stay in camp for several days. The people seem happy, despite their hunger. In the daytime, they sit talking in small groups. Mary is surprised to hear them laughing; it seems almost profane in the face of their troubles. As if they are laughing at their own deprivation.

In the evenings Mary watches Weetamoo unbraid her hair and shake it out so that it streams down her back to her waist. She dips her fingers into a pot of ointment and runs her hands through her hair many times. Soon it gleams in the firelight. Then she plaits it again, into two shining braids.

One night Mary touches her own head, where her hair is matted in a disordered tangle. It seems an impossible task, yet she begins to work at it with her fingers, picking and smoothing, until the strands come loose from one another and fall onto her shoulders and back. She senses someone behind her, then feels Alawa's hands move into her hair. Mary sits back on her knees while Alawa applies the ointment, smoothing it along the strands. They do not speak. The motion is almost like a caress. It is deeply soothing and the sensation reminds Mary of the times she and her sisters combed one another's hair when they were girls. Finally Alawa divides her hair into three sections and braids it into a long plait.

"Thank you," Mary says as Alawa turns away. Mary feels as if she's been ministered to in an extraordinary way. She feels contented and womanly for the first time in weeks. It is not until she slides under her sleeping skins that it occurs to her that she is becoming more Indian-like in her appearance and manner. She knows that she ought to fear for her soul. Yet she feels only comfort and peace. And gratitude.

The next morning, they break camp and set out on the trail. They walk for days, stopping only to sleep at night. Though the basket she bears on her back is heavier than anything she has ever carried, Mary feels her body gradually harden and grow strong. She sees many strange and kindly things in the Indians' treatment of one another. Once, she catches a glimpse of James as he carries an old woman on his back up a long hill. She remembers the kindness in his eyes and has the errant sinful wish that he might carry *her*, that she could lie against his back and feel the rhythm and warmth of his muscles moving beneath her breasts. Instantly she rebukes herself, knowing such thoughts contaminate her soul. She tries to concentrate on memories of her husband. Yet Joseph seems very far away.

They come to a wide river that tumbles with ice and white water. The women sit by the bank while the men work furiously, felling trees with their hatchets and constructing rafts. Mary huddles in her blanket, watching, her ears filled with the water's roar. She sees great lumps of ice spin and leap in the river.

There are so many people that it takes two days to ferry everyone across. When it is Mary's turn, she scrambles with others onto a pile of brush at one end of the raft and she crouches there while a warrior stands at the other end guiding it, swaying and tossing, to the far bank. The sound is deafening as the water rages, splashing icy foam over everyone. Miraculously, no one is tossed overboard.

As soon as they are across, Weetamoo directs the women to build wetus so all the people can rest and warm themselves. Mary works so quickly that her fingers crack and bleed; she is as eager as anyone for a wetu's comforting warmth.

The men dig a fire pit and boil a horse's thigh in a great kettle. Everyone is invited to sip the hot broth. The camp remains there for nearly a week. Mary has little to do but search for food and read her Bible. One afternoon, to busy herself, she begins to knit a pair of white cotton stockings with the needles and yarn in her pocket. When Weetamoo sees what Mary is making, she demands the stockings. Mary gapes up at her, pretending she cannot understand. Alawa, who is sitting nearby, tries to take them away but Mary jerks them from her and jams them into her pocket.

"They belong to me," she says. "The yarn and needles came from my own house. My skill was given me by the Lord."

Weetamoo picks up her war club and shakes it menacingly in Mary's face. "They are mine," she says in English. "All you make is mine. You are slave."

Mary is shocked to hear the English words coming from Weetamoo's mouth. When she raises the club again, Mary nods and says, "I will make the stockings for you." For the moment, Weetamoo seems satisfied.

Just after dawn the next morning, the warriors torch the wetus so the English soldiers will not be able to shelter in them. Then everyone marches north. As they climb a hill, Mary looks back over her shoulder and is surprised to see a group of English soldiers standing on the far bank of the river. She feels a throb of exhilaration, certain they will soon rescue her and the other captives. She wonders if Joseph is among them. Perhaps he even led them to this place.

Yet the English do not come, and after a time Mary realizes they are afraid to cross the river's fury. She catches glimpses of warriors running back and forth along the shore, taunting the English, and she feels a dark shame rise in her. She knows Indians despise weakness of any kind. She is humiliated that the English soldiers lack the courage and vigor to do their duty.

More troubling are the dark questions that underlie all her other fears: *Where is Joseph? Why has he not yet come?*

For hours, the air is thick with smoke from the burning wetus. From the top of a ridge, Mary watches flames licking up into the trees. Then the warriors lead everyone away.

The trail is narrow and steep and there are many people, all weary and weak from lack of food. Mary is faint with hunger and sore from the effort of carrying her basket. They go up a long hill, so steep she thinks her legs and heart will fail her as she climbs. As they descend into the valley, the trees thin out and reveal the abandoned fields of an English farm. Brown spikes of old cornstalks poke through the melting snow. Sheaves of wheat stand frozen in shocks.

The women move out over the fields to glean what corn and wheat is left. Mary wearily follows Alawa. After a while she finds a broken ear of corn, then a second. She loses one to a woman who snatches it from her hand. When Mary yells and starts to run after her, a group of women quickly surround her, blocking her pursuit. They laugh and point, mocking her. She stands with her head bowed, waiting for the dark flush of anger to drain from her face. After a while, the women lose interest in taunting her and gradually drift away.

They return to the trail and continue down the hill into a swamp. Dead trees and stumps rise in front of Mary. Vines run along the ground and reach out to bind her ankles and scratch her legs. More than once her foot sinks into the boggy ground. She feels she has descended into a dungeon from which she will never escape. She has heard that Indians often hide from their enemies in swamps because the treacherous footing makes it difficult even for those who live in the area to track people.

Men scout for patches of firm ground and decide where they can safely erect new wetus. They cut saplings, peel off the bark and then bend them into arches, pounding each end firmly in the earth. Women split the sapling bark into thin strips and use them to tie the wetu frames together. Men slice squares of bark from old trees and women lash them to the frames. The new village rises quickly; by nightfall the swamp is a jumble of domed huts. The men dig a fire pit and there is an air of excitement in the camp. Even Mary is caught up in the enthusiasm as the stew pots are thickened with grain and maize.

She is sitting outside Weetamoo's wetu when she sees James walking toward her, carrying a basket on his shoulder. She rises to greet him, but he does not acknowledge her. Instead, he stops to talk with a group of men lounging outside a neighboring wetu. He is so arrestingly happy that Mary cannot help herself—she calls his name. He turns, smiling, and approaches her.

"What have you there in the basket?" she asks.

"Ah—Mistress Rowlandson—I didn't realize 'twas you, sitting there as quiet and docile as a maiden." He laughs and slides the basket from his shoulder to set it on the ground. When she sees the slabs of meat piled there, her mouth fills with spittle and her belly twists in hunger.

"'Tis horse meat," he says. "Some warriors slew a mare and I was given the task of distributing it."

"Give a piece to me, then." She holds out her hand.

"What would you have?" His eyes dance. "A portion of liver?"

"I yearn to try," she says, "if you would but give it me."

He plucks a dark piece the size of his hand from the basket. It drips great spots of blood on the ground. The sight would have revolted her a few weeks ago, but now she stretches to get it. James raises it higher, out of her reach. Her face reddens in vexation at this child's game, yet she feels a tingling excitement. It reminds her of the early days of Joseph's courtship—how pretty and warm she felt in his presence, how exquisitely alive.

James finally stops teasing her and hands her the piece of liver, which Mary quickly spits on a stick and sets at the edge of the fire to roast. She is near fainting as the sweet odor fills her nostrils. As she closes her eyes for a moment to savor it, a girl runs up and snatches it out of the fire. Mary screams and grabs it, but the girl doesn't let go, and the liver rips in two chunks. The girl runs off and Mary stands holding the torn piece in both hands. For an instant, she wonders if she should finish roasting it, then realizes she will likely lose what's left if she does. She eats the half-raw liver like an animal. Blood runs from the sides of her mouth and dribbles onto her apron. Her mouth and chin are smeared with grease and blood.

She is so absorbed in eating, she doesn't see James return. When she finally looks up, he is standing a few feet away, watching her. He smiles.

"'Tis as I thought," he says. "You have become Indian."

Mary feels a wave of shame. "Nay," she says, shaking her head and wiping her hands vigorously on her apron. "I am an Englishwoman still."

His smile disappears and he bends to speak into her ear. "Do not fear this," he says. "'Tis your path to safety. You are strong and clever. If you can bring yourself to discard some of your English notions, you will flourish. I have no doubt."

Mary's face burns, even as she walks away from him, for she feels a strange mixture of disgrace and arousal. Why is it that she experiences such tremors in his presence? The sort of tremors that should be reserved only for her husband.

CHAPTER TWELVE

She is hungry all the time. She sleeps hungry and wakes hungry. Whenever Mary tends the fire, she scoops some of the pot's contents into her mouth when no one is looking. She does not want to think about what swims there. More than once she has seen Weetamoo drop a fresh-killed squirrel into the pot without skinning it or removing its head. She recognizes eyeballs, gray lumps of intestines, long tendons strung with bits of flesh, even scraps of fur. Only a few weeks ago she would not have brought such food to her lips, thinking it too vile even to throw to the pigs.

Before her capture, she was never without food when she wanted it. Now food is dispensed to her, bit by bit, by her enemies. She has only enough to keep her alive. She longs for a spoonful of cold porridge, or a scrap of stale bread. On the trail, thoughts of rich food invade her mind like whispers of the Devil himself. When she sleeps, she dreams of tables laden with sausages and beef and ham swimming in thick gravy. She dreams of sweet, hot grease running down her throat, of the sharp tang of newly cut cheese on her tongue, of loaves of bread torn open, exposing soft insides the color of winter grass.

She is aware that her suffering is no greater than anyone's in the camp. They are *all* hungry, all on the verge of starvation. She knows others also dream of food, for she hears them mutter *weyaus*—the word for meat—in their sleep. Food is so scarce that they smile and laugh when they find a root poking from the ground. Mary notices that whatever food is available, the men and women usually share with everyone, even their captives. She finds this strange, for she has always thought it a law of nature that a hungry man or woman will hoard food in a starving time. It strikes her that sometimes the Indians act like Christians, though few have been baptized. This is a great puzzle, one that she cannot work out, though she ponders it often as she sits sewing.

She encounters James again one afternoon in the woods as she collects sticks for Weetamoo's fire. She turns away without speaking, because she is still alarmed by her sinful arousal during their last encounter. But he takes her hand and slides something into her palm. She looks down and sees a small scrap of dried meat. In her surprise, she nearly drops it.

"Eat now," he says. "Before someone takes it from you." When he smiles, she knows he witnessed the corn and liver stolen from her. She blushes and pops the piece into her mouth. It is the size of her thumbnail and as tough as a stone, yet her spittle pools around it and slowly it softens between her teeth. She chews and swallows.

"Thank you," she says. "You are very kind." Her heart is beating too fast. She tries to meet his gaze, but finds it impossible. "I should go now."

He does not move.

There is a strange prickling sensation in the skin of her face. She tries again. "Weetamoo is a hard mistress. She will not think kindly on me if she wants me and I am not at hand."

"You should be grateful to Weetamoo. She has shown you great charity."

Mary thinks of the times Weetamoo kicked her awake, of her vicious blows, her relentless demands. "She has been pitiless and cruel. I have seen no charity."

James shakes his head. "She spared you Monoco's lust." He raises his right hand to adjust the blanket on his shoulder. She notices his fine, long fingers, the way they dance over the fabric. "He would have taken you for a wife, had she allowed it," he says.

"Wife?" She has lost the thread of their conversation. She looks up at him blankly.

"Monoco admires your hair. He wishes to marry you. Did you not know?"

She stiffens, as if an icy chain has encircled her neck. "I am married. I cannot be wife to anyone but my own husband." James says nothing, but stares at her as if her words make no sense. Another thought suddenly strikes her. For weeks she has been worried that Joseph has not come to rescue her. Has he been *prevented* from coming? Have Indians ambushed and killed him? Perhaps she is *not* married any longer.

"Is it—?" She can barely get the words out. "Have you word of my husband? Has some evil befallen him?"

James shrugs but there is something guarded in his gaze.

"Has he not tried to rescue me and our children?" Her voice is far more plaintive than she intends. She presses her hand to her mouth.

"I have not heard that news." He steps toward her.

"But you have heard something."

He looks briefly at the ground and then back at her. Directly into her eyes. "There are stories."

"Tell me what you know," she says. "Please."

Again he looks away, this time into the surrounding trees. "Some say"—he pauses—"they say that, believing you dead, he has taken another wife."

"No," she whispers. "It cannot be so."

"'Tis a story only."

She is silent for a moment, trying to absorb this. "Even if it be true," she says firmly, "I would never consent to union with an Indian."

"It is not a matter of consent," James says. "You are a captive here. Your approval is not required. You will be bought and sold at the pleasure of your mistress."

Bought and sold. Mary thinks of Bess Parker's babe and feels a chill that is not caused by the wind. "My mistress?" she says weakly. "Would not my *master* be the one to sell me?"

"You do not understand. You belong to Weetamoo. She is more powerful than Quinnapin. He gave you to her as tribute."

She frowns. "I warrant you speak nonsense. Surely Weetamoo derives what power she has from her husband."

He shakes his head solemnly. "She is the sachem of all the Pocasset people. She leads more warriors than Quinnapin. She is more respected. She holds more authority." He leans close to her, as if the intensity of his gaze might help her grasp the river of information he pours over her. "Her sister is married to Metacomet—the Wampanoag sachem the English call Philip. Weetamoo was once wife of his older brother, Wamsutta, who was sachem before Philip. When he was poisoned by the English in Plymouth, she wed again, but soon left him because her new husband sided with the English. Then she married Quinnapin because *he* sought the alliance, though he already has two wives."

Mary's mind spins as she tries to absorb all James is telling her. Weetamoo has had many husbands. She discarded them when they did not please her. It is preposterous. She wonders if James is trying to trick her. It is unseemly—and frightening—for a woman to have such power over men. It undermines the order of creation—the order that God put into the world.

"She will do as she wishes with you," he continues. "And no

one—least of all Quinnapin—will lift a finger to protect you." He places his hand gently on her arm. "The past is of no use to you, Mary. You must learn to make your way with what you have."

He has called her *Mary* again. She likes the sound of her name on his tongue so much that she almost lets down her guard. She feels the weight of the Bible where it lies in her pocket against her thigh and it occurs to her that she ought to take it out, as a defense against her disconcerting feelings. She wishes she could declare that she has not changed, that the past has made her who she is, that it gives her succor and hope. But she says nothing, for the thoughts that form in her mind refuse to move to her tongue.

"You should consider taking a new name," he says. "To signify your new condition."

"New name?" She suspects he is teasing her. But why?

"*Chikohtqua,*" he says. "Your new name should be *Chikohtqua.* Burning Woman."

The name instantly conjures the image of her dead sister as she was consumed in flames. Mary feels a bubble of nausea as she shakes off his hand and hurries away. Yet she cannot stop thinking of James's words and the name he bestowed on her. She tries to repeat the strange syllables but they twist on her tongue.

Burning Woman. Why does James think such a name would suit her? Does he mean it as an omen? Or a strange blessing? And what of Joseph? Is it possible that her husband thinks she is dead? Would he not strive by all means possible to assure himself of her safety? And the safety of their children?

She goes deeper into the woods, grateful for the shadows there. She has come to welcome the way the trees sift the light and soften the wilderness colors. There are still patches of snow on the ground but the earth is no longer hard as stone beneath her moccasins.

She recalls a conversation she had with Joseph not long after Joss was born. It was late summer and a sultry breeze had drawn her outside just as Joseph came up from the barn. They had sat on the bench by the front door for a time, slapping away flies. A wistful sadness overcame her as she thought of her mother. When Joseph remarked on her melancholy expression, Mary told him of how, as a child, she often sat with her mother on the door stoop at the end of a summer day while they talked of pleasant things.

Joseph looked at her thoughtfully. "Why has your father not remarried, I wonder? Your mother died many years ago and yet he has no wife."

She gaped at him in surprise. "Why should he remarry? My sister Hannah keeps his house well."

"It is not customary—or healthy—for a man to stay single so long." Joseph gazed at the low hills in the west, apparently unaware of her surprise. "Perhaps he still mourns her."

"I'm sure he does," Mary said, and immediately wished she had not spoken. She knew Joseph regarded mourning as a worldly sin—the sign of a man unable to submit himself to God's will. "My mother was a good woman. There are not many to match her in piety."

He nodded slowly but still did not look at her. "There are many women here in Lancaster who would be grateful for a husband who will provide well for them. And your father is the most prosperous man in town—by my thinking he ought to think beyond his own wants."

There it was—and not for the first time in their marriage—the suggestion that Mary's father was not sufficiently generous with his wealth. Although Joseph never said it, she had long suspected that his real grievance was that her father had not given more to *them*.

"He must do what his conscience commands," she said.

"As must we all," Joseph said. "Yet I believe Scripture makes it clear that it is a man's duty to marry."

"So, if I should die, you would soon propose to some young

maid?" She smiled and nudged him with her elbow, to show that she was jesting. But he was all sobriety that evening, and instead of laughing, he said he would do precisely that. He shifted on the bench to face her.

"You must know that my conscience would insist that I quickly wed," he said. "But you must also know that I pray daily that you will live for many years yet, Mary."

He had embraced her then, and she had quickly forgotten the conversation. But as she recalls it now, she wonders if his words were a foretelling of what is now unfolding in his life.

She begins to encounter James every day. At first she believes these are chance meetings. Later she suspects he has contrived them by watching her and learning her habits. He often appears suddenly at her side when she carries a pot of water from the river or searches for groundnuts on her hands and knees, poking at the frozen earth with a stick. He asks after her health and advises her on how to please Weetamoo. He shows her how to forage more profitably by searching for withered gray leaves under the snow.

One afternoon he brings news of Marie and Joss, reporting that they are both well and strong, adapting to Indian life. "As is the wont of children," he reminds her.

She is so filled with gratitude that she grasps both his hands in hers. "Thank you, thank you!" she cries. "I am rejoiced to hear this news! It gives me hope that we will someday be reunited."

He gives her the gentlest of smiles. It is not until she looks down, away from his gaze, that she notices she is still holding his hands. Yet she does not want to let go.

Gradually, her discomfort in his presence diminishes. He never shows her the slightest disrespect, nor does he ever make advances. She concludes that her earlier awkwardness and arousal were due to her agitated state after Sarah's death. It is not his fault that she was unable to master her feelings. She begins to trust him, to feel safe in his presence. She would never before have thought it possible that an Indian man and an Englishwoman could become friends, but this is what seems to be happening.

He tells her of Hassanamesit, the place where he was born, with its hills and forests and rivers of sweet water leaping with fish. He says that ancient ancestors built stone caves like wombs there, so sacred that only the *pauwaus* are allowed to enter.

He tells her he was very young when the English first came to Hassanamesit. "Mr. Eliot and his friend Mr. Gookin," he says. Mary frowns at the name, knowing she has heard it before. Then she remembers—the man who owned Bess Parker's lover was a Mr. Gookin. She wonders if it is the same man.

"We called them *wautaconog*—coat men," James is saying, "because they covered their bodies in stiff black cloth, even in seasons when the Nipmuc do not wear skins. They came in summer when we built our wetus and planted corn in the flat fields near the river. After they left, my older brothers mocked them. The *pauwaus* dreamed of snakes and hawks and smoked many pipes of tobacco to cleanse the air."

He tells her that Mr. Eliot came back many times. When James's father fell ill with a fever and the *pauwaus* burned herbs and chanted for him, it was not until Mr. Eliot prayed over him that he recovered. His father and Mr. Eliot became friends, and his father decided to send James to live with the English. He tells her that this is a common practice among the Nipmucs, who for generations have sent promising young boys to other tribes to learn their ways and language.

James describes the years he lived with Mr. Dunstan, the president of the college in Cambridge, where he first saw a printing press. He tells her of his enchantment with the press, and with the magic of words. He says that one day his master found him running his hands over the letters of type, his fingers black with ink. Instead of beating him, Mr. Dunstan said he believed God had shown James his vocation. Later he was apprenticed to a printer, where he set the type for Mr. Eliot's Indian Bible. Mary has heard of John Eliot's Bible, for it is famous throughout the Bay Colony as a work of great scholarship, a labor of love in the service of the Lord.

One day she thinks to ask James if he is married. He looks at the surrounding trees as if he does not know and might find an answer there. "Aye, I was," he says quietly. "But Nippesse died of a fever two years past. I have two young sons, Ammi and Moses." He pauses, regards her again with his dark, direct gaze. "They are not here. Children require a mother. My wife's sister cares for them in the north where they are safe, far from English towns."

She feels a flutter in her throat. "Do you not miss them?"

"Does the grass wither when there is no rain? Does the sparrow long for dawn?"

She looks down at her lap and pinches a fold in her apron.

"My brothers and father are here in camp. I am among my people." His tone is warm, forgiving. She wonders if he is seeking a new wife, but she does not ask.

One cold, cloudy afternoon when she encounters James as she is searching for groundnuts, she asks how he came to be among Philip's people. "If you are a friend of Mr. Eliot, why are you now among the warriors who terrorize the English?"

His eyes harden. "I am not a warrior. I have terrorized no one. Do you not remember who freed you?"

"I have not forgotten." She puts her hand to her throat, recalling the weight of the rope against her skin. "Yet you live openly among the rebels," she prompts. "You dress as an Indian; you go freely among them."

"As do you," he says, smiling. She feels her face flush as his words strike home. She has indeed adopted many Indian ways. She wears a deer-hide dress and moccasins, plaits her hair, and wraps a blanket around herself when she is outside. She smears bear grease on her hands and face to protect her skin from the elements. She has learned to carry heavy baskets and to weave mats and tie them on the wetus.

"You ask how I have come here," he says slowly. "I, too, have been a captive. I, too, have felt the rope bind my neck."

She looks at him in surprise.

"It is so." He points to his neck, and she sees what she has not before: a white scar cutting across his skin. "In August, when I was celebrating a successful hunt with my friends, English soldiers came. They put ropes around our necks and marched us to Boston. They put us on trial for killing settlers in the town of Lancaster. Your town."

A cold finger runs down Mary's back and she moves away from him. "You were among those who attacked the outlying farms?" she whispers.

"No. It was a false charge contrived by Captain Moseley."

"I have heard the name," she says. "'Tis said he is an excellent soldier, though his disposition is hard."

His eyes narrow. "He is more than hard. He is a cruel man. A devil. With a special hatred for Indians. He slaughters people as mindlessly as a deranged wolf, and with less reason. It is said he once ordered his soldiers to stake a grandmother to the ground and set hungry dogs upon her. A grandmother!" He looks at her closely. "While she screamed and begged for mercy, the dogs tore the flesh from her bones and devoured every morsel. Moseley looked on, laughing, though even his own soldiers turned away, sickened by what they had done."

"I cannot believe this," Mary says. "'Tis some lie invented by his enemies."

"'Tis no lie," he says, "for I witnessed his cruelty myself when he tied one of my friends to a tree and burned his flesh with brands from the fire because he would not speak a falsehood."

Mary closes her eyes against this image.

"In Boston they kept us chained in a filthy cell for a fortnight," he continues. "We could not see the sunlight or the stars or any green, living thing. We were not allowed to wash ourselves. They gave us tainted water and bread infested with worms." He leans toward her. "Do you know what happens to an Indian's spirit when he is confined? It withers and dies. We all sickened toward death. When we finally came to trial, the judge found us innocent. He said we must be sent to Deer Island until the war is over."

Mary tries to remember what Joseph told her about Deer Island, a barren strip of land in Boston Harbor used to contain friendly Indians during the hostilities. "I warrant it was for your protection," she says. "A safe haven where you would not fall victim to the attacks of enemy tribes."

He shakes his head. She notes the way the late winter light plays over his face, warming and softening his expression. "'Tis no protection. Deer Island is a sentence of death. The people sent there have not been provided food or shelter."

"I am certain the General Court has guaranteed their safety," she says, though she has no such certainty. "And surely the Lord will protect them."

He makes no response.

"Still, none of this explains why you live among Philip's warriors," she says. "Why did you not go back to your home village and live in peace?"

His eyes narrow. "That is what I wished to do. Tried to do. I fled Boston and returned to Hassanamesit. But in November Nipmuc warriors came and took all our stores and warned us that if we did not go with them, the English would seize us. The entire village followed them, save one family, which fled to its winter hunting camp." He strokes the scar on his neck and smiles. "Thus you see how it is. Though the Nipmuc captured me, I am able go about freely, for they understand that a man's spirit is free and will wither when confined. But the English do not understand the spirit and think it can be bound and caged."

His words trouble her. "True freedom lies in Christ," she says.

"No matter that an Indian is converted to Christ, to the English he will always be Indian." He gives her a sad smile. "I have lived many years among Englishmen. I have studied their books and worn their clothes and lived in their houses. But that does not mean I understand their ways." He leans in. "*Your* ways, *Chikohtqua*. Perhaps you will be able to explain them to me."

To her surprise, Mary finds herself smiling back at him. "I welcome the opportunity."

A few days after this conversation, Mary wakes to the cries of birds and the smoke of cooking fires. Though it is not yet light, the camp is already coming to life. She hears footsteps outside, the sound of voices. She is alone in the wetu. She sits up and pushes the heavy skin away; she can sense that the camp is already moving. There is no predicting how long they will stay in one place. Sometimes it is days, sometimes hours. More than once, when the word is passed, they have begun marching almost immediately.

The hide covering the doorway snaps open and Weetamoo steps into the wetu. "*Peyau yeuut,*" she says, gesturing. Mary has come to recognize Weetamoo's urgent tone and nods to show she understands she must go with her. Weetamoo touches her forearm with two fingers and surprises Mary by speaking English. "Today we cross big river. Meet Massasoit Metacomet. Philip." She spits the English name as if it is an epithet, but Mary has already grasped her meaning: She is to be taken to meet the leader of the Indian rebellion. Her heart contracts as she thinks of Ann Joslin's cruel death and wonders if a similar fate awaits her.

But Weetamoo will not acknowledge any of her questions. She pushes Mary out of the wetu, straps a basket filled with rolled furs on her back, and leads her up a hill to a rock outcropping.

A wide river lies below, twisting through a long valley. *"Quine-tukqut,"* Weetamoo says. Mary realizes she's saying the name of the river. She has done this before, offering her the names of places, as if they are gifts, a practice Mary has failed to appreciate. For the first time she understands how these names give a shape and significance to her new life as an Indian.

She feels an odd flutter in her chest and closes her eyes against the thought. She is *not* an Indian. She is an Englishwoman and a Christian. It is evil to embrace heathen ways.

Weetamoo slaps her cheek. Mary's eyes fly open and she stumbles after her down the hill to the river. Many Indians are standing on the shore; some have already boarded the heavy wooden vessels carved from tree trunks that they call *canoes.* Weetamoo points to an empty one that three warriors are putting into the water.

"Go," she commands and gives Mary a shove.

Mary is now certain that once she crosses the river the Indians will kill her. She is going not to meet Philip, but to her own death. She reminds herself that if God has ordained this day to be her last, she ought to welcome it. She should not shame herself or her faith by fainting. Yet she is shaking as she climbs into the canoe.

There is a sudden clamor downstream. A man roughly pulls her from the canoe and pushes her back onto the shore. The warriors begin to herd people together. With shouts and gestures they urge everyone north along the river. Then Mary hears a woman scream, *"Ynglees,"* and she understands that English troops have been spotted nearby.

Everyone is moving close together in an urgent, jostling mass.

She wonders briefly if she can slip away in the midst of the confusion and find her way to the soldiers. She looks around, seeking cover under the nearby trees where she will be able to shed the heavy basket. She pulls her blanket tighter and steps sideways, toward a likely copse of bushes.

She catches a glimpse of James, walking with another man several rods behind her. Though he does not look in her direction, she knows he has seen her. She has the distinct sensation that he is watching over her. That he knows where she is at all times.

She hesitates. James continues walking toward her, talking with the man, but not looking at her. Yet she is certain he saw her step away from the group. Her legs and arms are weak and her stomach fills with bile. She slips back into the hurrying crowd.

CHAPTER THIRTEEN

They walk beside the river for miles. When the warriors halt them at noon, Mary takes off her basket and sits with her back against a boulder. She is grateful for the chance to rest. A childhood memory comes unbidden—tending the fire while a young pig roasts slowly on a spit. Her mouth waters violently. She thinks of all she has cherished and lost—the plentiful stores of food, the comfort and security of her home. Her beloved sister Elizabeth. Her children. The support and love of fellow Christians. Yet in her hunger, she believes she would exchange all of them for a mouthful of sweet roasted meat.

"Mother?"

The familiar voice startles her. Joss! She looks up and cries out, for there he is—standing right in front of her. For a moment she thinks it might be a trick of her mind. But no—it is truly her son. She leaps to her feet and embraces him.

"How is it with you?" She holds him out at arm's length and then pulls him back in against her. Tears surprise her and she has to blink violently to check them. "Are you well?" She cannot stop

touching him—his shoulder, his arm, his face—though she can see
that it annoys him. His features are gaunt and he is bony from hunger, yet he tells her again and again that he is fit. He moves restlessly
as he speaks, jamming his hands into his sleeves and pulling them
out again, almost dancing on the balls of his feet. He asks no questions, and she does not tell him she fears she will be killed once they
cross the river.

It seems that only a few moments pass before the Indians begin
to march again and Mary knows that she must put on the heavy
basket and stagger along the trail with them. She embraces Joss one
more time, and off he runs, disappearing so quickly into the trees
that their encounter seems as insubstantial as a dream.

They come to a broad, flat place, where they sleep on blankets
on the ground. All night Mary lies awake listening to the water tumble and roll. At dawn, two warriors pull her to her feet and
put her in a canoe. She sits very straight, as if strapped into iron
stays. She is determined to keep her faith in the Lord, but when she
sees the crowd of Indians gathered on the far shore, her resolve
turns her spine to water. She grasps the gunwales, clenching them
so tightly that her fingernails leave crescents in the wood.

As they draw close to the far bank, she sees Weetamoo standing
onshore. When the sachem makes a small gesture with her right
hand, the warriors roughly push Mary from the canoe. She stumbles and falls, soaking her dress and blanket in the icy water. Weetamoo motions for her to hurry and then turns and walks into the
forest, as if Mary's obedience does not matter to her. The Indians
laugh as Mary rises and staggers out of the water. When she reaches
the bank, her legs buckle and she sprawls on the sand.

She begins to weep—great, rolling tears—fortitude running
out of her like the water that drips from the hem of her apron. She
is exhausted, spent. She cannot go on any longer. Someone touches

her shoulder. She raises her head and finds Quinnapin kneeling beside her.

"Why you cry?" His voice is gentle. She feels the weight and width of his fingers through the deer hide of her sleeve. She smells the bear grease on his skin and in his hair.

She sits up and wipes her face. His image blurs and shimmers before her. "Because I fear my hour has come," she whispers. "You are going to kill me."

"No." He shakes his head. "No one hurt you." He rises and gestures to someone behind him and a young woman comes forward, holding a scrap of meat. It is a moment before Mary understands the woman is offering it to her. She takes the meat and eats as another woman approaches with a small bowl of finely ground meal, followed by one who drops a handful of withered peas into her wet apron. Mary can make no sense of it. The Indians who just mocked her are now generously sharing their food. A moment ago, they stood in a circle around her laughing, yet now they are filled with kindness.

She sees James standing at the far edge of the crowd, watching. After a moment, he disappears into the forest. She feels oddly bereft, as if he has rejected her and is no longer her friend. She wants to go after him, but two warriors stand between her and the trees, and when she pushes herself to her feet, they glare at her so fiercely she sinks back to the ground.

The Indians gradually drift away, leaving her alone on the shore except for the warriors. She continues to sit where she fell, eating the food she was given, waiting for some vigor to flow back into her body as she ponders what will happen next.

Late in the afternoon, the warriors pull her to her feet and lead her up the hill to a wetu so long it has three smoke holes. The camp is a haze of sound and color. Smoke rises from hundreds of wetus. Sunlight slashes through trees and makes puddles of light on the ground. Snow has melted from the clearings, leaving patches of wet earth. Children squat in the mud, fashioning tiny animals from clots of black earth: deer, rabbits, dogs. Women come out of the wetus to watch Mary.

Inside, the two warriors squat on the ground and Mary finds herself standing in front of a man who sits cross-legged on a platform covered with many skins. She assumes this is Philip. He wears an English shirt and breeches. He looks to be about her age, though there is an extraordinary weariness in his gaze. He has a well-shaped head and wide shoulders. His chest is draped in a bone necklace and three wide belts of wampum. He has only one attendant—a short man whose right forearm is wrapped in a serpent tattoo and who looks at Mary with more curiosity than cruelty.

Philip surprises her by speaking English. He asks her to sit next to him and offers her a pipe to smoke. She looks at it longingly. For years, she has been fond of tobacco, yet she knows she cannot consent to sharing a pipe with an Indian, no matter how powerful, without compromising her honor. She notes the flicker of displeasure that crosses his face when she refuses. Yet it is quickly gone, like a flash of light on a river, replaced by a look of mild amusement.

He draws on his pipe and leans back comfortably against a reed mat decorated with feathers that hangs behind him. She notices that his right hand is misshapen. "You know Mohawk?" he asks, watching her.

Mary frowns, wondering if he is setting a trap. She remembers Alawa telling her she was born Mohawk and that James had once referred to the Mohawk as a savage, warlike people. "I have heard of them," she says cautiously.

"Mohawk foolish people," he says. "Do stupid things. Listen. One time, long ago, Mohawk people go to sachem and ask, 'Will winter be cold or not?' Sachem does not know but says go gather wood for winter fires and then he goes to visit *pauwau*. It is long walk to *pauwau*'s wetu. Sachem must go up mountain and down again, over many stones. When he finally reach him, *pauwau* says, 'Yes, winter will be cold.' So sachem goes back to people and says people must hurry, gather much wood." Philip draws again on his pipe; white smoke curls from the corners of his mouth.

Mary wonders why he is telling her this story. She wonders if it is true. The two warriors are watching him with little smiles on their faces.

"Ten days pass," Philip continues, "and sachem thinks again about winter and goes back to *pauwau*. 'Will it be *very* cold winter?' he asks, and *pauwau* says yes, it will be very cold winter. So sachem goes back to people and tells them hurry, gather every stick of wood in forest. Ten days more pass and sachem travels again to *pauwau*. He is weary from long walk. 'Are you sure winter will be very cold?' he asks *pauwau*. *Pauwau* says, 'Yes, I am sure it will be very cold winter.' Sachem asks, 'Did ancestor spirits tell you this?' *Pauwau* says, 'Not ancestor spirits.'" Philip pauses; his eyes flash. "'I am sure because I see Mohawk people gather so much wood!'"

He smiles and the warriors laugh, as does his attendant. Philip draws on the pipe, releases the smoke and laughs out loud. It occurs to Mary that his story must be a jest and, though she cannot see much humor in it, she forces herself to smile.

Philip shifts on the platform, leaning toward her. Apparently his jest was a customary pleasantry because his amused expression disappears and he begins to quiz her. He asks if her husband is wealthy, and when she says he is not, that he is only a poor minister working in the Lord's service, he laughs again. He says something to his servant that she cannot understand. Then he leans toward her. "I have plan," he says. "For you."

A ripple of alarm runs up her spine. "What plan?" she asks, but he does not answer. Instead he tells her that, as long as she proves herself a good captive, she will remain alive.

She bows her head, in what she hopes is a suitable gesture of deference. "My master treats me well," she says, thinking of Quinnapin's kindness on the shore.

Philip's smile disappears. "Weetamoo is sister." He pats his chest. "You honor Weetamoo."

She dips her head again.

"You not run away home," he says. "You live. Maybe we sell you back to English."

She feels a jolt of confusion. "You mean to release me?"

He does not answer. Instead, he tilts his head and asks, "Do you sew cloth?"

Mary slides her hand into her pocket and wraps her fingers around her mother's scissors. "Aye," she says.

"You sew shirt for my papoose?" he says. "I like English cloth." And he plucks at the sleeve of his shirt.

"Yes," she says, smiling. Relief washes through her. "I will gladly sew a shirt for your babe."

He smiles back before dismissing her with a flick of his hand. As she leaves, his servant presses a folded square of muslin into her hands, enough to make a child's shirt. The warriors escort her to Weetamoo's wetu, where she is immediately ordered to skin a freshly killed rabbit and scrape the hide clean. She obeys with suitable diligence. Yet she senses that her prospects are better than they were an hour ago because Philip has taken notice of her. Whether or not he decides to ransom her back to the English, he has opened the way for her to profit from her skill with needle and scissors.

She knows that Joseph would tell her that this new opportunity is God's guiding grace, but Mary has seen so little of God's succor since her capture that she has come to believe, like Ann Joslin, that He is absent from the wilderness.

They remain in Philip's camp for nearly a fortnight. When Weetamoo fails to assign her a task, Mary sits and sews, which gives her long hours of contemplation. She watches people come and go, notices that some of them exchange possessions for food—small baskets, belts, squares of cloth, fox furs, necklaces of feathers and bone. She thinks about Joss and Marie and frets over their welfare, praying that they have not been bewitched by Indians. When she is not thinking of them, she grieves for Sarah. She recalls the terrible burden of carrying her fevered and wounded body on the trail. She remembers thinking that very burden kept her alive. She thinks about Joseph and wonders what he is doing. Is he courting another woman? Is he married as the rumors say? She begins to accept the fact that he will not come for her and her affection for him shrivels.

Sometimes she thinks about Bess Parker. She wonders what became of her poor son. Has he been ill-treated by his master? Has he been sold not just once, but many times? How has he fared without his mother to care for him? How has *Bess* fared without him? She thinks about love and all she has been taught—that love belongs first to God, that mortal love is a poor imitation of divine love. That too much affection for her children and husband is sinful and dangerous because it might diminish her love for the Lord. Yet now it seems to her that love is a mystery that takes its own forms. Love goes where it will, and the attempt to redirect it actually corrupts it.

Few of the Indians speak English to her, except for James and Alawa. Weetamoo plainly understands Mary, and has demonstrated that she can speak English. Yet she rarely does, seeming to think it beneath her. Mary knows she must learn to understand the Indian language. But she finds it difficult and learns the words slowly, picking them up here and there, like scraps of food or discarded crumbs.

She asks James for his help. When Weetamoo has no chores for her, he teaches her useful words and instructs her in the complexity of Indian languages. He tells her that there are many different tongues spoken in the camp. "Every tribe has its own tongue," he says. "They are connected like the web of a great spider. Yet each is distinct."

She tries to make sense of this. It would explain why some of the Indians seem suspicious of others. Why they don't seem to understand one another plainly. Why they gather in little knots of people and cast sideways glances at one another. Perhaps this is the reason it has been so difficult for her to learn the words.

"Our tongues are not like the English tongue," he says. "English words are like small beads on a string. Our words are like relationships—some are very long and elaborate because that is the nature of some associations." He smiles and startles her by reaching across his knees and circling her wrist with his fingers. Her skin shivers. "A band that circles a woman's wrist—to the English it is a *bracelet*—but a Nipmuc sees it as a connection. So we call it *petehennitchab*, which means 'that which the hand remains put into.' So you see, the word explains what the hand *does*. We know things have no meaning if they are severed from their purposes."

She feels her face slowly redden under his gaze. His fingers still encircle her wrist. She tries to think about what he said. The idea is so strange, and her mind is so oddly misty and warm, that she can make no sense of it.

When he takes away his hand, she feels unexpectedly bereft.

When Mary finishes the shirt for Philip's papoose and presents it to him, he gives her a shilling. It is the first sign that her fortunes have changed. A few days later, Philip asks her to make a cap for his boy, and soon other Indians bring cloth and food to her and ask her to make clothes. She begins doing a steady business in trade. For the first time since her capture, Mary has food enough to satisfy her.

One morning there is a general tumult in the camp. At first Mary thinks they are preparing to move again. Yet after she has swept out the wetu and piled the sleeping skins on the platforms, Weetamoo dismisses her. Mary walks through the camp, looking for a quiet place to sew. The women, who are usually occupied with weaving mats or scraping hides, are instead clustered in small groups, engaged in animated conversation. In the evening there is drumming and dancing around a great fire in the center of the camp. Drawn to the ceremony, Mary sits beneath the overhang of a large boulder and watches the warriors dance. Quinnapin, his face painted in red and black swirls and his linen shirt unlaced to reveal his chest, dances until dawn.

When the sun rises again over the low hills in the east, Mary learns that the warriors have left for battle. It strikes her as strange and foolish that they weary themselves by dancing all night before a fight. So she is not surprised when, all the next day, men trickle back into camp, their glances wary and exhausted. A few are leading captured sheep and horses. Alawa tells Mary that they attacked the town of Northampton, where the English had set a trap for them inside the palisade. Many Indians were killed and many more wounded. The Narragansett sachem, Canonchet, was captured and beheaded by Mohegan warriors allied with the English.

That night the warriors blacken their bodies and form a circle around the fire. As the moon rises, they begin a slow, somber dance. The light flickers on their bent heads and blackened shoulders, over the shining patches of wet skin where the paint has sluiced away. Mary feels caught in the net of their sorrow. She thinks of Sarah lying alone in the cold ground. She thinks of Elizabeth sprawled dead in the snow. She begins to weep.

She is about to go back to the wetu when Weetamoo steps into the circle of dancers. She wears a coat of coarse cloth covered all over with belts of wampum. From her elbows to her hands, her arms are encased in metal and hide bracelets, and around her neck she has hung strands of shells and wood and stones. Bright stones dangle from her ears, catching the light and winking it back. She wears white shoes and fine red stockings. Her face is painted red and she has dusted her hair with red powder. Slowly she begins to dance.

Other women emerge from the shadows to join her, forming an outer circle around the men. The two circles move in opposite directions, like two great revolving wheels. Mary's gaze is fixed on Weetamoo, who, though moving with the circle of women, seems somehow to be the center of it all. Mary can neither explain nor understand this marvel.

The women begin to wail, softly at first and then louder and louder, throwing their heads back and crying to the sky. *"Naananto, Canonchet,"* they chant, over and over. Mary nearly joins them. She longs to cry her daughter's and sister's names into the blind night. She wants the fire to dance on her skin. She yearns to be swept into the double circle of mourning. Yet she does not move. Her bones feel shackled to the bedrock beneath her feet, her heart bolted as if in a box of iron.

Then she sees James. He wears only leggings and a loincloth. His hair is braided and adorned with three black feathers at his crown. His skin shines in the firelight. A necklace of shells swings back and forth across his chest. He lifts his knees high as he whirls and dances, his feet beating the ground in time to the drum.

She is spellbound. She cannot withdraw her gaze. Her heart begins to beat with the drum. She feels the dancers' sorrow enter her bones, as her own sorrow dissolves. She feels their wildness in her heart, and her feet begin to move on the earth.

CHAPTER FOURTEEN

The Indians mourn for three nights, blackening their faces and dancing and crying out the dead sachem's name. Quinnapin especially seems broken by this news. Alawa tells Mary that Canonchet was his cousin, and Mary's heart goes out to him, though she knows she ought to rejoice at the English victory.

The horses captured in the failed raid are picketed near Weetamoo's wetu. Mary hears them stamping and huffing in the night. A few days after the mourning ceremonies, two warriors come to the wetu and Mary is surprised to find she can understand them as they speak to Weetamoo. They ask if she will allow them to take the horses west into the hills to Albany and trade them for gunpowder, but she dismisses them with a wave of her hand.

Mary steps outside. The horses—a big chestnut gelding and two gray mares—whinny softly when she approaches. She is surprised the Indians have not already killed them for food. She rubs the flank of one of the mares, wishing she had some grass to offer. The mare reminds her of a horse her father bought when she was a young child—a mare so gentle Mary could safely ride alone on her back. She thinks about the warriors who want to go to Albany. She wonders if they will find a way to go without Weetamoo's permission.

She forms a plan, and goes in search of James. It is near dark when she finds him standing on a low bluff overlooking the river. The wind sings in the tops of the pines and the moon is rising over the low hills on the far shore, turning the river to silver. She approaches in what she believes is complete silence, for she has learned how to place her moccasin-clad feet so they make almost no sound. Yet before she reaches him, James turns, plainly having heard her.

He smiles and holds out his hand. His look is open, unabashedly happy to see her. She feels an electric ripple at the base of her spine. "I have not seen you for some time. I wondered if you had gone."

"Gone?" She does not give him her hand. "Where would I go?"

He shrugs. "You might have been sold and taken to some other camp. Or you might have left to find your way back to your home."

She laughs. "I am not so foolish. I have been making myself useful, as you suggested. I have been sewing shirts." She moves closer.

"So I have heard. You are becoming Indian."

He has made this accusation before and usually it irritates her. But this time, she is surprised to feel a flush of satisfaction. She wonders suddenly if she has been trying to become more Indian all along. Her reaction is disturbing. She pushes it away. "I need a favor of you." .

"A favor."

A slow heat climbs her neck. "Are we not friends?" she says carefully. "And fellow Christians?" She folds her hands in front of her waist, a sign of humility. "You know that Christians are commanded to help each other in times of trial."

He grunts softly. "What help?"

"I have heard that some of Weetamoo's warriors are planning an expedition west to the town of Albany."

"Who told you this?"

She shakes her head, dismissing his question. "I would like to make an arrangement. I want you to take me to Albany and trade me to the English. I will give you half my price."

"To Albany?" His face is partly in shadow, so she cannot read his expression, but his laugh is unmistakable. "Only an Indian would have the wit to negotiate her own barter so cunningly."

Her face burns. "I wish only to gain my freedom."

"What, you have no freedom here?" There is something unusually sharp in his tone. "Think on it. When you were among the English, were you ever allowed to roam the village at will? Did you have time of your own in which to start your own enterprise? Were you not watched constantly? Did you not labor for your husband from waking until sleeping?"

She cannot answer him, for he is uttering the very thoughts she has entertained for weeks now. "I have proposed a bargain to you," she says, the words like cold stones in her mouth. "You have not yet answered it."

He looks away, toward the rising moon. "More," he says after a time. "Half is not enough."

She is stunned. "I thought you a friend."

He makes a slight motion with his hand—a flexing of his fist. "Friend or no, you are not likely to fetch a high price. Surely you know that." He takes a step toward her. "You have lived with Indians," he says softly. "The English will never trust your claims of virtue."

She can say nothing. His words are cruel. But she cannot deny their truth.

"Abandon your dreams of returning," he says. "This is your home now. Your lot is cast with us."

She draws up her shoulders, stiffening them as if to protect her neck from a blow. "So you will not help me?"

She feels his gaze drawing her in, though neither of them moves. "I *am* helping you," he says. "I am trying to persuade you to surrender to your new situation. There is much happiness to be found in acceptance." He is silent for a moment. "And it is no small thing to slip from Weetamoo's grasp."

She feels a shiver along her spine, as if James had just dropped a handful of snow inside her dress. She turns and walks quickly back up the hill toward the camp.

M ary's plan of escape comes to nothing, for a few days later they break camp, cross back over the river, and march north. When they stop walking, Mary takes out her sewing.

She has never considered herself more than a clumsy seamstress, but her work pleases the Indians.

An old man gives her a knife in exchange for a shirt. A woman offers her a pouch of ground corn for stockings. She remembers what Joseph so often said: The Lord's hand is behind every opportunity. She sometimes misses Joseph, with his vast knowledge of the Bible and all of God's ways. All the years of her marriage she has taken refuge in him, as behooves a good Puritan wife, though it has not been an easy matter to curb her tongue or submit her nature to his authority. Something in her has always longed to strike out in her own direction, to express her own thoughts, not his. Perhaps, as Joseph himself has suggested, her hair signifies a fiery and disobedient temperament. Yet she always tried to discipline herself and act properly, so as not to shame either of them. So as not to bring down God's wrath on the whole community.

But thinking of Joseph does not bring the rush of longing that would have been seemly for a woman in Mary's circumstance. She has stopped petitioning the Lord daily for a safe return to her husband's protection. What prayers she manages to whisper have been for the welfare of her living children. She does not know if Joseph has remained faithful. She does not even know if he is still alive. If he lives, is he now rebuilding their house in Lancaster? Is he plowing the west field? There is a heavy stone in her stomach, as if an unborn child died there and lies waiting for a sad deliverance from the womb that has become its crypt.

The children begin dying. The youngest go first. Even Weetamoo's own papoose is wasting away. Mary frets about Joss and Marie. Are they finding enough food to stay alive? Are they suffering from fevers or dysentery? She begs the Lord to give them strength, to keep them well. She reads psalms in secret, searching for solace, but there is none to be had. Death walks through the camp like a sachem, taking one here and one there, at his whim.

Daily, the keening of women fills the camp. The sound is dreadful, like the howling of wolves. It makes Mary feel the same terror in her own throat. Her hearing has sharpened during her time in the wilderness. She has grown more aware of small noises and distant sounds. The waves of grief in the women's voices remind her of her own wild sorrow at Sarah's death, which is nearly as fresh now as the day her daughter died, though it is two months past.

They begin moving more often. Sometimes they walk for hours before they stop to set up camp. Then they are on the trail again early the next morning. Sometimes they build wetus and stay for several days. Mary does not know why they move or who decides. There seems to be no pattern to how long they will remain in one place and when they will move on.

The torturous job of rolling up the mats tears the skin of Mary's fingers and palms. She rolls and rolls, leaving coins of blood on the reeds. Yet the pain is nothing compared to the terrible fainting pains in her stomach. In spite of her sewing enterprise, she is starving. They are all starving.

The days grow longer and the sun is not so distant. The ground begins to thaw. Chickadees bounce through the air in front of her. One day, as they walk beside a river, Mary hears the buzzing trill of blackbirds. Then, from a small tree, she hears a familiar sound and recognizes it as the call of a sparrow. Despite her hunger pangs, her heart lifts and she is suddenly overwhelmed by the radiance of sunlight and the sweetness of birdsong. A great peace settles over her.

Until now, she has never observed anything but disorder and malevolence in the wilderness. Like her mother and father before her, she has always believed it is a place that harbors evil and danger. For the first time, she finds herself enthralled by its beauty. She senses something mysterious and holy lurking behind the apparent chaos of the forest.

Mary begins having peculiar, unsettling thoughts. She wonders if it is a delirium caused by the constant walking. If Joseph were here, he would likely tell her that God is testing her faithfulness. If so, she has already failed His test. James is right—she has grown accustomed to Indian ways. Though it is a hard life, without the comforts of civilization, there is a beauty in the Indians' wildness, and freedom in their ways that allows her to forge her own course. She has unexpectedly discovered an enterprising spirit within her nature. In exchanging her needlework for food and shelter, she has established a small place of usefulness and value within their society.

She begins to devise a plan to barter her own children back to her care. She imagines Joss and Marie living with her in a wetu of her own making. She pictures the three of them well fed and rested, going about their simple duties among a cluster of wetus. All of them at a circle fire, joining in the dance. She imagines sitting with Marie, their heads bent toward each other as they weave baskets side by side. She will tell Marie those secret things mothers must tell their daughters: that blood signifies both life and death, that men are sometimes cunning, that a woman's power lies in her composure.

The days spent on the trail are harrowing. Mary's basket is sometimes so heavy it rubs her back raw. The carrying strap cuts deeply into her forehead, raising two long welts that score her skin and sometimes bleed in rivulets down her forehead and face. She fears they will become scars to disfigure her face. But all she can do is apply mud poultices when each day's trek is done.

One morning, when Weetamoo points to the basket, some perversity makes Mary refuse to lift it. "It is too heavy," she says, signaling with her hands, pressing down on the top of her head and shoulders to show that she can no longer bear so great a weight.

"*Maninnapish!* Quiet!" Weetamoo's voice is as hard as the slap that follows. Mary does not see the blow coming and cries out, rocking back as she clutches her face.

"Go!" Weetamoo points with the air of a queen. Mary ducks to avoid another blow and lifts the basket, fastening the strap obediently across her forehead. Her anger gives her new vigor. She moves along the trail with determination, as if she has a destination other than the next camp. It is late morning before she realizes they are traveling east. Back toward Lancaster.

Slavery makes for an angry heart, the Devil's breeding ground. Mary recalls the biblical command that the slave must cheerfully obey the master, but she cannot make herself cheerful, cannot force herself to a Christian resignation. She is all resistance, chafing at her duty. Her heart is a cauldron. She wonders if this is what Bess Parker experienced when she was bound out. What Bess's enslaved son now experiences, wherever he is. She does not understand how anyone could require a slave to be cheerful.

Despite her defiant heart, she does all that Weetamoo asks, tries to satisfy her every whim. She finds that physical labor offers its own solace. When they set up camp, Mary throws herself into the tasks at hand: rebuilding the wetu, tending the fire, fetching water and firewood. When there is nothing Weetamoo requires—and there are many long hours of idleness—she takes up her needles. There has never been a servant more industrious in any English household.

Yet the dreadful ache in her stomach makes her so restless that she can knit only a few rows before agitation drives her to her feet. She walks constantly up and down the camp, and then into the trees. Her gaze sweeps back and forth inspecting the ground, and when she spots a decayed chestnut, she leaps forward and plucks it up as if it is her true redemption.

One day she finds three chestnuts and seven acorns. She eats the chestnuts and one of the acorns, despite its bitterness, then slips the others into her pocket. On the way back to the wetu she gathers sticks to feed the fire, for the icy edge in the air tells her it will be a cold night.

When she pushes back the deerskin flap, she is startled to find the wetu filled with people. Weetamoo's sister is there with her children and several other women Mary has seen before. Many more are there whom she doesn't know. They lean close by one another on the skins, legs stretched toward the fire or folded beneath them. A young man plays a flute and nearby a girl dandles a stick doll.

She sees James sitting near the fire. A warrior barks something Mary does not understand, and she squeezes all the way inside and lets the flap drop. Smoke scours her throat. Standing, she searches for a place to sit, but there is not a spare inch of space. Everyone seems to be talking. Two warriors dip their bowls into the stew pot of broth, which Mary knows is little more than hot water. She feels a wave of vertigo, and to prevent herself from falling, she clutches one of the hanging mats. This is beyond the light-headed hunger she has carried for weeks now. Perhaps it is the acorn she ate. Or the pipe smoke that now chafes her tongue, making it raw and sore. Still holding the kindling, she sinks to her knees.

A man shouts at her. Her brain swirls like water in a disturbed pond. Someone pushes her shoulder. She raises her head.

"Mauncheake!" the man says. *"Quog quosh!"* He makes a cutting gesture with his hand.

"I am ill," Mary gasps, and then surprises herself by saying the Indian word that means *very weak. "Sawawampeage."*

A babble of Indian words rise around her. A woman slides a hand under her arm and helps Mary to her feet. *"Netop,"* she says. "You must leave." Her English words are tainted with harsh, heathen inflections.

Weetamoo, who is holding her whimpering babe to her breast, speaks from the far side of the fire and for a brief moment Mary thinks she will defend her. *"Weetompaog,"* she says, gesturing to indicate the gathering. "My friends." But instead of smiling, she glares.

"I do not understand," Mary says.

Then James speaks: "She wants you to know we have many here tonight. There is no room for you."

It takes a moment for his meaning to penetrate her smoke-infused brain. "But where am I to go?" Her voice is mournful but there is no answer. She becomes suddenly aware that everyone has stopped talking. Her question—her tone—has struck exactly the wrong note. Indians do not look kindly on weakness. She begins to shake and her shoulders sag. The woman who spoke to her opens the flap and begins to pull her through the doorway.

"Mauncheake!" she whispers urgently. But Mary cannot make her feet move.

Then James is in front of her. She wonders dully how he has moved from the fire to her. There are so many people it does not seem possible that he has been able to set his foot anywhere. But here he is, only inches away, his hair shining with bear grease. He has painted menacing black stripes under his eyes.

"Go," he says. "Go from this place before I run you through." He raises his arm and there, two inches from her face, is the dark shine of his knife.

She glances up into his eyes—the briefest of glances, like lightning—for she wants to see if there might be a trace of Christian compassion residing there. She sees only the gaze of an Indian.

"Now!" he hisses.

She obeys, bowing her head and reeling out into the dark.

CHAPTER FIFTEEN

That night Mary sleeps in a shelter of her own making, like a rabbit in a burrow, safely tucked out of sight of night-wandering dangers. She wakes often because of the cold and the torment of her hunger pangs. In the morning, when she returns to Weetamoo's wetu, she finds a tumult of sorrow. The men are gone and Weetamoo sits in a circle of keening women. She has torn the sleeves of her shirt and blackened her face with soot. Her babe, tightly swaddled in a blanket, lies dead on the ground in front of her.

Though she has no affection for Weetamoo, Mary feels compassion. As she watches the circle of weeping women, she thinks of Sarah and Mari, and remembers feeling as if she had died with them, that her heart had been hollowed out, scraped raw, an empty husk. She nearly took leave of her senses, her sorrow was so great. She remembers wanting to mourn this way after Mari's death, how painful it had been to contain her tears. Her face had ached for weeks.

Mary suspects neither Weetamoo nor her family welcome her presence, yet she is loath to leave in case Weetamoo needs her for some task. And so she sits by, through the long mournful day, praying for Joss and Marie, whom she can only hope are still among the living.

In the morning, they begin marching again. On the trail, Alawa shows Mary how to dress her hair to ward off the spring insects, and then explains how to tell directions from the sun. Mary calculates that they are heading northeast again, toward Lancaster.

She sees warriors carrying those who, from weakness or illness, can no longer walk. Some have bound their bellies with cords. When Alawa explains that it helps to relieve their hunger pangs, Mary wishes she had a cord of her own. Most of the time they walk in silence, for hunger saps even the strength for talking. As they rest briefly at the top of a low hill, Alawa asks where Mary went when she was cast out of Weetamoo's wetu. Mary answers bitterly that she made a shelter on the cold ground. She says that she had considered James a Christian friend but now is convinced he is in league with the Devil.

Alawa gives her a strange look before she glances away to adjust the strap of her carrying basket. "You foolish woman," she says. "Wowaus—James—protects you. He save your life."

"Saved me? He drove me from the wetu at the point of his knife," Mary says. "He threatened to kill me."

Alawa shakes her head. "Did you not hear Weetamoo's words? She would take your head and put it on pike."

Mary stares at her blankly.

"He did not betray you," Alawa says. "He is still friend."

At midday murmurs of excitement pass along the line, and Mary understands enough of what is said to realize there is a rumor abroad that Philip plans to negotiate with the English. His people are dying—many have already perished. She overhears a woman lament that the grandmothers and babes always die first, as if the spirits of war wish to strip the people of both their wisdom and their hope.

They increase the speed of their march and set up camp for only a single night before moving on. Rain falls, turning the ground to mud. Mary thinks of the many years she planted her kitchen garden in this season, the pleasure she took in the cold slick of the earth between her fingers and toes. She wonders if Joseph is planting their fields.

As she walks, she tries to remove all thoughts of food from her mind, yet it is impossible, so great is her hunger. She is struck by how much of her life was dedicated to the getting and preparing of food. From early morning until near dark she labored with food, milking the cow, gathering eggs from the hens and ducks, churning butter, pressing cheese curds into their molds, kneading bread, sowing and weeding her kitchen garden, chopping onions, boiling meat, cutting turnips, slicing sausages into pies. Her mind conjures up pottages and cheeses, leek soups, fruit pies, sweet stews of pork and apples, bread and bowls of crusty cornmeal mush. Her mouth fills with spittle and her stomach roils. As she walks, her eyes constantly examine the trail for nuts and scraps someone else has dropped. Yet she finds nothing but acorn husks.

One evening warriors kill a deer, causing great excitement in the camp. Everyone gathers to watch as they open the animal and begin to strip off the meat. There is a whoop of delight when one warrior lifts out an unborn fawn and holds it high for all to see. They divide the food and Mary is given a small strip of meat the size of her finger. Later Quinnapin startles her by pressing a wedge of the fawn's shoulder into her hands. She thanks him with a pretty curtsy, a gesture that is difficult to execute in her Indian dress. When he laughs and calls for others to watch, she obliges him by curtsying again. A group of men and women gather around her; one of the women tries to imitate her but stumbles and falls on her knees, laughing. Mary demonstrates again, and then Alawa takes up the game. One after another they mimic her, even Quinnapin himself. A mischievous impulse prompts her to mimic them and, giggling, she begins to dip and stumble. Their laughter rises around her; soon everyone is laughing and bobbing up and down in mock curtsies.

Afterward, Mary feels depleted, but happy. It is as if a tap had opened and a heavy, dark liquid flowed out of her, leaving her many pounds lighter, more alert. She roasts the fawn piece on a hot stone, watching closely lest someone steal it. The meat is tender; even the bones are soft enough to eat. She is careful not to eat too quickly, for she knows how easily she could provoke her stomach into rebellion by overfeeding.

Weetamoo orders that a pouch of the slain deer's blood be boiled over a fire. Flames snap loudly in the wood, drawing people close. When the pouch is boiled, Alawa removes and divides it. The black jellied blood reminds Mary of the blood puddings her mother used to make; she savors her portion. The faces of the people look like ghosts as they eat.

Dark clouds boil up from the west, covering the sun. It rains all night. It is a cold, hard rain. Weetamoo tells Alawa and Mary to raise a bark wetu, and they rest comfortably dry, though many lie in the mud, their blankets pulled over their faces. In the morning, Mary sees them moving through the camp, wet and bedraggled, though those who wore hides instead of linen enjoyed some measure of protection.

The next day they begin to boil tree bark with the few groundnuts they have collected. Mary overhears an old man telling a hideous tale of killing captive children and roasting and eating them. She thinks of poor Joss and Marie, and it is with some effort that she tries to assure herself that this Indian's words are mere entertainment, that his intent is but to plague the captives. Yet the story chills her.

They continue on their way. Each morning they rise and lift

their burdens and walk east. Each night they set up camp. One bitterly cold evening, Mary comes across an English youth not much older than Joss, who sprawls moaning on the ground, wearing nothing but a shirt and waistcoat. Nearby lies a papoose, naked and shivering in the cold. The babe is clearly dying. His eyes, nose, and mouth are caked with dirt. Mary picks him up, wipes his face clean with her sleeve, and tries to warm him against her body. He groans and quivers and she thinks for a moment how sweet it is to hold a babe again. Then the child convulses once and lies still in her arms. She tries, but cannot revive him. Dark clouds boil up above the trees on the horizon and the wind comes up. A few snowflakes tumble in the trees. She puts the papoose back on the ground, wishing she had some scrap of cloth with which to cover his poor naked body, but she has lately lost her apron so she cannot even tear a strip from that for a shroud.

She turns her attention to the youth, and tells him he must get to a fire at once. He looks up at her, blinking, trying to focus. He shakes his head, and in a choking voice tells her he has the bloody flux and cannot stand. Something in his tone reminds Mary of Joss when he malingered. She finds the flint in herself to insist, "If you do not heed me, you will perish where you lie."

He moans and rolls on the ground. Annoyed, she bends and puts her shoulder under his arm and raises him to his feet. Together they move through camp as she searches for someone who will take him in. Mary asks one Indian after another for help, but they all refuse. Finally, one old woman points out a wetu at the far edge of the camp.

"Wowaus," she says. "English. Go there."

James's wetu. Of course. Mary hesitates, recalling how James drove her from Weetamoo's wetu, but the youth's suffering brings her to her senses. Summoning her strength, she presses on, wondering if James will again threaten her with his knife.

Night falls and it begins to snow in earnest; the wind howls

through the trees, driving the snow straight at them in long hori-
zontal slashes and gusting so powerfully that Mary staggers. Once,
the youth stumbles and they both fall to the ground. Mary struggles to pull him again to his feet, knowing they both risk freezing if
they stop moving.

Both are shuddering with cold when they reach the wetu. Mary
lifts the door flap and pushes the youth inside. He collapses on the
earthen floor as James rises from his blankets, taking up a club as he
stands. He wears only a loincloth and Mary looks away as she speaks.

"Please," she gasps, falling to her knees, "I beg you as a Christian, let this boy lie here by your fire."

James does not answer, but plucks a blanket from the ground
and wraps it around himself.

The youth tries to rise but cannot. He is wracked with tremors;
his naked feet and legs are blue with cold. "He has the flux," Mary
says, trying to push herself to her feet and staggering from weakness. "He has been cast out of his wetu."

James frowns. "Then why do you ask me to take him in? His
captor will hunt for him and be angry if he finds him with me."

"Please," she says. "He will die without help."

"What is he to you?"

The question takes her by surprise. She has not given any
thought to the boy's circumstance or situation—only to his condition. "He is nothing to me—save a fellow sufferer," she says. "Please.
Can you not find compassion for him, even though you feel naught
for me?"

He gives her a long look, with that penetrating gaze that has so
often unsettled her, before turning his attention to the youth. He
places a thick mat of skins next to the fire and together they carry
him there. James covers him—tenderly, she thinks—with a heavy
bearskin. Mary stands aside as he offers him a bowl of thin broth.
When the boy is unable to eat it himself, James turns to her.

"You are his protector," he says, pushing the bowl and a crudely shaped spoon into her hands. "It is your duty to feed him."

And so Mary kneels beside the boy, whose name she still does not know, and patiently feeds him broth until he falls asleep under her ministrations. Then she puts down the bowl, sinks back on her heels. She feels a wave of vertigo and drops her head into her hands.

"You are weary," James says. "You must sleep." She looks up to find him sitting on a mat gazing at her.

He gestures to the furs stacked on the platform. "This storm will last the night. It is warm here and you will be safe."

Her heart begins to beat too fast. She knows she should not stay a moment longer. Yet she cannot bear to leave.

A gust thumps against the sides of the wetu. The wind shrieks and rattles the door flap. "You will stay," James says firmly. He rises, hangs another hide over the doorway, securing it tightly so no draft can enter, then pulls two more hides from the pile on the platform and gives them to her, gesturing for her to lie down. She is too exhausted to refuse. She rolls onto her side and pulls the heavy furs over her, relaxing into the warmth. She hears the ragged breathing of the youth, and is aware of James moving quietly around the wetu. Later, he lies down a few feet away. She hears him murmuring Indian words in the darkness and wonders if he is praying. His voice seems to come from a great distance as she drifts into sleep.

CHAPTER SIXTEEN

Mary wakes in the middle of the night. She lies on her back, looking up at the smoke hole, wondering for a moment where she is. Then she remembers. The wind has died away, but she knows from the rapid ticking sounds outside that snow is still falling. She sits up and slides from beneath the furs to check on the youth. Low firelight plays over his features. He is still insensible, but when she puts her hand on his brow, it is cooler than it was a few hours before, which tells her that his fever has broken. She slips outside.

Snowflakes drift down, catching on the tatters of her cloak and in her hair. Shivering, she makes her way into the trees. Her moccasin-clad feet make no sound. She squats behind a rock and relieves herself.

As she stands, she sees someone moving through the trees to her right. She holds her breath and does not move, becoming one with the rock and the surrounding trees. There are two of them—warriors acting as sentries, watching the encampment through the night. They speak in low voices. She understands only a few words, but they alarm her, for they tell her that Philip is on the verge of surrendering, that the English soldiers will show no mercy. They expect all the men in the camp will be slain and the women will be violated.

Mary quickly makes her way back to the wetu. She is shaking, but not with cold. She recalls Elizabeth's warning the night before her death—it is as if her sister sits beside her still, and she can hear her voice: *"Before they kill the women, they defile them."* Elizabeth had been talking about Indians. Mary remembers her sick feeling at the words, her long-standing dread of capture, of how certain she had been that she would be assaulted and defiled. She remembers how she vowed that she would rather be slain than captured by Indians. Yet she has been captured, but she has not been assaulted. Despite her days of hunger and toil, she lives. Even with her lowly status as a slave and a captive, even with Monoco's carnal interest, no Indian has molested her. Her virtue is intact.

She pushes through the door flap, finds her way back to her pallet, and slides under the furs, still shivering. Her mind keeps spinning and she cannot sleep. She tries to untangle her conflicting feelings. She hated and feared the Indians, but after three months in their company, she has grown accustomed to their ways. They freely share their food and shelter—something she suspects no English soldier would do with an Indian captive. She has suffered much privation and hardship, but no more than her mistress, whose child has also died, and who has no more to eat than Mary. She has been given no advantages, yet most of the time she has as much freedom and respect as any Indian woman.

In his sleep, James rolls toward her on his mat. She watches him in the semidarkness, studies the contours of his face in the glow of the fire's embers. She thinks of his many acts of kindness—from cutting the rope from her neck, to protecting her from Weetamoo's wrath. She wonders why he chose to protect her. She can only conclude that it is God's doing, that the Lord has sent him to be her rescuer and friend.

Still shivering, she turns restlessly, trying to find a comfortable position.

"You are shaking." His voice startles her; she had believed he was asleep. Instead, he moves toward her. "Come." He wraps an arm around the skins that enclose her and pulls her toward him. She tries to murmur a protest, but it comes out as no more than a sigh. He draws back the bearskin and rolls her onto her side so that she is facing away and he presses himself to her, his chest against her back, his thighs along the backs of her legs, his shins touching her calves. Then he pulls another bearskin over both of them.

She knows it is wicked to lie there, that letting him warm her can lead too easily to wantonness and sin, that she should rise at once and flee. But his body is warm and strong and she is freezing. And so she lies, absorbing his warmth until her shivering stops.

"It is your thoughts that torment you," James says quietly. "You must share them, else they will give you no peace."

Tears spring to her eyes. "With you?" she whispers.

He is silent. She feels his heart beat against her spine. After a moment, he asks, "Am I not as good a friend as you have in these troubled times?"

She knows in that moment that he is as good a friend as she has ever had in her life. She begins to tell him, speaking into the darkness thoughts she has never imagined putting into words. It is a confession unlike any she has ever made—cleansing and thorough and nakedly honest. She tells him of her confused feelings about Indians, how disturbed she was at first, but how many of their ways now draw her. She tells him how she is attracted to the dances and strange songs, the power of the great drums, even the wildness of their grief. How she admires their stoic patience and generosity. How appealing are the freedoms their women enjoy, how surprised she is by the self-control of their men.

"You do not understand why you have not been raped." He states the question that has lain in her mind for weeks, states it so simply and straightforwardly that for a moment she wonders if she said the words herself. No one in her memory has ever been so direct about sexual matters. She cannot think of how to form a reply.

"Is that not so?" She feels his breath warm the back of her neck. His fingertips brush her arm as lightly as a butterfly's wing. "Have you not expected your virtue to be taken by a heathen?" As he says the last word, there is amusement in his voice, though she detects no derision. He is so close she can smell his breath, a sweet pungent scent like sassafras.

She shrugs, a movement intended to relieve the tension in her neck and shoulders, as much as to acknowledge his point.

"Indian men do not rape their captives," he says. "They adopt them as wives and daughters."

"Am I to be adopted then?" she asks, her voice a whisper. She welcomes the heat radiating from his skin, though she is warm now and knows she ought to move away.

He laughs gently. "I think you would like that," he says. "But I believe Philip has other plans."

She thinks of poor Ann Joslin, pictures her brutal death. "Do you think he will have me killed?" Her mouth is dry. She can barely speak.

"No, no." His hand, which hovers just above her arm, takes hers. His skin is warm, his fingers sure and strong. "No one will do you any harm. Have you not seen how I protect you?"

She does not pull her fingers from his. They curl into the warmth of his palm. "I have seen it," she whispers. "What I do not know is *why*."

He is silent for a long time. She can hear her heart beat in her ears. She wonders if he is going to confess his feelings for her. But when he finally speaks, he says, "Once, a few years after he baptized me, Mr. Eliot told me a secret. He said that God always weeps when men and women are cruel—to each other, to animals. To the earth itself. He said that Christ's kingdom will only come when we learn to be deeply kind. He told me to remember that while we draw breath, there will always be some way we can show kindness."

She does not know what to say. These are not the words she expected. Yet they move her, as if she has just witnessed a strange miracle.

"What will become of me?" she asks, after a time.

"Philip will redeem you to the English," James says. "When he is ready."

Her mind races. What of *us*? she thinks suddenly. What will become of this strange, unseemly friendship between an English wife and an Indian? No civilized Englishman or -woman will ever accept it. Yet she has come to a place in her heart where she feels she cannot live without it.

She is silent for so long that she hears James's breathing lengthen and knows he has slipped back into sleep, still holding her hand.

She wakes on her side, in the same coiled position in which she fell asleep. James no longer lies behind her. She sits up. The youth is moaning softly in his sleep, but James is not in the wetu.

She feels a wave of shame as she recalls what transpired in the middle of the night. Though there was no carnal act between them, the intimacy of her conversation with James distresses her. Mary cannot recall even one exchange with Joseph in which she so nakedly revealed her thoughts.

She pushes off the bearskin and gets to her feet. She is bending over the youth, trying to determine if his fever has returned, when the door flap opens and James steps into the wetu.

"You must go," he says before she has a chance to speak. "Weetamoo is looking for you. They say she believes you have run off."

"Run off?" Mary presses a hand to her forehead. "Where would I run to?"

He shrugs. "I do not know her thinking. But you must return to her wetu at once. She cannot find you here."

She understands what he has not said: that it will go badly not only for her but also for him if Weetamoo believes he is involved in her disappearance.

"I came here for help." She gestures to the youth. "The boy was dying. An old woman advised me to come here."

"*I* know why you came." His gaze does not leave her face. As if he has spoken what neither of them would ever say aloud: *The youth was not the true reason.* "You must go. *Now.*"

Her eyes fill instantly and unaccountably with tears, as if he has opened the ground of her heart and set free a hidden spring. She nods and hurries to the door. Her forearm brushes his as she passes. She looks up, into his face. "May I come tomorrow to see how the youth fares?"

"Of course. If Weetamoo consents." He lifts the flap and she steps out into the bright morning.

She is not free to visit James's wetu for two days—such is the fickleness of Weetamoo's demands. Her release comes when a warrior asks her to knit a pair of stockings to fit him. She looks for permission to Weetamoo, who signals that Mary might do as she wishes, that she may once again come and go as she pleases. It occurs to Mary that perhaps they are equally weary of each other's presence.

Mary goes at once to James's wetu and is pleased to find that the youth has come out of his stupor and is recovering. She talks with him for a while, cautioning him to obey James in all things, reminding him that he would be dead if James had not taken him in.

"He may be dead yet," James says, "for I have no more food. Nor muskets or arrows to hunt with."

The youth assures her he is grateful, but there is something

sullen in the curl of his mouth that she does not like. She leaves the
wetu, determined to scrounge food for James and the youth. Yet she
is able to find only two groundnuts and a scrap of bread so dry it
crumbles to dust at her touch. As she peels a strip of soft bark from
a chestnut tree with the intention of making a stew of the bark and
nuts, Alawa finds her and tells her that Weetamoo wants her to return to the wetu at once and mend a shirt.

The next morning, as Mary walks through the camp, she overhears a rumor that the English youth has escaped. She hurries along
the path and finds James smoking a pipe outside his wetu. He confirms that the youth is gone, that he left in the middle of the night.
"He has returned your kindness—and mine—with cowardly be-
trayal," he tells Mary. "No one seems to care for kindness anymore.
Perhaps we are well rid of him. He is one less mouth to feed, one less
body to take up space in a wetu."

"No!" She is unable to agree with this dark vision of the world.
"Kindness redeems our hearts, no matter whether we are thanked
for it."

He draws on his pipe, thoughtfully studying her face. Smoke
drifts in gray curls from the bowl.

Finally, he takes the pipe from his mouth and rests it in his
palm. "So I believed in my youth. But sorrow has come with the
English and infested our lands. We must learn new truths or die."
He gazes past Mary at the budding trees, as if he can see through
their branches into the future.

In the days that follow, Mary thinks about James almost constantly, recalling every encounter, from the moment he cut the
rope from her neck, to the night they lay side by side in his wetu.
She ponders the unsettling attraction between them, the way he
listens so closely to her, the respect he shows her even though she is
a woman and a slave.

Every day, the air is sweeter with the earth's perfume. There are buds on the trees, and small yellow and white flowers bloom here and there in the sunlight. Sparrows and warblers sing hidden in the forest. A mountain rises not far away, the trees on it tinged with red, as if dark blood flows through the naked branches. Mary stands watching, drawing in great draughts of air. She is struck by the realization that the wilderness has become a place of beauty to her. A place that is no longer filled only with danger, but also with mystery and peace.

The next day they pack up and begin to march again, through thickets and barren places, past swamps and over rocks. They are forced to stop often, for the streams are in spring flood and difficult to ford. They make camp and remain for a few days on the bank of a wide river. It runs fast and hard, throwing up white feathers of foam as it tumbles over rocks. When Mary is sent to fetch water, she stands on the bank entranced, watching the river dance in the sunlight until she hears Weetamoo call.

On the second afternoon of the new encampment, warriors return from a hunt with two deer and a moose. The people feast all night. Yet only a few young men dance around the fire. Mary does not see James there, nor has she seen him since the morning after the youth's escape. She misses him.

They wade across the river the next morning, through water so cold it numbs Mary's feet and legs. The force of the current makes her reel, and it takes a fierce effort to push through the water. With each step she is afraid she will fall. She hears the sound of laughter and looks up to see Alawa and two other women standing on the bank laughing at her. She feels a quick rush of anger, but it fades as she realizes how foolish she must look swaying through the water like a drunken woman. She smiles back at them, but as she reaches the far side, her foot slips on a stone and she crashes to her knees.

Her legs scramble and splash in the water, whipping up a froth of skirt and river; her hands claw the mud at the water's edge. Yet, as she manages to grasp a nearby sapling and pull herself up the sloping bank to a flat place at the top, she too is laughing. Alawa helps her to her feet and they start walking again.

After they cross the river, a contagious energy passes among the people and a strange lightness of heart comes over Mary. She listens to the women's chatter as they walk and learns that they will soon come to a great gathering place they call *Wachusett*. Philip and some of his warriors have gone ahead and are waiting for them.

They make camp again and Mary pours herself into doing the tasks Weetamoo commands: fetching water, gathering firewood, unrolling the sleeping mats and placing them in the lean-to shelter Alawa has erected. But she is soon left idle, and slips away.

She walks aimlessly. The stench of sickness is everywhere. People sprawl on the bare ground, groaning in hunger. Children cry piteously, clutching their stomachs. The few dogs that have not been eaten slink at the edges of the camp, seeking food and finding none. Mary keeps walking, trying to outpace her hunger.

She climbs a low ridge that opens onto a stone outcropping overlooking the camp. Low clouds the color of dung hang in the west. The trees are budding. She thinks of her kitchen garden in its spring growth. The onions and artichokes will come up on their own, but this year there will be no leeks or melons, no carrots or cabbages, for she is doubtful that Joseph—if he lives—has taken care to plant them. The lavender, if it blooms, will perfume no rooms or bedclothes. She idly fingers the stray flakes of dried lavender that have lain in her pocket all winter. Their fragrance is no longer strong enough to leave a scent on her fingers.

She remembers last spring, when Marie helped her care for the kitchen garden. How diligent the girl had been, how attentive to her weeding, determined to root out every threat to the tender shoots.

Mary had never contemplated before how diligently Marie attended to the details of her chores, how gentle she was in her character. Tears sting the corners of her eyes, and she quickly brushes them away.

She is struck by her strange situation. Though she is a captive, she experiences a remarkable liberty of movement. She recalls the many times in Lancaster she wanted to walk out the door and across the fields alone. How she had longed for the freedom to go where she wished—when she wished—free from neighbors' reproving looks and her sisters' chastening tongues. Yet she had rarely strayed beyond the yard by herself except the few times she visited Bess Parker. She had acted the part of the captive, though she was neither shackled nor restrained.

She thinks daily about Joss and Marie, prays they are well, and wonders if they have been rescued or ransomed back to civilization. She knows that Indians like to capture and adopt children from other tribes to replace their own dead children. Sometimes the children never return to their homes. Even when offered liberty, they choose to stay with their new families. She has also heard rumors that Indians sometimes sell children to papists in the French colony of Canada.

"Better that they die than forfeit their souls to Rome." She whispers the sentiment she heard Joseph express so many times. Yet something lurches at the base of her spine even as the words slip past her lips. The truth is that she desires only that her children *live*. Even if their fate is to be papists or Indians, she wants them *alive*.

Is she therefore willing to give their souls over to the Devil? Is she the most wicked of mothers? She forgets the terrible pangs in her belly and tries to summon some Christian remorse, using the most punishing reproaches she can think of. But she cannot wring a proper guilt from her heart. If she wants to repent of anything, it is of the harsh methods she used in raising her children. She recalls the times she struck Marie for impertinence, remembers the sturdy birch switch used to thrash Joss when sloth got the better of the boy. She punished her children with the dutiful regularity of all Puritan mothers, yet she now regrets every harsh word. What she once believed necessary now seems to her needlessly cruel. She often sees Indian mothers laugh with their children and indulge their childish antics. She knows she ought to righteously condemn them, but the truth is she longs only to imitate them. What harm could come if the English treat their children with kindness and mercy?

The scent of a cook fire reaches her on tendrils of smoke. In the camp below, women are fetching water from the river. She knows that Weetamoo will be vexed if she is not at hand. She makes her way down the hill into the camp.

It begins to rain; fat drops fall on her head and neck and shoulders. She runs for Weetamoo's shelter and slides inside. It is dry and hot from smoke and close-packed bodies. She creeps to the far wall, takes out her sewing and waits for Weetamoo to give her orders. But Weetamoo is absorbed in a conversation with Alawa. After a while Mary dozes off.

She wakes to a great crash of thunder. Everyone in the shelter is silent; they wait, heads turned toward the sound. But nothing follows. There is no new clap of thunder, no quaking of the earth. Mary finds her mat in the semi-dark and lies down. She falls asleep to the sound of the rain beating all around her like a hundred drums.

CHAPTER SEVENTEEN

In the morning, they break camp and walk toward a mountain that rises beyond the trees. Alawa tells Mary that it has always been a sign of hope and home for the Nipmuc people, a place to gather beneath the shelter of sacred spirits.

A feeling of dread comes over Mary, as if she is walking to her doom. Worse, she perceives she is not alone in this, but everyone around her is doomed as well; they are gathering not in hope but in desperation.

Everyone is starving. It is plain in the ravaged faces around her, in the exhausted strides of the gaunt warriors, and in the sorrow in the eyes of the old ones. They now eat anything they can fit into their mouths: insects, grubs, worms, tree bark, hides, even bones. One evening Mary is given a shard of boiled horse's hoof and sits on the ground, sucking and chewing until there is nothing left. A saying is passed around: Hunger masters the strongest warrior once it makes its home among the people.

She begins to hear rumors that Boston has offered payment for the captives. It is said that Philip will surely accept, for he needs more muskets, more bullets and, most of all, more food for his people. Mary feels a weight at the base of her spine, a dullness in her heart. It is as if she has already perished and has no need for rescue.

Late in the afternoon, they come to a half-built stockade. Beyond it, the land rises toward the mountain. Alawa tells Mary that they have finally reached Wachusett. Several wetus have already been erected; their domes make shadows across the greening meadow. Mary is faint from the long march and lack of food, but so is everyone else. She makes no protest when Weetamoo orders her to help build a new wetu.

M ary does not see James until two days later, when he approaches her as she gathers sticks for the fire.

"I have news," he says.

She feels a sweet flutter in her chest as she looks up at him. "Is it my children? Are they here in camp?"

He frowns. "I know nothing of them. I am sorry."

"Nothing?" The sticks seem suddenly too heavy to carry. Mary bends and places them carefully on the ground. Every movement she makes now is arduous. "Pray, then, tell me what news."

"The sachems are debating your situation. It is said they will soon redeem you to your people."

"Redeem?" Her eyes cannot seem to focus.

He nods. "It is all but certain. They wait on Philip."

She tries to absorb this information, but all she is aware of is a dreadful sensation of loss. Finally she manages to speak, her tongue sluggish and thick in her mouth. "Are Joss and Marie to be redeemed with me, then?"

"I have told you already—I know nothing of their fates." He tilts his head. "Come, *Chikohtqua*. Is this not the news you have longed for?"

Her cheeks flare. She has no answer for his question that does not bring her shame. Only a few weeks ago, she was begging him to help her escape to Albany. She licks her lips. "I cannot—" She stops. She does not even know what it is she cannot do. *Cannot go back to the English without her children? Cannot leave the wilderness? Cannot return to her husband?*

James looks at her as if she is a strange being, a creature not of this world. Then his expression softens. "You do not want to leave," he says quietly. "You have grown too fond of Indian ways."

She says nothing, though she knows he is expecting her to re-fute him. It is surely her hunger and fatigue that create this confu-sion in her heart. From the moment of her capture she has hated the Indians and their savagery. Has she not? Her strange thoughts are like cords binding her chest, cords pulled so tight she cannot breathe.

That night, Alawa cautions Mary to wash herself with extra care, for she will be brought before the sachems the next day. "Metacomet has called a council," she says. "The sachems will de-cide your fate."

"My fate?" Mary whispers. Fear makes a fist of her heart.

Alawa wrinkles her nose. "You English are always afraid. Is it because your god is so cruel?"

"The Lord is merciful and kind and greatly to be praised." The words fly automatically from Mary's mouth, a shield against heresy. Yet she knows, even as she speaks, that they are mere habit. She feels sick and wretched at the thought of going before the council. It is not the sachems she fears. It is the prospect of returning to civili-zation.

She believes that she has changed too much to ever fit easily into English society again. The wilderness—an abomination to her before her captivity—has now become her home. She can interpret the cries of birds and decipher the shifting patterns of clouds, perceive beauty in the unimproved forest. She has seen vistas that have stolen away her breath. She has learned to live in a new, free way, to be enterprising and to care for herself. She has come to see slavery as a great evil. Though other captives have despaired or died defeated, she has survived through cunning and perseverance.

With effort and discipline, Mary knows she will cope with a return to English life. Yet, even as she has these thoughts, something sad and desperate claws at her heart.

CHAPTER EIGHTEEN

It is James who comes for Mary the next day, who escorts her up the hill to the longhouse where the sachems are gathered in council. They are all there—Philip, Monoco, Quinnapin, Weetamoo, and the others—seated in a great circle around the fire pit. Many warriors are present, sitting behind the sachems or perched on the long sleeping platforms.

James tells her to sit quietly by the door until she is called forward. When she looks around to see if other captives are present, her heart leaps with joy, for crouched in the shadows is her sister Hannah, whom she has not seen since the day they were captured. Without thinking, she moves toward her, but James clamps his hand down hard on her shoulder and hisses that she must not look at anyone. So Mary sits on her heels, listening to the sachems discuss her fate. Philip says that the English have been humbled and now wish to pay tribute to him. They seek to redeem their captives and want the sachems to name a fair price.

Each sachem speaks in turn, some insisting that what they need most is food, while others ask for liquor and gold. One says that they should all surrender and ask for amnesty, but the warriors shout him down.

Philip raises his hand and everyone is silent. He lights a pipe and passes it around the circle. Each sachem smokes solemnly. It suddenly occurs to Mary that they are engaged in a sort of prayer. When all the sachems have smoked, Philip calls for the captives to be brought before the council, one by one. Mary is first. She moves quickly and sits before him, keeping her head modestly bowed.

"Stand up!" Philip says, gesturing to two of his servants, who quickly pull her to her feet. "This is council. Like English court. You stand." He turns to James. "You translate." Then he says something in his native tongue that Mary cannot understand.

James steps into the circle. "Tell the council what your husband will give to redeem you," he says.

"My husband?" She looks at Philip. "He is alive then?" The sachem's expression does not change, which she takes as confirmation. She wonders if they have known this all along.

"Mary." James's tone is gentle. "How many pounds?"

She stares at him. She is again being sold as a slave. But why are they asking her to name her own price? She has no idea what Joseph will pay to have her back. The very question is unnerving.

"Name a price," James says quietly. "Your court is waiting."

She sees something sad and anxious flicker in his eyes. He is serious, then. Perhaps this is the way Indians always negotiate their ransoms, but it seems unnecessarily cruel. He leans closer. "Now!" he whispers.

"Twenty pounds," she says. The number has popped into her head from nowhere.

A murmur of surprise goes around the circle. Out of the corner of her eye, she sees Quinnapin raise his eyebrows and smile at Weetamoo.

She knows at once she has made a mistake. "Mayhap it is too much," she says. "I beg you will take less."

Philip laughs. "Twenty pounds," he says in English. "Good price." She starts to say that her husband is not wealthy, but he waves her away. "Be gone." He then turns to James and orders him to write the ransom letter.

All day the people dance. Mary sits watching from the edge of the circle. Quinnapin wears an English shirt of lace decorated with wampum and coins and shows his strength by never resting, but dancing on and on, after the other men have staggered to the outside of the circle and collapsed. Weetamoo dances, too. Mary watches, entranced by the vigor and grace of her movements.

Suddenly, James steps in front of her. She has not spoken to him since the council. She meets his gaze, and feels a current jump between them, sparking like fire. "Has the council decided?" she asks. "Do you know what is to become of me?" Her voice breaks on the last word.

He shakes his head. "They say Philip is opposed to the bargain. Though I think he will yet be persuaded."

She bows her head.

"You priced yourself very high," he says. "Twenty pounds could buy much land. Is your husband a rich man?"

Mary looks at the leaping flames, at the dancers writhing before them. "He is not. I spoke foolishly."

"You do not wish to be redeemed," James says softly. "You are afraid to go home."

"Of course I wish to go home," she says quickly, angrily. "What other desire could I have?"

He continues to gaze down at her. Then he says something she cannot quite catch over the throb of the drums. Only when he says it again just before he walks away does she realize that he spoke the name he gave her: *Chikohtqua—Burning Woman.*

Mary's eyes sting and something hard lodges in her throat. It takes all her resolve not to leap to her feet and run after him. She turns her attention again to the dance circle, where she is surprised to see that Weetamoo is the only sachem still dancing. She whirls around and around in her red English stockings and white moccasins, her cloak of wampum and feathers flying out around her like the wings of a great hawk.

Mary cannot sleep. All night she rolls on her mat; only her regular thrashing marks the passing of minutes and hours. She hears the call of a screech owl not far from the wetu; in the distance, a lone wolf howls. James is right—she does not want to return to her former life as a Puritan wife under the restrictions of mutual watch, conformed in all her thoughts and mannerisms. She dreads the suspicious looks she will get, the interrogation by church elders, the distortion of her experience to create lessons in Christian piety for lectures and sermons. Yet she does not know what she wants instead. Could she turn her back on all things English and embrace Indian ways? What would become of her children? Her faith?

She thinks of James, of his protective kindness and compassion toward her, of his gentle ways, of the teasing affection in his smile. She thinks of how different he is from her husband. Despite the cold, she is sweating. She throws off the furs that cover her, gets to her feet, pulls a blanket around her, and slips out of the wetu. A gibbous moon lights her way as she walks through the village. She begins to hurry, as if her feet have a particular destination of their own, though she does not think about where she is going. Suddenly she finds herself in front of James's wetu.

For several minutes she stands there, trying to gather her thoughts. Yet when she pushes open the flap and steps inside, she still has no idea what she will say, how she will explain this inappropriate and unseemly invasion of her friend's home in the middle of the night.

It takes a moment for her eyes to adjust and find James's sleeping form. He is lying on a platform. She makes her way across the wetu. "James!" she whispers, crouching beside him.

Instantly, he is awake and sitting up, brandishing a long knife. She recognizes it as the weapon he threatened her with in Weetamoo's crowded wetu. She raises her hands, palms out in front of her face. "It is I. Mary," she whispers. "I mean you no harm."

"You should not be here." His voice is hard. "I could have killed you." He leans down and slides the knife under the platform.

"I am desperate," she says. "You are my only friend in this place."

"What do you want?"

She hesitates. Her ears fill with the sigh of the fire's embers, the anxious beating of her own heart. "I do not wish to return to the English," she whispers. "Please, let me stay with you." Instantly, shame sweeps through her; she bows her head away from his gaze. Yet she feels strangely liberated by what she has said. For once, she has spoken the truth of her heart.

"What of your husband?" James asks, but she cannot answer. There is no proper response she can force her lips to offer. She hears him shift and feels his hands on her shoulders. "You are anxious and weary and near-starving. You are not thinking clearly."

She knows he is right, yet anger flames through her at his words. She twists away, then instantly regrets it, for the pressure of his hands is the sweetest sensation she's felt in weeks. "I believe my mind is clearer than it has ever been," she says, but she realizes it is too late. He is already putting on his shirt, standing, moving to the door.

"Even if I wished this for you—"

"For *us*," she says, rising and going to him. "Have I not discerned your feelings rightly?"

But he is shaking his head. "It makes no difference," he says. "I have no power here. Like you, I am a servant. If you wish to stay, you must appeal to Philip or to Weetamoo. But—" He holds out his hand to prevent her from coming closer and touching him. She knows in that instant that she is right about his feelings, though he will not confirm it. For why would he resist her touch if it had no effect on him? "—I think it is too late. I believe your fate is already sealed." He reaches for the door flap.

She starts to move past him when he touches her arm. Instantly her nostrils fill with his scent. She feels an overpowering impulse to lean against him. She does not—cannot—move. His hand does not leave her arm, and she does not remove it. She stands with her head bowed, wishing that she could think of something fitting to say, but no words come. She slowly realizes that no words are necessary— that he already knows and understands her heart.

"You cannot escape your fate, *Chikohtqua*." She hears the kindness in his voice, the compassion that has always been there. "None of us can. I know you wish to stay. But there is no life for you here. There is no food, no safe village. The Indian ways are fading like a mist."

She turns to face him, nodding, acknowledging their kinship. They are caught in the same web of events, subjected to the whims of both sachems and magistrates. James cannot extricate himself. Nor can she.

She steps into his embrace, as easily and naturally as a child, and he wraps his long arms around her as if they had been made exclusively for this purpose. She feels ripples of desire course through her, which she knows will never be consummated.

She has the heartrending sensation that she has finally come home—but is not able to stay.

CHAPTER NINETEEN

When Mary wakes the next morning, the sun has risen in a clear sky, and Weetamoo is already bent over the stew pot. She still wears the red stockings and the bracelets of wampum from the celebrations. "Come! Hurry!" Weetamoo says, beckoning Mary to her side. She shows Mary a pile of dead squirrels and explains in clear English that Quinnapin trapped them and that Mary is to clean them and cut them into the pot. Mary bends to her work and is surprised when Weetamoo joins her in scraping the hides once the meat is simmering. Now that her papoose is dead, she spends most of her time making necklaces of wampum. Though the two women don't speak, Mary senses a new warmth from her, a strange companionship. She reminds herself that Weetamoo is likely pleased because Mary will soon bring money to her. Yet she cannot forestall a pang of sorrow.

Quinnapin comes to the wetu in the middle of the morning. He is obviously drunk. He staggers in and out of the wetu, calling out the names of his wives, one after another. When he sees Mary, he leers at her, grinning. Weetamoo is plainly vexed, but she says nothing, and when he stumbles past her, she presents her backside to him.

Mary has never seen a drunken Indian before, and finds it frightening. Quinnapin's behavior is in sharp contrast to the usual disciplined carriage and manner of Indians. Now she realizes that their rectitude would not be possible if they regularly imbibed the beer and hard cider of English tables. Yet it occurs to her that perhaps she can use Quinnapin's drunkenness to her advantage.

By late afternoon Mary is weary from hours of scraping hides and grinding corn from a basket Alawa fetched that had been stored underground. When Weetamoo finally dismisses her, Mary leaves the wetu with one aim in her heart—she will go to Quinnapin and plead her case. She will ask the sachem—she will beg, if necessary—permission to remain among the Indians.

Quinnapin is alone in the wetu, sprawled on a bearskin beside the fire, wearing only leggings and a breechclout. He looks up at Mary and smiles. It is clear that he is drunk beyond standing. If she were to flee, she does not believe he is capable of following.

"Sit," he says, patting the mat next to him.

She sits down beside him. Her skin prickles as though raked with quills, though he does not touch her. She smells his breath—a powerful muskiness mingled with the sweet scents of tobacco and beer. He touches her neck and lets his hand slide down her shoulder. His fingers drift toward her breast. Mary thinks suddenly of James and feels her secret parts swell with desire. Shame sweeps through her, a humiliation so profound she begins to shake. She moves away from Quinnapin. His hand falls and he grunts. "Why you not love Quinnapin?" His words run together, as if spoken underwater. He raises a pint of beer to his lips and takes a long swallow. He licks his lips and smiles at her. "Why you come here if not for love?"

She finds her voice at last. "I came because I must ask a favor of you," she says.

He nods, slowly. His eyes begin to close and he stretches out full-length. She sees that he is about to go to sleep. She has misjudged her opportunity; her plan has soured. She shifts toward him, puts her hand on his arm. His eyes open; she sees that he is having trouble focusing. "What favor?" There are flecks of spittle at the corners of his mouth.

"Please do not redeem me to the English. I wish to stay here. With your people."

He blinks again, starts to sit up, and collapses back on the mat. Then, suddenly, he is laughing, the laughter rolling up from his belly through his chest. He laughs and laughs; it seems he cannot stop.

She gets to her feet. He is far too drunk to understand her. There is no point in pressing her request. His laughter finally subsides and he lies watching her through half-closed eyes. She thinks he is asleep when he rouses again, pushing his torso up on his elbows.

"You go." He finds the pint bottle with his hand and drinks again, long and deep. "Go back to English where you belong." He is still smiling as he dismisses her with a flick of his fingers.

Mary makes her way back to Weetamoo's wetu, grateful for the late afternoon's long shadows. She is a woman with no people, no place of safety or comfort. Save her own corrupted heart.

In the evening, James comes to Weetamoo's wetu with the news that the sachems have decided on terms for Mary's release.

"Twenty pounds in goods and a pint of liquor for Quinnapin," he says. "To be delivered by Mary's husband."

Her fingers tremble and she drops the shirt she is mending. It makes a small pyramid of muslin on her lap. "I do not think my husband will be able to meet the price."

"It is the price you named." James regards her thoughtfully, as if trying to determine whether her words cloak some darker intention. "Surely he has friends who will help. And I think you shall be redeemed whether you wish it or no." James gives her a thin smile. "We all face redemption of one sort or another in these sad times."

She is frightened. And angry. "You arranged this," she says. "You have acted all along as Philip's servant."

His face darkens and he leaves the wetu abruptly. She realizes she has said too much. And, worse yet, none of it is true.

From that moment until her release Mary is never alone. Alawa follows her like a shadow everywhere she goes. It is unsettling after so many weeks of liberty—a sharp reminder that she is a prisoner after all, that her feelings of freedom have been illusory and fleeting. She knows too well that once she returns to English society the restrictions will be greater still. She will be constantly watched. She will never be free again to walk unobserved in the woods or to stray on a hillside to watch a storm roll in or to study the sunlight as it plays over the river. The natural world, which has unexpectedly become a solace in her captivity, will again be her enemy. And the wild stirrings of desire, the strange wings of joy she has experienced watching the Indians dance, will be gone forever.

In the morning, Alawa tells Mary that her time has come. She does not think she can bear leaving without her children. Sarah's body lies forsaken in the wilderness. Joss and Marie—if they are alive—are still with the Indians. She does not belong with the English anymore. Nor does she have any future with the Indians.

Two warriors come and bind her hands together. Alawa tells her not to be afraid; this is part of the ransom ritual. They put a rope around her neck and lead her to the great rock behind the council lodge. All the sachems are there except Philip. Quinnapin is dressed in his deerskin robe and headband, all decorated with fox tails, his hair lying loose across his broad shoulders. Weetamoo is regal in her long belts of wampum. She makes out James among a group of warriors nearby. Mary looks around the clearing for her husband, but he is not there. The only Englishman present is Squire Hoar—a lawyer from Concord.

The Indians make a great ceremony of releasing her, sharing a pipe and exchanging gifts while she stands bound before them. She bows her head as a shameful heat suffuses her face. She steals a glance at James, but he is looking away. Finally, they cut her bonds, and Quinnapin orders her to go.

"My children!" she moans, hesitating. "I cannot leave without my children!" Someone shoves her—she does not see who—and she stumbles away on uncertain feet, shrinking from Squire Hoar's welcoming hand and finally clutching it only to keep from collapsing. She is not able to stop herself from glancing over her shoulder. Like Lot's wife, she looks back, for she does not have sufficient faith to go forward.

There is Quinnapin, regarding her solemnly. Nearby, Weetamoo glares at her the way a hawk watches its wounded prey. Behind them stands James, his sorrowful gaze like an arrow, piercing her.

Squire Hoar catches her by the arm and hisses into her ear. "Do not show reluctance. We must hurry away from this place. The sachems are capricious and could change their minds in an instant." He steers her down the sloping land to where his horse is tethered and helps her to mount. She keeps her head down, so she will not meet James's eyes again. Yet, as the mare picks her way down the long trail and the rock recedes behind them, she begins to weep.

CHAPTER TWENTY

Perhaps he does not know she is weeping, because the squire offers Mary no comfort except for a thick slab of bread. As she eats, she gazes through blurred eyes at his back where a worn spot in his gray wool cloak reminds her of an eye. After a while she finds her voice and asks if he has any news of Joss and Marie. Have they, too, been ransomed? He answers that the authorities are hopeful there will be others, but as of this day, she is the only one to be redeemed. She feels as if a stone has dropped into her bowels and does not speak again. Her nose runs and she wipes her face with the corner of her blanket. Her dress is stained with grease and dirt, and her mouth feels similarly defiled. Yet the rocking warmth of the mare's flesh beneath her thighs provides an unexpected comfort.

She notices a sparrow flit from branch to branch above her head. She sees bars of late afternoon light slant through the trees and stares at tufts of new grass and at wet rocks in the stream when they stop to water the mare.

Two Indians accompany them, silent as the enveloping trees. They wear the garb of Praying Indians, a jumble of English and

Indian apparel. Mary suspects they are spies, though for which side she cannot guess.

After some time the squire begins to speak, and he talks on and on. He tells her that English soldiers had arrived in Lancaster before nightfall the very day of the attack. Her house—or what remained of it—was still smoldering. The soldiers counted fourteen bodies, two burned beyond recognition. They calculated that there must have been twenty captured. The squire reports these things in a dry, straightforward tone, as if he were counting felled trees. He talks of the hostilities and of the recent English victory on the western frontier, where Indians have been surprised in a great encampment and many slain. He explains in detail the arrangements made in Boston for her ransom, but she can no longer concentrate on his words. She thinks of James and wonders what will become of her children. She thinks of Joseph and wonders how she will greet him. What will he think of her when he sees how disordered she has become? How will she greet him knowing that he did not come to her rescue?

She recalls that the previous summer Joseph was offered a chaplaincy for English troops. It was a good position, a mark of the respect he had earned in the Bay Colony. Yet he refused it. "Out of a necessary caution," he answered when she questioned him. "I have a congregation to serve here."

Late in the afternoon they come to a clearing that Mary recognizes by the low slope of land falling down to a river. Unplowed fields run beside them, a sea of pale grasses and weeds. The river twists in a wide, black ribbon through the empty landscape. There is a charred hole in the field where a barn once stood.

Lancaster is gone. Not just in ruins, but vanished, as if God himself has swept it clear. Only the pastures remain, greening under the May sky, pale as quinces. The squire apologizes profusely, as if he were responsible for the destruction. He wishes, he says, there was another road that would not take them through the place of devastation. He spurs his horse to a trot as they approach the slope of land where Mary's house stood, as if speed might relieve her grief.

"Oh," she says, a low moan that comes from deep within. "Please. I would see the place."

He turns slightly, to look at her over his shoulder. "'Tis late," he says. "It will soon be night. And we are not yet in safe territory."

Mary is silent for a moment, but the urgent desire to see her home overcomes her restraint. "Please, Squire. Surely we will come to no harm if we linger just a short while. I wish to look on it." Her voice breaks as she says the last words and feels him turn the mare, relenting.

There is nothing of her home but the cellar hole, a dark smear on the hill. Not a stick is left standing. Mary slides off the mare and walks across the greening patch of ground that was once her dooryard.

"You must hurry. We dare not remain past dark." The squire has not dismounted, but sits his horse as if rooted there. The Indians, who have no horses, stand at some distance, their faces well shadowed by trees.

She crosses to the wide, flat stone that was her doorstep. As she steps onto it, some devil's spirit seizes her and her mind slips, tumbling back as a child might roll helter-skelter down a hill. She sees again the blood on the snow, hears the screams for mercy from the throats of friends and relatives, feels her heart scrambling in her chest as if trying to find its frantic way out. She stands as one bewitched, recalling all that transpired on that morning of horror.

Mary does not know how long she stands there before Squire Hoar's voice jars her from her trance. The sun has already fallen below George Hill and the long shadows of afternoon have become dusk. She looks at him as one deluded with visions. She scarcely perceives his features, the memories have so infested her.

"Mistress Rowlandson?" He dismounts and places his hand

beneath her arm to steady her. It is plain that he believes she has
suffered a fit of some kind; perhaps he expects her to fall to the
ground and convulse. And perhaps he is right to think so, for Mary
finds herself unable to speak. It is as if her tongue has been pulled
from its root and can no longer move in her mouth.

"We must find a place to tarry the night," the squire says. There
is a strained, fretful quality to his voice that she has not heard before. "We cannot travel in the dark."

She wants to ask why they cannot. Hasn't she walked over many
miles of rough trail in greater darkness? But her crippled tongue will
not permit her question. She manages to nod, and follow him back
to his horse, and clumsily remount. She keeps looking back over her
shoulder, even as the squire directs his mare along the road.

They take shelter in what remains of the garrison house belong-
ing to Cyprian Stevens. Its stockade is gone and half the house
has been blasted away. The front door gapes; wood shards rise like
teeth from the sill. When Mary examines the blackened chimney
bricks, the squire tells her that the Indians returned after their attack and used gunpowder to finish their work.

Squire Hoar builds a fire on what is left of the hearth and then
draws bread and cheese from his satchel of provisions and offers them
to her. Shadows rise and fall on the scorched plaster walls as they eat.
After a while he inquires about her treatment by the Indians. His voice
surprises her with its gentle concern and she soon finds herself pouring
out her trials to him. She tells of Sarah's death and the slow healing of
her own wound. She recounts the long days of marching, of forcing
herself to go on when she was on the verge of collapse. She speaks of
how hunger and privation taught her to take pleasure in Indian food.

He listens with a smile of pity. Finally she runs out of words.
"I forget myself," she says. "I fear it has been too long since I spoke
with an Englishman."

He nods slowly, then says, "You have not yet asked after your husband."

She feels as if he has just slapped her face. Her cheeks burn, yet she can manage no words of contrition. "He did not come," she says, the words scratching her throat strangely, as if they are filled with tiny barbs. "I thought—" She stops and swallows. "I have heard it rumored that he has remarried."

He dips his head as if complicit in a conspiracy, but then she sees he is only struggling to contain a smile. "I fear the Indians have tricked you," he says. "They are overly fond of making mischief, though the truth is they mean no harm. No, your husband has not remarried. He waits for you in Boston."

She expels a breath. "He is well, then, I hope?"

"Well enough. I know he will rejoice to see you." He takes a pipe from his satchel, pours tobacco into the bowl, lights it, and draws deeply. Mary has a sudden memory of Philip drawing on his pipe after telling her his story of the Mohawks gathering wood. She smiles and wonders why she did not detect the story's humor at the time. She was still learning Indian ways.

"He has been greatly occupied raising your ransom," the squire says.

She looks longingly at the ribbons of smoke. "The sachems said he would be present at my redemption."

"Mistress Rowlandson." He places his pipe carefully on his knees. He leans forward, his manner that of a king bestowing wisdom on his subject. "They asked a dear price for you. It was not a simple task to come by twenty pounds."

In the morning, they discover their two Indian guides have left sometime in the night. The squire does not appear surprised. Nor is Mary, for she is now well acquainted with the Indian inclination for stealth and independence of mind.

The squire tells her it is Sunday, and asks if she wishes to tarry longer at the ruined Stevens house, in observance of the Sabbath rule. She shakes her head. "I have not observed the Sabbath in many weeks," she says. "We had best continue on." She knows that if they linger she will be tempted to disappear into the forest like the Indian guides, and try to make her way back to Philip's camp.

As they ride past the hill where the meetinghouse stands guard over the stones of the burying ground, Mary recalls the last time she sat on the pew bench listening to her husband. The world has become so disordered, it seems as if years—not months—have passed.

They pass abandoned barns and houses. The squire tells her that all the frontier farms have been deserted. Everyone has fled east, taking refuge with friends and family who live in the towns near the sea. He describes the way the Indians butchered the English and burned whole villages. He says that now only soldiers venture beyond their yards.

When they reach Concord, the squire dismounts and walks through the village, leading his horse with Mary on it. At first she thinks the place is abandoned, but she soon sees that faces are peering from the tiny windows and half-open doors. Two young boys squat at the side of the lane playing a game with pebbles. A man comes out of a house carrying a yoke. Mary sees a woman in the shadowed doorway behind him. The squire calls out cheerfully and the man acknowledges his greeting with a solemn nod. Soon after, the squire stops in front of a large frame house set against a hillside.

"My home," the squire announces. "We will stop here for some refreshment and Christian fellowship. Which," he adds, as he helps her dismount, "I warrant you have sorely missed these past months."

"Aye," she says, though her agreement is accompanied by a shiver of trepidation. Will the faces of her fellow Christians be filled with judgment? Or pity? Instead of following the squire across the yard to the door, she finds herself staring at a wooden palisade a few yards to the east.

"Ah," he says, "I see you find my garrison of interest. But you need not fear for your safety, Mistress Rowlandson. You are perfectly secure now." He comes back across the yard to stand beside her. "I had it built for my Praying Indian friends, who lived there under my protection," he says. "Though there were many in town who wished them dead." Some of the ten-foot-tall posts no longer stand upright, but lean inward, as if in discouragement. The stockade is not very big, no more than fifteen feet square. She wonders how many people lived there.

Mary thinks of James. Of his family's exile to Deer Island. "What became of them?" she asks. "Did they join Philip's warriors?"

The squire shakes his head. "I have sometimes thought it would be better for them if they had. But Captain Moseley came to town one day and arrested every one of them. Women and children and old men as well as the young. It was a Lord's Day, and we were all at the meetinghouse. Yet in he marched with all his soldiers behind him, like the Devil and his minions, and there he declared his foul purposes."

Mary frowns, for this seems an unlikely tale. "He interrupted worship? Is it not against the law?"

"Moseley cares nothing for law. He came in during the sermon, stated his wicked intention and threatened to arrest any who sought to impede him. I slipped out and hurried home to defend my friends. But my striving came to naught." He turns his back on the palisade, as if to get more quickly away from his memory. "Captain Moseley and those like him are a terrible scourge on this land," he says. "It is one thing to be valiant in battle, quite another to visit tortures upon innocent women and children. It is said that he ordered one of his young Indian captives stripped of her clothes and he himself applied hot knives to her breasts."

Mary remembers James's description of Captain Moseley's tortures and tastes a dark bitterness on her tongue. She stares at the logs of the palisade. Bark has been stripped away in places, and woodpeckers have made holes in the wood in their search for insects and grubs.

"Come," says the squire, taking her arm. "We must go in and prepare ourselves, for I soon expect guests who I know you will want to see." He is smiling at her in a way that tells her that he has some surprise in store. She turns her head away from his gaze. She thinks of James, standing by the rock where she was redeemed. His sorrowful eyes.

Squire Hoar leads her into a room with a table and bench set before the fire. Two small windows slant triangles of sunlight onto the floor. He tells Mary to sit on the bench, leaves the room, and returns with a woman who carries a bundle in her arms. Her hair is long and straight; she has a triangular face with a sharp chin. She could be sister to some Indian women Mary has seen in camp. She sets her bundle on the table.

"English raiment, combs, shoes, everything you will need to refresh your appearance." The squire gestures to the bundle. "Delores will help you." He leaves the room, closing the door firmly behind him.

Delores smiles and looks deferentially down at her hands. Mary rises, curious to see the clothes, wondering if they will fit her. As soon as she moves, Delores leaps to unwrap the bundle and within minutes has spread out a new shift, bodice, skirt, apron, cap and a pair of latchet shoes.

Mary fingers the skirt, which is the deepest shade of indigo she's ever seen. Someone has paid many pounds to have these clothes made. She looks at Delores. "Where did these come from?"

Delores shrugs. She has not spoken a word. Mary suspects she is one of the Praying Indians that Squire Hoar sheltered.

She unties her pocket and lets it fall to the floor. She feels a wave of tears and has to swallow them down as she removes the deerskin dress and then her shift. Quickly, she pulls the new one over her head. The linen is cool and smooth against her skin. A moment later Delores is lacing Mary into the new bodice, buttoning her skirts. When she ties a fresh white apron around her, a faint whiff of lavender rises from the cloth and Mary almost sighs with pleasure.

Delores steps back and studies her. Then she makes a motion with her hand, fluttering her fingers over the cap that covers her own black hair. It occurs to Mary that she does not speak because she cannot.

Mary nods. "Aye, I suppose my hair must be presentable now that I am back in civilization."

A smile blooms on Delores's face, and she quickly produces a wooden comb from her pocket and begins to unbraid and comb out Mary's hair. It reminds Mary of the intimacy and comfort she felt the night Alawa braided it. It takes some time but after a while Delores seems satisfied. She hands Mary the linen cap, so white it reminds her of winter, and Mary settles it on her own head. It has been three months since she wore a cap and it feels both comforting and confining.

Delores looks her up and down, and solemnly nods her approval.

Mary runs her hands over her new apron and smoothes her skirts. "My pocket!" she says suddenly, and plucks it from under the discarded deer-hide dress. She straps it on, though the linen is filthy with grease. But she will not be parted from it, for it holds all she now owns in the world—her scissors and needles and the little Bible that James gave her.

"Thank you," Mary says. "I believe I am respectable now."

Delores nods, gathers up the old clothes, hurries to the door, teases open the latch with her elbow, and leaves Mary to face the squire.

• • •

They eat a simple meal of bread and milk, seated beside each other on the bench. "I would feed you more heartily," he says, "but the goodwives of Concord cautioned me that your stomach will be too tender for rich fare just now."

Mary's stomach roils as if in agreement with the unseen goodwives. Her hips and thighs ache. During her captivity she has grown accustomed to sitting on the ground; perching on a bench is no longer effortless. She shifts back and forth, trying in vain to find a comfortable position.

She asks about Delores and the squire confirms that she is a Praying Indian—a Nashaway who was widowed several years ago when her husband took a fever and died. "She took a vow of silence," he says, "and has not, to my knowledge, broken it." He shakes his head. "But I fear for her health. She does not have the usual stamina of Indians. Which is why she is still under my protection."

Mary would like to learn more about this woman and starts to ask, but the squire begins talking about his wife, who has gone to Ipswich to stay with her cousin. Many in Concord have moved close to Boston, he tells Mary, for with the burning of Sudbury, Groton, and Lancaster, Concord has become a frontier town.

Before she finishes her meal, Mary hears voices and then a knock on the door. As Delores hurries to open it, the squire rises expectantly. A group of four men and seven women come into the room. The squire welcomes them enthusiastically and encourages them to partake of their simple meal. Delores places a platter laden with bread before them. Mary resists the urge to hide some in her pocket and forces herself to smile back at the women, who crowd around. They speak to her soothingly, as if she is ill, making sympathetic sounds. She thinks she recognizes one of them, but cannot recall her name. She feels a moment of panic as they close in, as if she is about to be trapped and suffocated. Instinctively, she rises, moving away from the table, stepping back. But the women follow her deeper into the room and she realizes with distress that she's placed herself even farther from the door and its promise of freedom.

She steps to the side, bumps into a tall man, apologizes, moves the other way. She suddenly feels desperate to be outside in the air. She heads toward the front door and is halfway there when it opens and two more men step over the sill.

Mary cries out and claps both hands over her mouth. Abruptly, she is swept into the arms of her brother Josiah.

"Mary!" His voice is raw, almost a sob. He releases her, steps back, holds her face between his hands. "Praise God; you are alive!" His gaze is so filled with worry that her entire impulse is to soothe and reassure him.

"I am well, brother." She smiles, though her eyes are stinging yet again with tears. "And you? And our sisters, Joanna and Ruth?"

"We are all well. They are eager to see you face-to-face. But, sister, I have brought with me someone most keen to be reunited with you." For an instant, Mary is sure he is speaking of Joseph. Her heart thumps in her chest and her palms dampen. Then Josiah moves to the left, revealing the man who entered with him.

It is Henry Kerley, Elizabeth's husband. He stands by the open door, his long arms hanging at his sides. There is a pleading look on his face.

Mary frowns in confusion and looks at Josiah. "But where is my husband?" she asks. "Did he not come with you?"

Josiah touches her shoulder. "Nay, Mary, he had duties to attend. But you may rest assured he is most impatient to see you."

Not impatient enough to travel to Concord, she thinks, then pushes the unseemly thought away, for Henry is now standing before her, beseeching her with his dark eyes.

"Henry." She reaches out and puts both her hands in his outstretched ones. Already her eyes are brimming with tears.

"Mary," he says, with a quiet desperation in his voice, "pray tell me—have you news of my wife and daughters—and Henry? Do you know how they fare?"

She stares at him. She cannot think of a way to frame an answer. "Henry and the girls were captured when we were attacked," she says slowly. "But I have not seen them since."

"And Elizabeth?" He is holding her hands so tightly that she fears he will break the bones of her fingers.

She slips from his grasp and whispers, "Oh, Henry," choking on his name. She is vaguely aware that the room has gone quiet around her, that everyone is watching, listening, waiting for her response. She shakes her head and takes a step backward. She cannot continue to look into his fearful eyes. And so she stares at the floor as she tells him, in halting words, that his wife—her sister—is dead.

He says nothing, though his hands clench and unclench as she recounts Elizabeth's valiant defense of the garrison. She tells of the fire and the suffocating smoke that drove them out of the house. She explains how they gathered the children and she watched the Indians butcher John Divoll before her eyes. She describes Elizabeth coming out of the house carrying someone else's babe in her arms, demonstrating both charity and courage. As she speaks, Mary begins to tremble.

"She was struck down at once," she says. "The moment she stepped over the threshold, she fell. On the very doorstep."

Henry's shoulders sink so deeply into his chest that Mary thinks he will collapse. His face looks pinched and sickly. "Pray, continue," he says in a ragged voice. He has turned his face away.

"I am assured she died on the instant," she says. "She did not move. Soon after, the fire engulfed her."

He sways sideways and Josiah catches him before he falls, easing him onto the bench. Henry looks up at her, dazed. "I was there," he says hoarsely. "With the other soldiers. The house was still smoldering when we arrived. Bodies were strewn all over the yard. I saw two of my children—William, Joseph—stripped and mutilated—" He places his hands over his face. "I did not find the others or Elizabeth, so I hoped—I fancied—they had been taken captive." He is silent for a long moment, swallowing sobs. "It must have been she whom I buried," he whispers. "I did not know." His hands fall away. "There were two bodies burned beyond recognition—one lay before the door. I did not imagine—how could I have known?" He stares up at Mary, his eyes wide, as if he is looking through her, as if she is not there. "She was charred black as the earth itself." His voice is broken and raw. "A piece of her arm broke off when I lifted her."

Mary is pierced by a bolt of horror. She goes to him and takes his hands in hers. He bows his head and his tears fall onto the floor. She can think of nothing that will bring him comfort except to whisper that she wishes she had died in her sister's place.

CHAPTER TWENTY-ONE

Josiah and Henry offer to take Mary to Boston, where she will finally reunite with her husband. The squire lends them his wagon and two horses to draw it, and Mary arranges herself on the wide seat, tucked securely between her brother and brother-in-law. She tries to provide what comfort she can to Henry, who is miserable with grief. He cannot rid himself of the horror of having buried Elizabeth unknown. For three months he had held to the hope that she was alive among the Indians, and the destruction of this prospect devastates him.

They pass many signs of Indian raids—barns and houses lying in charred ruins, fields left unplowed. Josiah plies her with questions. Did she know that Indians were carrying out these depredations against good and gentle English people? Was she aware that they butchered people as if they were swine at harvest time? Mary shakes her head, though she vividly recalls the celebratory dancing around the circle fire after a battle. How she took pleasure in the wild drumming. She examines her heart for the shame that should stalk there, but feels only numbness and a general lack of sensation. She is as one dead, being carried through a foreign land.

As they draw near Boston, she recognizes the long stretch of gray salt marsh on their left and Gallows Bay on the right. Yet the town seems unfamiliar and strange. She pulls the blanket tightly around her although the sun shines brightly and the air is mild. Josiah repeatedly assures her that Joseph is eager for their reunion. Yet she keeps wondering why he did not accompany Squire Hoar to the ransom site. Why did he not, at the very least, go to Concord and meet her there?

She shifts to find a more comfortable position on the seat. The rhythmic creaking has chafed the backs of her thighs even through her thick skirts. Her hand strays to her pocket, where she finds her Bible and her needles and scissors, still secure, ready for when she might need them again.

The rock fortifications and Boston Gate loom up ahead, the towering wooden gallows standing just outside the gate. It is late afternoon. Mary is aware of a constriction in her chest as they ride through the gate, as if she is bound with heavy rope. She tries to dismiss the feeling, for there is no sense to it. She is not a prisoner or a slave. She is seated between two people who love her. She should feel free.

Yet her heart pounds frantically. Foolishly. Her face feels raw and sore though the breeze is gentle. There are few people abroad— an old man driving five swine along the road, a woman sitting in her doorway, three children running through a field, laughing.

She thinks suddenly of James and feels an astonishing wave of grief. Only a week has passed since she lay beside him in the dark, talking, as he warmed her with his body. A few days ago they embraced so tightly it seemed they would never be apart. Then he arranged her ransom. Now he is gone from her life. Forever.

She manages to find her tongue. "Where is Joseph staying?" Her voice is husky and strained. "Does he live with you, Josiah?" She wonders why she has not asked this before.

Her brother turns to smile at her. "I will bring you to him

directly," he says. "He lodges with Mr. Mather, who has been kind enough to shelter him in his distress."

Mary nods. Increase Mather is her husband's friend and counselor, renowned throughout the commonwealth, renowned in a way that Joseph has always wished to be.

The meetinghouse comes into view, its tall square walls gray against the sky. Mary notices that clouds have come up and now cover the sun. It seems like a bad omen. She smoothes her apron and, as Josiah turns the wagon into the Mathers' yard, she begins to shiver.

Both men leap off the wagon and Josiah helps her down. She hears the rattle of a latch and the squeak of a hinge. She turns to see Increase Mather standing in the doorway, his narrow body bent forward. Toward her. He smiles and reaches out a welcoming hand. Yet despite his pleasant manner, Mary cannot make herself step forward. Instead, her body stiffens as if a freezing rain has suddenly borne down upon her.

Standing behind him in the shadows is her husband.

Mary feels shackled to the cobblestones. She knows her heart should rejoice. A prayer ought to fly from her lips, praising God for bringing her out of the wilderness. Instead, as she looks at her husband, a pain sears her skull, so jagged it is all she can do to keep her eyes open.

"Mary!" Joseph slips past Increase, smiling and opening his arms in a wide arc that reminds Mary of a pulpit gesture. "Praise the Lord, who has given you safe passage through the wilderness!" Sunlight glints off his skin and makes his face look sallow and pasty.

"Squire Hoar gave me passage," she murmurs, but he does not seem to hear. He takes her face in his hands and kisses her forehead. She recognizes both alarm and pity in his eyes. She knows that weeks of hunger have transformed her, yet she has not realized until this moment that she wears the countenance of the dying.

She is dimly aware that Increase is talking with Josiah and Henry and calling for a servant to water the horse. His wife, Maria, appears in the doorway, a babe riding her hip. She is a plump, sweet-faced woman whose gray eyes seem charged with compassion.

"Come inside." She smiles at Mary and holds out her free hand. "You must take refreshment at my table."

Mary takes an uncertain step toward the door.

"We must give thanks to the Lord where we stand," Joseph declares loudly, in a voice intended to carry down the street. "Mighty are His works!" He bows his head and begins to intone a long prayer of thanksgiving and supplication, praising God for His mercy and begging Him for more.

Soon after the prayer, Josiah and Henry take their leave, and Joseph guides Mary to the door. She leans on his arm, for what is left of her strength has deserted her and she moves as jaggedly on her legs as a new calf.

"How fitting that the Lord has returned you to us on the Sabbath," Joseph says, as she steps across the sill. She hears the triumph in his voice and suddenly she is choking on fresh tears.

"Sarah is dead," she whispers.

"Hush!" He takes both of Mary's hands in his. His palms feel warm and smooth. "The time for tears is past," he says. "You have been redeemed."

She stares at him. "Sarah," she says, pushing the name past her tongue, so that it will not catch in her throat again. It sounds like a hiss in the air.

"I know, I know." He pats her hand. "'Tis the Lord's will, Mary. She rests in His care now."

So he knows. It is a shock—and a deliverance. Mary feels as if her spine has turned to dust; she sags against him as he leads her to the single chair at the table. At once, she begins to weep.

Maria presses a clean napkin into her hand and sets a steaming posset pot ornamented with blue vines and birds in front of her. The perfume of the ale and cream mingles with the spices, provoking in Mary a dreamlike state. She stares at the painted birds, suddenly remembering a particular afternoon when she had watched a sparrow hopping about the trees as she sat knitting outside Weetamoo's wetu. In the near distance a cluster of pine trees had risen dark green against the sky and beyond them a line of blue hills rolled away like the sea.

"Mary, you must eat." Maria's words startle Mary from her reverie. "Poor woman. Your skin lies upon your bones like linens set out to dry." She picks up the pot. "Come, drink." She puts the spout to Mary's lips. "Gently now," Maria whispers. "Gently. 'Tis over, Mary. You are free now."

Free. Mary blinks up at her through the blurring tears. She does not feel at all free. She feels as a bird must, one which has escaped its coop and flown away, only to be caught in a net, its wings clipped. She feels double-caged, having both found and lost a world.

Obediently she sips from the spout. "We must find Joss and Marie," she says weakly.

"May it please the Lord." Standing beside her, Joseph bows his head and begins to pray again, longer this time—thanking God for His gracious mercy and begging Him to spare the lives and souls of their children. As he goes on and on, Mary's mind wanders. She wonders if she has been out of the practice of communal prayer so long that she cannot attend. She thinks instead of Quinnapin and Weetamoo as she last saw them, tall and proud in their beads and feathers. She thinks of the great fire circle and the warriors dancing around it. She thinks of James and his piercing, compassionate gaze. She is uncomfortably aware of the walls that enclose her. She feels trapped, suffocated by the confinement.

When Joseph finally says, "Amen," and she opens her eyes, he is frowning at her. "You do not look well," he says. "Perhaps you would like to lie down?"

She is surprised by his consideration. She wonders if he has changed this much in the three months since she last saw him. Or is his solicitude for Increase and Maria's benefit? "No," she says, suddenly overcome by the same restlessness that was habitual during her captivity. She gets to her feet. "I would like to walk outside."

He nods as if he understands, though she does not think it possible.

For nearly an hour they walk up and down the street in front of the Mathers' house. A new bank of clouds comes up and swallows the sun, burdening the air with a damp chill, yet still they walk. Back and forth, back and forth. The movement soothes her, makes her feel herself again, for her legs have grown accustomed to walking many miles each day.

They do not look at each other, nor do they touch. Mary wants to ask her husband why he did not meet her in Concord, but she cannot seem to loosen her tongue. All her strength, all her *will* is in her legs. Instead, Joseph questions her. He asks for details of Sarah's death, and when she haltingly describes it, he takes three sharp breaths, but does not reproach her. He asks if she was able to watch over Joss and Marie. He bids her relate the details of the attack on their home. He wishes to know if her faith wavered during her time in the wilderness. Yet she says little, for her tongue is stiff in her mouth, apparently infected by an Indian reticence.

"I would know of your treatment by the savages," he says finally. She knows the reason for this question, knows that his concern is for her purity.

"They are a chaste people," Mary says. "I was not defiled."

He stops in the road and blinks at her. She realizes he does not believe her. She would not credit the words herself, had she heard them four months ago, before her captivity.

"I swear it," she says. "I have not been dishonored."

He closes his eyes a moment. "Praise God," he whispers. A gust of wind comes off the water and tugs at the cloak Maria gave her.

"Yes," she murmurs, drawing the cloak tightly around her, not only for warmth but to hide her form, for at that moment she feels a jagged, unwarranted pain in her belly, as if Maria's posset has turned to bile.

The evening is devoted to prayer. Everyone in the household gathers at the kitchen hearth. Increase and Joseph give thanks and pray for the safe return of Joss and Marie and the other captives not yet ransomed. Increase reads long passages of Scripture about God's mercy—the exodus of the Hebrews from Egypt, Jonah's release by the great fish, Jesus calming the storm. Joseph leads them in singing Psalm 124.

Maria sits on a bench, rocking her babe in her arms while her five older children sit at her feet. The oldest girl reminds Mary so much of Marie that her heart aches with longing. The oldest boy, named Cotton, is near Joss's age, yet his manner is as still and solemn as Joss's is lively.

Later, they all sit at table, women and men together, eating Maria's simple meal of bread and cheese and warm ale. Mary eats little and says nothing at all, for every bite of bread turns sour in her mouth.

Her mind is as sore as her belly. She thinks of Marie and Joss, who remain in the wilderness with the Indians. She thinks of Alawa, and realizes she misses her. She regrets that she never bid her farewell. She begins to weep yet again. It seems that her tears will not stop. Maria tries her best to console Mary, and Increase offers a prayer, but it is Joseph who finally stills her. He says her name in a stern voice, puts his hand on her shoulder, and prays that the Lord will give her strength to control her weak and womanly sobs.

The Mathers grant them use of the chamber over the kitchen for the night, allowing Mary and Joseph privacy and a bed to themselves. There is a fire in the small hearth set into the chimney;

they draw a bench before it and sit for a time, warming themselves. Mary finds herself entranced by the flames as Joseph tells her of his work while she was gone, of caring for the different members of the Lancaster church who had fled after the attack, of helping them find lodging in Boston and the nearby towns.

"We will remove to Charlestown," he informs her. "Our friends Thomas and Anna Shepard have agreed to take us in."

"Must we?" After her long march in the wilderness, Mary does not want to move ever again. She recalls with shame that she once thought her mother lacked a spirit of adventure because she complained of all the moving Mary's father required of her. Now, finally, Mary understands her distress.

"I have presumed on Increase's generosity for many weeks already, awaiting word of you," Joseph says. "And he is not overfond of visitors, for they disturb his study. Charlestown is only over the river. The move will not tax you."

"We could bide with my sister in Wenham," Mary says. She does not like Thomas Shepard, or his wife, Anna, who has always seemed a sour sort of woman. She chafes at the thought of accepting their charity. "Surely Joanna would welcome us until we have rebuilt our home in Lancaster."

Joseph looks down at his hands, which are still folded in his lap. "I have decided against returning to Lancaster. It is a forbidding place, filled with dangers. Too close to the savages." She cringes and she wonders if he noticed. "I no longer feel called to a mission on the frontier," he says. "Increase has suggested more established towns, perhaps in the Connecticut Colony."

"Connecticut Colony?" Mary finds her full voice at last. "Are we to go so far from what family I have left? Am I to be granted no rest?"

"Mary, Mary. You must calm yourself." His tone is gentle, meant to soothe, and he turns toward her in a kindly manner, though he does not touch her. "It is not for you to question the Lord's will. If He calls me to a new parish, we will go."

She looks away. "Promise me that we will not move before our children are returned to us." She makes her voice as even as she is able.

He responds as she knew he would. "Should we not leave such matters up to God? Has He not restored you to us for His glory?"

There is nothing she can say, no answers to such questions, save pious ones. Which she cannot at this moment give. And so she holds her tongue. Silence is one grace she has learned from the Indians.

After a long pause, he speaks again. "I fear there is another concern I must raise. There is the matter of your ransom. Twenty pounds is a steep price."

Mary feels a chill at her back, as if someone had just laid a cold hand there. She does not answer at once, but continues to look down at her lap. How sweet it would be to hear him say that she is a pearl of great price, that he would have sold all he had down to the last farthing to secure her safe return. "They said I must name a price," she says. "I had thought to set it fair. I feared too low a price would be my undoing."

"Yet Goody Kettle was released soon after you. And she was not so proud as to put a price upon herself."

Mary closes her eyes. She cannot think what to say that might satisfy him. "I did what I felt I must," she whispers. "I was given no chance to compare prices." Prices. Why does she suddenly feel more like a slave now than she did all those weeks in captivity?

"Do you feel no regret?" There is condemnation in his voice. "You placed a heavy burden upon me."

"Regret?" She thinks suddenly of James and is washed in sorrow. Try as she will, she cannot quell it. "Indeed, I have more regret than you will ever know," she whispers and begins to shake.

"Hush, Mary." He stands up. "Forgive me. It is not the proper time for this discussion. For now, you must rest." He draws her gently from the bench and leads her to the bed, where he pulls the blankets over her, and climbs up beside her. He draws the curtains and stretches out. He does not touch her, but lies very still, and after a few moments she realizes he has fallen asleep.

She lies staring at the patterns of firelight that flicker on the curtains, thinking of her children and James and remembering the Indians' sorrowful dance around the circle fire after Canonchet's death.

CHAPTER TWENTY-TWO

They remain guests of the Mathers for less than a week, until Thomas Shepard and his wife receive them into their home. Joseph attended Harvard with Thomas and they enjoy a collegial affection. Thomas's wife, Anna, grovels before him in an annoying manner, yet Mary is determined to like her, for she has a reputation as a good and charitable woman and her friendship could be of considerable value in restoring Mary to English society.

Charlestown's fortification walls are situated behind the Shepards' house, and the pungent odor of marshland wafts through their dooryard morning and night. Mary has not lived by the sea since she was a child in Salem and she finds the fetid reek of the tides disagreeable. She longs for the fresh, sweet scent of pine trees and meadows. She wants to feel a breeze in her uncapped hair and to gaze on long vistas of forests and mountains.

Mary's sister Joanna comes to visit. Mary tells her of Elizabeth's death, and they try to console each other, though no words can stanch their tears. There is still no news of Hannah's release. Mary assures Joanna that in the last glimpse she had of Hannah—

in the council house before the sachems—she looked as well as anyone.

In a private moment in the garden, Mary confesses her disappointment that Joseph did not travel to meet her in Concord, but Joanna cautions her not to dwell on such an inconsequential slight. "What matters is that you are returned to us," she says. "Why trouble yourself with an affront to your pride, after all you have endured?" And she takes Mary's shoulders lovingly and kisses her cheek. "Pray, tell me what transpired while you were in the wilderness," she says. "'Twill do you good to reveal your ordeals." There is a strange excitement in her voice, a prurience that irritates Mary. When she tries to answer, she finds her tongue has turned to stone.

"'Tis all right, Mary," Joanna says, wiping her face with a napkin. "There will be time enough to tell your tale. God will guide you. You must pray so."

Mary nods. She does not confess that her prayers have dried up like an exhausted spring, that she is unable to find comfort there.

Joseph no longer touches Mary the way a man touches his wife. Though they sleep beside each other night after night in the same bed, he does not take her in his arms, or explore her body with his fingers. She expected the consolation of union with him on her return and wonders if he finds her gauntness repulsive. He seems consumed by the thought that she might have forsaken God while she was in the wilderness. "My fear is that the Lord will withdraw His blessings from all of us," he says. "You must tell me all that befell you, Mary. For the sake of our family."

But there is no family anymore. There is just the two of them. "I did not knowingly forsake the Lord," she tells him. "Yet I sometimes believed that He forsook *me*." She turns away from his righteous frown. Yet, when she later reflects on her words, she is struck by the thought that it was Joseph, not God, who forsook her.

• • •

O n the Sabbath after her return, Mary attends public worship.
It is strange to sit across the aisle from Joseph with other
women instead of by herself in the foremost pew. Her days with the
Indians have made her restive, unsuited to perching for hours on a
hard bench. She is aware that the eyes of the congregation often turn
to her, especially when Mr. Shepard mentions her redemption in his
prayers. He speaks at length of God's special providence for His people, yet his sermon seems to her oddly tedious.

After worship, the women surround Mary and pester her with
excited questions. What did the Indians eat? Did they smell like
animals? Was it true that they danced naked in lewd ceremonies?
Did she encounter Satan while she was the wilderness? Was she able
to keep the Sabbath? Did she witness the roasting of children? How
many times was she defiled?

At first she is struck dumb by this onslaught. Then she tries to
answer. The Indians ate what they could find—roots and killed
deer and bear. They did dance but it was not lewd. She never once
glimpsed Satan. The women frown and shake their heads and ask
more questions. Clearly, her answers do not satisfy. She raises her
hands in a gesture of supplication.

"I pray you, if you will simply hold your tongues, I will tell you
what I witnessed," she says.

"Hush, let her speak!" someone cries.

"Aye, we would hear the truth, though it distress us," says another.

The women's expressions are greedy, stimulated, almost lustful.
Suddenly, Mary understands that they do not want the truth. They
want to hear details that will confirm their misconceptions, that
will validate their fears. For a moment, she is angry. Then a spirit of
mischief comes over her.

"I underwent terrible trials," she says. "I was made to listen to

birds and sit idly in the sun. I had to watch Indian ceremonies and
share their food. I had to build their shelters and carry their burdens
when we moved from place to place. They laughed at me cruelly
when I nearly fell crossing a river. 'Tis a wonder I lived to tell of it."

"By the Lord's grace," one woman says in an awed voice. Many
women nod. Clearly, they believe her now.

She apprehends that not one of the women perceive that she is
jesting. When she is repeating what they already believe, they do
not question her veracity.

"How many times were you dishonored?" calls a woman from
the back of the crowd.

"Aye, tell us!" chorus several others.

Mary shakes her head. "That I cannot tell you," she says. "For
there is no number at all." The women murmur, taking her words as
confirmation that the number is too great to admit. She regrets her
jest, but it is too late to mend her words. She is so plainly disturbed
that one kindly woman takes her arm and returns her to Joseph's
protection. In silence, he walks her back to the Shepards' home. She
does not attend the afternoon service with him, but sits in the parlor
and tries to pray. Her Bible lies open in her lap, yet God seems very
far away. It occurs to her that her jesting was much like the Indian
jests she witnessed during her captivity. She had become Indian, not
just in her dress and actions, but in her sense of humor as well.

She is distracted by the spring sunlight that dances through the
window and makes diamond patterns on the wall. It reminds her of
the way the sunlight fell through the newly budded leaves when she
walked with the Indians on the trail to Wachusett. For a few blessed
moments, the weight of her sorrow falls away.

News comes that Hannah has been ransomed with two of her
children. Mary flies into Hannah's arms when they meet and
begs her for word of Joss and Marie, but Hannah can tell her

nothing. She is emaciated and weak, but her cheerful temperament has not deserted her and she quickly adapts to her release. Mary wonders why she herself cannot make a similar adjustment, but her soul feels riven. In private, she weeps for the absence of her children and her ignorance of their welfare. Though Joseph warns sternly against heaviness of heart, she cannot stop sorrowing.

She begins to have terrible nightmares. Nightly she wakes, gasping, from dreams of death. The air in the upper chamber in the Shepards' home is close, nearly suffocating in its warmth, yet she rarely throws off her blanket. She has been cold for so many months, she cannot complain of this new discomfort. She forces her thoughts toward God, thanking Him that the sticky dampness down her back and neck is not blood but sweat. The fustian bed hangings do not stir as she rolls and thrashes on the bed. Beside her, Joseph sleeps, snoring lightly, unmindful of her distress.

She is afraid to let herself sleep. She listens to the night sounds—the call of owls, the regular cries of the night watchman as he walks the streets announcing the hour. Some nights she rises and bathes herself in secret, refreshed by the comfort of cleanliness. She thinks of James, remembering their long conversations and the night she spent in his wetu. How comforted she felt by his presence and the closeness of his body. She knows that any virtue she possessed before her captivity is gone, for she would willingly trade her soul for another such encounter.

One night she reaches out and strokes her husband's thigh. She thinks of the animal pleasure of conjugal union, of the great, sweet rush of joy that came over her sometimes when he did not hurry their lovemaking. Her hand slides up until she brushes his member with her fingertips. He stirs, half aroused, and for a moment she believes he will take her in his arms and caress her in the old, tender ways. Instead, he pushes her hand away and rolls over so that his back is to her.

She swallows a sob. She wonders if she is ever going to experience passion again. She resolves to try harder to return to civilized ways, to be a proper wife to her husband.

She dutifully attends to all the regulations and manners of society, but finds her restored life exhausting. Every morning she straps herself into her bodice and binds her hair under her cap. She ties on petticoats and fixes a clean apron over her skirt, wishing for the loose ease of an Indian dress. As she rolls stockings onto her legs and fits her feet into the stiff latchet shoes, she longs for the comfort of moccasins. She ties her pocket around her waist, the one thing that she still possesses from her years in Lancaster, a talisman she held fast to throughout her captivity. As she slides her hand into it and feels her needles and scissors, she has the thought that it is not Providence alone that saved her life, but her own enterprise and the contents of her pocket. A wicked thought that she dares not confess to anyone, least of all her husband.

She is living in another woman's house and cooking in her kitchen, and though Anna Shepard says nothing unkind, Mary knows from her frequent glances that the woman is scrutinizing her for signs of coarse and uncivilized behavior. Mary helps as she can, making bread and keeping the fire, washing clothes and bed linens, and spinning linen. She assists in tending the kitchen garden, and in plucking the geese of their soft down to make pillows and feather beds. But her fingers are strangely clumsy and the geese loudly squawk their complaints. The bread sometimes does not rise, and Mary's bodice and apron are often spattered with grease.

She eats with a solemn desperation. For the first few days, she wondered if her appetite would ever be restored, yet the time soon came when it seemed she could never get enough food. There is wantonness in her eating now, a hunger that goes beyond food, as if she yearns to consume life itself. She remembers eating horse liver at the Indian camp, remembers the blood smearing her chin and dripping onto her clothes. She recalls how deeply she rejoiced in the unseemly meal, how she cared nothing for her appearance or that she had grown wild as the forest beasts around her.

Joseph is patient, allowing her time to modify her behavior, to rid herself of what he calls the "savage ways" that have infected her. He insists only that she join him for prayer every morning and evening, certain that returning her to that discipline will ensure a correction in her spirit.

Then he begins to frown at her, and Anna comments on how agitated she seems. Once, after Sabbath morning service, she takes Mary aside and warns her that people are beginning to whisper that she was bewitched during her captivity. Some say the Devil himself possessed her while she was in the wilderness.

Mary's cheeks burn in fury, much as they had when Weetamoo ordered her about. Yet she holds her tongue, bows her head and thanks Anna humbly for telling her. As the days pass, Mary begins to realize that she will never be restored to her former self. The way is blocked, not only by her disordered nature, but by the citizens of Charlestown. Everywhere she goes she sees their wary looks and hears their mutterings. She comes to welcome her husband's search for a new and distant parish. The prospect of living in a town far from the Bay Colony's gossiping tongues appeals to her. She thinks of it as a new redemption.

Her constant concern—her obsession—is the recovery of Joss and Marie. She insists on journeying with Joseph as he travels through the Bay Colony towns north and south of Boston to earn a few shillings preaching as a guest in other ministers' pulpits. But the wilderness, like some great beast, has apparently swallowed their children and is not yet ready to spew them out.

When Increase Mather suggests that they seek ways to negotiate with the Indians, Joseph meets with Daniel Gookin, the man responsible for supervising the Praying Indians. He returns discouraged and anxious, fearing what neither of them dare say—that the children have been slain and, like Sarah, lie dead in some place they will never find.

Then comes a day when Joseph tells her that John Eliot, the minister of the Roxbury church, wants to meet her. "He has befriended the Indians and is familiar with their ways," Joseph explains. "He would know their actions, for he has striven to bring them to Christ." She thinks immediately of James and what he had told her of John Eliot, how he had visited Hassanamesit when James was a boy. How James had helped him with his Indian Bible. How much James admired him. Not only did Mr. Eliot baptize and befriend James, but he had secured his education in an English home. Mary shares none of this knowledge with Joseph, but eagerly agrees to the meeting.

Mr. Eliot calls on them the next day. He is a quiet, portly man with a small beard and graying hair that he wears to his shoulders. He sits easily in the Shepards' great chair by the hearth and smiles at Mary throughout the interview. Joseph perches beside her on a wooden settle, yet he is curiously silent as Mr. Eliot gently inquires about her thoughts and memories.

She does not say much, for she does not know how to answer his questions. She does not believe that anyone, including Mr. Eliot, can understand her experience. And she dares not ask him about James while she is in Joseph's presence.

"I have found Indians, on the whole, to be honorable men," Mr. Eliot says. "They are always willing to explain their practices, and are full of curiosity about our Lord."

Mary nods, trying to keep her hands still in her lap, though they twitch incessantly, even as her feet move beneath her skirts. "In truth, I have not found the Indians very different from English," she says.

Joseph's eyebrows vault upward. "I thought it common knowledge that they are overfond of mischief, much given to sport and dancing."

She struggles to hold her tongue, to prevent herself from contradicting her husband as Mr. Eliot leans toward her. "I know you were largely among the unconverted, and no doubt you oft feared for your life, but I trust you felt the Lord's providence through your many trials. And I would know, in particular"—he pauses as if uncertain how to best phrase his question—"I wonder—did you encounter any *Praying Indians?*"

She thinks at once of James. As heat rises into her bosom and neck, there is a choking sensation in her throat. She looks down at her hands twisting in her lap. Joseph is frowning. He takes her hand to prompt her response, but she begins to shake so badly that he doesn't persist.

Instead, he apologizes to the minister. "Pray, forgive her," he says. "She has been subject to such fits since her redemption."

Mr. Eliot expresses his concern, and soon leaves, after praying aloud that the Lord will unstop Mistress Rowlandson's tongue so that His light can shine more brightly for all.

CHAPTER TWENTY-THREE

Mary's silence—her "fit," as Joseph insists on calling it—in the face of Mr. Eliot's question troubles her. She thinks about it constantly, worrying it as she might worry a bit of thread in her fingers. She knows that her inability to speak was born of her guilt at wanting to stay among the Indians. No, it was more specific than that—she wanted to stay with James. Even after she learned that her husband was alive.

She spirals into depression and fear. Her distress is so monstrous that she soon finds herself unable to speak to anyone at all except Joseph and her sisters. Each morning, when Anna Shepard wishes her "good day" in her mournful voice, Mary can only nod and try to smile. Joseph apologizes for her and tries to explain that her strange behavior is due to the shock of her weeks in captivity. But Mary senses that not even he is convinced of this.

Joseph warns her that Mr. Eliot is only one of many who have requested an audience. She must find her voice so that she can answer their questions. Thomas Parker, Urian Oakes, Daniel Gookin, even Governor Leverett himself, have all asked to hear her tale. She begs Joseph to put them off, at least until she learns the fate of their children. She tells him that her tongue was stopped by some malevolent spirit during the audience with Mr. Eliot; that she fears she will be unable to do more than smile and nod in answer to their questions. Silence has descended on her like a heavy snowfall, muffling even her tears.

Her husband's fame has risen since her release. People are sympathetic to a man whose wife has spent so much time among the Indians. Who knows what depravities she has been subjected to, how tainted she is from living among heathens? They consider him noble for taking her back. He has been paid to preach in many towns throughout the colony, and people fill the meetinghouses, curious to learn what he will say. Mary accompanies him when she can, hoping to hear news of their children. They travel to Salem and Rowley, to Ipswich and Salisbury. Though Joseph is warmly received, people's curiosity is fixed on Mary. She is constantly plied with questions she is unable to answer.

Then, one afternoon as they travel to Rowley, they are overtaken by William Hubbard, the Ipswich minister. He is flushed with excitement as he tells them that Joss has been released in Portsmouth. Mary is rapturous. She begs God to forgive her for doubting His mercy. She promises Him that, if He restores her children to her, she will answer every question presented her.

As if in answer to her prayer, on the eve of their journey to reunite with Joss, word comes that Marie has come into Providence. Mary cannot contain her joy. She takes a brisk walk along the riverbank, listening to the bird chorus and watching the reflection of clouds in the water, just to clear her head. She gives thanks to God again and again. The distress she has felt since her return vanishes like dew on summer grass.

They travel to Portsmouth in a creaking wagon drawn by a hired horse. Mary has never felt so impatient in her life. She can hardly remain seated on the wagon bench.

Portsmouth is a jumble of houses clustered near the water. Several large wharves jut into the harbor, where three ships lie at anchor. Mary is surprised to see so many dark-skinned people in the crowded streets. They put her in mind of Bess Parker's son, and she resolves to locate Bess and pay her a visit. Joseph makes inquiries at a local tavern and learns that Joss is staying at the home of Major Richard Waldron, on the outskirts of town.

Major Waldron greets them with stately aplomb and requires that they take tea with him before sending a servant off to fetch Joss. The servant is clearly an Indian—he has the height and facial features—despite his formal green livery.

Mary leaps from her chair when Joss steps into the room. He is as thin as a skeleton. When he looks at her, his eyes widen and he stops and blanches, as if he has seen a ghost. "Joss!" She runs to him, takes his head in her hands, pressing his face to her bosom. Long after Joseph pries him away, tears run down her face and she cannot stop saying her son's name. She refuses to let him out of her sight. Through the rest of the afternoon and late into the evening, she watches him. She cannot stop touching him, patting his shoulder, dabbling her fingers in his hair, sliding her palm across his cheek. He is beginning to grow the fuzz of a beard and she repeatedly runs her finger over it, as if she expects it to disappear. She presses what food she can on him, yet her tongue can form no words other than his name. At times, she thinks she detects a crazed look in his eye, which causes her tears to flow again.

They take him home the next day. Joss, who is not stricken with Mary's reticence, talks all the way back about his captivity, describing it as a great adventure. Mary rides sideways on the wagon seat so that she does not have to remove her gaze from his face for even a moment.

As soon as they are back in Charlestown, Mary is desperate to be reunited with Marie. She does not even want to take the time to rest from their journey before leaving. But Joseph says they cannot go. "There are rumors that the savages are gathering in that area for yet another assault," he tells her. "I have been advised it is unsafe to travel that far from Boston. So we will wait for the soldiers to bring her."

"But Marie needs us!" Mary cries. "She will require her mother's succor."

"She will have it soon enough," he says. "We will discuss this matter no more. You must pray for patience and self-control, Mary. I fear heathen ways have tainted you." And he turns away. She wonders suddenly if it is fear of the Indians that prevented him from rescuing her, and she is too ashamed to continue her supplications.

Under English guard, Marie is brought to Dorchester, where Joseph meets her and returns with her to Charlestown. When the cart draws up in front of the door, Mary runs out and pulls Marie into her arms. Her daughter's face and form are even more skeletal than her son's, yet there is a cheerfulness about her that assures Mary her mind is not disordered.

Marie reports that her captor was a Wampanoag warrior who gave her to his sister. She was not beaten or bound though, like Mary, she was forced to carry heavy baskets as the woman and her family moved from place to place. For several weeks Marie feared she might be killed at any moment, but gradually realized that her captors treated her no differently from their own daughters. She asks what became of Sarah. As Mary describes Sarah's suffering and death, her voice grows hoarse and words fail her and soon she collapses into silence. She draws Marie close against her, clasping her for so long that the girl begins to protest.

As with Joss, Mary cannot draw her gaze from her daughter. She touches her face and arms and shoulders again and again throughout the day, to reassure herself that Marie is before her in the flesh, and not the phantasm of some sweet dream.

That evening, they sit before the hearth, a reunited family. After Joseph delivers up many prayers of thanksgiving, Marie confesses that she was not rescued by English soldiers, but by a Wampanoag woman.

"I was walking on the trail with the other women," she says. "I was last in line. I had my basket on my back and it was heavy." She touches her forehead, where the line of her basket strap still marks her skin. "One of the women—Motuckqua—came back to walk with me. At first I thought she meant to scold me, but when the others went round a bend and out of sight, she took my arm and dragged me off the trail into a thicket. We hid there for hours. I was frightened, but she made me understand she meant to take me back to the English."

"Surely, she risked her own life to do so," Mary says. "The Indians would regard such an act as treachery."

Marie nods. "I would not be alive without her help. She gathered food and found shelter and led me to Providence."

"I wonder what prompted her to such benevolence." Mary feels her eyes burn with tears.

"It was the Lord's doing," Joseph says. "A miracle of His grace."

Mary bows her head as he offers yet another prayer of thanksgiving, but she cannot stop thinking of the Wampanoag woman and her courage. She doubts she would have risked so much for an Indian child.

L ate on a Wednesday afternoon, a week after the children's return, Joseph insists on taking Mary to visit Daniel Gookin at his home in Cambridge. He tells her Mr. Gookin is an assistant on the Council of Magistrates and has the ear of Governor Leverett. He is now writing a book on the doings of the Praying Indians during the hostilities and wishes to question her. Although Mary does not want to be separated from Marie and Joss for even a few hours, she obeys her husband. As he reminds her, the Lord has shown her abundant mercy by bringing her out of the wilderness and restoring her children. Mary should feel obliged to thank Him not just in word, but in deed.

She has never met Mr. Gookin, yet the name is disturbingly familiar. She remembers that James mentioned it and she also heard it several years ago in a darker context. It is the name of the man who first owned Silvanus Warro, Bess Parker's lover.

As they draw up to the stately house, set back from the lane behind a sturdy fence, Joseph says he hopes she will find her tongue this time. A pretty servant girl greets them at the door, and takes their cloaks. She is about Sarah's age and her movements remind Mary of her daughter's quiet grace. They follow her into Mr. Gookin's parlor—a long clean room with freshly whitewashed walls and a sand-scrubbed floor. A wide table is situated before the hearth and a cupboard carved in ebony and oak stands against the wall.

Mr. Gookin is a tall, thin man with gray hair and a cheerful countenance. Mary judges him to be well into his sixth decade, despite his obvious vigor. There is an uncommon sadness about him, yet he greets them with a warm smile and a gracious manner, bids them sit at the table, then signals for the servant girl to bring food. Mary's eyes follow her as she bobs in and out of the room, bearing plates of small cakes and bowls of hot broth.

Joseph eats heartily, but Mary can do no better than pick at a cake and touch a few crumbs to her lips. Mr. Gookin smiles benevolently and speaks directly to Mary. "I want to be plain, Mistress Rowlandson," he says. "I am still seeking news of some friends—Praying Indians who were under my tutelage before these terrible hostilities started up last summer."

Mary nods. She wonders if James was one of his students, tries to carefully phrase a question. But before she opens her mouth, Joseph starts to speak on her behalf. He explains her late speaking disability, his concern that the Indians bewitched or corrupted her. She stares down at her lap in silence, though she longs to contradict him.

Mr. Gookin listens politely to Joseph, then addresses Mary again. "I am particularly curious to know if you encountered one Indian who goes by the name of James Printer."

She looks up at him, startled. "I met him," she says cautiously.

"Ah!" His face brightens and he runs his hands across his knees. "Tell me, how did you find him? I would know particularly of his loyalties. Were they clear in his dealings? Has he remained true to the English cause? Or has he gone over to Philip?"

Confused feelings tumble within her. She does not know what her answer should be. She is not even sure what the truth is. Finally, she says, "I did meet him, but I fear I could not discern his loyalties."

"Ah," says Mr. Gookin, nodding solemnly. "'Tis no surprise, in truth. He's crafty. One of the cleverest Indians I ever met, but not fully converted, I warrant."

Mary's impulse is to protest, yet she restrains herself, knowing that a passionate reaction would stimulate questions she does not want to answer. She says nothing, glances away at the small west-facing window, where she sees dark clouds rolling up the sky, lengthening the shadows in the room. She is surprised that Mr. Gookin does not light a candle or a lantern. Joseph asks him a question, and they embark on a long conversation about Indians, the hostilities, and the terrible toll the war has taken on English resources and lives, until Mary is no longer able to discern how one word is fitted to the next.

She senses a motion from the corner of the room, just beyond the firelight—an elusive deepening of shadows that reminds her of the stealthy, slinking walk of Indians in their night encampments. They always seemed just beyond her sight, like spirits or demons. At first she assumes it is the serving girl, but when she comes into the room bearing another platter of cakes, Mary realizes it was not her. She notes the shift once more, to her left, and this time she turns toward it. The movement again—not furtive and threatening as she first imagined—but humble, unassuming. She fancies she catches a glimpse of a dark brown arm as the fire flares up. She is suddenly aware that Joseph has stopped speaking and that Mr. Gookin is looking at her.

"Mistress Rowlandson?" He leans toward her. "Is something amiss?"

"No." She tries to order her thoughts. "I fancied I saw something—someone."

He smiles. "I assure you, there is no danger here. You are quite safe."

"I fear my wife's time in the wilderness has attuned her to shadows," Joseph says quickly. "She startles easily."

Yet even as he speaks in her defense, Mary turns again to look into the room's corner.

"Ah." Mr. Gookin has followed her glance this time and now he smiles. "'Tis but Silvanus—"

He continues to speak, but Mary is no longer hearing his words, for the name *Silvanus* has turned her cold.

"Silvanus?" she says aloud, breaking into Mr. Gookin's narration.

"Aye." Mr. Gookin smiles at her. "Pretentious, I know. But slaves are often strangely named. 'Tis not to be held against the man."

Her heart begins to beat fiercely against her ribs. She is surprised that Joseph does not hear it. "I would speak with him," she says, in such earnestness and excitement that she nearly rises from the bench. "Please."

Joseph puts a warning hand on her arm. "Please," she says again. "I would know if he has any knowledge of Bess Parker, lately of Lancaster. She is someone I once befriended."

"Once gave aid to," Joseph corrects her. "You showed her mercy. She was not your friend."

She wishes she could wave him away, like a pestering fly. "May I speak with him?" she asks again.

"Of course, of course." As Mr. Gookin rises and gestures, Mary turns to watch a tall black man come forward into the light.

CHAPTER TWENTY-FOUR

Silvanus is as dark as the shadows he steps from. Yet he exudes such a liveliness about his person that Mary instantly understands why Bess Parker was drawn to him. He listens closely to her questions, and answers directly, with no hesitation, no hint of awkwardness. He admits he and Bess sinned, that he is the father of her child. He says that the child has been sold, he knows not where.

"And Bess?" Mary asks. "Can you tell me where she might be found? I would speak with her."

Silvanus gives no answer.

Mr. Gookin shifts in his chair. "I fear she is dead, Mistress Rowlandson. By her own hand."

"No!" Mary puts her hand to her mouth. "Pray, tell me what happened?"

"I am told she drowned herself not long after she returned to service in Salem." Mr. Gookin glances at Silvanus. "I did not know the girl. But perhaps it was a mercy."

Mary cannot tell if the sag in Silvanus's shoulders is from grief or anger.

"I am sorry," she whispers, and it is to Silvanus, not Mr. Gookin, she speaks. "So very sorry." She swallows tears. Joseph presses his handkerchief into her hand.

Mr. Gookin looks distressed, and Silvanus still will not meet Mary's eyes.

"I fear my wife is not well," Joseph says, rising. "We must take our leave."

Mary stands beside him. She is, indeed, ill, but it is not a sickness that can be cured by leaving, or by any physic. "God go with you, Silvanus," she says, knowing at once from Joseph's frown that he believes she should not have spoken this blessing to a slave. Yet she cannot bring herself to regret it. She turns to Silvanus again. "Have you searched for your child?" she asks. "Have you any hope of finding him?"

He stares at her. "I am not a free man, Mistress. Mr. Gookin is my former master, but now I am the property of Mr. Jonathan Wade of Medford. 'Tis by his benevolence that I am here today to repair Mr. Gookin's roof."

She sees that Mr. Gookin is not looking at Silvanus and wonders if he is ashamed. But it is not something she can courteously ask. Besides, Joseph is already saying good-bye and guiding her to the door.

After the encounter with Silvanus, Mary takes to her bed. She lies feverish and spent, dreaming of Indians and black slaves, and meditating on Bess Parker and her child. She cannot stop imagining the poor woman's body as it is pulled, blue and bloated, from a river. She relives her own despair at the deaths of Mari and Sarah. She revisits her belief that all meaning in life has fled. Bess's son did not die in her arms, yet he was sold into slavery. Was that any better? Mary has been sold herself, has witnessed the arbitrary brutality of master against slave, has known the fear of being struck or slain at any moment. How can any mother bear the knowledge that her child is daily subjected to such cruelty, alone and unprotected?

Anna Shepard makes healing broths and possets, and Marie patiently feeds Mary. Joseph prays with her each morning and evening. He reads her long, cautionary passages of Scripture. Slowly she recovers her strength. She becomes more certain that God has allowed these terrible trials to fall on New England because they have embraced slavery. Instead of examining themselves, the English falsely and foolishly believe that whatever they do is approved by God.

As soon as Mary is well again, Thomas Shepard makes it plain that they have neither sufficient food nor room to give over to the entire Rowlandson family. When Mary suggests that they return to Lancaster and rebuild, Joseph dismisses her idea. "Has not the Lord harried us out of that country?" he asks and then pauses a moment to look closely at her. His eyes are narrow. *Like a snake's eyes,* she thinks, and feels a pang of guilt for her wicked thought. "Why would you want to return to a frontier town, Mary? Has not your contact with heathens been sufficient?" There is something hard and sharp in his tone, as if he delights in wounding her.

She turns quickly away, before he can question her further. Or detect the hot flush on her skin.

A week later, Joseph tells her that Increase Mather has come to their aid once more. He has persuaded Mr. Whitcomb, a member of his congregation, to allow them to live in one of his properties—a vacant house in Boston, not far from the meetinghouse. Joseph goes into paroxysms of thanksgiving. Mary packs their few possessions.

When she steps through the doorway and looks at the bare walls and floors of the rented Boston house, Mary's spirit plummets. How can she set up housekeeping when they have neither goods nor furnishings? Even though she will no longer have to share another woman's kitchen, they must still live largely on the charity of friends. Joseph finds her weeping before the empty hearth and scolds her for lack of faith. Does she not trust that God will provide? The truth is she does not, but within two days people come forward and by week's end they have a bed, linens, a table, a bench to sit on, and pots and kettles for cooking. Mary makes do with what is given, reminding herself daily that she recently had nothing at all. She finds herself reflecting, as the house slowly fills with goods, how few of them she would require if she still lived in the wilderness.

She spends many hours reacquainting herself with the tasks of an English wife. Yet she feels oddly cramped inside the house, and observes that her children do as well. Marie frequently opens the door and stands on the stoop, looking up at the sky. Whenever Mary permits, Marie takes her work outside into the yard and Mary often follows her. They sit on a bench and talk of their captivities. Joss is constantly restless, and whenever Mary is not watching, he leaves the house to roam. She does not know where he goes, and worries that he might get a notion to return to the Indians, for he has admitted that he sorely misses his life among them.

Mary's own gaze often flies to the door or a window. She sometimes follows it, stepping into the street in her apron. Several times, while sewing, or kneading bread, or making a broth, she thinks she hears a distant drum or the drone of an Indian chant. She stops and closes her eyes. She suspects her husband believes she's at prayer.

But she is not praying. She is listening.

Slowly Mary begins to understand that captivity has changed her son, and not for the better. Where he was once a lively and honest boy, he is now devious and sly. He often abandons his chores and runs off, she knows not where. Sometimes he is gone all day, not returning until well after dark. He offers Mary little help and none at all to his father. Mary can no longer depend on him to fetch wood and water, or tend the garden behind the shed. He acts as if he has no duties except to roam unfettered. He is often absent from family prayers and disappears on the Sabbath so frequently that the church elders have begun suggesting he be publicly reprimanded.

Joseph permits this freedom for as long as he can bear, then confronts Joss with his sins. "I fear the savages have corrupted you," he says, as the boy stands before him in the nearly empty parlor. "There is only one way to subdue a rebellious spirit. I must whip you, else you shall end up at the pillory or in the stocks."

Joss says nothing.

"Go and fetch the rod, boy," Joseph says.

Mary, listening from the kitchen, feels her heart clench. She thinks of the cruel wooden machines that stand in the town square. Of how often she has seen men and women fastened into them for hours or even days while their excrement runs down their legs and passing men and women spit on them. She cannot bear the thought of her son pinioned there. She also knows she can no longer stand by while one of her children is whipped in her own house, though for years she raised no protest against it.

Mary goes into the parlor and stands between her husband and her son. "You'll not whip him," she says to Joseph. "Not while I live."

Marie, who is spinning flax in the corner of the room, drops her distaff.

"Mary—" Joseph's voice rises in warning.

"No," she says, before he can continue. "I'll not have my son beaten—by you or by anyone. No more. The whipping of children is a cruel and unnecessary practice. The Lord commands us not to punish, but to love." Her voice trembles, for she knows that openly defying her husband is a grave sin, that she is risking severe punishment of her own. Yet she cannot remain silent.

Joseph stares as if she has gone mad. "You disobey me?" She knows he is angry—furious—and that he will not forgive this offense. Before her captivity, though she abhorred such punishments, she had always surrendered to what she believed was his greater wisdom. This time she is determined not to yield.

"You would risk his *soul?*" her husband asks in a voice that is barely a whisper.

"I would risk my own," she replies. And instead of dropping her gaze, she looks straight into his eyes.

To her surprise, Joseph dismisses the boy with only a reprimand.

Joseph does not—cannot—let the matter rest. It is his duty, as the head of his family, to bring all of them under God's order. Since she was a child, Mary has known by heart the Apostle Paul's words from First Corinthians: *Christ is the head of every man: and the man is the woman's head: and God is Christ's head.* She has always believed this is true—that there is no hope for her salvation outside of obedience to her husband and to Christ. When they retire behind the curtains of their bed that night and Joseph begins his long rebuke of her, she bows her head and listens in a spirit of submission.

She says nothing. Nor does she weep. She lets his angry words wash over her as if they are rain. When he is satisfied he has chastised her enough, he blows out the candle, draws the blankets over him and stretches out to sleep. Mary lies beside him as his long breaths turn to snores. Though she knows she is supposed to feel contrite, neither tears nor repentance come. Instead, she feels as if she has won a victory in a long battle. She wishes she could dance around a campfire to the music of drums. She silently pledges that she will never again allow any child to suffer a whipping in her presence. The Indians have raised kind, respectful children without

using the rod. If she can endure captivity and make a life for herself
in the wilderness, she can secure mercy in her own household.

Her mind turns to the many nights she slept in a wetu under a
warm deerskin. To the power of her legs as she walked the Indian
trails. To the startling beauty of wilderness vistas. She thinks of her
time in the wilderness not as an ordeal, but as an adventure. She
sees herself as a sojourner in a strange land who has returned richer
than before.

In the darkness she finds herself thinking, once again, of James.

Still, her husband does not touch her. Though they sleep beside
each other night after night in the same bed, he does not take
her in his arms, or explore her body. At first, she thought that he was
repulsed by her emaciated look, the way her sallow skin sagged
across her bones. But as the weeks pass, and her body begins to fill
her bodice once again, she suspects some other reason. For she has
noticed that he watches her when he thinks she is not looking. She
sees his gaze run up and down her naked body in the warm spring
mornings as she bathes herself with water and a cloth before slip-
ping her shift over her head. She sees the glint in his eye when she
bends over the grinding bowl and her breasts spill forward into her
bodice and she knows that he still desires her. Why then does he not
join with her?

She expected the consolation of his body on her return. They
both know it is his duty as her husband, that he is sinning by deny-
ing her conjugal pleasure. But she is reluctant to press the issue. She
begins to sense he believes she has betrayed him. That he believes
she has had relations with an Indian and is awaiting her confession.

One warm night in early June, as they prepare for bed, Joseph
tells her about a project Increase has planned. Mary has spent the
day with Marie doing laundry and her arms are tired, her hands red
and sore. Joseph is unusually cheerful and his good humor has

loosened his tongue. He mentions that Maria Mather is expecting yet another child and that there has been a fire in one of the houses in Charlestown.

"And Mr. Mather has designed a new scheme to help people perceive God's providence here in New England." He sits on the bed and Mary dutifully removes his boots and places them on the hearth. "He plans an anthology of experiences and trials of people during this late war. Especially those who have been captured or otherwise come under the influence of the heathens. He wants to make it plain that God has chastised us righteously so that we might submit more fully to Him."

Mary dips her head, as if to signal submission, though it is not what she feels. She wonders if any Englishman can write a true account of Indian captivity. It seems to her that few people know the truth of Indian lives and hearts.

She shakes the thought away as her husband continues talking. Wasn't her own sister slain by Indian wickedness?

She rises, blows out the candle, and climbs onto the high bed to lie down. The mattress shifts sideways as Joseph stretches out. He rolls toward her and for a moment, Mary believes he is going to take her in his arms. She feels the skin in her neck flush; her thighs grow warm. Instead, he continues expounding on Increase's project. Her attention wanders from his words; her limbs grow heavy and her brain swirls with strange images.

"Mary, do you not agree?" Joseph's voice is tinged with a rare excitement. "Such an endeavor would warm their hearts toward us. I warrant I will soon enough find a new parish once your tale is in print!"

She snaps back to wakefulness. "My tale?" *What is he talking about?*

"Have you heard nothing I said, wife?" There is a note of pique in his voice. "Mr. Mather wants you to record your ordeal, so that he might print it."

"I have given no thought to recording it," Mary says slowly. "It seems a better plan to forget those days."

"He means to use it to illuminate God's purposes."

She yawns. Sleepiness is claiming her even as she struggles to follow his meaning. "I fear I have no time for such an endeavor," she murmurs. Her eyes close again.

"Mary." He touches her shoulder and she shivers in response.

"What is it?" She forces herself to look full at him though he is but a shadow in the greater dark.

"Do not dismiss this. It will bring us both public prominence." His hand is still on her shoulder. She feels her flesh warming under his palm. It has been so long since he touched her.

"I have no desire for fame," she murmurs. "It is enough that my children are returned to me." She is so sleepy. Yet her words must be dutiful—and proper. But no, he is not content. He shifts restlessly, puts his mouth close to her ear.

"Promise me you will pray on it, Mary. Increase feels it is a most important project. I want us to be part of it."

Us, she thinks. Was it not her ordeal? If the story is to be told, is it not hers to tell?

As she drifts off to sleep, she finds herself frowning in the darkness.

In the morning, Mary recalls their conversation only dimly—it seems to her it might have been a dream. Daylight has washed away the shadows and makes her laugh at the strangeness of her imagination. She has no thought of recording her time among the Indians. Indeed, she does not know how she could begin to capture her experiences.

Nor does she believe Increase Mather would find any use for her thoughts. Even if he deigned to consider them, she has not been able to perceive God's hand in her ordeal. It seemed to her that God

was silent while she was in the wilderness. Though Joseph has reminded her daily that had God abandoned her she would still be
living among the heathen, she sometimes feels more abandoned
since her ransom. Yet she wonders briefly if, in writing down the
events, her mind might be somehow cleansed of them, and she
would be able to sleep well once again.

For the truth is, she has not slept soundly since her return. Night
after night she is awakened by dreams so terrifying and vile her heart
thrashes like a dying bird. She lies gasping in bed, as if drowning,
bathed in her own tears.

CHAPTER TWENTY-FIVE

Joseph continues to press Mary relentlessly to write a narrative of her captivity. He mentions the project several times each day, and talks incessantly about her experience as emblematic of God's chastising love.

Still, she resists. She says she is not sufficiently skilled in shaping sentences. She insists that there is too much she cannot remember. She says that much of what happened is too painful to recount. She pleads with him to cease badgering her. "Why do you seek to put me to this test?" she asks him one evening.

He gives her a startled look. "I do not think it a test," he says. "Does not the Lord say you must not hide your light under a bushel? Think how your trials exemplify the chastening hand of God upon His people. Think how often He spared your life, how your words might glorify His name." He pauses. "But perhaps you are right. Perhaps it is a test of your faith. Of your loyalty to the English cause."

It is the first time he has hinted that her loyalties may be divided and she reacts with a fury that she realizes only later is proof that his question has struck close to the bone. "How can you question my loyalty?" she snaps, throwing down her sewing and rising from her bench. "Have I not suffered enough but now I must be accused of disloyalty—*by my own husband!?*" She wants to throw something heavy across the room.

"Mary!" He leaps from his chair. "Calm yourself! I have not accused you of anything! I merely asked you a question."

"'Tis a vile question, then," she says, backing away from him. She thinks of James. She sees that her hands are trembling.

"Perhaps you could prove your loyalty by meeting with Increase. He would like to discuss his project with you directly."

She looks into her husband's face and in that moment comprehends that she has no choice. Her husband has cleverly maneuvered her into this position. "Very well," she says slowly. "I will talk with him. But I make no promises. I must allow myself to be led by the Lord."

His eyes narrow. And then he smiles. "Of course you must," he says. Not for the first time, she is struck by the thought that Joseph believes there is no difference between God's will and his own.

Mary sits with Increase Mather in his parlor, surrounded by his books. He smiles at her kindly. "How fare you, sister?" he asks. "Are you content with your lodgings in Mr. Whitcomb's house? Are you well treated?" His benevolence seems genuine, yet she remains cautious.

"Well enough." She thinks of the whispers and narrow-eyed glances of the women during Sabbath worship. She thinks of her husband's reluctance to touch her. "I praise God that our children have been restored."

"And that you are reunited with your husband?" he prompts, still smiling.

She looks at him and unexpectedly her vision blurs. Then,

suddenly, she is in tears, confessing a detail that she thought would never pass her lips. "My husband has not touched me," she sobs, pressing her fingers to her eyes. "Not since my return."

Increase sways back in his great chair, as if her words are a blow to his body. His fists curl over the carved knobs of the chair arms and knead the smooth wooden grooves. A shaft of sunlight suddenly wedges through the diamond windowpanes, then as suddenly shivers and disappears. Mary feels a responsive pang in her chest, prompted as much by her own plight as by the strange play of light.

"Have you done aught to offend him?" His voice is still kindly, though his question is not. "Have you not tried the womanly arts to bring him to you?"

She bows her head and looks into the black cup of her hands. "I have tried everything, sir. He thinks me tainted."

He says nothing. She feels his silence like some great-jawed monster lurking in the shadows, its tongue extruding between gleaming teeth, waiting to swallow her. Increase leans forward; she hears the dry buzz of his sleeves as they scrape the chair arms. His question seems to come from a great distance. "*Be* you tainted, woman? Have all your protestations been a mockery of truth?"

She keeps her head bowed. She does not speak. Cannot speak.

"Your silence condemns you," he says quietly, and sinks back in the chair, letting his head loll against the top rail. "But though you be stained, I warrant it is your own action that defiles you. The savages do not know Christ. They are devils."

"Not all are devils." She still cannot bring herself to look at him.

"Ah." He sighs. In the fireplace a log burns through and falls, sending a shower of sparks across the hearth. "You are right. Yet a good Indian is so rare as to be an irregularity." As he shifts again, sideways this time, his head tips forward so his solemn gaze rests on her once more. "But what has that to do with you, woman? You must confess your defilement and seek redemption."

"I was not defiled by the Indians," she says, her voice a hoarse croak in the darkening room. The cast of light coming through the window tells her that clouds have rolled in and a storm is brewing over the harbor. "No one defiled me but myself."

Increase frowns. "You confess that you have defiled yourself?"

She can think only of James, of the compassion she saw so often in his eyes, the many kindnesses he showed her. Of lying beside him in his wetu, of feeling his dark gaze upon her. She recalls stepping into his embrace, and the way she clung to him as he held her in his arms. She thinks of how her heart was pierced so painfully on the day she was ransomed that she could barely manage to look at him. Yet look she did, for she could not bear to walk away without a final glance.

She chokes back the memory, licks her lips and tastes salt. "My thoughts," she whispers. "I was defiled not by flesh, but by my own desire." She looks up and finally meets his gaze. "It is not what you think," she says. "The Indians. Their ways are different from ours, but they are not born of the Devil. They are most often chaste and kind—"

"Sister Rowlandson!" The words die in her throat as he rises from his chair. "What you say—if it be true—is of no consequence."

She rocks back on the bench. "What would you have me say? An untruth?"

"The only words that matter are those that God ordains." His voice ripples above her, like the disturbed surface of a pond. "I understood you came to discuss the writing of an account of your captivity. For the glorification of God. To show a lost people the chastening rod of His love. The question that lies before us has nothing to do with heathen ways!" His finger stabs the table, as if a manuscript already lies there, waiting to be read, when she has not written a single word. "It is plain that the Lord has used Indians as His rod. The question before us is"—he leans forward and down, so that his face is uncomfortably close to hers—"will you not record your story so that God may be glorified? That a lost people may perceive the mercy of His chastening love?"

She rises slowly, facing him. He is not a tall man, shorter than her husband, only slightly taller than she, and very thin. "I have not yet decided, sir," she says. "I wait upon the guidance of the Lord."

There is nothing he can say to this, no way to refute what she has claimed—the full authority of God over them all.

"Pray, sit down." His voice has softened. It is almost melodious. He has immense control of his tone, more than any other minister she has heard. "Perhaps you do not fully understand why I bid you write this book."

She sinks back onto her bench.

"You have suffered a great ordeal," he says, sweetness and compassion now emanating from him, the sweetness of Christ. His collar is starkly white against his dark brown coat. "Yet it is not your story alone, but ours—all of us here in New England." His arm sweeps out to encompass the room. "It is *God's* story—the story of a covenant people lost in the wilderness. As you were lost." He pauses; he seems to be waiting for his words to penetrate. Perhaps he expects some reaction on her part, some word or gesture to indicate she understands. But she says nothing.

"Do you not see, Sister Rowlandson? *You* are the emblem for all of us. Your story is our own, writ small." His voice rises. "Your ordeal is a testament to God's mercy. To His promise of redemption." To her surprise he sighs; his shoulders sag. "We have suffered beneath His rod for many months. The Indians have slain hundreds of our people." He pauses. "It is never easy to discern God's will. Yet we know He keeps His covenants. So I ask you to write this account that we might all better understand His purposes." He peers at her again. She wonders if his eyes are failing, if he has difficulty seeing her in the dim house light. "You are well now, are you not?" Again, the soothing voice, the tone that softens the stone in her heart. "You have recovered from your tribulation? You and your children have a roof over your heads? All the earthly comforts?"

"Aye," she says.

He nods gravely. "And your husband—surely he is seeking another parish?"

"Yes, I trust he is." And she does trust—she must have trust, for she has no evidence. Since her return Joseph has done little but brood when he is in her presence. The rest of the time he seeks other company, going out at all hours visiting, calling it ministry though she knows it is escape from the spiritual captivity that her return has imposed upon them both. She recognizes it, for doesn't she, of all people, know captivity? Isn't she most intimate with all of its deceits and cunning ways?

"So"—Increase says, leaning forward once again; she feels his movement as a shift in the air, as if a cold cloth has been pressed to her face—"you will demonstrate God's will? His glory?"

"I fear I cannot, sir," she says, "until I understand His way."

"Then I shall tell you how it is to be done." His voice is very low. "You will write down the particulars of your ordeal and I will make of them a testimony. You must leave it to me."

A bitter taste comes into her mouth as she understands his intent—he means to take her story from her and shape it into something she will not recognize. He is requiring her to relinquish her experience to him—just as she relinquished the body of her dead child to the Indians. Nausea flows through her and, with it, a stubborn anger is born.

"I will pray for the Lord's guidance," she says carefully.

He nods. "Ask your husband to come to me," he says. "I have word of a parish that might have need of him. And I will also encourage him to resume his marital duties—"

"No!" She cuts him off, alarmed. "He must not know I told you

of this difficulty between us. It would shame him beyond bearing!"
She reaches toward Increase, beseeching him. "Pray, promise me
you will say nothing. 'Tis best left in the Lord's hands, is it not?"

He folds his hands together and places them on the table. Mary
finds herself staring at them. They look more like a massive fist than
hands in prayer. "I will give you that promise, if you will give me one."

She waits for him to continue, but he seems to be waiting for
her assent. Finally, she dips her head in a submissive nod.

"Promise me that you will not only pray on this project but that
you will ask the Lord's blessing upon it. That you will ask Him to
open your heart to it."

She looks up at him. "I will do what I can, sir." She sees from
his expression that he knows she has promised nothing. Yet they
both smile in the pretense that she has agreed.

J oseph badgers her with questions about the meeting. Did Increase persuade her of the rightness of the endeavor? When will
she begin to write her narrative? How long will she delay? When she
explains that she has agreed to pray on the matter, he informs her
that he will pray, too—pray that she will perceive the wisdom of the
project. Pray that she will quickly perceive that the salvation of New
England depends on her compliance.

She does pray—or tries to. But God is silent. If she is procrasti-
nating in her duty, as Joseph suggests, God has not yet seen fit to
correct her, or soften her heart toward the project. Or toward her
husband.

Nor does she see any sign that God is softening Joseph's heart
toward her.

B y summer, all of Boston is saying that the hostilities are nearly
over; the Indians are beaten. All that remains is that the last of
the rebels be rounded up and punished. Many are captured and

executed. Among them are Praying Indians. Mary thinks often of James. She wonders if he has been arrested, if he will be hanged. Or worse.

Joseph decides that she should attend the executions of those Indians judged guilty of treason. "It will benefit you to see justice brought upon our enemies," he says. "I warrant it will settle your mind."

"Nay, Joseph, I beg you not to require this new duty of me." She looks at him, struggling to keep her face from revealing her horror. "I have witnessed sufficient suffering during my captivity. I would not look upon any more."

"'Tis those guilty of causing all the suffering who will be hanged," he assures her.

"While some are surely guilty," she says carefully, "many have only committed the crime of being born Indian. Which, surely, is no crime at all."

"But they are the very ones who defiled you," he says. "You must agree that the gallows is too merciful for them."

"No one defiled me!" she cries. But he bids her hush and will not listen. Despite her pleas, he is not moved. So she obeys and accompanies him to the hangings, standing beside him as witness, watching the guilty as they are dragged up the gallows ladder to the platform. She hears them cry out their final words; she watches them drop into the air and hang twitching at the end of the long ropes.

Yet she refuses to cheer with the crowd or join Joseph in his prayers of thanksgiving. The spectacle sickens and haunts her. When she walks past the common, where the heads of the condemned are speared on pikes, she turns away from the sight, lest it stop her heart.

The governing council declares an amnesty for any Indians willing to repent their association with Philip and come to Boston. When Mary hears this news, she feels a flutter of excitement—something close to joy. "God is merciful," she says to

Joseph, and asks him what he knows of the amnesty. She wants
to know how it will work. Will the Indians be allowed to return to
their homes? Will some test of loyalty be exacted?

"I cannot say I favor this declaration," he tells her. "It seems
to me it puts us all at risk. Fortunately, the period of the amnesty is
short. And"—he gives her a meaningful look—"I have heard that
each Indian who accepts amnesty must bring in a dozen others with
him. Then he will be indentured to an English family. That, or serve
with a militia unit until the Indian threat is over."

Mary feels a tightening in her own neck. "Enslaved?" she whispers. All she can picture is James shackled in chains. She shakes her
head, as if it might remove the image from her mind.

"Nay, I said *indentured*," Joseph replies. "You will find some
comfort in that, I warrant," Joseph says. "For every Indian restored,
an English family's lot will be improved."

For one vivid moment, she actually hates him.

A fortnight later, all of Massachusetts Bay withers under a three-
day scourge of hot, humid weather. The sun rises dark orange
in a crimson sky. The heat is searing, causing strong men to collapse
as they go about their work. Mary is reminded of the day Bess
Parker gave birth to her son—she recalls the blistering sunrise, how
the air was so thick and hot she found it hard to breathe, how her
sweat-soaked shift clung to her back and thighs all day.

She stays in the house as much as possible, keeping to the down-
stairs rooms when she can, venturing into the cooler cellar for relief.
Marie works beside her without complaint. Joss, however, continually laments his confinement to the house, remarking on how cool
and refreshing the wilderness must be. He frets at the lack of activity
and has begun to talk about going back to the Indians.

Mary's sleep remains restless, filled with dreams. She wakes often in the night, feeling suffocated, trapped. In the morning she

steps outside and draws in great breaths of warm, sea-laden air. She sometimes pretends she is back in the wilderness and the air is winter-cold.

On the third night, long after Joseph and the children have gone to sleep, she slips out and walks up and down the yard in bare feet, wearing only her shift. The moon is full, like a yellow bubble of cream in the black sky; the stars wink softly in the haze. She wishes it would rain.

She hears a footstep behind her and freezes. How many times has Joseph told her that renegade Indians roam the Boston streets at night and that she must stay inside where he can assure her safety? She holds her breath.

"Chikohtqua." The name spoken in the sweetly familiar voice sends lightning through her arms and legs. She turns, her hand to her mouth. James steps out from the shadow of the tall fence that bounds the property.

She sways backward, her eyes wide. He is wearing English breeches but his chest is bare, covered only with a necklace of black beads. His hair is longer than before, plaited and tied with feathers.

He takes a few cautious steps toward her, as if she were a deer, easily startled. She does not back away, does not take her eyes from his.

Then he is standing right in front of her, so close that if she reaches up she can put her arms around his neck and draw him down to kiss her. She squeezes her hands into fists. She does not touch him.

CHAPTER TWENTY-SIX

"James!" she whispers. She hears a sound from inside the house, one she can't identify—the creak of a floorboard perhaps, or the soft shudder of the building as it settles on its foundation. She snaps into the acute awareness that, from a window, she and James can be seen standing together in the yard. That the next sound she hears could be someone raising the alarm.

She takes his hand and quickly draws him into the empty cow-shed. She pulls the door shut and stands before him in the darkness. Her heart is beating fast and she is conscious of his nearness. "How did you find me?" she asks. She has a wild, wicked thought that he has come to claim her and take her away with him.

In the dim light, she detects the flicker of a smile. "'Twas no great feat. You are the most famous woman in the colony now."

"You should not be here," she says quickly. "There is a bounty posted on Indians."

He nods. "I know. 'Tis why I travel by night, for I know you English regard darkness as your enemy. Is it not why you white-wash the insides of your houses? Why you endlessly dip candles and press oil for your lamps? Why you are forever talking about light?"

She wonders why he is taking the time to make this little speech. It is as if he is preparing for debate before a court and wants to practice on her.

She shakes her head, dismissing his rhetorical questions. "Where have you been? Why have you come?"

"Because you can help me. If you speak to the right people, you can make it possible for me to live."

She smells his scent over the mustiness of the shed. "What influence do you imagine I have?" A streak of moonlight slices through a broken board and lies across the slope of his left shoulder. Her eyes have adjusted; she can see his face now. "Have you forgotten I am but a meek and humble woman?"

"I could never forget you are a woman." The flickering smile again. "But humble you are not. Nor meek. Else you would not have prevailed during your captivity."

She cannot deny this. Nor does she wish to. Her heart is beating wildly. Foolishly. "And why should I help you?"

"Surely you have not forgot that I helped you," he says. "Many times. Now it is your turn."

Her face flushes with inner heat. Yet she pretends she is not moved—the habit of concealment is strong. She narrows her eyes. "I recollect that you refused me. When I begged your help in getting to Albany, you said you would not."

"I cut the rope from your neck," he says. "I gave you shelter in the storm."

She shudders slightly, a tiny movement of her shoulders. "You betrayed me and arranged my ransom to the English," she whispers, so softly that at first she thinks he cannot hear. But his frown—a flash of pain on his brow—tells her otherwise.

"*Chikohtqua*," he says, his voice reproachful, disappointment laced with sadness, "you *know* I did not deceive you. You know I did all I could to protect you. There was no future for you among my people because there is no future for any of us. Apart from life among the English."

She bows her head, all her anger and doubts crumbling away. What bitterness toward him she felt disappears in an instant. It requires all her willpower not to touch him, to stroke his face or his chest, to move into the circle of his arms.

She hears the sound of his breathing, the skittering of a mouse in the corner. "Can you not come in under the amnesty?" The musty air bores into her nostrils.

"The amnesty is for those who are guilty of nothing more than being in the wrong place at the wrong time. I am"—he pauses—"not in that category. A special case. There are many who think me the Devil's colleague, who consider me the worst of traitors and would like nothing better than to see me hang."

She thinks of Joseph, of his fervent cheers after each execution.

"I have more guilt upon my head than most who have hanged," he says.

"Guilt?" She tries to imagine what he might be guilty of. "What harm did you do?"

"I went with the Nipmuc on raids. I carried a musket. I met with Philip."

"But the Council does not know these things. What evidence is there?"

"In truth, I have provided them evidence by my own hand. Though the Council needs no evidence to hang an Indian."

"What do you mean—by your own hand?"

He sighs. "After we burned Medfield, I posted a letter in my hand warning the English that if they continued to fight, they would lose not only their lives but also their houses and cattle. I wrote that we would fight for twenty-one years if necessary."

She is silent, absorbing this news. "But surely you know some who could help you better than I. You have mentioned Mr. Eliot."

"I have already seen him," he says. "Last night I surprised him in his kitchen and asked for his help. He told me he had already petitioned the authorities on my behalf and they refused to listen. War is a stern mercy, he said, but it is God's mercy."

"I think it is no mercy at all," she whispers.

"Aye," he says softly. "You speak true—it is not. But Mr. Eliot was right in one thing—for he told me what I have told you—that the Indian way cannot prevail. That, though God may chastise the English, yet He protects them. For they belong to Him. They are His people."

She sees no evidence that the English are any more God's people than the Indians or the Irish or the Spanish, but she can think of no good response. Mr. Eliot's words are much like Joseph's— proclamations she no longer believes are true. They reflect a vision of God that now seems to her cruel and whimsical, a God whose wrath no man can stay, through prayer or by any other means. This is a God she cannot worship.

"And you believe I know someone who can be prevailed upon to save you from the hangman?" she says slowly. "Someone who has more sway than Mr. Eliot?"

He shrugs. "I know you have had the ears of many powerful men since your release. I ask simply that you try to persuade them to show mercy."

His words resonate as she casts about in her mind for anyone she has met who is powerful enough to help James. "I will do what I can," she says. "Yet I fear no Englishman will listen to a woman."

"In truth, you are my last hope, *Chikohtqua*." He takes her hand and presses her palm to the center of his chest. She nearly gasps with the longing that strokes through her. His skin is warm and damp. She wants desperately to kiss him, to feel his arms around her. She has the thought—the sinful, depraved *hope*—that he will ask her to leave everything and go with him. But she says nothing for she knows as well as he does that they are both caught in a web of circumstance not of their making, but from which it is impossible to escape.

They stand together in silence for several minutes. She takes a deep breath, and slides her hand out from under his. The beads on his necklace glint in the moonlight.

"You had best leave," she says. "Before someone sees you and sounds the alarm."

He says nothing, but brushes her cheek with his thumb, a touch as light as the wing of a butterfly. Then he slips out the door and is gone.

She stands in the shed. She can smell his skin on the tips of her fingers. She must think of something she can do to help him. She does not want to be his last hope.

For days, Mary ponders whom she should approach to beg for James's amnesty. She has met with several important magistrates since she first returned and she once dined with a group of ministers and their wives. She remembers being introduced to prominent officials from Boston who studied her as if she were a curiosity, brought back from an alien shore. Yet none stand out as useful to James's case, and she is at a loss to remember their names.

She considers asking Joseph to introduce her to someone on the Council. If she approaches the matter cleverly, he might reveal an important connection. The trick will be to make *him* feel sufficiently important and powerful.

In the end, she turns for guidance to God—though she is no longer certain she believes in His ability to affect events. She prays, humbling herself several times each day. She knows that her increased show of piety pleases Joseph. Though he does not discern the reason for her prayers, he praises her devoutness and patience. He assures her they will be rewarded in due time.

But Mary knows that the one thing she does not have is time.

Quite unexpectedly an answer presents itself. Joseph reports that Increase has grown impatient with waiting for her response to his proposal. He demands an audience. And suddenly Mary discerns a way she can help James.

She sits on a bench against the wall, facing Increase in his great chair by the empty fireplace in his parlor. Sunlight spangles the tiny diamond panes of his windows, yet the room is still dark. He presses the palms of his hands together.

"So my prayers have been answered." He smiles at Mary. "God has guided you to record your ordeal. To shine His light upon New England."

"I have received His guidance, aye," she says. "Though it is not quite as you may think."

He raises one eyebrow. "I do not understand."

She wets her lips and takes a deep breath. "The Lord has made it clear to me that He requires of New England a sacrifice. Else all my efforts will be in vain."

"A sacrifice?" He taps the tips of his fingers together, and she senses annoyance in the gesture. "Have we not already sacrificed much? Please explain yourself." She senses that he suspects she is thwarting him. She must make him believe her proposal is God's will, not her own.

She settles her hands in her lap, composes herself. Looks up at him. "I must confess that sometimes, during my captivity, I strayed from—nay, I *doubted*—God's providence. I came to believe He was not present in the wilderness."

Increase shakes his head sadly. "Our Lord inhabits every place." Sweetness and compassion permeate his voice. "It is our task to discern His presence, not His task to discern ours."

She nods. "I understand that now. But I underwent a great trial—a *testing*—and I want to impart its meaning in my narrative."

He nods. "And so you shall. I shall see to it." He lowers his head so that his mouth rests briefly on his templed index fingers. Then he looks at her. "But what is this added sacrifice that you believe the Lord requires?"

"'Tis a sacrifice of mercy," Mary says slowly, cautiously choosing each word. Her mouth and lips feel dry. "There is one Praying Indian—James the Printer"—she tries to ignore his sudden grimace—"who must be returned to Boston to carry on his trade." She pauses, waits for his face to resume its normal expression. "The Lord has a particular mission for him."

Increase nods, but his lips are pursed; he clearly does not accept her claim. "The Lord is rarely so explicit." He places his hands on his knees. "Especially toward one such as yourself."

He means toward a woman, she thinks. Her hands have balled into fists of their own accord. Yet she nods as if she agrees, then says carefully, "I am told that you are able to clearly read His meaning in signs and portents, such as in the shapes of clouds and the position of constellations. That you prophesied the Indian rebellion."

His eyes narrow as he looks at her, yet she catches the ghost of a smile. He is obviously flattered; she has touched his secret pride.

"So surely you cannot deny that sometimes God is both clear and precise in His messages."

He nods slowly. "This is your requirement? Freedom for James the Printer? In exchange for your narrative?"

"Not *my* requirement. I believe it to be *God's* will," she says in the softest voice she can manage.

"How well do you know this James?" His gaze is bright with suspicion.

"He was one of many I met during—"

But he is not listening to her. "Are you aware that he is a deceitful traitor and mischief-maker? That there is a great price on his head?"

She looks at him dumbly. She cannot allow her face to show any emotion.

"You are asking on his behalf for mercy. For amnesty." He shakes his head. "I'm afraid I cannot grant such a demand."

"Not even if it be God's will?" She knows she risks being accused of heresy. She has not forgotten Ann Hutchinson. At best, he will regard her question as disrespectful and insolent. She could end up pilloried or locked in the stocks. Or banished from the colony. Yet she continues. "I believe you *can*—should you wish to. I believe most of the authorities heed you closely."

Again she sees he is flattered, that he likes thinking of himself as a man of great influence, that he *wants* to believe her. She leans in toward him, as if she is about to offer a secret.

"The Printer showed me mercy," she says quietly. "He is the Lord's servant."

"Showed you mercy," he murmurs.

"Aye, more than once. I believe the Lord wishes to reward him for his faithfulness. I think that is why He has instructed me to write the narrative you want—once the Printer is granted amnesty."

There is a long silence and Mary suspects that the sun has shifted behind clouds, for the room has grown suddenly darker.

"I must pray on it," Increase says. "And consult with others." And now he leans toward her. "I warrant you do not comprehend the profound impact your story will have. Not only upon its readers—but upon you as well. I believe it will mean your redemption back into society."

She feels herself begin to tremble. He is telling her that he will accept the bargain.

CHAPTER TWENTY-SEVEN

A few days later, Increase again summons Mary to his parlor. It is raining, a warm drizzle that soaks through her cloak and renders the cobblestones slippery under her shoes. She thinks of how the deerskin dress she wore during her captivity had shed the rain, how surely her feet had gripped the ground through the soles of her moccasins.

Increase does not smile at her this time; his face is solemn and pale. He does not even invite her to be seated. He sits in his chair and speaks slowly in a low voice, carefully choosing each word. "Arrangements have been made to grant James Printer a special amnesty. He must come in during the two-week period assigned by the Council. And because of his past, he is subject to an additional obligation."

"What is this obligation?" She can see his jaw working. She wonders if he is angry.

"He must present the heads of two of his Indian compatriots to the authorities in Boston. In token of his loyalty."

Mary stares at him. Her mouth feels as if it has suddenly filled with dust. She tries to imagine James's reaction to this decree. How could he possibly accept such an arrangement? He will flee instead, head north, deeper into the wilderness.

"That is too much to ask," she says, her voice rasping in her dry throat. "He will never agree. You must remove this requirement."

Mr. Mather shakes his head. "It is not mine to remove. It comes from the authorities by way of Daniel Gookin himself."

Daniel Gookin. Mary recalls her encounter with Silvanus in Mr. Gookin's house. Mr. Gookin, who once *owned* Silvanus. A chill runs down her back.

"He has done a great deal of work with the Praying Indians," Increase continues. "You should know that it is only through his advocacy that the authorities even *considered* James Printer's case for amnesty."

Mary cannot think what she should say. She is certain that James will not agree to this condition. She cannot parse out whether she should withdraw her agreement to write the narrative of her captivity. She must speak with James, must learn his wishes given this new stipulation.

But Mr. Mather is not waiting for her response. "You will begin writing your narrative at once," he says. "I shall edit your pages, and provide all such guidance as you may require, so that your work may be an emblem for the enlightenment of New England."

She stares at him. She feels a dull throb behind her eyes—the beginning of a headache.

"There is one additional condition to our covenant." He leans forward over his knees, his back slanting over the space between them. Her feet shift uneasily beneath her skirts, making small tapping sounds on the wooden floor. "That pertains particularly to you. A condition upon which the Printer's freedom—his very life—depends."

She feels trapped. She has foolishly failed to anticipate that the authorities would require something beyond a manuscript of her story. "You have pledged to preserve his life in exchange for my narrative," she says slowly.

"Aye," he says, "but it will only be possible if the connection between those two things is completely hidden from public view. The exchange must be kept an absolute secret. Not even your husband can be told."

"I don't understand." Her mouth and lips are very dry.

His eyes go hard. Mary feels as if she's failed some test. "I cannot be seen bartering for the life of a *savage*." His voice is a hiss. "Surely you can understand *that*!"

"I had not thought—"

"No, apparently you had not. So I will make it plain to you: There cannot be the slightest *whisper* of any involvement on my part—or yours—in his reprieve. If James Printer is to live, you shall have no contact with him. Ever. You shall not seek him out to find out how he fares. You shall not speak to him if you encounter him on the street. You shall not communicate with him by letter or messenger or any other means." He pauses, slides back so that his head is resting against the knot of decorative scrollwork at the top of the chair. "He will be as dead to you. Else, he *will* be dead—arrested, tortured, and executed. As he no doubt deserves."

She stares at him, trying to absorb his words. She feels dizzy, ill. The price she must pay for James's freedom—for his life—will be his complete removal from her life. And the price he must pay is even more horrific.

She does not think she can bear it. She will never see him again. James—*the man she loves*. She is stunned by the thought. It jars her so violently that for a moment she sees nothing but a blank oval where the minister's face should be. Since childhood she has been taught that love belongs to God, that love of things and people is a certain path to damnation. It is the reason Joseph warned her against loving her children, the reason he never said he loved her. The reason he forbade her from ever saying she loved him.

And indeed, she realizes now, as she sits facing Mr. Mather in his dark parlor, that she never has loved Joseph. It is nothing like the mixture of passion and devotion, gratitude and longing she feels for James. The feeling that she cannot bear to be alive without him.

Yet before this moment, she had no idea her feelings for James were in any way related to love. In fact, she has rigorously avoided examining those feelings. Was she afraid of the truth she would find there?

Dazed, she looks around the room and focuses again with difficulty on Mr. Mather's long face. "He is Christian," she says quietly.

"Pardon me?" He seems genuinely puzzled by her statement.

"James Printer is a true Christian," she says. "Baptized in the Lord. He is not a savage. He was kind to me."

He shakes his head. "I fail to see how that pertains," he says. "This covenant is between you and me. And it is binding. It cannot be broken without consequence. You must agree today—now—or there will be no amnesty for the Printer."

She feels cold all over. As if the rain that soaked her clothes has turned to ice against her skin. She holds herself erect so that she will not shiver.

"I agree," she says. "I shall begin writing my story directly. This very afternoon."

Mary sharpens one of the quills from Joseph's writing box, then sits at the small table in the parlor, where she has already arranged the bottle of black ink and the two precious sheets of paper she purchased in the market. The table, donated by a member of Increase's congregation, is so wobbly it can be used only when pushed against the wall. She arranges a sheet on the wooden surface and carefully smoothes it under her hand. She has to force her thoughts away from James. How odd—now that she is banned from seeing him, she is filled with longing. Only a month ago she felt anger and bitterness toward him, counted him as one who had betrayed her. Now she knows he is the only man she has ever loved. Her mind races, inventing one ruse after another to outmaneuver Increase so that she can see James again. She *must* find a way to meet him. She needs to know if he will comply with the grisly requirement sent down by the Boston authorities. And she must be certain that he knows what she has agreed to do, that she has repaid all his kindnesses in full. That she has saved his life. As he saved hers.

She stares down at the blank paper in front of her. First, she must make good on her promise so that Mr. Mather will have no excuse to break his part of the covenant.

She dips the quill into the ink. She cannot think how to begin. With the selectmen's order to garrison the town? With her husband's departure for Boston? With the snowstorm the night before the attack? With the shriek she confused with the wind? She recalls kneeling on the hearth and hearing the first musket shot as she tried to bring the fire to life.

She sees that the ink has dried on the quill while she sat thinking. She dips her pen again and begins to write. The words come with difficulty, with painful slowness, one or two at a time. She starts with the day of the attack, that terrible morning of death and destruction that still plagues her dreams and shortens her sleep.

On the tenth of February, 1675, came the Indians in great numbers upon Lancaster. Their first coming was about sun-rising.

Her words cover less than half the page when Marie comes through the door carrying a basket of goods from the market. Mary quickly blots the paper to dry the ink, realizing that she foolishly has not thought of a place to keep her narrative. She cannot leave it sitting on the table in plain sight, for it will quickly be stained with grease and all manner of other substances.

She rises, takes the page and slides it under the mattress of their bedstead. It will have to wait until she can spare another few minutes to add to it. She wipes her hands on her apron and turns to greet her daughter.

"Did you find some good onions?" she asks, taking the basket from Marie's arm and setting it on the table.

Marie nods but does not answer, and Mary's stomach knots. A maternal response, as much a part of her being as her bones and blood. "What is it? Did something vex you at the market?"

Marie dips her head—a gesture of submission all girls learn at their mothers' knees. *It can also signal evasion,* Mary thinks.

"You'd best unburden yourself," she says, pulling the towel off the basket and briskly taking out three onions, a small wheel of cheese, and a loaf of bread. "Did you bargain well for this?" she asks, sniffing, confirming her suspicion that it is not fresh.

But Marie does not answer. Her glance slides sideways and she appears unduly busy with her apron.

Mary sets the loaf on the table and steps directly in front of her daughter. "I'll have no more of this. Speak the plain truth, child."

Marie sobs and covers her face with her hands. Mary takes her by the wrists and gently draws her hands away. "Come, tell me."

And finally Marie confesses what she overheard in the market. "I heard a woman say your name when I was near the weaver's stall. I peeked over the bolts of cloth to look. There were two of them— finely dressed they both were, with great wide sleeves and lace collars. They spoke exceeding ill of you, Mother." Her eyes are swimming with tears.

"Tell me," Mary says—although, in truth, she does not want to hear.

"They said you are unclean. That you brought back queer manners from the wilderness. That you cannot rule your children. That you are tainted."

Mary feels the air in her lungs go cold. She bites down hard on the words she longs to say. "Go on, child," she says instead. "Tell me all."

Marie takes a shuddering breath. "They said if nothing happened, why do you not speak freely of your time in the wilderness?"

A laugh burbles up through Mary's chest, but she does not release it. "'Tis ignorance, plain and simple," she whispers.

"'Tis *malice*, Mother," Marie says, looking at her directly now. "And it infects others."

Mary cannot deny this. She recalls the many conversations she had with her sisters and friends about Bess Parker, how quickly rumors and falsehoods had spread from one woman to another. She had not thought of the stories as malicious, but they had certainly been infectious.

"'Tis fear that is infectious, daughter," she says. "And one thing alone casts out fear."

"Perfect love casteth out fear, for fear hath painfulness, and he that feareth, is not perfect in love," Marie recites dutifully. But her face is still sullen with anger and it is plain she does not believe the words.

Or even understand them, Mary tells herself. *But then, who among us does?*

She thinks of her captivity, how terrified she was in the first weeks, how desperately she wanted to believe that Joseph was coming to rescue her. How James had frightened her at first. For she had believed he could not be trusted—not because of what he had done, but simply because he was an *Indian.*

How strangely things had been turned and twisted. How poorly her experience had matched her expectations. It was James she had failed to trust, but he had saved her. And Joseph, whom she trusted, had not come for her. *Not even as far as Concord after her release.*

Love. She is required to love, honor, and obey her husband. But what does such love mean? It is not desire; it is not affection. *It is simply one more duty.*

Mary writes her story as she has time, and slowly the words and sentences accumulate. Though it is a duty she did not choose, to her surprise she finds that the more she writes, the more she wants to write. She ponders which words she can use to best express her terror in the days after she was captured, how she can explain her frantic grief when Sarah died. Her waking thoughts are consumed with how to convey her experience.

She longs to hear news that James Printer has come in under the amnesty but she dares not ask anyone. Joseph is clearly pleased that she has agreed to Increase's plan, and credits himself with persuading her. She does not contradict him. He believes he will benefit in some important way from her labors. She is startled to find that she does not care. Her future—her security and safety—has been inextricably linked to his since the day she married him. Always, before now, she did all she could to ease his life, since whatever was in his interests was in hers as well.

She knows, by the way Joseph watches her when she is writing, that he wants to read her pages. But a perverse caution grips her. She purchases a wooden box with a key in which to keep the pages and she shows them to no one. She finds a loose board in the wainscoting by their bed and hides the box there when no one is looking.

She has known for weeks that she is the subject of gossip. Still, she has to go out among the people of Boston and strive to be accepted. The men are courteous and kindly, though she notes a hesitation behind their smiles. She suspects that their benevolence is more in deference to Joseph and his friends than a mark of personal regard.

Mary reads the women more easily. Their glances and whispers plainly proclaim their doubts about her virtue. It is now common knowledge that she came to Bess Parker's defense the evening before the attack on Lancaster. This leads many to conclude that she was unchaste when she lived among the Indians.

One afternoon in late July, Joseph informs Mary of a more vicious rumor. He finds her in the yard, bent over the laundry kettle, scrubbing a stained apron. He asks her to put down her work and attend to him. She shakes the water and soap from her hands and wipes them on her apron, glad for the respite, however brief. Hands clasped behind his back, he paces back and forth between the garden and fence that separates their yard from the neighbor's. His head is bent so that his gaze falls on his shoes.

His manner unnerves her and Mary feels her stomach clench. *What has he heard?* She has the terrifying thought that it has something to do with James.

Finally he stops pacing and faces her. "You have sworn that you were not violated during your time with the Indians," he says. "Yet there is now word among the good people of Boston that you were wife to a savage. What am I to make of this?"

She sucks in a sharp breath. "You must not make anything of it," she says slowly. "'Tis but the idle nattering of gossips, for I had no intimacy with any savage." Yet even as she speaks, she is thinking of James, how his kindness had opened her heart, how his warm glances had roused her. She draws up her shoulders so her back is as straight as a board. She knows she must face Joseph boldly, must show no fear, for he will surely interpret it as guilt. "Who is it I am said to have been joined to? Or have these scandalmongers not even troubled themselves to supply a name?"

He gives her a hard look, assured that his gaze will ferret out the truth. "There *is* a name. One-Eyed John. A Nashaway sachem, recently hanged. He is not unknown to me for he was often in Lancaster."

Monoco. Mary recalls the sachem's ruined eye and the shameless way he clutched her hair. She remembers Weetamoo's mocking dismissal. She recalls James telling her that Monoco had ordered her capture and that he wanted to take her for a wife. And that he had supplied the horse on which she and Sarah rode to Menameset.

"He was in the Indian camp," she says. "But I did not become his wife."

"Did he not violate you?" Joseph's hands are still tucked behind his back where Mary cannot see them. "Did you not prevail upon this Monoco for protection? Did you not trade your virtue for food?"

"As God is my judge, I did not." She presses her own hands against her waist, forcing them to be very still. "As I have told you, again and again, no one violated me."

"Then wherefore this tale?" Joseph looks bewildered. "There must be some truth to it, else it would not have spread so far."

"'Tis the Devil's work," she says. "These are vile lies. Rumors! Am I to be punished for sins I have not committed?" She does not know who is behind the story, but Monoco's interest was no secret in the Indian camps. "Rumors do not need evidence to grow," she reminds him. "All they require is an evil tongue and an eager ear."

He says nothing. He appears to be waiting for her to say more.

She looks at the ground and sees that her wet shoes are powdered gray with dust. "I believe Monoco wished to purchase me from my mistress," she says after a silence. "But she would not sell me."

"Ah," he says. "There it is—the kernel of truth that feeds the lie." He straightens, drawing to his full height, as he so often did when facing the congregation. "We must do what we can to repair your reputation. Lest we both become outcasts."

She thinks of Bess Parker, and how she was shunned in Lancaster. How cruelly the women spoke of her. Now Mary has become the outsider, the subject of scorn and gossip, the banished exile. Perhaps she deserves no less.

Joseph steps toward her, his hands falling to his sides. "Yet I still perceive guilt writ upon your face."

She meets his wounded gaze. "If there be guilt in me, 'tis not because I was unchaste, but because I could not save our poor Sarah's life."

"Aye, 'tis a pity you could not mend her," he says. "But you should not let it burden you unduly. The Lord will use her death for His purposes."

"His purposes?" she says in a thin voice. "How can the death of a child suit His purposes?"

He gives her a long look. "That is not ours to answer. Only your prayers can shed some light in that darkness."

She knows he does not mean his words unkindly, but they scorch her heart. She pictures Sarah's inert body lying on the floor of Quenêke's wetu. She thinks of the terrible cries Bess Parker uttered when her son was taken from her. She hears again the eerie keening of Indian women when their babes died. None of these seem to have any purpose except sorrow.

CHAPTER TWENTY-EIGHT

The summer deepens and Mary grows languid in the heat. One afternoon the air is so hot that she sheds her shoes and stockings. When Joseph finds her sitting on the front stoop mending a pair of Joss's breeches, he yanks her to her feet and steers her quickly inside.

"This is not an Indian camp, Mary." His face is almost purple. "You know their ways are sinful."

"What do you know of Indian ways?" She jerks her arm from his possessive fingers and angrily stuffs the thread and needle into her pocket. She is no longer willing to passively submit to his ignorance.

He is startled for no more than a moment. "I am your husband," he says. "Do not shame me." He points to her feet.

She looks at her dirt-caked toes. "How does the comfort of my feet bring shame on you, husband?" she asks, though she knows the answer—bare feet and uncovered legs are signs of a whorish nature. Yet how is it that the Indians can dress as they choose—for comfort and freedom—without chastisement from their fellows? The severe conventions of English dress, which fall most heavily on women, seem old things, relics of some dark age before she was born.

He shakes his head. "I know you are still suffering from your ordeal, Mary. But these spells—"

"*Spells?*" Her back goes as rigid as the floorboards beneath her naked feet. The threat of witchcraft is palpable in the air. She remembers the times Joseph was called to consult over the signs of witchcraft in towns near Lancaster. How he always returned home agitated and frightened. "I suffer no spells, let me assure you."

He closes his eyes and goes to the chair in the corner of the room—the chair given by the members of Increase's church—and sits down. He carefully places his hands on the arms and looks up at her. "Please, sit ye down." His tone has changed. He addresses her as a farmer speaks to a fretful animal—patiently, gently. "I have news that will interest you."

Mary drops onto the bench by the hearth and tries to feign interest despite her anger. But her pretense quickly fades when he tells her the authorities have taken custody of many Indian children orphaned in the recent hostilities. "Some are old enough to be bound out as slaves," he says.

She narrows her eyes and hardens her jaw at the word *slaves*. She starts to say something, but Joseph cuts her off.

"Most will be sent to Barbados, of course. But there are some"— here he smiles at her—"some who are young and docile enough to be suitable in English homes. And I have been honored"—he pauses again, a technique he has long used in his sermons for dramatic effect—"nay, *we* have been honored to be offered one of those children."

Mary's heart leaps at the prospect of another child to care for. To love. "I would be pleased to adopt one," she says, eagerly nodding. "Perhaps a girl. Though she cannot replace Sarah in my heart."

Joseph frowns. "Adopt one? Mary, these children are *Indians*. They are being offered as *slaves*."

Finally she perceives his meaning and in that instant her happiness turns to revulsion. "You would bring a slave into our house?" Her fingers twitch so violently in her lap that she has to push her hands under her apron to still them. "Have you so quickly forgot that *I* was a slave? Joseph"—she leans so far toward him in her earnestness that she almost rises from the bench—"I was sold like an animal at market. I was dragged everywhere against my will. Made to do the meanest task for no reason. Threatened with death many times at the whim of my mistress." Her words come out in a rush, so quickly that she gasps for breath when she stops. It is only then, as she stares at Joseph's stunned face, that she realizes she has told him more about her captivity in a single moment than she has in all the weeks since her release.

He shifts in his chair, and by his expression she can see that he is carefully weighing his words before he speaks.

"I know you have suffered greatly," he says. "But you are not of a race born to slavery, and your feelings are more finely tuned—"

She interrupts him. "Do you think *Indians* are born to slavery? They value freedom above all things. They bow to no one. Their children are raised up strong and unfettered, disciplined not by chastisement, but by love."

He sighs and slowly shakes his head. "These heathen ways you speak of are not *God's* ways, as well you know. Their liberty is not the freedom of Christ. They do not know the Lord and thus are subject to every corruption and temptation. Think on this: Slavery's yoke may yet be their salvation. And you must not forget that God has ordained slavery and set down His ordinances for it in Scripture." He slides forward on the seat of his chair so that his knees seem to point accusingly at her. "What of Timothy? The Nashaway boy whose poor service we suffered for months until he ran away? You had no pangs of conscience then. Do you now imagine we oppressed him? That we were not kind masters?"

"I know 'tis in the Bible." She bows her head, stung as her own guilty part in the matter assails her. "Yet it is wrong. I *know* it is wrong. It is blood on our hands." She looks up at him. "I believe God Himself has given me this knowledge."

She sees his frown and knows that she has vexed him.

"You would condemn all the good Christian men in this colony who keep and sell slaves." His voice is little more than a hiss. The room's shadows have folded over his face in such a way that she can no longer see his eyes. "And with them good Mr. Whitcomb, who has loaned us the use of this house."

"Mr. Whitcomb?" Mary's hands tremble beneath her apron. "What has Mr. Whitcomb to do with slaves?"

"He ships them to Barbados and sells them for profit. Did you not know this? 'Tis his most lucrative business."

Mary thinks of Mr. Whitcomb, who has always seemed a kindly and generous man. Recently she sewed a shirt of fine linen to thank him for his beneficence. Yet this news that he trades in slaves turns her gratitude to repugnance.

"Then we shall bide here no longer." She gets to her feet. "I cannot bear thinking of it. I cannot." As she speaks, her voice rises and she begins to tremble. "We must remove to some other dwelling at once."

"What foolishness is this?" Joseph rises. "We are in no position to refuse Mr. Whitcomb's charity over some foolish sentiment. One would think you had never poked your nose into the Bible, the way you jabber. Be silent!"

But Mary is unable to obey. Her tongue has been torn loose from her palate; she is filled with indignant fire. "I'll keep no slave anymore, husband. Not while I live! 'Tis the greatest of sins!" She knows her own words are not only disobedient but also heretical, and that such rebelliousness has cost more than one woman her life. Yet she is no more able to prudently still her tongue than she was in the Indian encampment when she railed against Weetamoo's demands. When outrage overcame her there, she thought it was an effect of her hunger. But perhaps it was born of something else.

Joseph gawps as if she has become suddenly deranged. In two strides, he crosses the floor to her. "Quiet yourself," he says, placing his hands on her shoulders, a gesture that has sometimes soothed her in the past. But this time his touch burns through her clothes like fire. "Your weeks among the Indians have demented you," he says.

"I am quite sane," she tells him. "I have sworn—to the Lord— that I will never again keep a slave. It is too humiliating. Too despicable. It is not a fit position for any man, woman, or child."

"Mary, they are *Indians*—not beasts. Calm yourself."

"Nay, we *treat* them as beasts. And I'll not have such corruption in my house." She turns and goes back outside, leaving him standing alone in the gloom.

That night, Mary does not retire until long after Joseph has gone to bed, pretending the need to finish mending Joss's shirt. So it is not until the next morning, after family prayers, that Joseph chastises her. She stands before him obediently with her head bowed and listens as he reads long verses of Scripture that justify the keeping of slaves. Yet she does not yield. She refuses to apologize or recant her words. Even when he commands her to pray for God's forgiveness, she feels herself grow stronger and more determined to resist the outrage of slavery.

In the days that follow, Mary cannot rid her thoughts of the certainty that slavery is the vilest of sins. She is no longer able to walk through the rooms where they live without remembering that the owner trades in human flesh.

She hopes that Joseph will soon find a new ministry. Living in the house sickens her and the early kindnesses of the women of Boston have turned to whispers and stares. The longer Mary stays in town, the more the gossips' tongues are fed. She knows—as she always has—that a woman's reputation is easily lost on the slimmest of suspicions and, once lost, impossible to regain.

The only solace she finds is in her children. She minds them with an animal ferocity. She will not allow Marie out of her sight and daily pleads with Joss to keep close to the house. That he does not heed her is a trial to her all summer. His restlessness drives him to frequent the docks, where she fears he mingles with disreputable men and boys. He neglects his chores and comes and goes as he chooses. He begins to adopt Indian ways and spends hours in the woods and swamps beyond Boston Gate, setting cunning traps for squirrels and rabbits. He takes knives from the kitchen so he can clean the animals and wear their skins on his belt. Mary reports none of this to Joseph, knowing that she will not be able to tolerate his remedy.

Joss, who had in the first few days after his return talked endlessly of his captivity, is now so rarely present that Mary hardly speaks with him at all. Yet Marie is ever at her side, and so they speak often of their time among the Indians, comparing masters and wetus, and the taste of Indian food. Marie frequently speaks of an Indian girl she befriended, confessing that she still prays for her welfare. Once, as they sit sewing in the dooryard, Marie confides that she was fond of her mistress, who treated her kindly, slipped extra food to her from time to time, and even taught her some Wampanoag words. When Mary tells her about Alawa and Weetamoo, Marie's eyes grow wide.

"My Indian mistress and the other women spoke often of Weetamoo!" In her excitement, Marie jumps up, dropping the stocking she has been mending. She is still somewhat wasted from the rigors of her captivity, yet her girlish vitality has returned and Mary is pleased to see that she grows stronger each day. "They said she was a warrior queen, known everywhere for her courage. Tell me, Mother, what was she like? Was she very beautiful?"

Mary blinks in surprise. It has not occurred to her that Marie would have heard anything of Weetamoo. "Perhaps she was beautiful to Indian eyes," Mary says. "I saw no display of courage, though it was plain that many venerated her." She remembers the times that James warned her of Weetamoo's power. She had given his words little heed, for it had seemed absurd that a woman could have such influence.

"But she must have had courage," Marie says. "There are many tales of her noble deeds as she led her warriors in battle."

Mary frowns, trying to imagine this, but she cannot. Even Weetamoo, with all her pride, was not so unnatural a woman. She had a child, whom Mary saw her lovingly attend. Mary cannot picture her taking up a musket. She wonders what has become of her. Has she gone into hiding in some wretched swamp?

"Come sit down and finish your mending," she commands Marie. "We'll talk no more of Indians this day."

Mary visits her sisters as often as she is able. Yet the journey to Wenham, where Hannah is living with Joanna, is neither easy nor safe, and so she does not undertake the ride often. Hannah is in deep mourning. Her husband, John, and her son Josiah were butchered during the attack. Two of her children remain in captivity. All that is left of her family is four-year-old William, who was released at the same time as Joss. When Mary sees her, she tries to comfort her, yet she has little solace to offer. They usually spend their time weeping as they exchange recollections of the dead.

After Mary's third trip to Wenham, Joseph forbids future visits. When Mary protests, he reminds her that she always comes home filled with despair. "You must set the past aside and gird yourself for the future," he tells her. "Such mourning is an affront to God's will." Mary knows this is true, but it angers her that her husband holds such authority over her that he can forbid her visiting her own sister.

She begins to yearn for another child. It occurs to her that if she could hold a babe in her arms once more, it would soothe the soreness that invaded her heart when Sarah died. When will her husband again seek the tenderness of marital union? Joseph is a man bound by duty and law, and he knows full well that a husband has an obligation to satisfy his wife's carnal needs. Yet, he still has not joined with Mary, or even embraced her. As the days pass, what began as Mary's mild annoyance becomes desolation. One night, as they prepare for bed, she confronts him.

"You have not touched me as a man touches a woman," she says. She sits on a stool by the open window. It is very warm and there is a skim of perspiration on her fingers as she plaits her hair.

Joseph sways back on his heels, as if her words are a blow to his body. His fingers curl over the cuffs of his nightshirt and he kneads the fabric there. The candle on the mantel suddenly flares up, and then shivers and sinks down. Mary feels a responsive pang in her chest, prompted as much by Joseph's stricken look as by her own plight.

But she is resolved to know what can be done to restore their marriage. "Have I done aught to cause you to lose desire for me as your wife?" she asks.

"Nay," he says quietly. "I still have a husbandly desire for you."

"Then why will you not cleave to me?" She puts down her comb. "Do you think me contaminated?"

Joseph sighs. "You have sworn to me that you are not, and so I must believe you." The glow from the candle flickers along the bridge of his nose and chin. "Yet the Lord has told me the time for our reunion has not yet come. I have prayed long and hard on this." He shifts sideways and his head tips forward so that his solemn gaze rests on her face. "You must trust in the Lord, as I do."

There is no response she can make to this. If he believes God has commanded him to abstain from lovemaking, he will pay no attention to her. She is distracted by the worm of light on his face and the dry buzz of his sleeves as he crosses his arms. She suddenly recalls the way James looked at her after her release. She thinks of how much yearning lay between them.

"—the only actions that matter are those that God ordains," Joseph is saying, his voice rippling around her like the disturbed surface of a pond. "You rebuke me for not performing my husbandly duty, yet you do not answer my questions."

She chokes back the memory of James, licks her lips and tastes salt. "I have told you what I could." She rises and faces him.

He is not a tall man, yet he seems at that moment to tower over her as he tells her, "Yet every night you thrash upon our bed, and sometimes you wake weeping." He puts out his hand. "Come, Mary, let us have done with this foolishness. We need our rest."

She stares at him. She did not realize he was aware of her nightly distress, the terrible dreams, the strange weeping fits that assail her in the dark. "I would that we might conceive another child," she says softly, and then it is done—she has spoken the secret desire she had been harboring for weeks.

But he seems not to have heard her. He smiles gently, takes her hand and leads her to the bed, speaking in a voice one uses to calm a fractious horse. She is not surprised that he makes no move to join with her that night, but simply strokes her hair until she falls asleep.

CHAPTER TWENTY-NINE

Mary sits outside the meetinghouse with other women of the congregation. It is a Sabbath afternoon in August; morning worship is over and the afternoon service has not yet begun. The women are arranged on two benches in the shade of the building, seeking to catch any breeze that might come off the water. The air is very close and still. Dark rain clouds loom in the west. The women fan themselves and discuss the likelihood of a storm. Then Eliza Rogers begins to tell news of Indians she has heard from her husband, who had recently traveled to Plymouth.

"He assured me that the rebellion is all but over." She takes a square of linen from her sleeve and dabs at her brow. "The savages are surrendering everywhere. And those who refuse are captured or slain."

"Thanks be to God," Constance Hobart whispers. She is a small woman with tiny hands and a round face.

"Aye," Maria Mather says, looking at Mary. "Mistress Rowlandson must be especially gratified to see our enemies cast down."

Mary keeps her head bowed. Her Bible lies open in her lap, though she cannot make her eyes focus on the words.

"'Tis said they found the body of an Indian queen," says Eliza. "She was drowned in a river, trying to escape."

"A queen?" Constance laughs. "Indians have no queens."

"Aye, they do," insists Eliza. "They say she led her men on the field of battle."

The skin at the back of Mary's neck prickles and she raises her head. "Do you know her name?" she asks.

Eliza shakes her head. "No, I did not hear it."

"No matter," says Constance. "I have heard that savages have many names. To confuse us."

Mary leans forward. "Was there someone with her? A young woman servant, perhaps?"

Eliza looks at her. "I heard naught of one. But what matter is it? They are all devils, are they not?"

Maria reaches over and places her hand on Mary's arm. "Are you ill?"

"Nay." Mary tries to make herself smile but her lips feel as if they have hardened into a grimace. She thinks of Alawa, of her deft fingers tying a reed mat to the wall of a wetu, of their gentleness as they smoothed and braided Mary's hair.

"I thought perhaps the heat—"

"I am well enough." Mary shifts her arm so that Maria's hand falls away. She imagines Weetamoo swept downstream in a churning river, sinking under the surface of the water.

"I have heard it said that pagan women marry whom they please," Constance is saying. "This one was a slattern with many husbands, one of them brother to Philip. Her last was a Narragansett king."

"He too has been captured and executed," Eliza says. "His head was carried on a pike to Hartford."

"Aye, I heard news of that," says Constance. "He had one of those heathen names no one can pronounce. Quinny-nap or Quinny-hog." She pinches her face into a smirk.

"Maybe it was Quinny-ninny," Eliza suggests. The women giggle.

"Quinnapin," Mary says.

All the women look at her.

She gets to her feet, for her eyes are burning and her heart races in her chest. "His name was Quinnapin," she says. "He was once kind to me." She leaves them gawping as she walks away. She does not care where she goes. She wants only to be alone.

She heads toward the harbor, thinking of Weetamoo dandling her babe and dancing in the circle. Thinking of Quinnapin with his wide shoulders and proud bearing, of the long belts of wampum swinging on his chest as he danced. She remembers his generosity as she wept on the shore of the river. She imagines his fine head cut from his shoulders and mounted on a pike. Her stomach churns.

She bends and vomits into the gutter.

She cannot confess her distress to anyone in Boston, for there is no one who will sympathize. She briefly considers confiding in her sister, but knows that Hannah is currently being courted by a man from Wenham and Mary doubts she will want to resurrect memories of her captivity. Even if Mary does tell her, she doubts Hannah will appreciate her attachment to James.

She prays for a swift healing of her spirit. But the days go by and she continues to brood. One night she dreams she is accompanying Weetamoo back to her home village.

Alawa sits beside her on a raft on which they are crossing a raging river. Suddenly a wave comes up and sweeps them off the wooden timbers. Instantly, they are sucked beneath the boiling, gray current. Mary watches Weetamoo and Alawa thrash in the water, their long braids writhing, their faces clotted with terror, even as Mary sinks to her own grave.

She wakes gasping and bathed in sweat, her heart pounding. It is a moment before she is able to reassure herself that she is alive,

FLIGHT OF THE SPARROW

that the vivid images came not from her memory, but from a dream. Yet all the next day she cannot shed the powerful feeling of breathless choking. The dream seems to her more than a dream; she becomes convinced it was a visitation of some sort—a warning of what would have happened to her had she stayed with the Indians. In the middle of the afternoon it strikes her suddenly that in arranging for the ransom she had not wanted, James had once again saved her life. She would likely now be dead if it had not been for him.

The fact that she has sworn she will never see James again twists her heart. Yet she consoles herself that in sealing the covenant with Increase, she has finally paid James in kind.

There are more public hangings of Indians. Mary hears rumors that many, including Philip's wife and son, have been captured and sold into slavery. Then comes word that Philip himself has been killed—shot by an Indian in a swamp near Providence. His body was drawn and quartered and his head set on a pike and displayed in Plymouth.

The Council declares that the Indian hostilities are over.

Mary longs for word of James. She desperately wants some assurance that he is safe and well provided for. But she cannot make inquiries, cannot even show an interest in the fate of the Indians who came in under the amnesty. All she can do is concentrate on writing her narrative, as she pledged. All the news events must wash over her now, as if they had never occurred.

Yet whenever she hears a whisper of news about Praying Indians, she listens closely, longing to ask questions but holding her tongue for fear any inquiry might risk James's life. She thinks often of the Indians confined to Deer Island during the hostilities. She wonders if those who survived have been allowed to return to their homes. Then, in September while in the marketplace, Mary overhears a conversation between a cobbler and the wife of a shipbuilder as she looks over his wares. The wife is boasting that one of her husband's ships has been used to transport captured Indians to Barbados, where they will be sold as slaves.

"I warrant few will outlast the trip," the woman says. "'Tis said Indians make poor slaves and even poorer sailors."

The cobbler nods and feigns a polite laugh, though Mary notes his expression shows little interest.

"The lucky ones are confined in Natick," the woman continues, fingering a blue velvet shoe embroidered in gold and silver. "My husband says they keep a close eye on 'em there. No Indian can step outside the town limit, on pain of death. 'Tis too dangerous to allow them to come and go."

The cobbler draws the woman's attention to a pair of red and yellow silk brocade shoes, and smiles when she emits a gratifying *Ahhhh!*

Mary moves on to a fabric stall where bolts of bright cloth are stacked in a colorful wall behind the vendor. She prays that James was not forced aboard that ship. Her fingers shake as she examines a length of cotton printed all over with small red flowers. She wonders if he has even come in under the amnesty. Perhaps he fled north to be with his children.

She thinks about the cruelty of a law that restricts Indians to one town. She knows how bitterly they abhor confinement. She recalls James's harrowing description of his brief imprisonment in Boston. She remembers him telling her that many Indians believe they will die if they cannot freely walk the earth. In the midst of her own captivity, Mary found a singular pleasure in moving about as she wished. Her greatest misery, apart from Sarah's death, was on the few days when she was closely confined in Weetamoo's wetu.

Then one morning the town crier calls out the news that James the Printer and two hundred other rebellious Indians have come in and submitted to the authorities. The town buzzes with excitement. Mary is surprised, for she had not known that James was famous enough to create such interest. She longs to know more, to find out where he is. But there is no one she can ask except Increase Mather. She considers showing him what she has written, on the pretext of seeking his approval. When they are alone, she could ask after James's welfare. But before she is able to implement her plan, Joseph finds her pages.

Mary does not know how he found the box, for she hid it well behind a loose wainscot board near their bed. She suspects that Joss saw her conceal it and told his father. Ever since his return from the wilderness, the boy has been plagued by bouts of unpredictable behavior; sometimes he is secretive and sometimes unruly. Joseph has suggested that the Indians hexed him, but Mary assures him that is not their way. "More likely 'twas one of the Boston gossips," she says smartly, and then regrets it when her husband hushes her with a warning frown.

"These 'gossips,' as you brand them, have only our welfare in mind," he says. "Please remember they are the very ones who contributed their monies to your ransom."

She closes her mouth and bows her head, for this seems to be what Joseph requires of her since her return. He has long since stopped pestering her for details of her ordeal, though she knows he still believes her silence cloaks a guilt of such enormity that she can never be forgiven it.

She finds him with the box on a cloudy afternoon in late September. She has just come from visiting Abigail Whiteman, invalided after a fall. She carries a basket of food that Abigail generously pressed on her. Joseph is seated at the table before the open box, poring over her pages.

She is so startled she drops the basket. A pork loin rolls out from its cloth onto the floor, but she ignores it. She rips the page from his hands, gathers up those scattered across the table surface, pushes them into the box and firmly shuts it. There is no thought in her, only anger. She is trembling with fury. She clutches the box to her breast, so outraged she cannot speak.

Joseph rises. His face has gone pale and he looks very solemn. He reaches for her, but Mary, the box clutched to her breast, backs toward the open door. Then he speaks, and the timbre of his voice startles her with its tenderness.

"I had not known," he says softly and she thinks she sees a tear rise in his eye. "Why did you not tell me?"

She shakes her head, for she has no answer to his question. She sees that she wounds him still further with her silence, but she does not know how to mend it. Her mouth is as sealed as a tomb.

"I had not thought your time was so hard there," he says. "You have been sorely tried. Yet you have been the Lord's faithful servant." He moves around the table to her and this time Mary does not step away. She lets him touch her—her shoulder, her arm. He raises his hand and strokes her cheek. She begins to tremble. Not this time with fear or fury, but with grief. Wracking shudders course through her as a great sorrow overwhelms her.

He takes her in his arms. It is the first time he has embraced her since her return, and it undoes her. She presses her face into his chest, sobbing. She feels his hand caressing her back in long, almost amorous strokes. He whispers something in her ear that she cannot hear. When at last she gathers herself enough to lift her head, she sees him looking down at her with a sorrowful expression that matches her own.

"I am sorry you did not feel you could tell me these things," he says. "How faithful you were to our child! What courage you showed in caring for her."

Mary's tears well anew and she wipes her eyes with the back of her hand. She feels as limp as wet cloth, as if grief itself has melted her bones. And for a fleeting moment, she has the absurd wish that she could tell her husband about James.

CHAPTER THIRTY

Summer slides into fall, and Mary works on her pages every day, striving to finish the narrative so she can present it to Increase. The leaves turn crimson and gold and the nightly temperature drops; Joseph begins to spend every evening with friends. As soon as he has consumed the simple meal Mary prepares, he leaves the house, claiming he must be about the Lord's business. Sometimes he does not return until nearly morning. Despite her own exhaustion, Mary dutifully waits up for him, writing as long as her eyes will allow, and then sewing by the light of a candle while Joss and Marie sleep on their pallets in the room's shadows. She wonders bitterly what sort of business compels him to abandon his family night after night. She imagines gathering enough courage to demand an explanation.

Instead, one evening in October as he is leaving to call on the Mathers, she asks if he will take a message to Increase. "Tell him I am ready to show my pages."

Joseph blinks. "I did not know you were so near finishing. Should I not read them first to determine if they're satisfactory? 'Twould be a sorry business to trouble Increase if they are poorly done."

She feels a pinch of anger. Why must Joseph always question her abilities? Why must he always prove an obstacle to her wishes? She knows, even as the rebellious questions rise in her, that he is merely doing his duty as head of the family.

She sees that he is waiting for an answer. "I have done the best I can. 'Tis time he saw them."

His frown deepens, but she perceives it is more impatience than annoyance, for he keeps glancing at the door, eager to be gone. "I may be a good while," he says. "You need not wait up for me this night."

She does wait up, as he knows she will, sitting at the hearth, knitting a pair of stockings from discarded thread. Though the night is cold, she does not light a fire. Joseph has denied her that comfort, reminding her that the home is not theirs and they are not in a position to overly concern themselves with fleshly ease.

What he means is that *they are poor*. Until she was captured Mary had never wanted for warmth or food or any necessary thing. Since then, she has become well acquainted with deprivation—of food, of comfort, of safety—but she has not imagined it would extend past her return to English society. It has not escaped her notice that the comforts Joseph deprives her of in the name of household economy are ones he freely partakes of by visiting friends. She feels a dark and tangled bitterness growing in her.

It is well after midnight when Joseph returns. He stumbles as he comes through the door into the kitchen, alerting Mary to the fact that he has consumed more ale than usual. She is reminded of Quinnapin's drunkenness, though Joseph is at least able to walk. Lately he has been going directly to bed, saying nothing beyond his prayers. But this night he is cheerful and his good humor has apparently loosened his tongue. Before she has a chance to inquire if he delivered her message, he says there is good news—the Mathers are expecting yet another babe. A cord of envy tightens Mary's womb. Joseph knows that she longs for another child, yet he seems insensible to how this news strikes her, and instead goes on and on about his friends' joy. Mary watches him, carefully controlling her expression so that it will not betray her feelings. He sways before her as she puts away her needles. Finally he says that Increase is eager to see her narrative. He presents this news as if it bears no relation to her message.

"He has great hope that it is a true account of the Indians," he says, sitting clumsily on the bed. She dutifully kneels before him and removes his boots, even as she bites back a retort. She doubts that any Englishman or -woman could write a true account of the Indians. It seems to her that no one but Indians themselves know the truth of their lives or their hearts.

"When will he see me?" she asks. "I would meet him sooner than late."

"Tomorrow you will bring your work to him. I warrant he is as eager to see it as you are to show it." Smiling, Joseph reaches out and fingers a curl that has come loose from her cap. "Do you imagine I cannot discern your sin of enthusiasm?" He smiles. "It is no secret that you are an impetuous and headstrong woman. Let us have no more dissembling, wife. Meekness is a tiresome virtue."

She has never heard Joseph speak this way about meekness. It surprises her that he has lost patience with the most womanly of virtues, the very one she has constrained herself so often to practice. Would he prefer a woman who orders her husband about? She thinks at once of Weetamoo and her imperious manner, of how she commanded Quinnapin and he obeyed without a murmur.

He reaches for her again, and draws her head into his lap. He places one hand on the back of her neck and pulls her face against his loins. He moans and Mary has the terrible thought that he wants her to perform an unnatural act. With a shudder, she wrenches away and stumbles to her feet.

"Go to bed, Joseph. You are overweary." She does not add that he is also drunk.

He gives her a bewildered look. "Are you not coming?"

"No," she says, turning away. "I cannot yet. I still have chores that must be done before morning."

Mary does not retire to bed until she is sure Joseph is asleep. She is frightened and disturbed by what he has said and done, and she lies staring into the dark for a long time before she sleeps.

She dreams she lies naked in a small wetu. Sunlight slides through the smoke hole and she can smell venison boiling in the stew pot. She turns her head and sees that Quinnapin lies beside her. At first she thinks he is sleeping. Then—to her horror—she sees that he is dead. His head has been severed from his body and the flesh is rotting away from his skull.

Mary wakes abruptly, her heart thrashing and her stomach heaving. For a moment she thinks it is morning, but she hears no birdsong and the sky is not yet the pearl gray color that signals the hour before dawn. She sits up and tries to pray, to reassure herself that the dream means nothing. But her prayer does not come. When she stretches out again, she is unable to return to sleep.

Even as she looks forward to the meeting with Increase, she worries that he will tell her nothing of James. And she suspects he will find her narrative wanting, for she has not been able to perceive God's hand at all in her ordeal.

In the morning Mary packs up her box of pages and walks to the Mather home. A maid lets her in and shows her into the parlor, where Increase sits at his table, writing. He does not look up.

"Mr. Mather, I have brought my manuscript. My husband said you would be glad to see it."

He raises his head and peers at her. His eyes are bloodshot. "Sister Rowlandson." He gestures for her to place the box on the table. "You may leave it in my care." He turns back to his writing.

"But I would speak with you," she says.

He does not stop writing. "I will read it soon, if it be God's will."

The scratch of his pen on the heavy paper annoys her. "I have questions on another—"

He cuts her off. "Rest assured I will treat your words gently." He glances up to give her a thin smile. A carriage rattles past on the cobblestones. "Now you must grant me the peace to work." He rises and holds out his hand to take the box.

Mary's tongue feels as if it has been suddenly coated with dust. "Will you not allow me to speak?" she asks hoarsely.

"'Tis not the time." He leans across the table and takes the box from her. "Fear not, for I will discern the hand of God in your trials where you have not. I will insert the appropriate Scriptures and make plain how the Lord aided you, how He has raised you up to transcend the evils all around you." He clasps the box to his chest, as if it were as holy as the Bible. He taps his index finger on it, twice. "Once I have improved your text and published it, you will regain your former status as a good and pious wife."

Finally, she understands he is telling her that the manuscript seals their covenant. It has secured James's safe passage back into English society. And hers as well. James will live and she will regain the respect and status she lost during her captivity. Joseph will resume his husbandly duties. He is telling her that she will no longer be the subject of gossip and suspicion; she will have the support and sponsorship of the most respected minister in the colony.

Yet the stark truth is that if she could choose, she would rather live among the Indians than be restored to English society. She closes her eyes and heat suffuses her neck and face as she thinks of James. She recalls his words: *The Indian ways are fading like a mist.* The fact is that she *cannot* live among them, for they are now a defeated people. Their ways are no more. Only one path lies before her.

When she opens her eyes, Increase is smiling as if he has given her a gift. Clearly, there will be no chance for her to ask about James. He gestures toward the door. "God go with you," he says.

"And with you."

She is startled when he reaches forward and touches her shoulder before resettling himself in the chair, but she understands it is a blessing and an assurance that he has not forgotten his pledge.

At home she finds Joseph in an unusually buoyant mood. He presses her for details of her encounter with Increase. "You are certain he will publish it soon, then?" he asks. He says the stories the gossips tell of her in Boston and Cambridge are growing more malicious with each passing day. He tells her some have even asserted she is carrying Monoco's child. Mary feels a choking sensation, as if a stone has lodged in her throat. Once again, she assures her husband that no Indian has defiled her. That sadly, as he well knows, she is carrying no child at all.

Her desire for news of James does not leave her. She lingers when she goes abroad in the market, hoping to overhear gossip about him. She considers taking Joseph's horse to Cambridge and searching the shops for him, or traveling to Natick to see if he is there. She asks Joseph if they might attend worship in Cambridge one Sabbath, but he disapproves—whether out of loyalty to Increase or dislike of the new minister in Cambridge, she is not sure.

Then, in answer to her prayers, an opportunity presents itself. In late October, Joseph begins complaining of a sore on his leg. Mary treats it with salves and poultices, but the sore does not respond, growing daily in size and tenderness. He no longer goes out but stays in the house, sitting in his chair with his leg propped up on a stool. When Maria Mather tells Mary that Hannah Eliot, wife to John Eliot, is renowned for her healing arts, Mary easily persuades Joseph to travel with her to Roxbury.

The Eliots' home is more humble than Mary expects, considering Mr. Eliot's reputation as the great missionary to the Indians and author of the Indian Bible. Mr. Eliot himself opens the door and invites them into the small, dark parlor, and while Joseph consults with his wife at the hearth, Mary speaks privately with the minister in a corner of the room. Above them, dried roots and herbs hang from the ceiling, pungently scenting the air.

Though Mary dares not inquire specifically about James, she questions Mr. Eliot on the current situation of the Praying Indians. He shakes his head sadly when she mentions Natick, and reports that conditions there can only be described as wretched.

"'Tis the only remaining praying village," he says. "So all Christian Indians are confined there, no matter their tribe or homeland. I'll warrant there are many unconverted who have sought refuge in Natick to escape slavery and death. 'Tis dirty and overcrowded, little more than a prison for the poor souls who occupy it." He sighs. "I travel there as often as I am able, bringing them food and raiment and the hope of the Gospel."

Mary tries to imagine the Indians she knew living in such conditions, but all that comes to her mind is a memory of watching them dance around the circle fire. She can still hear the deep, rhythmic beat of the drums, feel her heart keeping time with the dancers' feet. She is so caught up in remembrance that at first she doesn't realize that Mr. Eliot has asked her a question.

"Mistress Rowlandson?" he says.

She blinks at him. "Forgive me. I fear I did not hear you, sir."

"I said perhaps you and your good husband would like to accompany me on my next visit, a fortnight hence." His smile is hopeful, encouraging. "It would be a fine act of Christian charity."

Mary's face is suddenly so warm that she puts her hands to her cheeks. For the first time in many weeks, she speaks directly from her heart. "I would be honored, sir."

CHAPTER THIRTY-ONE

Mary sits perched on the narrow wooden seat of the cart, wrapped in a blanket and wedged between her husband and Mr. Eliot, who has hired the cart, oxen, and driver, Samuel, a member of his church. Samuel walks the whole way, guiding and encouraging the two oxen. They are not well matched, and Mary regularly bumps shoulders with both men as they make their slow way from Boston to Natick. Joseph, his leg now well healed, is nevertheless in an ill temper. He has made plain to Mary his doubts about the wisdom of this journey.

"What perversity could make you wish to be among Indians again?" he asked her, wrinkling his nose as they rode away from the Eliots' home after their visit. Mary expressed her surprise because, in Mr. Eliot's presence, Joseph had pretended a great desire to minister to the Indians. She was relieved when he did not demand an answer to his question, for she dared not confide the truth, nor could she think of any fabrication that would have satisfied him.

In the cart bed behind Mary are two large bundles—one of blankets and one of linen shirts. Mary has collected them from members of Increase's congregation for distribution in the praying town.

They will stay in Natick overnight, a prospect she knows Joseph dreads. Throughout the journey, Mary has kept silent as Joseph and Mr. Eliot discussed the latest news of the plague raging in London. As they descend a long hill through a forest of oak trees, the cart-driver walks in front of the oxen, bellowing at them to slow down so the wagon will not break an axle on the stones and ruts. Even before she glimpses the stockade fence, Mary smells the smoke of the cook fires, the faint gaminess of stew pots. The trees thin out and she sees the rounded domes of wetus. Braids of smoke twist toward the sky.

The cart enters the town through a broad gate and Samuel halts the oxen in a litter of spiny burs under a chestnut tree. It is the only big tree left standing inside the stockade. The wetus are clumped close together; the frozen ground is strewn with stones. A breeze carries the stink of feces. *There is not enough land for all the people here,* Mary thinks. *This is worse than the crowded conditions at Wachusett.* Mr. Eliot climbs down first and then Joseph, who offers Mary his hand to steady her. Her heart is beating so hard she feels light-headed. She stumbles as she steps onto the ground.

"I thought Praying Indians were supposed to live in *English* houses," Joseph says in a disgusted tone.

Mr. Eliot regards him thoughtfully. "I think it best they live as they choose. In whatever circumstance they deem comfortable."

Joseph scowls. "How can *this* be called comfort?"

But Mr. Eliot has turned away to greet two Indian men as other men and women emerge from the wetus. Mary has a vivid memory of carrying Sarah into the village of Menameset three days after the attack. Her heart had been pounding then, too—with terror. Now it is anger that animates her. The two men call out to Mr. Eliot. *"Koonepeam!* Welcome, Eliot!" They approach with both hands out-stretched, to show they carry no weapons. Mr. Eliot's smile is so wide Mary imagines his face might split. *"God wetomuakquish!"* he says, grasping each hand in turn.

Mary studies their faces but does not recognize the men. A group of young boys darts out from behind a wetu, then retreats. A crowd slowly gathers, making a circle around them. Mary is shocked by the gaunt bodies and tattered garments and blankets. With the hostilities over, she assumed the Indians had been provided with sufficient food and clothes. It is clear that they are still starving. She is washed in fresh anger. She remembers sitting on the shore of the river near Philip's camp, weeping, surrounded by Indians. Remembers that though they laughed at her, they had been generous and kind—sharing what little food they had with their terrified captive.

Out of the corner of her eye, Mary glimpses a familiar figure at the rim of the crowd. Her heart thumps in her chest. Although the light is behind him and all she can see is his silhouette, she is certain it is James—tall, broad-shouldered, his head canted forward in a familiar way. He is not looking at her; his gaze is fixed on Mr. Eliot. Her skin feels as if it has been suddenly sheathed in ice. She remembers Increase's warning—any whisper of a connection between her and James could cost him his life. She forces herself to look away, to stare at the stockade walls and empty her mind. Beside her, Joseph puts his hand on her arm. She jumps away as if she has been burned.

"Mary?" He leans down so that his mouth is near her ear and she alone can hear his words. "What has distressed you? Did you see one of your captors?"

She shakes her head. She steals another glance in James's direction, but he is gone. For a moment she wonders if he was even there at all. Was he a phantasm of her imagination? Or is James as mindful as she of the perils of meeting? She takes a deep breath and smiles at her husband.

"I am perfectly well," she says, struggling to keep her voice even. "I had a sudden memory of my captivity. But—'tis of no concern." She lowers her arm so that his hand slides from her elbow. "I worry, though, that they want for food and raiment. They do not look recovered from their ordeal."

"What ordeal?" Joseph frowns. "Do you speak of their surrender? They are *Indians,* Mary. If they are hungry, 'tis no more than they deserve. Remember who incited the hostilities. We English are a peaceful people. We have always dealt fairly with the heathen."

She has the wicked urge to slap him. She draws her shoulders together and turns to face Mr. Eliot. "Is it not a good time to distribute the blankets?" she asks. "While everyone is assembled?"

Mr. Eliot directs two Indian youths to retrieve the bundles. As they scramble onto the wagon, Mary notes that she can see their ribs through their shirts. *We should have brought more food,* she thinks. *How difficult would it have been to carry a side of beef? The cart was half empty.*

The bundles are placed on the ground before Mr. Eliot, who unties them, and for the next twenty minutes, Mary hands the blankets, one after another, to the women, and then passes out the shirts. Mr. Eliot is looking around the circle, greeting people by name, introducing some to Joseph. Mary is aware that, as people attend to Mr. Eliot, they are watching her. The women are silent. They do not even speak to one another while they stare at her. She is mindful of her clean, confining clothes—the tight bodice and sleeves, the hard shoes that pinch her feet, her cinched-in waist. She becomes abruptly aware of how her clothes restrict her and promote her submission.

When Mary is finished distributing the blankets and clothes, Mr. Eliot turns to Joseph. "Come with me. I would have you meet one of my prize Indians." And before she has a chance to question him, Mary is hurrying behind her husband and Mr. Eliot.

As they approach a wetu, the door flaps open and James steps out.

"My friend!" cries Mr. Eliot, hurrying forward and clasping his hand. "Ah, it is *good* to see you. You look well."

Mary stops in midstride and rocks back on her heels. She feels as if she has suddenly been taken by a sweating fever. She watches

James's face, recognizes the flicker of worry at the corners of his eyes, the tiny twist of his lip.

"I am fortunate to be alive," James says. "We all are."

"I have come with a request, my friend," she hears Mr. Eliot say. "Goodman Green has asked that you return to Cambridge as his apprentice. As soon as you are able."

"It is a long walk from Natick," he says and Mary hears the bitterness in his voice. A chill goes down her back. She looks away.

Mr. Eliot laughs. "Nay, you will not live here, but in Cambridge, as before."

"I am an Indian," James says. "I will be arrested."

"Of course you shall have papers to prove your exemption from the regulation. It is already arranged."

Mary leans in. There are three men between her and James. He shakes his head. "I cannot leave my people. It is a dangerous time."

Mr. Eliot nods slowly, fingering the cuffs of his shirt. "You will be paid for your work," he says. "You will prosper and be of help to them." He pauses. "I would like to give Goodman Green my assurance of your return."

James nods. "I will think on it."

"And I will pray for your discernment." Mr. Eliot puts his hand on James's shoulder. "I offer my condolence on the death of your father," he says. "Naoas was a good Christian man."

"Aye, he was," James says, but his voice is hard. "Good enough that he left Philip's camp and returned to the English. They repaid him by sending him to Deer Island."

Mr. Eliot shakes his head sadly. "It is my people's great shame," he says. "Your people will long remember the devastations we have perpetrated there."

"We will never forget."

Joseph clears his throat. Mary can feel disagreement emanating from him like viscous smoke. She is grateful that he says nothing.

Mr. Eliot turns to Mary. "James, I wonder if you have knowledge of Mistress Rowlandson, lately redeemed from captivity. She has great concern for the welfare of Praying Indians."

James glances at Mary, studies Joseph, looks back at Mr. Eliot. "We have met," he says. His expression betrays no feeling.

With great effort, she looks at James. "I recall no meeting," she says. Will he take her warning? Has he been told of the arrangement between Increase and the authorities? Will he understand that she is assuring his safety?

When his eyes finally meet Mary's, she feels as if a bolt of lightning has struck the top of her head. Her hair feels set afire; her scalp pulses. "Aye, but we have met, though you deny it." His expression reminds her of the time he threatened her with the knife in Weetamoo's crowded wetu.

She nods, once. "My mind was greatly muddled with fatigue and hunger during my captivity. No doubt I have forgotten much."

There is a flash of pain in his eyes, which vanishes so swiftly Mary is not certain it was there at all. She shivers. Joseph takes her arm and turns to Mr. Eliot. "I fear my wife suffers a chill. Is there a place where she might shelter from this wind?"

"A wetu has been prepared for your use," says one of the men who first approached Mr. Eliot. Apparently he is a leader, though Mary notes that he does not carry himself the way sachems do. "For all who visit us—" He gestures toward a grove of young pine trees along the north wall of the stockade. "I will have someone take you," he says, addressing Mary. At his signal, a woman steps from the crowd, takes Mary's arm, and quickly leads her away from the men.

A white cross has been painted on the door flap and the wetu is newly made—Mary can smell the fresh-cut saplings and recently stripped bark. The walls are lined with woven mats, the platforms draped in skins. A pit has been dug, lined with stones, a fire

already laid. She cannot help herself—she emits a little sigh of pleasure.

The woman gives her a quick glance, then says in halting English, "You warm here. Sleep. Be glad."

"Thank you," Mary says, then remembers the words she learned
from James. *"Kuttabot'mish wonk."* She is instantly rewarded by the
woman's smile. "We celebrate tonight," the woman says, opening
the door flap. "You come."

"Kuttabot'mish," Mary says again. She wonders if there will be
dancing.

The celebration is held in the longhouse. The meal is preceded
by a lengthy sermon and prayer delivered by Mr. Eliot. There
is no dancing and Mary does not see James. Yet she feels unexpectedly content, as if she has come home, even though she is mashed
between Joseph and a short Indian woman who eyes her warily.
Mary listens to the woman talk with an elderly woman. She manages to catch a few words, but is unable to decipher the general
meaning. There is food; trenchers of maize cakes are passed around
with bowls of thin stew made of beans, onions, and squash. There is
no meat. When Joseph grumbles under his breath that Indians are
miserly hosts, Mary flushes in anger. She knows they pride themselves on sharing all they have. Mary eats with a relish she hasn't felt
in weeks. Beside her, Joseph picks at his stew. He seems to understand that he must eat something out of courtesy, but it is obvious
to Mary that every swallow is arduous for him, that he is worried he
might not be able to keep the food down.

A pipe of tobacco is passed around after the meal, and the
smoke settles Joseph's stomach. Mary is grateful that no one is
watching her, for she feels faint with longing and she suspects it
shows on her face. Longing for what, she is not sure—what she feels
is a strange combination of desire and remembrance.

Tobacco smoke drifts in great loops through the longhouse. Mary closes her eyes and breathes it in. The sound of the people talking reminds her, oddly, of a river. Their voices have a deeply soothing quality, as long as she doesn't try to parse each word.

After they retire to their guest wetu, Mr. Eliot, Joseph, and Samuel sit by the fire and smoke another pipe. Mary, pleading fatigue, lies down on a thick mat of furs and pulls a deerskin over her. Staring up at the smoke hole, she feels that she is in a dream she has dreamed a hundred times since her release. Firelight flickers across the dome of the wetu. The smell of earth and hides mixes with the smoke. She hears the men's low voices. She closes her eyes.

She wakes in darkness to find Joseph beside her. He is restless, tossing on his mat. He whispers her name, tells her he can't sleep. "There is no comfort in this foul place," he murmurs. He thrashes and rolls, whispering complaints about Indian ways—everything from their food to their dress; he insists that their creature comforts are of the Devil. No matter that they are Christians. She puts her hand on his arm to soothe and comfort him. She wonders why he doesn't think of praying to quiet his nerves, but dares not suggest it, for she knows he will take offense. She tries to summon up a bit of pity for him, to sympathize with his revulsion for all things Indian. Instead, she feels only growing irritation and a longing for the deep peace created by many Indians sleeping in one wetu. Somehow, she manages to relax back into sleep.

When she wakes, Joseph is snoring beside her. She slides out from under the deerskin, rises, and goes to the door. She pushes open the flap and slips out into the night.

The moon hangs above dark clouds rolling in from the west. Tomorrow it will rain. She takes deep breaths, stretches, and makes her way to a band of spindly trees along the north wall of the stockade. The trees do not look healthy; there are only a dozen of them. She looks back at the clustered wetus—dense black mounds against the darkness—and sees that it is not a village, but a prison.

She stands under the trees for a while, and is still there when she hears the snap of a branch and the rustle of dead leaves to her left. She freezes instinctively, but then realizes that whoever is there wants her to know she is not alone. No Indian would make such sounds without intent. She turns and sees a figure approaching her. When the moon slides briefly from its sheath of cloud, she recognizes James.

Her entire body is aware of him. She makes a slight movement—turning her shoulders, her head, in his direction. He stops a few feet from her. His arms hang at his sides. She cannot read the expression on his face.

"I did not expect to find you here," she says. "And I"—she pauses—"I am glad you were not hanged."

"'Tis no thanks to you." The words rush from his lips like a hiss. It is as if they have been filling his mouth for weeks, pressing against his teeth.

She feels as if she has been slapped. He does not know, then. He has not been told of her part in his redemption.

"You have no idea what it has cost me to be here," James continues. "What it has cost all my people."

She turns to face him directly. "Nay, I do know," she says, and she wants to tell him more, but his hardness frightens her. "I am familiar with the requirements of your amnesty."

He is silent for several moments. Mary can hear her heart beat in her ears. "Why did you come?" he asks, finally.

"I thought it would bring me peace if I were among Indians again." She spits the words out, as if each one sears her tongue.

She cannot bear his gaze; she bows her head and keeps it bowed.

"You will find no solace here," he says. "We are not your people. You must stay among your own."

"I have no people." A broken whisper. She is not sure he even hears her. She wants to turn away, to go back to the wetu, but she does not. She can smell him—the familiar musk of his clean skin, the tang of bear grease in his hair, his breath laced with sweet tobacco. She thinks of all the things she wishes she could say—chiefly that she heeded his plea for help as they stood in the cowshed all those weeks ago. That she has repaid her debt to him, that she has sacrificed her desires in exchange for his life—but her throat is locked. She cannot bring even one word forward onto her tongue.

He grunts softly. "Nor do I," he says. "I am neither English nor Nipmuc now." He is silent for a long time. Tears burn her eyes. She must not let herself weep. She must be strong, though her heart is breaking at his words. She feels him looking at her. "At least you have your church and your English town," he says slowly. "You have the English army to protect you. You have a minister for a husband, a leader of his people. At least you are a free woman."

She looks up at him—a swift, furtive glance—and then down at her hands. "Nay, I am not," she says. "I am not free at all." She fumbles for her pocket and draws out the little Bible he gave her in Menameset. She holds it out to him.

"Please," she says, "take it. It is yours."

At first he does not move. Nor does he speak.

"I beg you." She wipes her face with the fingers of her free hand. "You gave it to me. Now I want to give it to you."

"Why?" he asks. Still, he does not take it.

"Because it is all I have on my person of any value," she said. "And because you have been my true friend."

When she says the word *friend*, she sees something break in his face; the stoniness dissolves like a clay mask in the rain. He opens his hand and takes the Bible. Then he turns, walks away from her, and is gone.

CHAPTER THIRTY-TWO

Mary does not sleep again that night, but lies awake, thinking of her encounter with James. She recalls every word, every inflection, every motion—the slant of his shoulders in the clouded moonlight, the clench at the base of her spine when he looked at her, his outstretched hand as he took the Bible. She goes over and over these details, burning them into her memory, setting them there like a brand. She recalls other moments—trembling as he cut the rope from her neck, sitting with him outside Weetamoo's wetu, lying beside him in the winter dark. She examines all her recollections until she knows them by heart, as if she were carefully preparing a story to hand down to her children and grandchildren. Yet knowing that she will carry all these tales untold to her grave.

As the sky grays toward dawn, it begins to rain. Slowly at first, then harder. By the time the men wake, rain is crashing on the dome of the wetu. Mary feels as if she's inside a great drum.

She stirs up the fire and they break their fast quickly. An Indian man comes to announce that the oxen have been hitched to the cart. They are given extra blankets and a deer hide to cover their heads and they take their leave without witnesses, except for the man who tended the oxen. No one steps out of the wetus to say farewell as they roll through the village gates.

For most of the journey, only Samuel breaks the silence with his periodic calls to encourage the oxen. Mary is grateful the rain is too loud to allow conversation with Mr. Eliot and Joseph. She has no desire to say anything. She wonders if she will ever want to speak again. The word *friend* beats in her heart like the rain.

They are still an hour from Boston when Samuel gives a shout. Mary pushes back the hide covering her face and peers in the direction he is pointing. Through the rain, she makes out a dark smudge along the horizon, a smudge that gradually resolves into thick, black smoke.

"I fear some dreadful calamity," Mr. Eliot says.

"Aye," says Joseph, his tone ominous. "God is not yet done with New England."

They proceed up a long hill, and at the top, they see it clearly: Boston is on fire. Flames lick through the smoke. In the distance they observe a great clamor at the water's edge, and many boats in the river.

"I dare not return you to your home," says Mr. Eliot. "You must bide with me in Roxbury until we know it is safe to enter Boston."

A spasm of panic passes through Mary. "I must be with my children," she cries. She leaps to her feet in the wagon, making it creak wildly as it begins to descend the hill. Joseph grabs her arm and pulls her back down onto the seat.

"What are you doing?" he hisses. "Sit still and don't move, lest you overturn the cart!" He turns to Mr. Eliot. "Pray, take us to the gate. My wife has been through too many ordeals of late."

Mr. Eliot signals Samuel to continue, and so they do not stop but pass through Roxbury toward Boston. It takes every bit of Mary's willpower not to jump down and run ahead, but she manages to restrain herself as they move forward into the smoky haze.

By the time they reach the Neck, it is apparent that half the town is on fire. Samuel stops the cart, for he can go no farther against the tide of swarming people pouring toward them. Some are running wildly; some carry bundles; others push carts filled with their children and goods. Smoke boils over a house near the harbor.

Mary takes the opportunity to clamber down. She begins running, weaving among those fleeing the town, through the gate, following the streets north to their house. She sees a gaping hole in the roof of the meetinghouse; the streets are covered in a dark gray mud that she quickly realizes is wet ash. She hears Joseph's footsteps pounding behind her, but she does not turn or slow down to wait for him. All that is in her mind is the desperate need to find Joss and Marie. She is determined that this time she will not fail them. This time she will lead them to safety.

She runs down alleys and side streets, for the main streets are flooded with people. Finally, she reaches their rented house. It is— praise God—unscathed. She nearly falls to her knees as she pushes open the door and stumbles into the kitchen. She hears Marie cry out and sees Joss crouched in a corner. Mary throws her arms around her children. It is only after she feels their solid flesh against her body that her tears begin to flow.

When Joseph lurches into the house a moment later, panting heavily and clutching his chest, he finds the three of them kneeling on the hearth, their arms wrapped around one another. He collapses into his chair, but says nothing. Mary does not invite him to join them.

When the rain stops in midafternoon, they venture out into the streets. The news is terrible. Fire has destroyed more than forty buildings, including the meetinghouse and two houses across the street. Increase Mather's home has burned to the ground, destroying all his furniture and—most tragically—most of his books and papers. Mary wonders if her pages are gone and the thought tugs at her with a strange mixture of bitterness and relief. People shuffle through the smoldering and sodden ruins. The stink of wet ashes is dreadful. Mary will not let herself be parted from the children. She insists they stay close enough to hear her voice should she call them. Joseph warns her against such foolish affection, but she does not repent.

The town is in tumult for weeks. Increase is laid low with a fever and lies in bed, unable to preach. Mary makes a broth of chicken, beef, and healing herbs and carries it herself to the house where the Mathers are temporarily staying, hoping that she will be allowed a private moment with the cleric. But a maid meets Mary at the door and, gesturing to the shuttered windows, tells her that Mr. Mather is too ill to receive visitors. A few days later, Joseph sorrowfully reports that the doctors fear that Increase will soon die.

He lies near death for several weeks, then begins a slow recovery. Everyone says it is in answer to the people's fervent prayers. All agree that God is punishing Boston for some grievous sin, though they cannot agree on the sin itself. Some claim the calamity is chastisement for the colony's adoption of the Halfway Covenant on baptism. Some say it is a sign they must strengthen the laws against licentiousness. A few voices proclaim that the fire is a reprimand for selling Praying Indians into slavery.

Mary continues to ponder her encounter with James. He was so cold to her in Natick, she is certain he did not know of her bargain with Increase. Perhaps he believed that she had done nothing at all in response to his request for help. Their brief conversation in the dark had revealed only that they were alike in their separation. Just as she declared she did not belong among the English, he no longer considered himself Nipmuc. They are both without a people. She wishes now that she had followed him when he walked away, that she had tried to break through his wall of resentment and rekindle the old affection between them. Yet he had accepted the Bible, and she finds some measure of comfort in that.

Winter comes down hard, filled with wind and ice. Snow falls and blocks the streets, so it is a trial to make their way to public worship in the half-built new meetinghouse. Even Joss rarely goes out, but stays close to the fire with Mary and Marie. Only Joseph ventures forth, to visit the sick in the parish and to seek a new call whenever he has word of an unpastored church.

For months Boston is rife with pestilence and fear. Despite the defeat of Philip's alliance, dread plagues the town, fed by tales of new Indian depredations, of spies in their midst, of rumors of another confederation of Indians forming to the west, a confederation that will rise up and drive all the English back into the sea. Even when the snow packs down and makes it possible to go out, people rarely venture beyond the gate. No one ever goes anywhere alone.

Spring finally comes, and with it a gradual relaxation of dread. It seems as if the sun melts not only the snow and ice but also something hard and cold in people's hearts. Mary thinks of how much has changed in the past year. She remembers the day of the attack and the ordeal of Sarah's death. She remembers her terrible hunger and the humiliation and fear she experienced as a slave. She remembers hours spent sitting in the spring sun outside Weetamoo's wetu, sewing shirts and stockings. She remembers long, searching conversations with James at the rock by the edge of camp.

She visits her sisters, Joanna, Ruth, and Hannah. In March she learns from Joanna that Henry, Elizabeth's husband, has removed to Charlestown and is pledged to marry a woman in April. Mary feels a pang for Elizabeth on hearing this news, though she is glad for him. She hopes his new wife will bring him happiness and solace. Yet in the darkest corner of her heart, she envies him and the hope of future joy his new life represents. It seems to Mary that *her* life has grown more bleak and gloomy since her redemption.

Soon after Henry's wedding, the long-awaited change in their fortune finally comes: Joseph receives a new call to the church at Wethersfield in the Connecticut Colony. He is jubilant and Mary finds herself infected with his cheerfulness at the prospect of this new beginning. It will be good to live again in a place where she is not the center of town gossip. She packs the few things they own into a chest, and arranges farewell visits to each of her sisters and brothers, knowing she may never see them again.

CHAPTER THIRTY-THREE

Wethersfield, Mary discovers, is a pleasant town situated on a wide stretch of the Connecticut River. Renowned for its fields of sweet onions, it is a place where Joseph promises she will find relief from her afflictions. Yet she cannot look at the river without remembering Weetamoo standing on the bank and presenting its name to her like a gift. It seems that the ghosts of her captivity are determined to haunt her wherever she goes.

She takes pleasure in the task of setting up housekeeping in a home that is her own. The Wethersfield parsonage is twice as large as Mr. Whitcomb's Boston house, almost as big as their destroyed home in Lancaster, with a lean-to behind the kitchen and parlor on the ground floor, and two chambers above. There is space for a kitchen garden behind the house and broad fields set aside for their use on the west side of town. The outbuildings include a large barn and shed. There is even a ladder beneath a board in the parlor that leads to a small cellar where Mary can store root vegetables in the winter.

Marie is always at Mary's side, cleaning and arranging their goods in proper order. Joss also stays near at hand for the first few weeks, attending to the small chores that come with relocation.

Though Mary hoped that Wethersfield would prove a new beginning, where she would be free from the burden of suspicion born of her captivity, she soon finds that her reputation has gone before her. The pitying and disapproving glances of townswomen quickly inform Mary that there are already whispers about her. Only a week after her arrival a round-faced woman appears at the door, bearing a pot of savory beans and a cluster of questions. She introduces herself as Esther Allen and insists that Mary must not hesitate to apply to her for any need. "Even the smallest want we will happily supply." She gives Mary a wide smile, displaying the gap in her front teeth— a gap so large and black Mary can scarcely tear her eyes from it.

"Ye must tell me what befell you—amongst the savages, I mean." Esther sets the pot on the table with a bang and perches on the hearth stool. "Surely, 'twas a terrible trial. Your fortitude inspires us all." She glances around the room but does not seem to notice the disarray that nearly drives Mary to despair. The kitchen is cluttered with chests and unwrapped bundles. A tall stack of Joseph's books stands in the far corner, awaiting a new cupboard.

It is clear that the woman wishes to trade kindness for gossip. Mary thanks her for her visit and confesses that she is too weary to easily tell her of her trials this day, but will consider how to best share in the future what she has learned.

Esther nods, but her mouth has hardened. Mary is stunned by the boldness of her next comment. For all the gossip in Boston, little of it was told directly to Mary's face.

"It's been said you were forced to marry a savage," Esther says. "That you didn't want to return to your husband." Mary stares, her mind momentarily frozen. She wonders how to reply, knowing that whatever words she chooses will be repeated throughout the town.

"No," she says slowly. "'Tis a vicious lie, perpetrated by one of the Indians who had power over me."

Esther studies her skeptically. "Well, of course you would have to say so now, would you not?"

Again, Mary is shocked by the woman's impudence. She can think of no polite reply. A memory of Weetamoo flashes through Mary's mind—she sees the sachem sitting beside Philip before the council fire, proud and regal in her belts of wampum and braided hair. Oddly, Mary finds herself considering what Weetamoo might say if she were in Mary's situation.

She straightens to her full height and touches her breast, as if a necklace of wampum hangs there. She can almost feel the cool beads beneath her fingers. "Goody Allen," she says, "please be kind enough to remember that you address the wife of your new minister. And remember as well that a gossip who prejudices the public against an innocent person can be sent to the stocks."

The color instantly drains from Esther's face. She sways back on the stool, so hard that for a moment Mary fears she will crash to the floor. Esther hastily takes her leave and Mary bids her farewell, though the woman's hard countenance tells Mary she has not bested her. Esther will quickly spread the first rumors against her.

The encounter disheartens Mary. It seems that she will never escape her captivity. If, as Joseph and Increase believe, the Lord sent her afflictions as a judgment against New England, then why does Mary continue to suffer at the hands of the very people her ordeal was meant to save? She shakes her head in bewilderment and goes back to ordering her house.

The next morning, Joseph confronts her in the kitchen garden by the back door. She is on her knees digging up the soil to plant the thyme and coriander seeds she has brought from Boston. Before she even wipes her hands clean on her apron, he begins scolding her for offending Goody Allen.

"Do you plan to disaffect *all* the women in my new congregation?" His eyes flash. "I will not have my good name damaged by"—he pauses, and for a moment Mary thinks he has finished, but before she can collect her thoughts to respond, he continues—"by your—your *savage ways.*" His face is bright red and spittle flies out between his lips.

"Savage ways?" She struggles to her feet. "What hateful rumors have the gossips in this town already spread? And I have not yet dwelt here a fortnight!" She cannot bear to look at him, so she rushes into the house. She flies past Marie, who is making a beef pasty in the kitchen, and hurries into the parlor. There, Mary sets about unpacking a chest of crockery. It takes all her self-control not to throw every bowl into the fire. She recalls the time she rushed from Weetamoo's wetu in a fury and paced up and down the camp. The walking had brought her some measure of calm and it strikes her that it might do the same now. If nothing else, it would help her think. She pulls her cloak from its peg in the front entryway and goes outside to walk the road, she knows not where.

She passes houses and fields and comes to the river, where a flock of black ducks paddles by the bank. No one is in sight, so she sits in the grass and watches the ducks. She is charmed by a mother duck leading four ducklings into the water. The spring air and the sunlit water gradually restore Mary's spirits and after a time she returns to the house.

Joseph meets her at the door. She sees at once that his anger has disappeared. He looks shaken. "Where were you? You frightened me." He takes her hands and pulls her inside where he surprises her by kissing her cheek, though it is broad daylight.

"Forgive me," he whispers. "My words were unjust. I was over-wrought." He releases her and looks into her eyes. "But you must promise me that you will not run off like that again."

Mary's first impulse is to reassure him. Yet the short time by the river has been such a blessing—a brief taste of freedom she has not experienced since her time among the Indians.

"Please, Mary. Promise me you will keep to the house and yard."

She looks at him. His eyes are kind and pleading and she feels her heart soften in response. Yet the thought of confining herself to the house dismays her. No, it *frightens* her.

"I cannot," Mary murmurs, so low that he does not hear it at first. He frowns. "What do you mean you *cannot*?"

"I cannot promise to keep to the yard," she says more clearly, no longer murmuring. "I must be allowed to walk, Joseph. I must feel myself a free woman." Something catches in her throat and she reaches out and grasps his hand. She knows that she has sinned in resisting her husband's wish, yet she cannot hold her tongue. "You must understand— so much has been taken from me. You must allow me *that*."

She is stunned when he squeezes her hand and gives her a half smile. She perceives it as a sort of reassurance. She is certain he does not understand how her hour by the river has comforted and provided her with the solace her prayers have not. Still, he seems willing to overlook her rebellion. At least this time. Perhaps she has misjudged him.

She does not confront Joseph on the subject again. Yet from that day on, she goes out walking regularly—to the river and along the unfrequented paths at the edge of Wethersfield—where she finds the refreshment and peace that enable her to bear the barbed tongues of the congregation. She feels profoundly grateful for this small freedom.

Mary goes daily to market with Marie, carrying a basket on her arm. People smile at them and women often stop to talk. They explain that Wethersfield was once a frontier town like Lancaster, but has been long-settled and the surrounding Indians subdued. One summer morning, Goody Wickers tells Mary about the Pequot Indians, whom she says were once a warlike people until the English victory over them in 1637. Mary does not learn the details of the battle until several weeks later, and when she does, she is so repulsed that she can no longer bear to hear it spoken of. For it had not been a battle at all, but a massacre of women and children.

English soldiers had surrounded a Pequot fortress and set it on fire. Seven hundred Pequots burned to death. Mary cannot rid her imagination of the death screams and the anguish of the poor mothers as they watched their children being consumed by the flames. It sickens her and brings to mind once again the memory of Elizabeth's body wrapped in fire.

Mary tries to explain this to Joseph, to put into words how her captivity has changed her perception of Indians. She tells him that the Indians treasure their children more than anything, and that death by fire is surely the most brutal of all possible deaths. She says that the history of the Pequot slaughter has surely spread among all the tribes. Perhaps it is why Philip's Indians fired the English towns, believing that using their own tactics against the English was a just recompense.

Joseph listens closely, and waits until Mary finishes before he speaks. They are sitting on the bench in front of the house, for it is a warm evening and the kitchen is hot and stuffy. When Mary runs out of words, Joseph sighs and takes her hand from where it lies in her lap. "Have you forgotten the sovereignty of God? Remember, the Lord has chosen us to do His work here in this place. That means we must sometimes be the rod of His chastening."

Her hand stiffens in his. "But surely we are not called to"—she can hardly speak the words—"*burn the children?*"

He makes no reply but brings her hand to his lips and kisses her fingers. "You must not let yourself be afflicted by a battle that took place when you were but a child in England."

"Nay, 'tis not this only that afflicts me." She withdraws her hand and presses it back into her lap. "It is but one instance of what I fear is a greater sin."

"And what would that be?" He has shifted on the bench to face her. In the growing dusk, she feels the sharpness of his gaze, like a knife scraping against her face.

Mary takes a moment to find words for her thoughts. "I wonder if we can be so certain of God's purposes. Is it not possible that God also counts the Indians as His children?"

Joseph looks at her as if she has spoken nonsense. His silence is so heavy that she briefly looks away. She expects him to correct her, reassure her of God's mighty presence. Remind her that the Bible is the only necessary source of understanding. At least he will accuse her of apostasy. But he says nothing.

The evening darkens and folds around them. Mary feels she can hardly breathe, yet the thoughts that have been ravishing her mind and heart for months seem to have a life of their own, and she fills the silence with them. "Is it not true that we can never be certain of God's will? That even His wonders and signs may be wrongly understood? How can we claim righteousness when so many have suffered at our hands?" She utters these last words as a cry, for she is shaking. "Lately I have begun to think I can count on nothing but my own love for my children. And even that is sorely tested. Especially by Joss."

Mary thinks she hears a rueful laugh escape Joseph's lips, but she cannot be sure it is not her own sobs. He places his hand on her back. "Shhh. Mary," he whispers. "You are overwrought. We will talk about this matter another time." He rises and takes her hand and leads her to bed, where he joins with her for the first time since her redemption.

Afterward, she weeps in wonder and relief.

The next day, when Joseph returns from making parish visits, he tells Mary he has brought her a gift.

"A gift?" she says, looking up from her spinning. "What possessed you?"

"Hush." He puts a finger to his lips. His eyes are dancing as they sometimes did when he courted her. He beckons her outside where, hanging from a hook on the gatepost, she finds a birdcage. It is bell-shaped, formed of thin strips of iron. Inside is a sparrow.

She stares at the bird, which flutters up and down, chirping.

"Do you not like it?" Joseph's voice is filled with disappointment and confusion. "I had the cage made for you by Wethersfield's own blacksmith."

Mary turns to him and makes herself smile. "'Tis beautiful, finely wrought. I thank you for your kindness."

Joseph seems satisfied with this, but Mary is stunned with melancholy. All she can think of is Sarah's love for Row, her refusal to leave the bird the morning of the Indian terror, and the wretched ordeal that preceded her death.

She hangs the cage by the west-facing window in the kitchen. When Marie comes in from gathering eggs, she sees it and bursts into tears. One of the eggs rolls out of her apron and smashes on the floor. Mary comforts her and tells her not to mind the broken egg, but Marie is still sobbing when she turns away from the cage and places the remaining eggs on the table.

"It reminds me so of Sarah," Marie whispers. "I do not think I can bear it."

Mary nods, but can offer no more consolation, for she feels exactly the same.

The new sparrow does not sing, but spends its days sitting in its cage. Occasionally it utters a series of harsh chirps. Mary feeds it and gives it water each morning, but every time she opens the cage door to scatter crumbs, the sparrow pushes against her hand, trying to escape.

CHAPTER THIRTY-FOUR

With Joseph's resumption of his conjugal obligation, Mary hopes she will conceive another child. Since Sarah's death her womb has ached with emptiness. But after four months in Wethersfield it is apparent that she is now barren, that the woman's time of life has come upon her. She feels that God has once again forsaken her. When she expresses these thoughts to Joseph, he is surprised and suggests that she has misread the signs. When she assures him that she has not, that she no longer has her flows, he tries to soothe her with the thought that she should perceive her barrenness as a gift. The Lord is sparing her the dangers and sufferings of childbirth, and she should praise His holy name.

Yet Mary cannot bring herself to praise God for unfruitfulness. She continues to secretly yearn for a child. For many children. She longs to be surrounded and distracted by them. She wants them hanging on to her skirts as she goes about her duties. She wants to hold infants in her arms and press them against her breasts. She wants to kiss their necks and bellies, to delight as their laughter fills the rooms of her house. She wants their warm, lively bodies around her all the time.

Marie senses her sadness, and gently questions her about its cause. Mary tells her the truth—that she wishes for another child, but is past conceiving. Marie looks her full in the face and speaks words that could have come straight from her father's lips: "God wills only what is best for us, does He not?"

Mary murmurs that she is right, that her desire is probably sinful, and she will strive to turn her thoughts to other matters. Yet whenever Mary chances to meet a woman whose belly is swollen with child, she feels a sharp pang in her own womb.

Over time Mary settles back into her old routines. If she was formerly contaminated by Indian ways, as her husband believed, she is now infected again with English customs. She keeps a clean and orderly house, and prepares savory meat pasties and sweet breads for Joseph and the children. She attends public worship and visits the sick. She reads the Bible with Joss and Marie and oversees their prayers. The fact that she is no longer able to pray herself is a dark secret she reveals to no one. She bows her head and sits in respectful silence at the proper times, so no one but the Lord Himself knows her transgression. It is clear to Mary that she is not saved. But no one—not even Joseph—dares to accuse her of any lapses. In Wethersfield, she is known as the woman who suffered at the hands of the Indians. Since her encounter with Esther Allen, she has not been pressed to divulge the particulars of her story. Gossip and imagination have already supplied those details.

Marie seems to adjust well to her new life. Like Mary, she has experienced some relief in moving to a new place. She, too, had been reluctant to describe her experiences during the time she was a captive. But one morning, six months after their resettlement, Marie reveals something of them to Mary.

They are in the stillroom off the kitchen, making mustard plasters, when Mary asks her what she knows of Joss, for he has spent little time at home in the previous month. "I fear that some wildness has tainted him," Mary says. "He cannot be still. I do not know where he goes."

"To the riverfront or the woods," Marie answers quickly, and then seems to regret the telling, for she glances furtively around the room, as if her brother might be hiding in the shadows. "Please, do not tell him I told you."

Mary drops more black mustard seeds into the bowl and quickly grinds them to powder with the pestle. She hands it to Marie so that she can add the proper amounts of flour and water to make the plaster. "But what does he do there? I can think of nothing—"

"Mother, he wants to be a sailor. He cannot bear staying in one place day after day. He wants always to be moving." Marie bends over her work as she speaks. Her words flow out like a swarm of bees, as if she cannot release them fast enough.

Mary wonders aloud if his restiveness is born of his time among the Indians and, though Marie does not answer directly, she mixes the plaster so violently that it slops onto the table. The girl quickly wipes it away with the corner of her apron. "I oft dream of Indians. Sometimes the dreams are sweet."

"Aye, I understand," Mary says softly. "'Twas a powerful time. It cannot help but change us."

Marie goes back to stirring, but Mary sees that her arm is shaking. "Marie." Mary places her hand on her daughter's wrist, so that she has to drop the spoon. "You may tell me anything. It will not shock or dismay me." Mary wonders suddenly why she has not sought her daughter's confession before. Has she been so absorbed in herself that she cannot perceive Marie's sufferings?

"It was a hard life," Marie says. "The first days there was so much work I sometimes thought I would rather die. But then"—she takes a shuddering breath—"once I grew accustomed to the toil, they treated me like one of their own. They were kind and tender. Sometimes it was even fun." She pauses again and Mary releases her arm. "I do not think the Indians are devils, Mother. The woman who saved me risked her own life when she brought me back to the English. If any had caught her, she would have been slain."

"That was an act of extraordinary kindness," Mary says.

"*Christian* kindness." Her daughter's tone surprises Mary with its force. "Is it not Christian to risk your life for another?" Before Mary can respond, Marie continues. "Yet she had no faith in Christ. She was not Christian, but heathen." Her voice fades, and again she starts to wipe tears from her face with her apron. Mary yanks the apron corner from her hands, fearing that she will blind herself with the plaster. Marie seems not to notice. "I do not understand this. And I cannot ask Father."

"No," Mary whispers. "You cannot."

"And it is worse because I do not know what became of her," Marie says. "There is so much hatred—so much fear. I worry that she has been sold for a slave."

Mary nods. Tears burn her eyes. "I, too, mourn. So many I knew died or were subjected to English cruelties." Her voice thickens; she cannot continue. All she can do is take Marie in her arms as if she were a small child again.

Her daughter's anguish sharpens Mary's. She broods about her captivity, wondering what has become of the people she lived and worked with for three months. She knows that Philip and Quinnapin and Weetamoo are dead. But what of the others? What of Alawa? Did she die with Weetamoo? What of the boy who carried Sarah with him on the horse, whose name she never thought to ask? And what of James? Did he return to his apprenticeship, or is he still in Natick?

She thinks of her narrative, regretting that she left it with Increase. She tries to imagine how she might better tell the truth of her experience. It is not enough simply to remember what happened.

She wants to understand and explain what it *signifies*. She wants to give her captivity its true meaning and weight.

She considers confessing her spiritual dryness to Joseph, but she knows already that he will counsel her to prayer and fasting, will read long passages of Scripture to her. She knows none of this will lift the weight of her discomfort and confusion. During their family prayer sessions, as Joseph reads the Bible and prays over them, she sits listening with her eyes downcast, even though her heart is in turmoil. One evening she is surprised to find that she is not alone in this. Joss, perched on a stool with his face turned to the floor, leaps suddenly to his feet and blurts, "Not everything is a sign from God. Some events just *happen*."

Mary lets out a small gasp. Not in shock, but in recognition of the truth.

"Nay, I'll not have you blaspheme," Joseph chides darkly.

"Is it not a sort of blasphemy to avow that God is always chastising or rewarding His people?" Joss asks. "Might not some things be beyond our knowing?"

"Aye," Mary says. "Is it not conceivable that God may act on whimsy?"

Mary is astonished when these questions silence Joseph. For a moment he glares at her, but then bows his head and closes his eyes. Mary does not know if he is praying or contemplating her heresy, but she is no longer interested in finding out. She rises and announces that the hour is late and they must all go to bed. Then she quickly leaves the room.

Joseph is not silenced for long. On Thursday evening, in public meeting, he delivers a stinging sermon on the terrible consequences of forsaking God—a sermon he preaches with rare venom. A sermon Mary knows he has crafted especially for the ears of his family.

"Consider the signs of our forsaking God," he cries. After two hours of exhortation, his voice has grown hoarse, yet the force of his conviction stills everyone in the congregation. "Chief among them is a deep and high ingratitude." He looks at Mary, and then up at Joss, who sits in the back gallery. "Hear the word of the Lord, from the book of Amos, chapter eight: 'Behold, the days come, saith the Lord God, that I will send a famine in the land, not a famine of bread, nor a thirst for water, but of hearing the word of the Lord. And they shall wander from sea to sea, and from the North even unto the East shall they run to and fro to seek the word of the Lord, and shall not find it.'"

Mary looks down at her lap. Beside her, Marie also bows her head, though Mary suspects it is from fear of her father's anger as much as the Lord's. When worship is finished and the congregation has filed out, Mary continues to keep her eyes averted from her husband's, for she does not want to acknowledge the truth of his words, nor the fear they have set in her heart.

She hurries home and does not speak with Joseph until that night, long after the children have gone to bed. He sits late by the fire writing while Mary reads her Bible, or tries to. Her eyes cannot focus on the page but keep jittering off in all directions. As he puts away his pen, she speaks.

"I know you meant your sermon for Joss and me," she says. "And I am grateful for your attempt to guide us."

He rises and steps toward her. She closes her Bible and stands to face him. "You must not misunderstand what I have to say, Joseph. But the truth is, I can no longer claim a hope of salvation. I do not believe I am one of God's Elect."

He shakes his head. "Nay, Mary, you cannot be the one to know such things."

"No." She raises her hand, palm out, to keep him from touching her. "I know that God has forsaken me—and I Him. That is enough, surely, to condemn me to eternal damnation."

His scowl deepens. "Did you not hear a word I said this night?"

"Aye, I did." She extends one of her hands toward the fire, in the hope it might warm her, but her fingertips remain numb. "I heard every word, Joseph. I heard myself in your condemnation of sinful New England. In your description of those who forsake the Lord."

He gives a loud sigh. She sees that he is agitated, that she has angered him yet again. She knows that she must say what she has to say quickly, before she loses courage. "The truth is—the truth that you do not want to recognize—is that my time in the wilderness has changed me. Forever. I am not the helpmeet you once had. I am no longer the meek and godly Christian wife you married and fathered children upon. I am lost in the wilderness, far from God's presence."

Then Joseph surprises her. In spite of his rigid bearing and stony gaze, he takes Mary's hands and draws her to him. "We must pray for guidance," he says gently. "You must not lose hope. Truly, God has not forsaken you. Not after all you have suffered."

Mary is nearly moved to tears by his rare tenderness. "But that is my point, Joseph," she finally manages to whisper. "If my ordeal was of God's making for New England's redemption, then it appears to have failed. For I see no benefit to New England or myself that compensates for the great oppression—the injustice—of what we have done—are doing—to the Indians and the Africans."

He releases her then, almost pushes her away. Mary is not surprised, for she knew before she spoke that he would find her thoughts repellent. His scowl returns and an angry flush rises in his face. For a moment, Mary thinks he might strike her. Instead, he turns and begins to pace the length of the room.

"You try me severely, Mary. Have I not exhibited an extraordinary patience with you? Have I not counseled you and prayed for you and read Scripture to you day after day? Yet this is your recompense—this stubborn refusal to submit to my wisdom?"

She shakes her head. "God alone can save me, Joseph. You yourself have said so."

"Aye, God alone. But you must exhibit a proper *inclination* toward His will. You must soften the soil of your heart so that He may plant the seed."

He waits for her response, but she says nothing. Nor does her face or body betray any inner tumult. She has, somehow, in the long months since her release, fashioned a kind of peace with herself.

"'Tis a dangerous business to try God's patience, wife. He will not endlessly indulge your obstinacy."

"So you have oft told me," she murmurs.

"And you think my words idle?" His voice rises.

Mary takes a step backward, for his look alarms her. "Not at all," she says. "Nothing about you has ever been idle."

Whether he perceives the insolence in her remark or not, he does not say, but quickly turns his back and leaves the room. Mary does not know where he sleeps that night, for he fails to join her in their bed. She does not see him again until morning, when she comes in from milking the cow and finds him sitting at table, awaiting his breakfast.

Neither of them mentions their argument. Neither apologizes. Mary is sure that he will eventually raise the issue again, but that time never comes. Only three days after his sermon, when they are all seated at table on a bright Saturday afternoon, Joseph dips his spoon into a meat pie and raises it to his lips. As he opens his mouth, a troubled look contorts his face. He drops the spoon, clutches his chest, vomits and slumps sideways in his chair, dead.

For a moment Mary has the odd thought that he has been shot. It is as if she has suddenly returned to Lancaster and is reliving that terrible day. Even as she gets to her feet, she glances at the window, her eyes searching for some sign that an arrow or bullet has pierced the glass. But there is neither arrow nor bullet. Joseph has been slain not by Indians, but by God.

Mary stands with her hand pressed to her mouth. Only after several minutes pass does she think to look at Joss and Marie. They sit, staring at their dead father. Mary finds her voice and sends Joss for the doctor, though it is plain her husband is beyond reviving. She sends Marie to fetch a neighbor. And for a few moments she is left alone.

She stands very still in the middle of the room. She thinks briefly that she should be doing something, but she cannot make her limbs move. She becomes aware of the hiss of the fire in the hearth and the sweet yeasty smell of the bread she set baking. A gust of wind shudders against the house clapboards. The sparrow utters a sharp chirp and begins hopping up and down, flapping its wings.

An odd feeling comes over her. It is the same sensation she felt when James cut her free of the rope around her neck—a confused and startled elation. She finds herself whispering over and over the one thought that stands alone in her mind: *how surprising are the providences of God.*

CHAPTER THIRTY-FIVE

In the early days and weeks after Joseph's death, Mary is shrouded in a haze of activity. The people of Wethersfield surprise her with their kindness and generosity. Women come to sit with her day and night. They bring her kettles of fish stew, meat pasties, rounds of cheese, and loaves of bread. They read psalms of consolation and pray with her for God's comfort and mercy. The men come and cut her wood, milk the cow, and feed the ox and horse. The church elders vote to allow her to stay in the parsonage and provision her with Joseph's salary while they seek a new minister.

Mary is properly somber and assures people she trusts Joseph's soul to God's care. No one tells her she should not mourn. Some of the women try to console her by informing her how difficult it is to bear an unexpected and sudden death. She wonders if they have forgotten that she witnessed the brutal murders of her sister and nephews and brother-in-law. Joseph's death was, by comparison, exceedingly gentle.

The truth that she confesses only to herself is that she has experienced an unexpected freedom in her husband's absence.

As the days pass, she falls into a contented acceptance of her widowed state. She knows she cannot remain in the parsonage
indefinitely—the congregation will soon call a new minister—but
she has a strong inner assurance that she will be able to find a way
to survive this new misfortune. She wonders if this is the fruit of
enduring her captivity—or something else, more fundamental to
her character.

She frets over Joss and Marie, worries that witnessing their father's death is one too many blows in their young lives. Without a
man to provide food and shelter, no family can survive intact for
long, and Joss is not yet of age to assume a man's duties. Marie takes
to her bed until Mary reminds her that her usual chores are now
compounded by her father's absence. Marie tries to bear up cheerfully under this new burden, but Mary knows she feels vulnerable
and frightened. Mary wonders why she has not noticed before how
truly her own feelings are reflected in her daughter's heart.

Joss says nothing about his father's death. He makes no change
in his conduct, but continues to leave the house and disappear into
the forest for days at a time. One morning, Mary comes into the
kitchen to find him trying to conceal a long knife in his jacket. He
spins to face her, but it is not a look of shame or embarrassment that
he turns on her, but an unfriendly scowl.

"You already have a knife, Joss." As Mary crosses the room to
him, he backs away. "Why do you take mine?"

"I have need of it," he says, grimly.

"What need? I cannot imagine what use you might have for it
that is greater than my own."

"'Tis a secret," he says, and before she can question him further,
he runs from the house. He does not return for two days and Mary
never sees the knife again.

It takes her several months, but Mary slowly comes to understand that Joss, as surely as Sarah and Mari, is lost to her. She

considers the possibility that he has been lost since the moment of his capture.

Mary knows she cannot enjoy her single condition for long without rousing the concern of her neighbors. In Connecticut Colony, as in Massachusetts Bay, it is the law that every man, woman, and child must live in a well-ordered household, ruled by a man. She knows she will have to find a new husband, or return to Massachusetts to live under the roof of one of her brothers while her children are bound out.

Then, as she is taking tea and warming herself at Dorcas Walsh's hearth one February afternoon, a tall man walks into the room and announces he is looking for Dorcas's husband, Abiah. He introduces himself as Samuel Talcott, a solicitor and the commissioner of Wethersfield. He tells Mary he has heard of her plight and he offers his condolences.

As Dorcas hurries off to find her husband, Mary looks up into Samuel's pleasant face and her breath catches in her throat because something in his eyes reminds her of James. His gaze has the same compassion, and the same fierce penetration, though his eyes are gray instead of brown. They talk of the recent snowstorm and discuss the Test Act in Parliament that requires all in the House of Lords and the House of Commons to take an anti-papist oath. When Abiah appears and Samuel takes his leave, she notices how completely her hand disappears in his warm palm. It seems to Mary that he holds her fingers for a moment longer than he should. "If there is aught I can do to help," he says, "I trust you will send for me."

"I shall," she says. Her cheeks are still flushed long after he leaves.

On a sunny morning in March, Mary and Marie begin the weeklong process of spring cleaning. They fill the barrel in the yard with hot water and spend the morning washing the linens and draping them over bushes to dry in the sun. In the afternoon they carry the furniture outside and scrub the floor with sand until it shines. They sweep out the hearth and the small brick oven set into the wall. As they prepare to wipe down the walls for a new layer of whitewash, Mary carries the birdcage into the yard and sets it on a stump. The sparrow chirps and flutters, beating its wings against the iron. "Yes, little one," she murmurs, unlatching the cage door. As soon as the door swings open and the sparrow flies out, she knows she has wanted to release it since the day Joseph presented it to her.

She watches the bird as it bounces through the air in its scalloped flight. It turns and swoops down over her head and lands on the low branch of a tree. A moment later, it begins to sing.

Though Joseph's estate is small, it still must be properly executed. When Mary is granted administration rights in April, she is at first honored, and then alarmed. She has no knowledge of the law or the complexities of inheritance. Dorcas reminds her that Squire Talcott has offered his assistance; he knows the law and is well respected in town. "And he needs work to keep his mind harnessed," she says. "His wife, Hannah, died a year ago this past February."

Mary seeks Samuel out on a gray afternoon and finds him at home, fitting a new window into his parlor. He puts down his tools and wipes his hand on his apron. He seems inordinately pleased to see her and offers his help again, even before she has the chance to present her plea. He insists on discussing the matter at once and so they sit in his kitchen drinking tea served by a merry-faced young woman. The house is brimming with children and servants. When Mary leaves it is almost dusk and there is a buoyancy in her step that she has not possessed in years.

Samuel calls on her the next day and together they begin sorting through Joseph's papers. There are many—it appears that papers are the chief part of Joseph's estate—but Samuel is undaunted. He comes daily, sometimes bringing one or two of his children with him. Mary is delighted, especially with little Nathaniel, who is not yet two. She is pleased to note that Marie quickly forms a friendship with his eldest daughter, Hannah.

Samuel is a scholarly, quiet man who graduated from Harvard College six years after Joseph. The way he looks at Mary and gently guides her decisions quiets her mind and heart. When he begins to touch on matters more personal than Joseph's estate, she encourages him. He is honorable and highly regarded, a landowner, a man of boldness and daring, active in the militia. He tells her that he has eight children, five of them in sore need of a mother's guiding hand, especially Ruth and Nathaniel, who are too young to remember their mother. Mary's heart goes out to them.

Samuel begins openly courting her in May. He is as gentle in temperament as he is strong in body and mind. He tells Mary that he admires her steadfastness as well as her passionate spirit. He listens to what she has to say with concentrated interest. He encourages in her a freedom of tongue and temper that Joseph condemned.

Mary begins to wonder if her growing affection for Samuel is sinful or liberating. She argues with herself at night, lying awake in her bed. Is it possible for a woman to marry for love? Could it be that a shared sense of humor is more important than wifely obedience? When she sleeps, she often dreams of Samuel. Sometimes she is walking with him beside the river, watching canoes filled with Indian warriors cross to the other side. Sometimes she is on the trail behind him, cheerfully carrying a heavy basket despite the forehead strap digging into her skin. She wakes, wondering: is she in love with Samuel Talcott?

When Samuel proposes marriage, Mary happily accepts, though she fears she has little to bring to the union except for her body and her nearly grown children. But that is enough to satisfy him. They are so well suited that neither sees any reason to wait. They are married on the sixth of August.

It seems to Mary, as she becomes wife to Samuel and mother to his children, that the desires of her heart have been fulfilled. She cherishes her new husband's kindness and compassion, as well as the vigor and strength of the young ones who daily surround her. She cuddles and caresses Nathaniel, Rachel, and Benjamin in a way Joseph chastised her for doing when her own were young. When she forbids any punishment beyond scolding, Samuel raises no objection. Mary applies the practices she saw Indian mothers use with their children, and her new charges respond joyfully, with love. Sometimes, in private moments after they are married, Samuel calls her his "sweet savage," a jest that Mary enjoys, for indeed, she *is* savage at times when they lie together in their great bedstead.

Samuel is curious about her captivity, and she willingly answers his questions. When she mentions that she wrote a narrative of her experiences at Increase Mather's request, he asks to read it. She explains that she no longer has it, that she gave it to Increase long ago and has heard nothing of it since. She suspects it was destroyed when his house burned in the great fire of 1676. Or, if it was saved, perhaps he found repairing her writing deficiencies too difficult a task to pursue. Samuel questions her closely. Is it possible the manuscript was saved and misplaced? Or put aside and forgotten? He declares that she must write to Increase and ask him what became of the narrative, for if it still exists her husband wants to read it.

Mary gives him a merry smile, for she knows Samuel as a forceful man who usually finds a way to get what he wants. "I warrant it will be a waste of good ink and paper," she tells him. "It has been so long since I gave my pages over, I doubt he even remembers them."

But Samuel continues to press her. Finally, more than a year after their wedding, Mary writes a letter of inquiry. To her surprise, Increase responds within the month, informing her that he still has her pages, that he has recently had the opportunity to improve them, and is planning to publish them within the year. Because of its length and importance, her narrative will be printed as a separate volume. He adds that he has made some important additions to it, including appropriate Scriptures and lessons. Surprised to learn that the manuscript survived, Mary does not object, though she suspects that he has twisted much of what she has written to his purposes. The blessings of motherhood have so thoroughly pervaded her life that she has little time or interest in anything else.

Increase assures her he has crafted a preface designed to secure Mary full acceptance as a woman of faith and piety throughout the colonies. He has arranged for Joseph's last sermon to be included. In the spring, she receives a package of proof pages of the book along with a note from Increase informing her that the type is already being set in Cambridge.

Mary carries the pages outside and sits under the great chestnut tree behind the house to read them. The youngest children scamper around her in the grass like newborn lambs until they finally tire, lie down beside her, and fall asleep. She reads as if it were not her own story, as if she does not know it by heart. In truth, she does not—for Increase has transformed it from a ragged tale of hardship, endurance, and grief into a polemic on steadfast faith.

That evening, as she shows Rachel how to set the dough for the morrow's baking, she tells Samuel that she regrets submitting the narrative. "Mr. Mather has corrupted my story and savaged the Indians in ways I did not intend," she says.

Samuel, who has pulled his great chair near the open door to catch the breeze, is cradling a sleepy Nathaniel in his lap. He tilts his head and smiles at her, a now familiar gesture that Mary has come to cherish. "But he has preserved your record of their

generosity and fortitude. And shown your courage and forbearance
in the face of adversity. You have naught to regret."

"Nonetheless, I fear I shall," Mary says.

In May, Mary travels with Samuel to Boston, leaving the youngest
children in the care of Samuel's older brother John and his wife.
It is the first time Mary has returned to the Bay Colony since she
moved with Joseph to Wethersfield. Samuel has arranged for them
to stay with a distant cousin who lives near the harbor in Boston.
After they settle in, he rents a stylish hackney coach imported from
England. It is fitted with red leather seats, and heavy green fustian
curtains to draw over the windows to keep out the road dust.

Over the next few days, Samuel and Mary travel to visit her
sisters and brothers and their families. Despite the luxury of the
coach, Mary feels jostled about like a mouse in a box. Yet she is
delighted to be reunited with her family. Her sisters Ruth and Joanna are still neighbors in Wenham, both married and raising large
families. It is good to sit with them in Ruth's parlor and talk as
sisters again. Their concern for Mary is sincere—driven neither by
curiosity nor false interest. She walks with them through the town,
marveling at how it has changed since her girlhood there.

The next day in Ipswich, Mary is joyously reunited with her sister
Hannah, who married Samuel Loomis the year after Mary moved to
Wethersfield. Hannah is plainly content with her new situation, her
sweet disposition unchanged despite her weeks in captivity. Mary
greets her two-year-old son, Samuel, for the first time. She covers him
with kisses and caresses, which she never would have done in Joseph's
presence. "You have changed, sister," Hannah remarks, eyeing her
thoughtfully as Mary dandles little Samuel on her lap.

"That is a good thing, is it not?" Mary asks, laughing.

"Indeed it is."

A few moments later, when Hannah touches her waist in a

particularly tender way, Mary gives a little cry. "You are with child again!" She places Samuel on the floor and rises to embrace her sister.

"If it's a girl, I mean to name her Elizabeth," Hannah says. Mary sees the tears in her sister's eyes, and her own throat tightens so suddenly she cannot speak.

While their husbands inspect the fields, the women talk for more than four hours, sharing all that has happened since they were ransomed.

"I was grieved to hear of Joseph's death," Hannah says. "After you came safely through such torments, to lose your husband was surely hard."

"Aye," Mary says, nodding solemnly. "But the Lord has provided for me. Abundantly." She does not tell her that Joseph's death presented her with only a few hardships, all quickly mended once she came to know Samuel Talcott. In private, she did not mourn very much. She soothed her guilt by reminding herself what Joseph himself said so many times: A Christian should not know grief, for all things are in the hands of God. "And I take great pleasure in my new life as Squire Talcott's helpmeet," Mary adds.

"Are not all his children a burden to you?" Hannah asks.

"Nay, they delight me. I love them all as my own." Mary thinks suddenly of Joss, who left Wethersfield three months before. She has not heard from him, nor been able to trace his whereabouts. "'Tis Joss who troubles me," she confesses and Hannah's brow knits in sympathy. "I fear he is corrupted somehow. Ever since his captivity, he has been restive and guarded. He told me he wished he had not been redeemed. He disappeared into the forest for days without telling anyone his plans. And now"—she draws a handkerchief from her sleeve, in case her tears start to flow again—"I do not know where he has gone," Mary adds. "Marie says he often spoke of going to sea. Perhaps he has stowed away on a ship."

"I am sorry," Hannah says softly. "Do you think him bewitched by the Indians?"

"I know not," Mary says. "In truth, I think it just as likely he has been corrupted by the English as by Indians."

Hannah does not seem to grasp the import of Mary's words. "I oft dream of them," she says. "The Indians. I still wake in the middle of the night weeping."

"Aye," Mary nods. "As do I." She is grateful for the chance to leave behind the subject of Joss. "But not every night. And Samuel is very kind to me."

"As is *my* Samuel. Though I confess, I still miss my children." Hannah's next words catch in her throat. "I know Josiah is gone, yet I have not lost hope that I will someday be reunited in this world with John and Hannah."

The scenes of the February morning in Lancaster leap into Mary's mind. She again sees Elizabeth's fiery death, the bloody torments visited on her brother-in-law and nephews and the long line of bound captives, though she closes her eyes against the visions. "Aye," she whispers. "It must be a terrible thing not to know their fate. I will pray that they are alive, even if they be captives still."

Hannah nods and wipes her eyes with her fingers. "Does your wound still pain you?" Mary realizes Hannah is changing the subject for both their sakes, yet she blinks at her in surprise, for no one has inquired about her wound in more than two years.

"I am well healed." Mary touches her left side, where the ball that had passed through Sarah dug a narrow trench. "There is a stiffness there I fear I will carry to my grave, but it is of no consequence."

Hannah smiles sadly. "I have sometimes wished I carried some mark of my captivity upon me as you do. It is an emblem of your courage, your fortitude."

Mary feels washed in shame. During her captivity, she did whatever she could to survive, even plucking food from the mouths of children to feed her own hunger. Since her return, she has acted the coward's part, allowing Increase Mather to twist the story of her trials to his purposes. Adding to the great English deception. She shakes her head. "My dear sister," she says, "you are wrong. 'Tis an emblem of my iniquity."

Hannah frowns in puzzlement and Mary wonders if she should try to explain her new understanding of what happened during the captivity. Yet her husband's voice in the hall and the shaft of late afternoon light slanting through the front window signal that they must soon be on their way back to Boston.

"'Tis you who have come through this affliction without stain, Hannah. Not I." Mary rises, goes to her, and gently puts her arms around her. "My gentle sister, whom I have so oft neglected. You have been sorely tried," Mary whispers. "Yet you have been the Lord's faithful servant. And now He has blessed you with new life."

Mary does not understand why she is speaking such pieties, when she is no longer certain that God even hears English prayers. Yet she continues to stand there, comforting her sister with the very words Joseph once used to comfort her.

CHAPTER THIRTY-SIX

The next day, Mary and Samuel call on Increase Mather. The cleric has aged in the three years since Mary last saw him; his hair is as wispy and gray as smoke, his sunken cheeks furrowed with wrinkles. Nevertheless, he exudes the same rigor and determination that she remembers. He is filled with plans for distributing Mary's book. He tells them that the type is being set this very day at Printer Green's shop in Cambridge. Then he casually mentions that the Indian printer, James, works there. "He is one of Mr. Eliot's protégés," he says. "A remarkable man—for an Indian." He glances at Mary.

She stares at him, wondering if he is testing her. Is he waiting to see if she has broken their covenant? Has he forgotten it? Or does it no longer apply? Though Mary has told Samuel that James helped her during her captivity, she has not mentioned her part in securing his amnesty.

"You say James Printer, the Praying Indian, is setting the type for the book?" Samuel asks, leaning forward.

"Aye." The cleric shifts in his chair. Mary senses that he is in some pain, that he cannot sit comfortably. "God's mercies are sometimes strange, are they not, Squire Talcott?"

"Indeed they are. Exceeding strange." Samuel smiles at Mary. "I would like to meet this printer," he says, turning back to Increase. "And I warrant my wife would like to witness the making of her book."

Mary sees a shadow pass across Increase's face, the hint of a warning frown.

"Could you make the arrangements soon?" Samuel asks. "Tomorrow, perhaps? We would like to make a donation to the printing costs, once we have seen the operation. But we have few days to spare; we must make a long journey back to our home in Connecticut Colony." To Mary's surprise, he reaches over and takes her hand. "Our children are expecting our return."

Mary cannot keep from smiling at her husband. Two years ago, she would have condemned herself for taking pleasure at seeing someone best a cleric. But now she feels a bubble of happiness that is so sweet she cannot think it evil. She squeezes Samuel's hand and is suddenly so overcome by warmth she puts her free hand to her cheek. She wonders if her face is flushed. Such spells of unexpected heat, she knows, are a common tribulation for women at her time of life. Yet she suspects this one is caused not by her errant body, but by her wayward mind.

Increase is looking at Samuel and nodding slowly. "You may consider it arranged," he says quietly. He keeps his gaze carefully averted from Mary.

Though Mary has grown used to wearing the lace collars and velvet sleeves that display her new husband's station, for her visit to the printer's shop she wears a plain bodice and skirt and a simple linen collar. She carefully plaits and coils her hair and secures it under her cap. She straps on her pocket—a new one, embroidered in doves—though she carries nothing in it.

Outside, Samuel helps her into the coach and tells the driver where to take them, while Mary settles into the slippery leather seat. She doesn't draw the curtains to keep out the dust until they begin to move. The coach creaks and sways, jostling Mary and Samuel so that they repeatedly bump shoulders. At one point they are jostled so violently that Mary lands in Samuel's lap. He takes advantage of this opportunity by kissing her soundly on the mouth. She lets out a squeal of counterfeit protest, but her face is flushed with excited pleasure, and she is unable to contain her laughter.

When the coach stops, Mary lifts the corner of a curtain and peeks out. They are in front of a narrow one-story building set between two large houses. The coach has caused a commotion in the neighborhood. Dogs bark and children flock close to the great wheels; the driver tries to shoo them away, to no avail. A few women are gawking from their dooryards. A light breeze carries the stink of rotting garbage. The driver opens the door. Samuel climbs down and holds out his hand for Mary, just as a short man emerges from the shop. He wears a long printer's apron and leather breeches; his gray hair is bound at the neck. Clearly, the presence of the carriage has drawn him outside. He gives Samuel a small bow and runs his hands over his apron, in a vain attempt to wipe them clean.

"Goodman Green at your service, sir." He looks first at Samuel, then at Mary. There is something shrewd and calculating in his face.

"Samuel Talcott," her husband says. "Mr. Mather tells us you are printing my wife's book."

He frowns. "I have not heard of any Mistress Talcott."

"I was formerly Mary Rowlandson," Mary says. She looks past him at the closed door of the shop. The single small window is dark. "I wrote a narrative of my captivity."

"Ah! Mistress Rowlandson!" Goodman Green extends his hand, and then quickly withdraws it to wipe it once again on his apron.

"You must forgive me for not recognizing you." He stares at her left cheek, where a wisp of hair has escaped her cap and dances beside her ear. "'Tis an honor to make your acquaintance." He regards her as if she is a great curiosity. "Yours is a fine book, Mistress. 'Twill be a sensation. All New England will profit by it." He sounds as if he is about to go off on a long discourse until Samuel interrupts him.

"May we go in?" He indicates the shop. "My wife and I came out of curiosity—to see how the book is printed."

"Ah, yes." The printer smiles broadly. He hurries to the door, opens it, and stands back to let them pass through. "You are most welcome."

They step into the shop. The room is smaller than Mary expected. It contains a desk and stool, a cabinet and small table. Most of the room is taken up by the press. She stares at the tall wooden machine, which reminds her of a gibbet, with its timbers and struts. There is a great lever protruding from its center, like a blunt-tipped spear. She imagines James's hands on the machine, his fingers clamped around the lever, the muscles in his shoulders tensing and stretching as he operates the press.

But James is not in the shop—the three of them are alone. Mary is suddenly aware that she had expected—had *hoped*—to meet him. A sharp, damp smell pervades the room. Over their heads hang sheets of paper like small white curtains, clipped to lines of twine strung from wall to wall. Mary glances out the window, which offers a view of the street. The coach driver is talking with a woman carrying a child. A man drives by in a cart loaded with straw. An old woman shuffles along, carrying a basket on each arm. Three young boys run, laughing, after a squealing pig.

Goodman Green appears at her elbow and hands her a sheet of paper. Printed on it is the title of her book, *The Sovereignty and Goodness of God*. He is practically twitching with worry. "'Tis a fine work, Mistress," he says. "May I show you how it is printed?"

"Aye, I would like that," she says.

The printer leads Mary and Samuel slowly around the room, pointing out the wooden letter case with its sorted letters of type, the composing stick, and the frame that holds the completed page of type. He shows them where he mixes the pots of ink, the stacks of paper, and then turns to the press itself, carefully explaining how each sheet of paper is held over the bed of inked type. He demonstrates how the screw-lever secures the ink to the page. *All of these things are touched by James every day,* she thinks. *This is his world now.*

She feels overwhelmingly sad. She cannot believe James thrives here, confined to this small room. She remembers him as she last saw him—shadowed in the winter night under the stars, opening his hand to receive her Bible. He must perceive his life in Boston as a cruel redemption. Her own redemption has cost her much, as well—her integrity and, perhaps, her faith. She thinks of the many changes Increase made to her pages, how he took out entire sections, how he added Scriptures and pieties, how he cast the Indians as agents of the Devil. How she voiced no objection to his authority to make her experience fit his purposes.

She touches Samuel's arm. "We should leave and let this good man return to his labors." She is suddenly desperate to get out of the shop.

"I am honored by your visit," the printer says amiably. "We hope to have the first copy printed within the month. As you can see, we are exceedingly busy." He gestures to the press. "My apprentice has been setting type a fortnight past."

"James," Mary whispers and pinches her lips together. She had not intended to say his name aloud.

Goodman Green gives her a startled look, even as he nods. "Aye, his Christian name is James."

"I would be grateful if you would thank him on our behalf," Samuel says.

The printer raises one eyebrow. "Thank him?"

"For his good work," Samuel says. "And for showing charity to my wife when she had great need of it." And he presses a small pouch of coins into the printer's hand.

Without warning, tears sting Mary's eyes. She turns away while the printer is thanking her husband and steps over the doorsill into the gray light. Then she sees him: James, walking quickly toward the shop, his head down, eyes on the cobblestones; it is plain he does not see her. He looks much as she last saw him, though his hair is cropped short and he wears only English clothes under his printer's apron. There is a sad urgency in his gait and his back seems to sag, as if he carries a great burden.

He raises his head suddenly and blinks at her, as if the gray light is too bright.

Mary stumbles toward him. She feels as if she is walking a great distance, though it is only a few yards across the cobblestones. Everything looks sharp and jagged—the intersection between the cloth of James's shirt and the air seems to vibrate. She reaches out and brushes the cloth with her fingers.

He looks down at it as if her hand is a rare curiosity he has not seen before. He says nothing.

"I had not thought to see you again," she ventures.

"Nor I you." He glances past her, and she turns to follow his glance. Samuel is now talking with the carriage driver, deliberately giving her privacy. "Is this man your new husband?" James asks.

"Aye," she says quickly, "I am wed to Samuel Talcott now."

"I trust you have found happiness, *Chikohtqua*."

His use of her Indian name stops her breath. She recalls the clear, luminous moment in Increase Mather's parlor when she realized she loved him. "Happiness," she says softly. "Yes, I can rightly call myself a happy woman." She is aware of his gaze, how it still pierces her heart, after all this time. "And you? Are you not happy?"

He tilts his head, as if in thought. But she sees the anger in his eyes. "I will be happy when my children come back to me and I return to Hassanamesit, where my mother gave me life."

"Then you must go soon," she says firmly.

He shakes his head slowly. "The English have forbidden it. They keep close watch, lest Indians rise up again to oppose them. Even though so few of us remain. They threaten the people with death if we leave Natick. And now they are trying to persuade us to sell our land, since we cannot live on it."

A bolt of anger goes through her at this flagrant injustice. Her throat clutches at some words, but she cannot utter them. Two women hurry past, throwing dark looks her way. Mary watches them proceed down the street, heads tilted toward each other.

James leans closer. "Aye, you ought to have a care for your reputation. If you are seen talking with an Indian and recognized, all your efforts at restoration will be in vain."

"I made no effort at restoration," she says.

"Then what is your book but an attempt to redeem yourself in English eyes? I have read it many times, for I set the type and know each letter."

She bows her head.

"You could have told the story true," he says. "But you have salted it with lies."

It takes her a moment to find her tongue. "It has been altered by another," she says. "It is not the story I wrote. It is the story they *required* me to tell."

"You should not have allowed your name to be attached to it," he says.

Blood pounds in her ears. "Would you have me driven into exile like Anne Hutchinson for saying what they do not wish to know? How long would it be before they banished me?"

He leans toward her. "But what have they left you? What has this book cost you?"

"I have my place in society," she says weakly.

"The English used you." He pauses. "As they used me. We are alike in that." He gives her a smile that she cannot interpret. "Perhaps it is a mercy. Those they do not use, they kill. We have both bought our redemption at a terrible price. You had to forge a lie. I had to bring in the heads of innocent men. We have both sold our souls to gain acceptance in this new and terrible world."

His words scorch her. She stares at him until his face ripples and shimmers. "Does love mean nothing?" she whispers, but he does not seem to hear her. "I am sorry," she says, reaching for his hand. "So very sorry." And she clasps his fingers as desperately as Weetamoo must have clutched the raft before the river tossed her to her death.

CHAPTER THIRTY-SEVEN

Mary rides back to Boston in silence, going over and over her conversation with James. She thinks of the many Indians sold into slavery and of those confined in Natick, without the freedom to roam through the wilderness that was once theirs. They are a dying nation, their towns burned, their lands appropriated, their very bodies starved and crushed and sold. All in the name of God.

It seems to Mary that she is trapped in a great web of English deceit and cruelty. That she has unwittingly allowed herself to become one of the sticky strands. Yet she has sometimes acted rightly—in giving aid and succor to Bess Parker, in refusing to allow her children to be whipped, in repudiating slavery, and in refusing to keep slaves in her own house. She is suddenly struck by the thought that the times she felt redeemed were when she *ignored* the counsel of the clerics and goodwives around her and followed the promptings of her own heart. How strange that venturing away from accepted wisdom was the very path by which she found herself.

It is a sweet relief to lie in Samuel's arms that night. Yet even the blessed joining of their flesh does not assuage the terrible new ache in Mary's heart.

They make the long journey back to Wethersfield on horseback, accompanied by two traders and a Mohegan scout. Though the Indians have been subdued, it is widely feared that rebellious warriors might still attack lone travelers. Mary sits behind Samuel and they talk of their sojourn in Boston. They discuss Mary's conversation with James and the sorrow that overcame her when he spoke of what had happened to his people.

"Something must be done to help him return to his home," Mary says. "You are an influential man. You know many people of consequence in both the Connecticut and Bay colonies. Surely you could persuade the authorities to open the Indian towns."

Samuel laughs. "I think you overrate me, wife. I warrant it is your influence that will be most keenly felt in these colonies, thanks to your pen. Why don't you write to the new governor of the Bay Colony and make your case?"

She considers his words. It would be a bold endeavor for a woman. One she would not have considered before her captivity. Yet now she sees that it is not only the right action, but the necessary one.

"Perhaps I shall," she says, shifting to a more comfortable position on the horse.

"Nay, I spoke in jest, Mary," Samuel says. "Clearly, the authorities are convinced it would be dangerous to allow the Indians to return to their homes, else they would not have required them to live in Natick. It is plain they must be closely watched."

"Plain?" she says. "How is that? We have slain and enslaved them and taken all their lands." Samuel knows her feelings on slavery, but he clearly does not fully agree with her new concern.

"I suspect it is more a point of wisdom than principle." Samuel is a practical man. Unlike Joseph, he does not admonish Mary with verses of Scripture, but uses reason and persuasion to bring her around to his thinking. "The prospect of success in English endeavors here requires the regulation and containment of the natives."

Mary falls silent, thinking again of the Indians. Samuel is wrong. It is *not* a practical matter, but one of principle. She recalls again what James said the night she slept in his wetu: *While we draw breath, there is always some way we can show mercy and kindness.*

"Yet I trust you will not constrain me, Samuel, should I try to do what I can to bring this matter into the light."

"*Constrain* you?" Samuel laughs. "I doubt I should be able to if I tried." He turns to look at her. "Nay, wife, you must follow your conscience wherever it takes you."

Mary leans forward to kiss him on the cheek. In broad daylight.

The journey home is long and wearisome. They do not draw near Wethersfield until late on a Thursday afternoon. They ride slowly past fields of onions and winter rye. The sky is sheathed in low clouds, thick as the fleece on unshorn sheep. Mary hears the lowing of cows and the throaty song of blackbirds from the river. She peers at a low barn on one side of the road and an orchard on the other. Beyond the orchard lies impenetrable forest. In her fatigue, she thinks she sees a flicker of light among the trees, and the sound of Indian drums. She leans away from the broad comfort of Samuel's back and rubs her eyes with her fingertips, trying to penetrate the forest gloom. Did she glimpse the glow of a circle fire, or was it her imagination? Has she mistaken the cadence of the horse's hooves for drums?

"Samuel." She taps him on the shoulder. "Did you hear something just now? Drums? Or chanting?"

Samuel half turns on the horse and peers at the forest, where

she is pointing. "I heard something, but I doubt 'tis drums. I suspect we heard nothing but the wind and horses." He smiles and
reaches back to grasp her hand. "You are weary. 'Twas likely your
imagination." Mary appreciates the gentle affection in his voice, yet
she knows what she heard was not the wind.

She leans forward to rest against his back and closes her eyes.
She thinks of the flickering lights and the pulsing drums. She is
certain she heard and saw *something*. Perhaps it was a phantasm of
the past—a shimmer of ghostly impressions in the afternoon air. Or
maybe an omen of a future not yet born. The Indian resistance has
been shattered, but she cannot conceive them a wholly broken people. Perhaps—and Mary finds herself praying this—the Indians
will find a way to prevail. Perhaps their drumming will be loud
again. Perhaps the people will rise from the ashes.

Mary has no chance to determine the truth of her perceptions,
for a moment later Samuel says, "Home!" in a cheerful voice and
turns the horse into their lane. As they approach the house, the sun
breaks through the clouds and casts its rays over the fields on their
left and right. Then the front door opens and the children come
running out—Benjamin and Rachel first, their curls golden in the
light, then Elizur and Hannah and Mary's own Marie, who carries
little Nathaniel on her hip. Samuel slides off the horse and helps
Mary down, and the two of them hurry forward, arms open for an
embrace. The children tumble around them, their warm bodies jostling Samuel's legs and Mary's skirts and limbs, their excitement
filling the air like a rising breeze.

Mary kisses each child, tells them over and over how glad she is
to be home. Then Elizur begs Samuel to toss him in the air and
Hannah and Rachel run off to collect wildflowers by the brook.
Marie leads Nathaniel in a little dance.

Mary stands for a moment gazing at the scene as waves of pleasure and fatigue rush over her. She considers all that has happened

to her since the attack. How much she has lost. And all she has gained. She looks at the front door. In a few minutes she will go inside to pick up her domestic work again—the long hours of toil for her family that both exhaust and satisfy her.

She closes her eyes and tips back her head, to let what is left of the afternoon sunshine fall on her face. For a moment, in her weariness, the sound of the children's laughter reminds her of Indian women singing and she sees again the great circle fire at Wachusett. The white and purple ropes of wampum swing on the sachems' chests. The women chant and sway. The warriors dance with feathers in their hair, their long braids thrashing. And the people raise their arms to the sky, their faces lit with a terrible, wild joy.

AUTHOR'S NOTE

The characters in this novel are based on real people who lived in Massachusetts Bay Colony in the seventeenth century. The broad outlines of their lives are consistent with historical records. However, those records are sparse and sometimes contradictory. Thus, I have freely interpreted their personalities and interpersonal relationships, adding details, events, and encounters to serve the needs of the novel.

Mary White Rowlandson was the fifth of nine children of John White, owner of the largest landholding in Lancaster, Massachusetts. She was born about 1637 in England and emigrated to Massachusetts Bay Colony with her parents and older brothers and sisters in 1639. The family first settled in Salem, then moved to the new town of Wenham. Her mother, Joane West White, joined the Wenham church pastored by John Fiske, whose journal provides a fascinating and myth-busting window into the life of a congregation in Puritan New England. John White again moved his family—this time to Lancaster around 1654. A few years later, Mary married Joseph Rowlandson; at about the same time he was ordained pastor of the Lancaster church. They had four children, the first of whom died at age two.

In August of 1675, a small group of natives attacked a section of Lancaster and killed eight people. The following February, a massed group of warriors under the leadership of the Nashaway sachem, Monoco, attacked Lancaster again, burning houses and barns and taking captives, including Mary and her three living children. Her son, Joseph, and daughter Mary (whose names I have modified for clarity) were separated from her. Her youngest child, Sarah, died of wounds eight days after the attack. The Indians marched Mary and other captives through western Massachusetts, then north into southern Vermont and New Hampshire before returning to central Massachusetts. She was ransomed back to the English in early May, and reunited with her husband in Boston. Soon after, their two living children were released.

Largely dependent on the generosity of their new neighbors, the Rowlandsons lived in Charlestown and then Boston for nearly a year before Joseph was called to pastor the church in Wethersfield, Connecticut. He died suddenly in November 1678, about a year and a half after the move. The church elders pledged Mary the rest of her husband's annual salary and allowed her to remain in the parsonage.

In August 1679, Mary married Samuel Talcott, a militia captain and lawyer who helped administer her husband's estate. Samuel had eight living children by his first wife, Hannah. In 1682, a book in which Mary recounted her experiences in captivity was printed by Samuel Green in Cambridge under the lengthy title *The Sovereignty and Goodness of God, Together with the Faithfulness of His Promises Displayed, Being a Narrative of the Captivity and Restoration of Mrs. Mary Rowlandson*. Her husband's last sermon was bound with it. The book sold out, forcing demand for a second and third edition.

Mary turned up briefly in court records in 1707 when she

posted bond after the arrest of her son, Joseph, for having sold his brother-in-law as an indentured servant. She died in January 1711, at the age of seventy-four.

Her book, which quickly became famous, is considered the first "best-seller" in English America. She is widely regarded as the originator of the Anglo-American "captivity narrative."

There is less information on James Printer, also known as Wowaus. He was a Nipmuc Indian who came from Hassanamesit ("place of small stones"), established by John Eliot in 1654 as a Praying Indian village, located on land that is now the town of Grafton, Massachusetts.

When he was about five, James was taken to Cambridge to serve in the home of Henry Dunster, minister and president of the new Harvard College. James likely enrolled in Elijah Corlett's Cambridge Grammar School, but there is no documented evidence of his presence in Cambridge after 1646 until he is listed as a printer's apprentice to Samuel Green. His apprenticeship coincided with the publication of John Eliot's Indian Bible, and it is likely that James helped Eliot and other Indian assistants in their translations. Eliot himself gives credit to James for being the one man who was able to compose and "correct the press with understanding."

James fled his apprenticeship to join his family in Hassanamesit and was living there in 1675 when the war began. In early November, Nipmucs allied with Philip came to the praying town and captured all but one Hassanamesit family. The same group participated in the attack on Lancaster three months later and took Mary Rowlandson captive.

James acted as a scribe for the sachems during negotiations for Rowlandson's release, and historians generally agree that he wrote the gloating message nailed to the bridge after the attack on Medfield.

After the war, James came in under the English amnesty and returned to his job as a printer's apprentice, where he was the typesetter for the first edition of Mary Rowlandson's book in 1682. In the same year, the colonial government partitioned the "empty" Hassanamesit land for English settlement. James and twenty-one other Nipmucs (only two of whom were originally associated with Hassanamesit) signed a deed, which allowed them to retain their claim to the village.

In 1698, the Hassanamesit Indians were finally permitted to leave Natick. No more than five Indian families returned to Hassanamesit. Among them were James and his family, including his sons, Ammi and Moses. In less than three decades, most of that land had been sold to English proprietors.

James was apparently still alive in 1712. His date of death is uncertain, though it is sometimes listed as 1717.

A four-and-a-half-acre "reservation" in Grafton, Massachusetts, is all that remains today of the once vast Nipmuc lands.

There is no record of Mary Rowlandson ever acting on behalf of Native Americans or African-Americans. John Eliot, however, donated seventy-five acres of land in 1689 to support a school in the Jamaica Plain district of Roxbury. A condition of the donation was that the school would educate Native Americans and African-Americans as well as colonial English children.

The site of Mary's ransom back to the English is preserved as Redemption Rock, a one-quarter-acre historic site in Princeton, Massachusetts. The granite ledge where she was released in 1676 overlooked a vast meadow (now forested land) where the Indians camped.

John Hoar, the English emissary who secured Mary's release, was a lawyer and a social maverick who fiercely protected a group of Praying Indians that he sheltered on his property in Concord,

Massachusetts. Nearly two hundred years later, Bronson Alcott, the Transcendentalist friend of Ralph Waldo Emerson and father to Louisa May Alcott, purchased the property. He renovated John Hoar's house into the two-story, nineteenth-century home where Louisa wrote *Little Women*, and which is now a beloved museum.

Mary Rowlandson's story would not have been possible to write without extensive research. The list of books and articles I relied on is much too long to include here. An indispensable source was Neal Salisbury's edition of Mary's narrative with related documents. Other crucial sources included Diane Rapaport's *The Naked Quaker*, which introduced me to the story of Elizabeth Parker and her lover, Silvanus Warro; Jill Lapore's *The Name of War: King Philip's War and the Origins of American Identity*, which thoroughly explored the riveting and tragic history of that conflict; and Dennis A. Connole's *The Indians of Nipmuck Country in Southern New England, 1630– 1750, An Historical Geography*, which provided detailed information and context about the Native Americans who lived in what is now central Massachusetts.

About the Author

Amy Belding Brown is the author of *Mr. Emerson's Wife*. Her publication credits include *Yankee, Good Housekeeping, American Way, The Worcester Review,* and other national, international, and regional magazines. Married to a United Church of Christ minister and the mother of four grown children, she currently teaches writing at Granite State College.

CONNECT ONLINE

amybeldingbrown.com
facebook.com/amybeldingbrown
amybeldingbrown.wordpress.com/

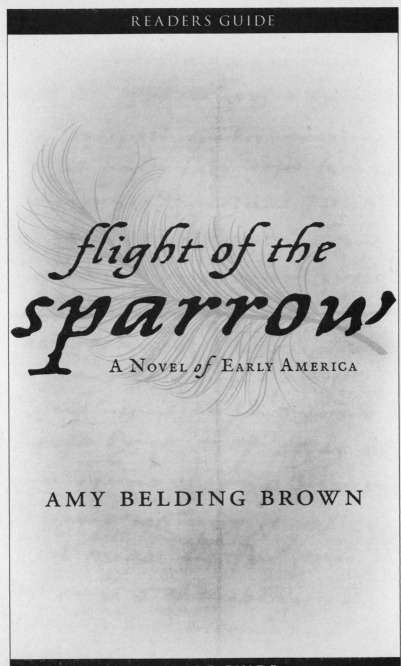

flight of the sparrow

A Novel of Early America

AMY BELDING BROWN

A CONVERSATION WITH
AMY BELDING BROWN

Q. Can you explain what originally inspired you to choose Mary Rowlandson as the subject of your second novel? Originally you wanted to call it "Redemption." Why?

A. I wanted to write something set in the Puritan era in New England, partly so I could learn more about it myself. I became aware when I wrote my last novel about the New England Transcendentalists that they were reacting to the Puritan culture, which had dominated the area for nearly two hundred years. But, like most Americans, I didn't know much about that time besides the Mayflower Pilgrims and the Salem witchcraft trials. I first stumbled on Mary Rowlandson's narrative in a museum gift shop when I was doing research on *Mr. Emerson's Wife*. When it came time to start a new novel, I turned to Mary's story.

As I researched the novel, I kept encountering references to "Praying Indians." This prompted me to investigate John Eliot and the fourteen villages of Nipmuc converts he set up in the second half of the seventeenth century. At the time, I was living in Grafton, Massachusetts, which was the site of Hassanamesit, one of those "Praying

Towns." When I first moved to Grafton, I noticed a sign on the town common that mentioned James Printer and he struck me as an interesting person. When I started to dig into the history and learn about the Praying Towns and the Natives who lived in them, I was fascinated. I began to understand what a remarkable man James Printer was. Then I read a reference to him in Mary Rowlandson's narrative and knew I had to include him in the book. He became one of my favorite characters, and central to the story I wanted to tell.

My working title—"Redemption"—related to the novel on several levels: the Puritan religious theme, Mary's reentry into English life, the unfulfilled promise of restoration for Nipmuc peoples, and the impact that simple acts of kindness can have on a fellow human being. Also in my mind was "Redemption Rock," the name of the historical site in Princeton, Massachusetts, where Mary was ransomed.

Q. *What do you most hope readers will take away from reading* Flight of the Sparrow?

A. I hope readers will come away with a sense of what it was like to live in Puritan culture and society, an appreciation of the importance and terrible cost of King Philip's War, and an awareness of the complexity of English-Native relationships in the 1600s.

Q. *Does Mary's original narrative still exist, and did you consult it as part of your research? Can you give us a sense of her language? Do we know which words are hers and which were altered by Increase Mather?*

A. Mary's original narrative is in the public domain and available in many print and electronic versions. I consulted it many times throughout the research and writing of *Flight of the Sparrow.* I found Neal Salisbury's edition especially useful because of its informative introduction and additional documents that provide invaluable context to her experience.

Mary's language is typical of seventeenth-century Puritan writing, so it takes some getting used to, not only because of when it was written, but also because her narrative is so full of biblical references and authorial asides. The more times I read the book, the more I saw three separate layers that I could pry apart fairly easily. The first is the straight story of her experience, which moves quickly from one event to the next. The second is a layer of cultural platitudes and moralistic conclusions that, interestingly, don't always match the story itself. Third is a layer of biblical quotations and references, likening Mary's experience to the trials of the ancient Israelites.

Most scholars agree that the preface was written by Increase Mather. But there's no way to know for sure if Mary's original text was altered, though many believe that it was at least "influenced" by someone other than Mary herself.

One problem I ran into as I read and reread Mary's narrative was that many of her views offended me. While she points out that the Indians were unexpectedly generous with their food and sometimes even kind to her, much of her commentary is disparaging, judgmental, and even vicious. Overall, she comes across as a pious Puritan woman with a narrow and bigoted point of view. I didn't like her until I read some scholarly articles that suggested the book may not have been entirely of Mary's making. They pointed out that she likely wrote it under the guidance of clergy—either her husband and/or Increase Mather—and that it would not have been published if it hadn't conformed to Puritan thinking. I took that possibility and enlarged it until I found a woman I could relate to.

Q. You present Mary as a woman who is profoundly changed by the three months she spends with the Native Americans who take her as a captive. Were you guided by historical clues, or purely by your imagination? Was it part of your intention all along to show a woman who comes to question the accepted practices of her own society?

A. Mary's changed viewpoint as I've presented it in the novel is fiction. There's no evidence that her opinion on Native Americans (or slavery, for that matter) was any different from the majority of other seventeenth-century Puritans.

Although there are no historical facts suggesting that Mary wished to stay with the Indians, I knew from other reading that it was not uncommon for captured English colonists to stay with the Indians when they had a choice. During her captivity, Mary demonstrated an entrepreneurial, survivalist mentality that was outside the norm. Pious Puritan women were supposed to submissively resign themselves to their fates, assuming that whatever happened was God's will. Mary seems to have had more spunk than she or others expected, a quality that was not considered appealing or appropriate in a woman at that time.

Near the end of her narrative, Mary does make a few references to hurtful rumors and nightly crying bouts. It struck me that she was treated as if she had been "tainted" by her captivity. Whether she said anything to trigger the rumors, I don't know. But I think it's at least possible that, witnessing what she did during her captivity, she might have questioned some of the fundamental assumptions of Puritan culture. However, she would never have been allowed to express such doubts in her book.

Q. I found Mary's relationship with James Printer very moving, although sad. The fact that their lives did intersect, and they may have known each other, makes their relationship especially compelling. Did you learn anything about James that did not make its way into the novel? How typical was his experience compared to that of other "Praying Indians"?

A. James Printer was an extraordinary man, known for his great intelligence, ingenuity, and piety. The more I dug into his story, the more interesting and impressive he became. He was apparently comfortable in both the Puritan and Nipmuc cultures—a remarkable accomplishment in itself. He could read and write; he had a formal English education; he lived with the president of Harvard College in his childhood; he helped John Eliot translate the Bible into the Massachusett (Algonquian) language; and he was also a respected leader in his own Hassanamesit community.

When hostilities broke out, James fled his apprenticeship and returned to Hassanamesit. Daniel Gookin later wrote that James did this for "love of his homeland." He was one of the Hassanamesit Indians taken by Philip's forces, where he was apparently trusted to inscribe a warning note to the English after a battle and play a part in Mary's ransom negotiations.

I was struck by the fact that he came in under the postwar amnesty without suffering execution or imprisonment. Many of the Indians who had been less flagrant in their "rebellion" against the English were hanged. I never found a satisfying explanation for how James managed to return to English society.

I think James's experience was typical of other Praying Indians in that he lost family, friends, and homeland in the war. But thanks to his intelligence and early education, he was able to negotiate the Puritan/Indian collision more successfully than most.

I did find some interesting information about James's family that didn't make it into the novel. Shortly after the Hassanamesits were captured by Philip's followers, James's father, Naoas, his brother Tuckapewillin and his wife, and several children tried to escape and return to the English. Unfortunately, they encountered an English scout who robbed them and imprisoned them in Marlborough. There they were so threatened and abused that Tuckapewillin's wife, afraid she would be killed, escaped into the forest with three children, leaving behind her nursing baby. Naoas, Tuckapewillin, and the remaining children were sent to Deer Island.

Deer Island was a bleak, windswept island in the middle of Boston Harbor. The living conditions were extremely harsh. About five hundred Natives were interned there without adequate food or clothing. Though they built wetus with the few available materials, the shelters were too insubstantial to adequately protect them. They had no access to their stores of winter provisions, were prohibited from cutting the trees for firewood, and were forced to eat what they could find—mostly clams and other shellfish. Disease and starvation made the death rate soar. Meanwhile, people in the English towns petitioned to have all Christian Indians put to death; others called for their deportation.

Q. I knew so little about English/Native American conflicts in New England before reading this novel. Can you tell us more about King Philip and the war that bears his name? Your description of the Native Americans in defeat is heartbreaking. In your research, did you find any brighter stories to soften that bleak picture?

A. "King Philip" was the English name for the Wampanoag sachem who was the second son of Massasoit, friend to the Pilgrims. Late in his life, Massasoit asked that his sons receive English names from the Court; the oldest (Wamsutta) took the name "Alexander" and the younger (Metacomet) took the name Philip. When Massasoit died, Alexander inherited his title, but within a year he died after testifying in front of an English court and Philip became the tribe's sachem.

Convinced Alexander had been poisoned, many Wampanoag warriors began to advocate for retaliation. Resentment had been building for some time. One of the chief flash points was the differing Indian and English practices of land use. So tempers were already flaring when John Sassamon, a Praying Indian (and someone James Printer almost certainly knew and worked with), informed the authorities that Philip was preparing to attack the colony. The colonial officials required Philip to face charges. Although the Court found no proof of his wrongdoing, they warned him that further rumors—whether or not they were based on fact—would result in the confiscation of all Wampanoag land and guns. Soon after, Sassamon's body was found under the ice in a nearby pond. The English assumed he was murdered by Philip's supporters and arrested three Wampanoag men who were tried, convicted, and executed.

In response to the executions, warriors attacked Swansea, killing several people and destroying the town. Colonial forces retaliated by destroying a Wampanoag town. The hostilities quickly expanded, drawing other tribes into a loose confederation, including the Narragansett and Nipmuc. The English colonists found allies in the Pequot and Mohegan tribes, as well as many of the Praying Indians. Meanwhile, the Mohawk tribe, long-standing enemies of the Nipmuc, began to press Philip's forces from the west.

The war was devastating to both sides; when compared to other American wars on a per capita basis, King Philip's War is still the bloodiest to this day. More than half the Puritan towns were attacked and twelve were completely destroyed. More than six hundred men, women, and children were killed. The colonial economy verged on collapse. But the Indians fared even worse, losing more than three thousand to war, disease, and starvation. After the war, many were executed or enslaved and sold onto slave ships bound for Bermuda. Others fled north and west to join other tribes. Those who remained were closely controlled; all the surviving Praying Indians were crowded into one Praying Town—Natick—and they lost their self-governing status.

Unfortunately, I didn't find many heartening stories. The exception is the few English individuals who spoke out against the cruel treatment of Indians and slaves. One of these was John Eliot, who also donated funds to establish and maintain a school that educated African-American and Indian students as well as the children of English colonists.

Q. *My first knowledge of Indian captives during this period comes from having read* The Light in the Forest *by Conrad Richter, a classroom standard when I attended public school in New England. There was also a movie, I recall. Were they in the back of your mind when you started this project?*

A. It's been years since I read *The Light in the Forest* and, though I remember liking it, I didn't revisit it in writing *Flight of the Sparrow*. There are many Indian captivity stories in print, both fact and fiction, but Mary Rowlandson's was the first and happened much earlier than the action of *The Light in the Forest*. I did reread *Black Robe* by Brian Moore, which takes place at approximately the same time as Rowlandson's captivity, but is set in what is now Canada. Some of those images were in my mind, I suppose, but mostly I drew on my reading of Rowlandson's narrative and the research on New England Natives and colonists in the second half of the seventeenth century.

Q. When the English and Indians were not at war in the early colonial period, what level of interaction existed among them? Was it mostly limited to trade?

A. It was largely trade. Early on, Massasoit's decision to seek an alliance with the Plymouth colonists ensured their survival, since he provided them with food and essential knowledge. Not all the English colonies were so fortunate. The English both feared and reviled the tribes around them. Indians reminded them of the Irish, whom they considered barbarians. Like the Irish, Indians lived in small, domed dwellings; they also danced in strange ways and mourned their dead loudly. Indians, whose populations had already been devastated by disease when the colonists began to settle New England, were generally tolerant of colonists as long as they didn't interfere with their way of life.

Indians traded furs and land for English tools. As the English either bought or took more and more land, there was increasing friction. The English, who believed the land belonged to them because it had been chartered by the King, felt entitled to claim all land that wasn't being "used," by which they meant actively farmed. Indians resented having their hunting grounds parceled up into little English farms and the subsequent destruction of their crops by English animals.

Q. Despite the prejudice and self-righteousness of many Puritans, there were clearly some men such as John Eliot who took more enlightened views. Can you talk a little bit about how well freedom of thought and religious diversity were tolerated, and when—as in the case of Anne Hutchinson—they were punished?

A. Massachusetts Bay was a theocracy, especially in its early years during the Great Migration from England. The religious freedom the Puritans sought was self-interested and applied only to them. They saw themselves as refugees from the tyranny of English religious laws. As I understand it, the English were relieved to be rid of them because the Puritans were seen as religious zealots and troublemakers. Most of the laws they set up in Massachusetts were attempts to codify Old Testament commandments.

Though it's sometimes thought that the clergy were in charge, in fact the Puritans established their government on the assumption that everyone was a deeply pious Christian trying to live according to biblical ideals. Their "mutual watch" system requiring every church member to keep an eye on every other member was one mechanism of enforcement. Interestingly, this was not to ensure the personal salvation of each individual. As Calvinists, they believed that everyone's salvation had already been determined by God before birth. Their fundamental concern was the behavior of the group; they believed that one person's bad behavior could jeopardize the safety and success of the whole community. They took as their prototype the ancient Israelites, whose "angry God" punished His people when they were disobedient, sometimes wiping out entire villages.

On the other hand, the New England Puritans were in some ways progressive (for their time). They prohibited wife beating and child abuse. They required parents to teach their children to read. They didn't condemn "heretics" to death. Instead they banished them from the colony—as in the cases of Anne Hutchinson and Roger Williams—and usually only after repeated offenses. Hutchinson and Williams were part of the first generation, living in a time when the colony was still struggling for survival and was fixated on religious "purity." After the second generation, differences of opinion were more common, and more generally tolerated.

Laws of that time included specific regulations on everything from spinning, galloping horses on Boston Common, to the wearing of lace and silk, fences, marriage, and profaning the Sabbath. Most of the punishments involved fines, though repeated offenses could result in imprisonment or whipping.

The Puritans tried to establish a perfect Christian colony, leaning on the letter rather than the spirit of the law to accomplish their goal. Their laws and punishments grew out of a belief that the bad behavior of one person was a threat to the entire colony. In their view, it was less punishment than self-preservation.

Q. We often forget that slavery was deeply embedded in early colonial society, and that well-respected men actively participated in the slave trade by selling Africans and Native Americans to sugar planters in the Caribbean. Can you explain how slavery contributed to New England's growth and wealth, both among the English and the various Indian tribes?

A. One of the things that surprised me when I researched *Flight of the Sparrow* was that I kept bumping into matter-of-fact references to slaves, both Indian and African. It was just an accepted part of life in the 1600s. There were both African and Indian slaves serving in families, but the colonial economy in New England wasn't dependent on slave labor as it was in the South. The slave trade, however, was an economic gold mine. Not long after the Puritans settled in New England, they began importing slaves from Africa, shipping them to the West Indies, selling them there and buying sugar for rum-making. The slave trade made some businessmen and investors very rich and created jobs for thousands of others in the trade itself and in the industries dependent on it.

Q. *This is your second novel, following* Mr. Emerson's Wife *(St. Martin's Griffin, 2005), which was also set in Massachusetts, a century and a half after* Flight of the Sparrow. *What keeps drawing you back to New England history?*

A. It's partly provincialism on my part, I guess; I grew up in New England and have spent most of my life living here. My forebearers were part of the Great Puritan Migration. The landscape itself speaks to me in a profound way. I was raised on New England stories and the ideas of New England people. I feel my background allows me to understand regional history from the inside out. And there's certainly plenty of material to inspire me.

Q. *What were your beginnings as a writer, and what do you most enjoy about writing?*

A. I wanted to be a writer for as long as I can remember. My parents always read to me, and once I could read myself, my nose was always in a book. I think, like many writers, my desire to be a writer grew out of my love for the books I read. When a book moved me or made me think in a new way, I found myself wanting to have that impact on others. I remember, at a very young age, loving to hear Margaret Wise Brown's books because of the way she used words and the enchanting pictures those words painted in my mind. It was a special joy to revisit her when I read to my own children.

I like to write poetry because it allows me to play with words in that way, but I've always been especially drawn to stories. My father used to tell wonderful, imaginative stories that he made up on the spur of the moment, and that model of creative magic also had a powerful impact on me.

What I enjoy most about writing is discovering something unexpected. I write the way I read—to find out what happens next. My writing process is pretty messy; I don't usually know where I'm going and it takes longer than I'd like to get there, but the payoff is encountering the unexpected—a new character, a plot twist, something I didn't know in a character's background, etc. Writing historical novels gives me a little less imaginative leeway, since I try not to contradict anything that's historically documented, but the research process makes up for it. I love delving deep into historical books and articles and coming up with intriguing details.

Q. What do you read for pleasure? Have you been particularly inspired or influenced by the work of other writers?

A. An early influence was Louisa May Alcott, whose Jo March was the model for many women writers in my generation. When I was in my teens, I loved Ernest Hemingway. I even copied out a quote of his in calligraphy, framed it, and hung it on my wall: "Once writing has become your major vice and greatest pleasure only death can stop it." It's pretty extreme, but for quite a while it was my credo.

I'm an eclectic reader; I don't limit myself to one genre. I read a lot of literary and mainstream fiction; I read history and biography and memoir, poetry and classical literature, and occasionally some reader-friendly science. I have a fairly long list of favorite writers, including Anne Patchett, Marilynne Robinson, Barbara Kingsolver, Hilary Mantel, Richard Russo, Nathaniel Philbrick, Geraldine Brooks, Mary Oliver, Frederick Buechner, and, of course, Jane Austen. But I also really love reading a fantastic book by a writer I've never heard of before.

Q. What might we expect from you in the future?

A. I'm currently working on a novel about Emily Dickinson. Or, rather, about Emily Dickinson's circle. It's in the early stages, but I'm really excited about it. Dickinson is interesting in her own right, as a sort of literary mystery, but many of the people around her lived dramatic and captivating lives. Also, Dickinson lived in an interesting time when the nation was going through incredible changes, a time period that overlapped the Transcendentalists. In fact, I recently learned that Dickinson was a big fan of Ralph Waldo Emerson, who had a major influence on her view of the world.

QUESTIONS
FOR DISCUSSION

1. What was your overall response to the novel? What did you feel? What did you learn?

2. Discuss Mary Rowlandson's relationships with the three men in her life—Joseph, James, and Samuel. What does she give and what does she receive from each relationship?

3. Mary Rowlandson lives in a society ruled by men in which women were allowed few of the freedoms that we take for granted today. Identify those constraints, discuss how they might have helped or hurt the Bay Colony's survival, and discuss how women might have found meaning in life despite them.

4. As an Indian captive, Mary feels freed from the constraint of "mutual watch," the "relentless scrutiny of each other's conduct required of all church members." Discuss the idea of mutual watch as it plays out in the novel, and what it might be like to live under such a system. Can you think of any modern-day equivalents?

5. Mary experiences both cruelty and kindness at the hands of her Indian captors. Compare their behavior toward her to the cruelty and kindness shown her by her husband Joseph and other members of English society.

6. Discuss the various forms that freedom and imprisonment take in the novel. What role does the sparrow play in the author's exploration of those ideas?

7. While living with the Indians, Mary begins to find beauty, peace, and sacred mystery in the wilderness. How does she initially view the natural world and what inspires this change? Compare her experience of the natural world to your own.

8. Mary becomes convinced that slavery and physically punishing her children are wrong, and she stands up to her husband Joseph on these issues. What makes her so sure she is correct to reject them? Is mere conviction enough, or is something else required?

9. James Printer tells Mary, "We have both bought our redemption at a terrible price." And Mary realizes that she felt redeemed when she followed the promptings of her heart. Discuss the many meanings of redemption in the novel.

10. The Puritan worldview differs markedly from our own. Discuss their beliefs as they relate to God's love and punishment, child rearing, grief, the infectious nature of sin, slavery, obedience to authority, and salvation. In what ways are these ideas still part of current thought and practice? In what ways has our thinking changed?

11. Because their exposure to another culture has changed their beliefs and perceptions, both Mary and James feel estranged from their original people. Have you ever felt estranged from your own "group of origin"? Care to share your experience?

12. Have you read other "captivity narratives," either those from previous centuries or those written by recent, contemporary captives (such as Elizabeth Smart and Jaycee Dugard)? How do they compare with Mary Rowlandson's story?

13. What do you most admire about Mary? What makes her story relevant today?

14. What do you hope to remember about this novel six months or a year from now? Do you think that some part of it will remain with you for even longer than that?